THE TWIN FLAME

K.T. ANGLEHART

The Twin Flame: The Scottish Scrolls Book II

Copyright © 2023 by Katrina Tortorici

ISBN: 978-1-7773317-3-3 (Print)
ISBN: 978-1-7773317-5-7 (Hardcover)
ISBN: 978-1-7773317-4-0 (eBook)

Cover Design by Melissa Williams Design

Published by The Magic Dwarf Press

Maps designed by Riccardo Caimano | @fantacities

The boldest fae flees from our neighbour land
Her charge, the Wise One, and she the key
Whence the ancient passage tomb stands
United their magic, and so shall it be.

—Scottish Scroll II, 1576

ATLANTIC OCEAN
NORTH SEA
SHETLAND ISLANDS
ORKNEY ISLANDS
OUTER HEBRIDES
ISLE OF SKYE
INVERNESS
ABERDEEN
SCOTLAND
EDINBURGH
GLASGOW
GIANT'S CAUSEWAY
NORTHERN IRELAND
BELFAST
ISLE OF MAN
GREAT BRITAIN
IRISH SEA
LIVERPOOL
DUBLIN
IRELAND
WALES
ENGLAND
CARDIFF
AVEBURY
LONDON
CELTIC SEA
ENGLISH CHANNEL
N

N
ATLANTIC OCEAN
BALLYCASTLE
GIANT'S CAUSEWAY
NORTHERN IRELAND
BELFAST
THE BOYNE VALLEY
CONNEMARA
GALWAY
DUBLIN
THE BURREN
REPUBLIC OF IRELAND
LIMERICK
IRISH SEA
CORK
CELTIC SEA

N
ATLANTIC OCEAN
NORTH SEA
ORKNEY ISLANDS
INCHNADAMPH
OUTER HEBRIDES
UIG
ISLE OF SKYE
PORTREE
LOCH DUICH
LOCH NESS
INVERNESS
FORT AUGUSTUS
SCOTLAND
ABERDEEN
THE FIVE SISTERS OF KINTAIL
GLENCOE
LOCH LOMOND
LUSS
EDINBURGH
GLASGOW
GLASGOW NECROPOLIS
NORTHERN IRELAND
BELFAST
ISLE OF MAN
ENGLAND

Book One's Last Moments

The Vast In-Between

Nissa was being followed.

When her ferry docked that morning at Port Soderick, she had the strangest feeling: Someone would be expecting her.

It was stupid, of course, and highly unlikely. Her mind must've dreamed it up because, Heaven knew, she was in way over her head, and she no longer had Mckenna to take charge. How did Mckenna always know what to do? She made it all look so effortless.

"Excuse me, sir! How do I get out of here?" Nissa asked one of the dock workers.

"Where you looking to be, girl?" the man said, his accent a cross between Irish and British.

"I'm not really sure. I'm looking for an orphanage, but I don't know which. Is there maybe a town nearby?" If records of her existed, she would finally discover whether the notorious Feblands she learned about, nicknamed the *Free Felons,* were in fact her parents.

"I don't know about no orphanages, girl, but the port's got shuttles going to Douglas, the capital. You'll find loads more there." This sounded like a sensible enough plan, not that she had another to go on. She glanced at the gloomy, grey overcast sky looming above her head, and that about decided it for her; she was in no mood to wander around aimlessly in the rain.

A loud cough behind her made Nissa jump. She breathed a sigh of relief when she spotted a kind-faced old lady, smiling apologetically. Offering a polite smile in return, she continued towards the shuttle.

Within ten minutes, the sky released a furious downpour, and she was let off in Douglas, where she scrambled to the nearest café for shelter. It was then that Nissa knew her instincts had been right.

She *was* being followed.

The old lady from the docks was loitering behind her, drenched from head to toe, and waving keenly in her face. Funny, had she been on the shuttle all this time?

Nissa waved back and drew nearer, thinking it impolite to ignore her, when the lady lifted a thick, wrinkly index finger and pressed it against Nissa's mouth. Too stunned to react, she merely stood there, letting the strange woman silence her like a schoolgirl.

And then the situation grew even more perplexing. Without a word, the old lady trotted out the door, pressed her face into the front window, and beckoned Nissa over. She obliged, seeing the rain had now turned into a drizzle. There was no harm in indulging an old lady; she was probably just lacking a bit of company—or her marbles.

"Hello, ma'am," Nissa said cheerfully outside the café. "I'm Nissa."

The lady nodded, then began walking ahead of her. Perhaps she was mute, Nissa thought. Bewildered, she called after her.

"Excuse me! Was there, um, something you needed from me?" The lady looked over her shoulder to throw Nissa a brief glance and once again, gestured for her to follow. Odd, she thought, but she couldn't very well leave a helpless, elderly woman to wander off on her own.

The next thing Nissa knew, she was walking for twenty minutes down a country road, trailing behind the lady like a duckling.

"Where exactly are we—?" Nissa cut herself off as she lay her eyes on what she always imagined would be her dream home. They stopped in front of a modest little cottage that looked to be a couple of centuries old, with warm red brick, copper shingles, and rustic wood shutters, which were always featured in her favourite storybooks. It was perched in the centre of a green expanse, probably larger than the soccer field in Abredonia Woods.

"Is this your home?"

The lady nodded as she stepped onto the thick lawn, then turned around to wave Nissa over.

I'm in way too deep now, Nissa thought, entering through the wood-panelled gate and into her backyard. What she walked into was something out of a faery tale: Cottony rabbits hopped around a vegetable patch, nibbling away greedily at carrots and lettuce leaves; a flock of chickens strutted about, pecking at nothing in particular; and a handful of tabby cats roamed around like guard dogs, one of which had its nose in a stream that flowed along the edge of the yard and into the woods that bordered the land.

And just when she deemed it all too perfect, sharp rays of sunlight beamed through the dark clouds, hitting her cheeks. She felt as though she was in a trance as she walked leisurely around the grounds, greeting the animals and smelling the various plants, until a hard tap on her shoulder snapped her out of it; for a second, she had forgotten she wasn't alone. The old lady was standing behind her, pointing at two steaming cups of tea on a round, cast-iron bistro table near a sunflower patch. When had she gone inside to make tea? Apparently having no choice in the matter, Nissa sat down.

"The tea will warm you up, pet."

Nissa spat out her tea. "You can talk!"

"'Course I can talk. I've still got my tongue, haven't I?"

"But why didn't you say a word this whole time?"

"There are ears everywhere," she said gravely. "And so that you didn't ask too many questions."

Nissa's expression was blank. "I just walked a mile in the rain to sit here and have tea with a stranger."

"Oh, I'm no stranger, pet. My name's Arethusa. I'm your grandmother."

BELFAST, NORTHERN IRELAND

It was 3:00 a.m., and Cillian was drenched in sweat. Back in his guestroom at Ms. Beattie's, he was awoken, yet again, by the High Priestess's transparent silhouette.

"What do you mean, she's gone and LEFT?" the High Priestess's astral form bellowed, making Cillian flinch. The last thing he wanted was to tell the High Priestess he'd failed her. While he still believed in the Priestess's larger plan, he didn't want Mckenna to have to carry it out under protest. With some more time, he could sway her.

"She's gone to Ballycastle."

"I'd gathered that. Am I to thank you for your astuteness?" she said through gritted teeth. "Why aren't you *with* her? You told her you'd *bring her there,* did you not?"

"Of course, but she and her friend got into some sort of quarrel. The inn owner said they'd both left in a hurry, separately." Cillian didn't dare admit he prompted their fight. He knew Mckenna wouldn't see reason with her friend around—she made her much too soft. But he hadn't anticipated *this.*

"You do realize you can't cross the border now, not without the Wise One with you! That plan's gone to shite, thanks to you."

"What do you mean, we can't cross?"

"When you said the last time that she thinks her mother's in Ballycastle, I tried astral travelling there. It's impossible. Which means Abby has it protected. Going in by the Wise One's side would have been the only way to enter."

"But that kind of magic is . . . advanced. How is that possible?"

Her expression was envious. "It just is."

"Perhaps I can enter, High Priestess. I see the darkness inside her. And she fancies me, so—"

"Congratulations, you've got yourself a girlfriend. Did you think that'd grant you special entry? Meanwhile, she's sipping tea with her new mum, chatting about the Scottish Scrolls." Her astral face inched closer to his, and his body went rigid. "Was it too much to ask for you to *simply* guide her into fulfilling the first Scroll—"

"I have—"

"—and *remain* with her until she found our dear Abby? The rest, ah, the rest would have been child's play," she said, every word icier than the last. "Do you remember? DO YOU REMEMBER HOW IT WAS ALL SUPPOSED TO GO?" And then her face transformed into Mckenna's, pouting like a misbegotten child. Cillian rubbed his eyes, knowing what he was seeing wasn't real. Of the Priestess's many talents, it was her ability to hypnotize that frightened him most.

"I can get her back. I can get her to see what we see. I'm nearly there, let me—"

"I will let you do *nothing* else. You're a disappointment, Hayes," she spat. "We're done here. With any luck, my stone will find her the second she steps out of that town. And when she does, it's my way from here on."

"Please, if you let me, this *will* work—"

But she was already gone.

Nissa leaned back, mouth agape. "You're my grandmother?"

"I've startled you, haven't I? 'Course I have . . ."

"No, no . . . I mean, well, I'm surprised, yeah . . ." Question after question hit Nissa like a heap of falling snow, and she lay buried beneath, unmoving.

"You have questions, surely."

"My parents," were the only words she managed.

Eyes filled with sorrow, Arethusa began her story: "My daughter, Annie, met Simon at a young age. He was visiting from England, and she worked at a shop down the road. Oh, and what a beauty Annie was, like yourself. You're the spitting image."

Nissa didn't know how to react to this, so she listened on.

"Simon went in there every day, doing everything to get her attention. 'Course, it didn't take very long. He was . . . experienced. And she was, well . . . Annie. Lovely and full of heart, but as naïve as a child sitting by the chimney on Christmas Eve.

"But Simon, he was a rotten influence. Poisonous from the start, he was. They grew inseparable fast. I begged Annie to leave him, but poor, clueless girl that she was, she fell hopelessly in love. Did I mention she was young? Just sixteen at the time. Before I know it, she's moving to England with him. She'd write to me, yes, but when I started asking too many questions, she stopped. I found out Simon was involved in very *bad* business . . . drugs, I'm afraid," Arethusa added, seeing Nissa's eyes widen. "Not a year down the line, the two were wanted for drug-trafficking."

Exactly what the librarian had told her. "Annie, too?"

"Only 'cause she wouldn't leave his side. Still, she'd gotten into bad ways. They'd come back to the Isle every so often 'to see you, Mum!', Annie would say, but I knew the real reason; he had bank accounts here. See, the Isle of Man's a self-governing nation, so for Simon, a foreigner living outside of the law, this was a tax haven. I imagine this is what brought him here in the first place."

Nissa cringed, wondering if this would get any worse. It all sounded unreal, like an Al Pacino film.

"But something happened when they had you," Arethusa went on. "They started running into . . . hurdles. Things would go wrong left, right, and centre; and Annie, she started opening up to me. It turned out some of Simon's men were betraying him. He was losing loads of money, and one of them, he discovered, was working with the police. Things got so bad, Simon came to believe you were a changeling. Very superstitious man," she said, shaking her head.

From the sounds of it, this couldn't be good. "What's a changeling?"

"Oh, dear, you *are* American, aren't you? A changeling is a baby whose human soul's been swapped for a faery's."

Nissa laughed, but her grandmother showed little humour. "Wait, are you kidding?"

"No, ducky. You're not a changeling, of course, but it's not so far-fetched to assume." Before Nissa could ask what she meant by this, Arethusa continued. "I'm afraid this next bit won't be easy to hear." She placed her hand over Nissa's. "Simon, he grew angrier and, well, he became violent. Your mum—oh, she loved you so, you must know that—she wanted to protect you; she kept you here with me, but Simon's luck still hadn't changed. So, the truth is, he . . . he . . ."

"He wanted me gone."

"Annie and I were afraid of what he might do. We arranged to have us on the next ship to America."

"Us?" And then it hit her. *Arethusa Febland.* How could she not have realized it sooner? She was the foreign family member listed on the passenger list.

"Simon wouldn't let your mum out of his sight, so I snuck you away and brought you to Boston myself. I had a cousin there, and she was thrilled to take you in. But not a year after you arrived, I found out she'd died in a car accident."

Was Nissa just a walking bad luck charm? "That's how I ended up in foster care? Couldn't you have come back for me?"

Tears stung Arethusa's eyes. "I wanted nothing more, pet. The plan was always to return to the Isle to save your mum from Simon, and then we would come find you again, together. But when I returned home, Simon was here, waiting for me. He told me Annie was gone," she said, her voice shaking, "and demanded I tell him your whereabouts. Said one way or another, he'd find you, and he'd always keep an eye on me. So I couldn't risk coming and putting you in danger, you see."

Nissa swallowed the lump that had formed in her throat. "Did he—he didn't *kill* her . . .?"

Arethusa exhaled, squeezing her hand tighter.

The first tear fell, and the rest flowed like a river breaking through a dam. The walls she'd built over the years crumbled, and she was left there, in hollow skin and bones, her every fear realized. She was parentless, and her own flesh and blood a murderer.

Arethusa came around and held her granddaughter's head to her chest. Nissa didn't know how long she'd sat there, hysterical, until the dryness in her throat drove her into a fit of coughs.

"Drink up, pet. Tea soothes the soul."

Nissa let out a stifled laugh through her cries and finished off her cuppa, which was now lukewarm.

"When you found Simon here, what happened?"

"Oh, you wouldn't believe it. I was saved by three enormous dogs . . ."

A typhoon of emotions, Nissa let out another laugh. "How?"

"It's thanks to an insufferable neighbour of mine, Peter. Annoying bloke, him and his bloody dogs always stomping on my petunias . . . Well, I've since bit my tongue because his three huskies saved my life. Simon was on my porch, see, and those dogs—never minding their own business—sensed I was in trouble. Came dashing up my porch and straight for Simon's groin! He almost didn't make it out alive, I tell you. I never saw him again."

So, her mother was dead and her murderous father on the loose.

"There's something I don't understand."

"What's that, ducky?"

"Why didn't the foster system have my last name? The ship records did, I found it on the passenger list."

"Your mum did register you as 'Nissa Febland', hoping you'd find us some day. But when I found out my cousin passed and you'd be in the foster system, I begged them to remove your surname. I couldn't risk Simon tracking you down. Oh, but I'm ever so glad you did find me," she said, stroking her cheek, "and I suspected you would."

"How?"

Arethusa leaned in, like she had a secret, and spun Nissa's bracelet around her wrist.

"It was you?"

Arethusa winked, tears streaming down her made-up cheeks.

It was like a sunbeam hit Nissa's chest. She fingered her bracelet, amazed at how far it had brought her. "And today, at the docks? How'd you know I'd come?"

Leaning in closer, Arethusa whispered, "Let me show you."

That afternoon, after a much-needed hearty lunch (smoked salmon and capers, fresh-baked bread, traditional Manx broth—a mix of beef celery, leek, and turnip—and more tea), Nissa was being led blindly, yet again, down a quiet country road.

"Almost there, pet."

"Where're we going?"

"Kewaigue Hill."

It didn't look like much. There was nothing but a farmstead and an old primary school in sight. "Is it, like, a famous hill? Where's the hill?"

"This way," Arethusa said brightly, steering Nissa towards a footpath beside the farmstead. Some untamed bushes came into view, and soon they'd entered a woodland crammed with tall, slim trees. They walked in silence for some time, listening to the sounds of the birds singing, leaves rustling underfoot, and the flow of water in the distance. When they reached a footbridge over a small, shallow river, Arethusa bypassed it, instead turning down an unseen trail alongside the water.

"Look ahead, ducky."

Through the trees was a site that quickly rendered Nissa in a state of calm. A very old-looking bridge stood between the surrounding trees and fallen branches, somewhat camouflaged by the vines that clung to its stone walls, as though nature was helping to keep its secret. Beneath it, a stream flowed through the rocks, bright autumn leaves drifting in its shallows.

"This is the ancient faery bridge. Not many know of it—only those who've already been here."

"More faery stuff?" Nissa blurted.

"Shhh, you don't want to offend them!"

Nissa wrinkled her brow. "Offend . . . the faeries?" She held back a chuckle, seeing that her grandmother didn't look to be kidding.

"Oh, faeries are very much real, pet. I can assure you of that."

"Have you seen them?"

"I don't have to. They show their presence in all sorts of ways. Through blessings, gifts, signs . . ."

"What kind of signs?"

Arethusa trod towards the arch of the bridge, where about a dozen stones lay on the ground, and smiled down at them. Nissa stepped closer: Each stone had a message written on it in thick, black ink:

> *Thank you for the great weather!*
>
> *Thank you for helping my family through this tough time.*
>
> *Please help Mom feel better.*
>
> *Please give my son strength.*

"Some of these are wishes," Nissa said.

"Go on . . ." Arethusa said, and pointed down at the rest. Nissa read every stone, her heart warming with each message.

> *Please help Nissa find her way home.*

"I've been coming here every day since my return from Boston, leaving offerings to the fae folk. When I got here early this morning, I found this resting on my stone." She held up a long feather, a striking blend of yellow, orange, and indigo. "Feathers are messages from the divine, see? And this one, well, I'd never seen one so beautiful. Naturally, when I saw it . . ."

Nissa was lost for words. She reached out and squeezed her grandmother's hand and allowed the tears to fall, touched beyond measure that someone in this world had loved her all this time.

PORT SODERICK, ISLE OF MAN
PRESENT DAY—OCTOBER 30, 1991

The moment she stepped off the ferry and onto the Isle of Man, Mckenna felt a surge of energy enter the base of her feet and shoot upwards, as though magic lurked beneath the earth.

Perhaps it did. Esme's words rang in her ear: *Your intuition is stronger than you ken. You must always follow it.*

If the past two weeks under Esme's wing had taught her anything, it was that grounding was the only way to 'listen inward', as Esme would say. And so there, in the middle of the port, never minding the curious onlookers, she closed her eyes and inhaled, then let out a long, slow breath. Centring first, she released any tension trapped within her chakras, and grounded, picturing roots sprouting from the soles of her feet and into the pavement. The chatter around her dissolved, and she zeroed in on the noises of nature around her: the boats swaying in the harbour, the wind whistling high notes.

"Lead me to Nissa," she mouthed to the ether.

A buzzing sounded in her ear, followed by a hard tugging at her chest. Her toes tingled, then her feet, and her legs and onwards, as though every one of her limbs was falling asleep.

Was she . . . vibrating?

The tugging grew stronger. Instinctively, she resisted, putting as much weight on her feet as she could, but if she fought it any longer, she was afraid she'd rip in two. She loosened her muscles and let herself go.

POP.

She was lighter than a feather, floating upwards, her unconscious body lying beside the docks hundreds of feet below her.

Whoa.

Two dock workers ran to her aid. She squinted, trying to make out the scene, but it was drifting away as she soared higher . . . and higher . . . and higher still. She was a goddess, rising above land and water, omniscient; and there, the Isle of Man rested in the heart of the Irish Sea, an equal distance away from England, Ireland, Scotland, and Wales. It was literally one vast in-between . . .

This is like one huge faery doorway.

Another *POP.*

She was hovering above a woodsy area, not far from a farmhouse. Down the road below, a sign read: *Kewaigue Hill.*

Nissa felt at peace on the Isle of Man, and she was quite taken with the faery bridge. She and Arethusa walked over to the site every day to pay the fae a visit, leave out honey, chocolate, and silver coins ("They *adore* shiny objects!"), and pick up any trash left behind, something Nissa learned they most appreciated.

She also learned that faeries were sort of like angels, but for the earth. They tended to nature, and therefore were known in some cultures as nature spirits. Arethusa went on to explain the inner workings of devas, who smoothed weather conditions, and of nymphs, who oversaw the water and the woods.

"Leprechauns are faeries, too."

"No way! Aren't they known for being tricksters?"

"As are all faeries. They find it amusing to play wee pranks—you know, hide objects, spoil the milk, that sort of harmless thing. But if you *really* anger a faery, it won't be such a *wee* punishment."

Nissa's mind jumped to the tale of the old man who ended up paralyzed after kicking a faery hill. "It sounds like they just want to be treated with respect. I see nothing wrong with that!"

"I quite agree, ducky."

There was a rustling sound behind them. "Same here," uttered a familiar voice, one Nissa had wished for weeks to hear again. Mckenna stood at the foot of the stream, her eyes hopeful, apologetic. Nissa ran over and threw her arms around her.

Mckenna returned her embrace. "I'm so sorry, Nissa. I didn't mean a thing—"

"No, don't! *I'm* sorry, Kenna. I just left you there. It was a crappy thing to do."

"Yeah, it was pretty crappy."

"*So* crappy."

"Lying to you was worse, though," Mckenna said solemnly. "But I'm ready to tell you everything."

"Like how you managed to find me here . . .?"

Mckenna laughed. "That, too."

Nissa's grin spread from ear to ear. "I'd like to think I had something to do with it, though."

"What d'you mean?"

Nissa glanced over at the wishing stones under the bridge, then at Arethusa. "I'll explain later."

Arethusa winked. Feeling giddy, Nissa linked her arms with Mckenna's, then with her grandmother's. "I'd like you to meet my best friend, Mckenna. Kenna, this is Arethusa—my grandmother."

Mckenna looked both stunned and elated. "It's an honour to meet you, Arethusa."

"How do you do, Mckenna. What an interesting name. Scottish, is it?"

"I'm actually not sure."

"And the honour's mine, my dear. Nissa's talked my ear off

about you. She thinks highly of you, this one does. A very wise person, indeed."

Nissa noticed Mckenna flinch. "Should we head back for some tea?"

Arethusa clapped her hands together. "Excellent idea!"

As Mckenna led the way out, Arethusa placed a hand on Nissa's shoulder and leaned into her ear. "I daresay she needs you as much as you need her, ducky."

THE POWER OF SAMHAIN

Andre slammed the phone down on Seán and kicked the kitchen chair. Seán had been with Abby all this time—the woman who deserted her family through a vague explanation on a piece of paper.

Seán said he and Abby had a strong feeling Mckenna was in Ballycastle and that they would find her together "when the time was right." What did that even mean? *Immediately,* that was when the time was right. And this woman had no business *feeling* anything about *their* daughter.

"Abby says it's the safest place she could be," Seán had said, trying to reassure Andre.

"Right, if that's what Abby says," Andre scoffed. "Why are you letting her influence you?"

"Come off it, Andre, I'm not *letting* her do anything. She knows what she's talking about. You can't understand."

"Whose fault is that?" And that was when he had hung up. Something wasn't right. She just happened to show up when Seán happened to be visiting the very spot they'd met seventeen years ago?

Andre was tired of waiting around. Seán was either being tricked or being drawn back into Abby's world; Andre had seen the way Seán spoke about her before he left. He'd never gotten over his grief, his heartbreak. He was still in love with her.

It was time Andre fought for him.

Cillian sat cross-legged on a sandy beach, staring out at the water drifting across the bay and playing last night's dream over in his mind. Mckenna had appeared to him so vividly, her hair wilder than ever and eyes piercing his own the way they so often did. But he couldn't make out what she way saying.

In a desperate attempt to locate her, Cillian had been practicing astral projection every day since she left Ms. Beattie's. He hadn't been successful the first several tries, but it must have been due to Abby's protection enchantment cast over Ballycastle. That, and the fact that he still couldn't astral project. His attempts failed each time, and he was about ready to give up all hope. The Priestess was right—he was a disappointment. As a high-level practitioner, he should have been able to master astral projection by now. He would never be able to warn Mckenna, to keep her from the High Priestess's grasp.

To be with her again.

Fear and self-loathing permeated his bones. The very thought of Mckenna being tortured into carrying out the High Priestess's plan made his chest rip to pieces. And to think just a month ago, Cillian's one desire had been to gain the Priestess's trust, to be the one to help the Wise One meet her fate.

Now, he cared little about the Priestess. In the end, they might have the same goal, but he could achieve the same outcome another way—one that allowed him and Mckenna to be together. He remembered how appalled he was, at first, when the Priestess disclosed the old witch's prophecy, that peace came at a cost: *billions of souls shall expire upon this Earth.* He was not a murderer, he'd said. "It's not a killing spree," the High Priestess had replied. "We are merely halting the reincarnation of souls—souls that should remain in the spiritual realm, that no longer have a physical place here on Earth." And in time, he understood: The Scrolls incited a righteous path, not an evil one.

Mckenna would understand that, too. She would come to believe in the new Earth, just as he had.

A thought occurred to him. What if she wasn't in Ballycastle anymore? There was a small possibility her mother wasn't there at all. What if he didn't focus on getting to Ballycastle and instead focused solely on *her?* In all his years as a mystic practitioner, he had only ever tried astral projecting to a location, but never to a person. It was a long shot, but he had to try. He knew the High Priestess would stop at nothing until she got her way. He'd been suspecting all this time that that thing she was working on had to do with lifting Abby's protection spell. And to be able to break a bond that strong, she would have to do it on the most magical night of the year—Samhain.

It was now or never.

It was this fervent desire that triggered what happened next: A loud buzzing noise sounded in his ear, and his body began to vibrate like it was mildly in shock. Then something popped, and he began to soar, leaving behind his dormant body.

In this new state of consciousness, limitations were a mere myth, and time was but a concept; with the power of intention, he could bend it. He suddenly found himself in a wooded area, floating above a stone bridge. He could feel Mckenna was here, wherever this place was, and that Nissa was with her. The magic here was strong and ancient, like faery magic. This was an in-between place.

The largest one there was.

DOUGLAS, ISLE OF MAN

She didn't know whether it was because she and Nissa had reconciled or if it was due to the three-course meal Arethusa whipped up the night before, but Mckenna awoke on Halloween morning bursting with energy.

"I slept like a log," Mckenna said, scooping up a mouthful of treacle tart, leftover dessert from last night's feast.

"A snoring log," Nissa said with a yawn.

Arethusa came around to fill their coffee mugs. "Happy to hear you got some rest—heard you girls chit-chatting 'til late last night."

Mckenna looked across at Nissa with mock guilt. She'd told her everything ("Took you long enough!"), from the incidents on her birthday, to Petronella's vendetta against Alice Kyteler, to being a Wise One tied to a terrifying prophecy. Nissa had been attentive to every word: "Where do you think Abby is, then?" Nissa asked.

"I don't know, maybe Scotland. I thought I'd try that thing I did to find you. But first, I was thinking we should go back to Belfast; last night, I dreamt of Cillian . . ."

Nissa sat up, propping her pillow behind her back. "Was it hot?"

Mckenna slapped her on the arm. "He was telling me to come back. He said it was important that he see me again."

"Do you know if it's a real message?"

"I don't know. I was thinking of the book you borrowed in Kilkenny. Remember the Wise One's ability to dreamwalk?"

"Oh, *right!* Freaky . . . of all books. I mean, it's fiction, but maybe some things are based on truth."

"I tried it."

"You tried to project yourself into someone else's dream?"

"Yeah, Cillian's—to talk to him somehow. I hate how things ended, you know? And there's something about him, it's like he can really see me."

"Mhm." Nissa winked.

Mckenna rolled her eyes. "*Anyway,* it didn't work. I don't even know if dreamwalking is possible."

"Kenna, did you think maybe you only dreamt that because you *want* him to want you to come back?"

Mckenna's face flushed.

That night, the girls stood out on Arethusa's porch, packed and ready to catch the ferry back to Belfast.

"Be good—both of you. And pick up a phone and call once in a while," Arethusa warned, squeezing them in a tight hug. "Look out for each other, whatever you do. I mean it, duckies."

"We promise, Gran," Nissa said. "And don't worry, we'll come visit!"

Arethusa beamed. "Mckenna, a word?" She placed her hands on Mckenna's shoulders and steered her out of earshot. Mckenna waited for the "keep my granddaughter safe" speech, but instead, Arethusa placed a smooth black stone inside her palm. "Black onyx. It absorbs negativity and helps the bearer resist negative influences. Think of it as a shield of sorts."

Mckenna found it strange but thanked her nonetheless. She couldn't shake the feeling that Arethusa knew more than she let on.

They waved at Nissa's grandmother from the road, and just as they began making their way to the town centre, Mckenna stopped in her tracks.

"You okay, Kenna?"

"Yeah, I just feel . . ." she started to say, but she couldn't put it into words. From the moment the wind stirred that morning, she had felt a mysticism drift through the air. "Is it okay if we make one last stop at the faery bridge? I'd like to say good-bye."

What Mckenna thought would be a peaceful walk down to Kewaigue Hill turned out to be the exact opposite. Dark shadows appeared out of the corner of her eyes, some at their heels, some gliding alongside them, and others appearing close enough to brush her cheekbones.

No doubt spirits that roamed the Isle, she thought. She could feel they were drawn to her, vying for her attention.

Shit. Not now.

"Do you think Halloween has something to do with it?"

Mckenna shrugged, then flinched at the sight of the shadow of a brawny man. "Can we just, like, quicken the pace?"

They half-walked, half-ran up the footpath and into the woods. At the sound of the water trickling from the stream, Mckenna's footsteps slowed, and she allowed herself to listen to its calming sounds. The spirits, whoever they were, seemed farther away now, like she had pushed them back somehow.

There was a rustling up ahead. They turned the corner and the bridge came into view, along with a visitor.

At the sight of Cillian sitting by the water's edge, Mckenna's stomach became the stage for a trapeze show again. "How did you . . .?"

Eyes growing wide at the sight of her, he jumped to his feet, took three long strides towards her, and grasped her hands in his. "You have to come with me, lass."

Mckenna swallowed, the touch of his skin shooting fire up her arms and down her body. "Where? What's going on, Cillian?"

"There's someone after you. And if you don't come with me now—"

"Whoa, whoa, Casanova, relax," Nissa said, stepping beside Mckenna. "Where she goes, I go. And whatever you mean to say, spill it."

Cillian turned to Nissa. "It's too dangerous for you."

"Nissa's not leaving," Mckenna said, pulling her hands back.

Cillian ran a hand through his hair. "Fine. Then you both have to leave with me right now."

"Where?"

Cillian sighed. "Ballycastle." *Did he know . . .?* "I'll tell you everything on the way, promise." When Mckenna hesitated, he said, "You see I'm telling the truth, don't you?" He took her hands again and lifted them to his heart, which was beating like a base drum.

She could. But Mckenna could also feel all sorts of other things—anxiety, fear, affection, guilt. "You've been lying to me."

Cillian bit his lip. "I have. I'm not now." His eyes were filled with pain as he gazed at her, unblinking.

Nissa looked from him to Mckenna. "Hang on. Kenna, maybe we should . . . deliberate?"

Mckenna turned to her friend, muttered, "It's okay," and then looked back at Cillian. "You'll tell me everything?"

He nodded, his hands still covering hers.

WILTSHIRE, ENGLAND

"Come on, for old time's sake," Abby urged Seán over dinner. It was the evening of Samhain, the harvest's end and beginning of a new year. A time to honour their ancestors and leave offerings for the dead.

There was a magic around this time that had always pulled him in. Back in the day, he even participated in one of Abby's ritual ceremonies. But he felt it best not to get entangled with all of that again.

They'd been spending quite a bit of time together, meeting up every other day—Abby supposedly had 'business to attend to', but as always, she kept her explanations short. In the meantime, Seán hung back at the café and worked on his illustrations. The publisher would expect them soon, and he had fallen far behind.

"Would you watch, then?" she pleaded.

He looked into her persuasive eyes, which for an instant, he could've sworn flickered to a deep blue, like sapphire.

"Well . . . will you?"

He gazed down at his mushy peas, admiring the volcano he had shaped, then out the window. The town was growing still; children had already finished trick-or-treating, and the moon was at its brightest, a signal of the night's end.

"Fine. For old time's sake."

Looking as pleased as she did the day they met, Abby excused herself to freshen up.

Mckenna and Nissa followed Cillian back up the path.

"Wait, Cillian," Mckenna called after him. "Stop!"

Cillian turned, looking impatient.

"Why Ballycastle?"

"There's no time—"

"Tell us, Cillian, or we're not coming," Nissa said firmly.

Heaving a heavy sigh, he closed his eyes for a moment. He looked like he hadn't slept in days. "I think you need to go back there."

"Why?"

"It's the only place where you're protected. And I think it's the key to sensing where your mum is."

"How did you—?"

"I know who you are, Mckenna," Cillian said. "I've always known."

It was like she was falling from a hundred-storey building. Of course he did. Mckenna felt like a massive imbecile. What were the chances a perfect stranger would be there to chauffeur them around Ireland, offer them places to stay? "Who are you?" was all she could muster.

"I'm a mystic practitioner." Instantly, Mckenna felt faint. How could she not have sensed it? Could she have been so blinded by her attraction to him? "I've gotten good at hiding it," he added, looking both proud and ashamed. "I was sent to protect you on your quest to find your mother. It's important that you do, and you're the only one who can. There's someone after you; it's because of an old prediction . . ."

Elizabeth Dunlop's prophecy. He knew about that, too. Her mind froze and vision doubled, and her body went still, fighting hard to process the words that left Cillian's lips: *Prediction. Mystic. Scrolls.* Finding her breath, she uttered, "Do you know what the Scrolls say?"

"Afraid not," Cillian said quickly. "Listen, there's a High

Priestess who wants to use you to lead her to Abby. She needs both your powers to succeed. But when she's done with you . . ."

Maeve. "She'll kill us," Mckenna finished.

Nissa's hand flew to her mouth. Mckenna had known she was in some kind of danger, but not that her life was at stake. Nissa cleared her throat. "So . . . the, um, High Priestess can't find Abby without Kenna?"

"That's right. When Abby left you as a baby, she cast an enchantment on both of you—that you'd be the only one to find her when you came of age; that's seventeen for a Wise One. But the Priestess is performing a ritual *right now* to lift that enchantment *and* the one protecting Ballycastle."

"So that she can find us both no matter what." It was all starting to make sense.

"Exactly. She uses this ancient stone to dowse—dowsing is like searching for an answer or location using a pendulum," he added. "That's how she's known where you've been all this time."

"Why didn't she just find me and kill me then?"

"She needs both your powers, Kenna," Nissa said gently.

"Right, and if her ritual works tonight, there will be nothing stopping the stone from tracing Abby anymore. But if you find Abby first, you can warn her."

Mckenna let out a bitter laugh. "Impossible. How the hell am I supposed to warn her—?"

"Through astral travel," he said, his eyes desperate, pleading. That was how she'd found Nissa. She stared into them, sensing their sheer urgency.

"And the ritual—why tonight?"

"A complex ritual like this one needs all the power it can get. Tonight is Samhain, where the veil between the living and the dead is thinnest. The spirits, the ancestors she'll be able to invoke . . ." He trailed off, his expression grim.

Nissa gave her a light slap on the arm. "That must be why you're seeing ghosts! Because of Halloween—uh, Samhain."

Mckenna felt like she was having another one of her

nightmares. "How do you know all this? Who sent you to 'protect me'?" she said, using elaborate air quotes.

Cillian hesitated. "I'm sorry. I can't give them away."

Surely, it couldn't be her mother. "Esme?"

He cast her a remorseful glance, implying he couldn't say. Mckenna tried to read him, but all she could feel were her own emotions—of pain, betrayal, confusion. This was too much for her to bear. The feelings she had for him, the feelings she thought he had for her, had it all been merely based on his duty to protect her?

It was Nissa who broke the silence. "Um, so, how would going back to Ballycastle help Kenna sense Abby?"

"I believe she needs to be in a place she's connected to. One that's sacred to her." He stepped closer. "That's where your mum had you, and that's where she knew you'd one day come back to. We have to hurry, though . . ."

Mckenna seized his arm. "Wait. I know of a pretty magical place." Her eyes darted around the trees that loomed over them. "Right here. And I think I know how to find her." Spinning on the spot, she made for the faery bridge, Nissa and Cillian at her heels. Wind whipped her hair as she tore through the trees, imagining her mother's proud face when they set eyes on each other, and praying the High Priestess hadn't yet begun her ritual—

The shadow of the brawny man appeared again out of thin air, making Mckenna stumble backwards onto the path. His energy was heavy, dark. Frozen, she peered into its spectral eyes, black as the earth beneath her feet. *I'm not afraid of you,* she thought, keeping her head level with his. *I'm not afraid of you . . . I'm not afraid of you . . .*

A gravelly inner voice spat back, one that was not her own: *You should be.*

Gulping hard, adrenaline surged through her, her insides flooding with what felt like boiling water, and her eyes wide with fright; her heart was the spout of a kettle, about to burst and sizzle over. She was sweating, too. Was this what a panic attack felt like? Her knees buckling, she reached out to grab what was nearest, but her hand only snatched up air. *Uh-oh,* she thought stupidly, feeling nausea flowing up from her sacral chakra and straight for her head, and the trees blurring through her watery eyes.

Please don't faint. It'll be too late . . . the . . . the Priestess. As the world around her faded, her entire body began pulsing, then vibrating.

POP.

She was standing in some sort of back alley, the clattering of plates and cutlery sounding through the metal doors. Casting down was the glow of the moon, ominous in the dark passage. If it weren't for the graffitied walls that flanked her, she could've sworn she was back in that creepy alleyway in Kilkenny, where Petronella had flogged her until she practically passed out. No, this place was different. Where was she?

One of the metal doors swung open, and stepping out was one of the most stunning women Mckenna had ever seen. She was slender and leggy, with white-blond hair that poured down her back; she had pointed features, smooth and alabaster, like she'd been carved from clay; and her eyes were a deep, penetrating blue.

"You've learned to astral travel, I see. Such a quick learner. Beautiful form . . ." She took several paces towards her, admiring Mckenna's spectral silhouette.

"You're Maeve." From the moment their eyes locked, she knew; she held herself like no other: frightening but bewitching, graceful but commanding, imposing but transcendental. The woman was a walking paradox.

"It's a pleasure to finally meet you, Wise One."

"Where am I? How did you know I was here?"

"I sensed your apparition. What does it matter where we are? Your soul's found me, and for a reason, I'm sure." She waited, her lips forming a slight smile that didn't quite reach her perfect cheekbones.

"I'm here to tell you to stop. Just stop whatever you're doing! Even if you manage to counter Abby's spell, you'll never get us to do what you want. You can screw your Scrolls."

"Hmm," Maeve began, feigning an innocence that didn't suit her. "I don't have to get you to do anything—you'll do that all on your own."

Mckenna's gut twisted. "What are you talking about?"

Her plump lips lifted into a full smile. "You were Elizabeth Dunlop. Don't you remember, Bessie?"

The name Bessie crashed in her ears like a gong. "You're lying," she spat. And yet she recognized the nickname as she did a childhood friend.

Maeve was scrutinizing her. "And those humans, how cruelly they treated you. An unforgivable punishment . . ."

Like a tidal wave, the image of an angry crowd and roaring firepit flooded her mind. The ropes straining her wrists. The shouting. The troll-like man. *"A quick snap of the neck, aye, Bessie girl?"* The flames catching her leather boots . . .

"My dear, it was you who had the prophetic vision, who wrote the Scottish Scrolls."

No. It couldn't be. "There's no way. I'm . . . I'm not evil!" she shouted, though was not the least bit convinced.

Her brow lowered slightly in concern. "Evil? I should think not. You, as Bessie, envisioned a utopia. Peace and harmony on Earth. The natural world thriving."

"At the cost of billions of lives!"

"Not lives, dear—souls. Oh, you've still so much to learn. I've forgotten how young you are. But I've faith in you; you'll soon ken that this is the only path. Tell me, which is the real evil: preserving the natural world, or allowing those who will cause its destruction to continue to have their place here on Earth?"

Before she could protest, she felt a tugging at her chest, like a yarn being pulled from a sweater, unravelling, loosening, until—

POP.

She was back in the woods, lying on the paved path and staring up at the concerned faces of Nissa and Cillian, the latter's warm hand cradling her neck.

"Kenna! Are you okay?"

"Are you hurt? You've hit your head—"

"I'm fine, I'm fine," she insisted, her voice hoarse. "There's no time. Help me get to the bridge . . ."

"What happened, lass?" Cillian asked as he lifted her to her feet.

She gulped. "A ghost came up in my face. I panicked and fainted, that's all."

Her head aching slightly from the fall, Mckenna sat cross legged at the edge of the stream. The mere act of touching the earth sent an outpouring of power through her body, like a current taking the path of least resistance. Only the leaves rustling, stones turning, and flow of water filled her ears. She felt for the small feather inside her coat pocket, the very one that flew into her bedroom window the night she left home. Raising it to her lips, she whispered to it her one wish, then tossed it into the running stream. She waited, hoping for some kind of vision to flash into her mind, like the one she'd had of Seán tucking Abby's note into his wallet. But nothing happened. "Lead me to my mother," she said aloud.

Still, nothing.

"It's not working. I can't do it."

Cillian dropped to the ground to face her. "You can. You're a Wise One, lass."

"I feel like I still don't understand what that really means."

"It means you've got centuries of magical abilities right inside of you. You've got it all, right here." He placed a hand to her heart. She wasn't sure why, but her eyes welled with tears.

Nissa rushed to her side. "You've got this, Kenna." She sat down, too, so the three formed a triangle. She took Mckenna's hand and nudged Cillian to take hers. He nodded and grasped it.

"Lead us to the Wise One's mother," Nissa said.

Cillian joined in. "Lead us to the Wise One's mother."

At last, Mckenna: "Lead us to the Wise One's mother. Lead us to the Wise One's mother."

The wind picked up, and steadily their voices grew stronger.

"Lead us to the Wise One's mother. Lead us to the Wise One's mother. LEAD US TO THE WISE ONE'S MOTHER."

Like flickering tea lights, hundreds of faeries appeared out of the air—specks of blue, yellow, green and white danced around the bridge, stream and trees, flooding the woods with light and radiance.

"Are those . . .?" Nissa whispered in awe.

Mckenna nodded, giving her hand a tight squeeze.

AVEBURY HENGE—WILTSHIRE, ENGLAND

When Seán and Abby reached the stone circle, he stopped just outside of it. "I'll watch from outside the stones."

"If you wish," she said, and stepped inside.

"Did you ask permission?" Seán grinned, remembering their first encounter.

"I always have permission." That wasn't the answer he expected. He meant to ask what she meant by this, but what happened next made words escape him altogether. Her eyes fixed on his, Abby undid her frock's buttons one by one.

Seán couldn't look away. He caught his breath as she lifted the garment over her head and tossed it aside, leaving a stone necklace as the only thing touching her silky skin. Oh, how she lit a fire in him still—one he couldn't seem to put out. Before he knew it, he had stepped past the stones and joined her in the centre of the circle. Then, piece by piece, he removed his clothing, too. She took his hands in hers and, together, they thanked nature for its gracious gifts, promising to continue giving back, from one living entity to another.

On the altar Abby created, a gust of wind blew out two candles, leaving just one to burn. In the dim light casting over her body, Seán found her lips. His mind didn't wander past the moment. He let himself fall at her mercy, their bodies greeting each other for the first time in seventeen years.

"Seán . . ."

"Yes?"

"Will you say something with me?"

"Yes."

"Briseadh an ceangal . . ."

"Briseadh an ceangal," he repeated in a daze.

"Eadar nighean is màthair."

". . . eadar nighean is màthair."

The High Priestess looked down at Seán—the Wise One's flesh and blood and Abigail's one love. It was he who connected them, and so it was only he that could break their magical bond.

She waited for his body to give in, until all senses vanished and only his soul remained, overcome with ecstasy. Bridged with the divine.

"Briseadh an ceangal eadar nighean is màthair." They repeated the Scottish mantra for the final time.

Break the bond between daughter and mother.

Mckenna's body vibrated, until she felt the familiar *POP*. She was soaring through a dark tunnel, fast. *This isn't how it happened last time . . .*

Perhaps because now she was travelling much farther.

She landed in a valley, through which a narrow river rushed, and found herself standing in the shadows of a range of stony mountains; wisps of mist touched the green mountainside, dotted with sparkling pools of water. Had she entered a magical realm?

"Mckenna."

Slowly, she turned, hardly daring to believe who was staring back at her, looking pale, wild-haired, and beautiful. "Mom?"

Abby smiled a smile so warm, it could heat an entire island.

"You found me." Her voice was velvety soft, and her accent resembled Esme's. It was everything she'd imagined it would be.

Mckenna reached out, but she couldn't touch her.

"You're not really here, you're astral projecting," Abby said sadly, but there was pride in her eyes.

"Where am I?"

"Isle of Skye. You must leave now and come to me. I'm in the village of Uig."

"Mom, there's so much I don't understand—"

"You are the bridge, Mckenna. The bridge between all of existence. But your destiny is not written. You *must* remember that."

She could feel herself being pulled away—her body was calling her back. "Mom—"

"I love you, swan."

"Mom!"

POP.

"MOM!" The woods echoed with Mckenna's cry. She was back on the ground with Nissa and Cillian, who was grasping her face in his hands.

He heaved a sigh of relief. "Thought we'd lost you."

"What happened, Kenna?"

The woods were dark again, but a brand-new light shone within. "I found her."

EPILOGUE

Mathis was too late. He surveyed the Wise One as she embarked on the ferry leaving the Isle of Man, his once ethereal body now fully flesh, blood, and bones.

He had been watching over her since she'd left on her journey. The Wise One's third eye was opening, he could tell from the glances she'd cast his way, likely feeling his Arcturian presence. But hovering around in his energetic form wasn't nearly enough—he had made his choice now; without warning the Council, he had left Arcturus and entered the third dimension. Though, his incarnation on Earth was only temporary—just until he completed his mission. The fate of the universe depended on it.

The Council would understand. How much did the girl know? Did she know of the Scrolls? He felt for her, truly. She had little idea what would become of this world if she continued on with Cillian by her side. How had his brother come to choose such an unrighteous path?

He examined their course. They were headed for Scotland. That was where the Akashic Records said it would all begin.

And he had to stop it before it did.

THE TWIN FLAME

I

Thomas Reid

Andre carefully folded his map and slipped it into his back pocket before wearily climbing into the cab. After enduring a grueling six-and-a-half-hour flight from Logan to Heathrow, followed by several uncomfortably lengthy train rides, he was amazed he could stand upright.

The wretched feeling in the pit of his stomach when he spoke to Seán on the phone had lit a fire in him. It defied all reason that Seán would linger with Mckenna's mother for so long when just before his departure, nothing could deter him from searching the world for their daughter.

Their one-of-a-kind, mysteriously mystical, "Wise One" of a daughter.

He'd waited far too patiently for his family to come to their senses. This was about all the foolishness he could take.

"Avebury Henge, please," he said to the cabbie, whose

salt-and-pepper moustache was much too large for his face. He didn't quite know where Seán was staying, but he was certain it was within walking distance of the monument—he visited several times daily, just in case Mckenna turned up.

"It's past midnight, mate," the cabbie grunted. "The monument's closed at this hour."

"That's fine. They must have inns around there, right?"

"In the town, sure."

"To the stone circle, then."

Shrugging, the cabbie stepped on it.

During Andre's seemingly endless journey up to this point, he'd had plenty of time to go over what he was going to say to Seán. For one, how could he have just upped and left without him—in the middle of the worst parental crisis imaginable, no less? Had they really drifted that far apart? It had been a challenging year for them, what with Mckenna's consistent misbehaviour and their ongoing disagreements about how to handle it. Andre had always felt strongly that they needed to be honest about her past, about the inherent powers she surely possessed. But Seán . . . he was hellbent on keeping their daughter from having anything to do with *that world*.

Andre hadn't realized how truly afraid Seán was until he sat Andre and Mckenna down and recounted the whole story. Andre had never known the extent of Abigail's struggles—that someone was after her. All he knew was that her *world* was growing dangerous, and Seán wanted Mckenna far from its poisonous grasp.

But how could Andre ever truly forgive his partner for concealing his true sexual preferences? Seán had, long ago, confided in Andre that Abby had abandoned him and Mckenna when he came out as gay—a falsehood that Seán had perpetuated until just a few months back when he finally revealed the truth: Abby had left her family to shield them from danger. Recently, Andre had discovered that Seán's attraction extended beyond just men; he had expressed to Andre and Mckenna that he was attracted to a person for reasons independent from gender. That he simply loved that individual for who they were in their heart.

Supposedly, Seán had kept this minute detail from Andre because, in his view, it didn't hold significance. Although he might have been in love with Abby in the past, Andre was undoubtedly the love of his life now—and had been since Seán emigrated from Ireland with newborn Mckenna—and there was no reason to introduce any doubt into their relationship.

The cab came to a screeching stop.

"How much?"

"Twenty quid."

Andre rummaged through his pockets. "Will you take thirty American?"

"And what d'you reckon I'm to do with that?"

Andre sighed. "Come on, please. I didn't have a chance to change my money."

"Fifty."

"Forty." Andre slapped two twenties in his hands. The cabbie rolled his eyes, which Andre took as a reluctant *yes*. "Thanks," Andre muttered, and let himself out before the cabbie changed his mind.

The air was both brisk and humid, the kind of cold that crept into your bones and dawdled until your skin was wrapped in goosebumps. Andre buttoned his trench coat and slung his duffel bag over his shoulder as he stepped onto the grass closest to the road, encircling the vast field like a racetrack. In the field's centre, several structures huddled together—most likely homes, but it was difficult to see through the darkness. The entire area remained shrouded in dimness, with the sole sources of light emanating from within the cluster of buildings.

He pressed forward with purpose, his hurried steps guiding him towards the nearest porchlight, all the while silently praying that he'd stumble upon an inn fast.

It's past midnight on Halloween, and I'm a Black man knocking on doors asking for a place to stay. Superb timing, Andre. Should have stayed at the airport hotel until morning . . .

He continued on the path towards the porch, noticing a crooked sign out front that read *The Henge Inn*.

Sighing in relief, he made his way towards what he could now make out was a kind of historic carriage house-turned-cottage, its weathered brick centuries old. *Please have a vacancy, please have a vacancy, please don't kick me to the curb . . .*

His thoughts trailed off when he heard voices shouting in the night. It sounded like a man and a woman, whose muffled grunts and gasps were mixed with the rustle of clothing.

His parents had taught him as soon as he could speak not to get involved in fights. Because at the end of the day, the harsh reality was that he would most likely be the one deemed at fault.

But the struggle, although faint, carried an unmistakable sense of urgency that he couldn't possibly ignore.

". . . WITCH!"

Andre halted. "Witch?" he muttered under his breath. Heaving a heavy sigh, he darted in the direction of the cry.

AVEBURY HENGE, ENGLAND
OCTOBER 31, 1991

"Briseadh an ceangal eadar nighean is màthair."

The moment the foreign words escaped his lips for the final time, Seán found himself staring into blue eyes as deep as sapphire.

Eyes that were not Abby's.

He scrambled backwards, and only then did he become aware of his bare body lying on the dank field. Quivering uncontrollably, he reached for his jeans. "Maeve? What the h-hell happened . . . ?"

He could never forget Abby's witch friend, Maeve. She'd visited Seán and Abby in Ballycastle quite a bit, and before then, they had been inseparable while growing up together in Aberdeen, Scotland. Abby, Maeve, and their other friend—Esme, if he remembered right—were like the three musketeers. Always together, always seemingly planning, plotting.

But what was Maeve doing *here,* at Avebury Henge, in the

middle of the night? He hadn't seen her for over seventeen years. And why on Earth were they both on the ground, stark naked?

He remembered earlier that evening Abby pleading with him to join her Samhain—Halloween—ritual. He remembered walking together from the café . . . and then nothing. Like he'd slipped into a coma.

Why the bleedin' hell *was* he about to join Abby in a ritual?

Maeve chuckled, apparently amused. "You're still such a pure belter, Seán." His whole body cringed at her Scottish slang and thick accent—it'd always been much less endearing than Abby's. "This has been fun." She tousled his hair, and he instinctively pulled back at her icy touch. She chuckled again and grabbed her white frock, which was strewn on the ground beside them.

Seán ripped his eyes away. "Would you put that on and tell me what the Jaysus is going on! Where's Abby?"

She pouted. "Oh, you poor thing. I'm sorry, Seán, but Abby was never here."

He snapped his eyes back towards her, no longer phased by her nakedness. "What are you talking about?"

"Think."

His mind rewound like a cassette tape, all the way back to spotting Abby around the stone circle weeks ago. Why had he been here for so long? He felt as though he'd just snapped out of a dream. When he arrived at Avebury, he vowed to find Mckenna as soon as possible, but every time he suggested they seek Mckenna out, Abby convinced him to stay—and he, for whatever absurd reason, obliged.

He tried to make sense of it. All this time, he *had* been aware of the goings-on around him, but had he been in full control? It felt like he'd been watching himself in a horror film, making stupid decision after stupid decision, unable to intervene. And if he knew Abby as well as he thought he did, she would have pushed to search for their daughter straightaway rather than stay put like a bloody hermit.

Instead he'd been here. Wasting time. Biding time . . . for *her*.

And Abby was never here. Where was his shirt? He scurried

around, searching the ground under the dim glow of the moon and one candle that withstood the breeze. "What did you DO TO ME, WITCH?" his voice echoed around the clearing.

Maeve put a hand to her chest. "You say *witch* like it's a bad thing."

He stood up, nearly tripping over himself. "Where I'm standing, it fecking well is."

She rolled her eyes, and finally slipped the frock over her head. As it cascaded down her slender frame, she smoothed out any wrinkles and took a moment to flatten her pale blond hair. "I'm not certain what our dear Abby's told you in the past, but I'm quite adept at hypnosis, did you ken?"

Seán clenched his jaw. "You Aberdonians and your *ken*. Speak from this century, will you?"

Eyes narrowed up at him, she flashed him a wicked grin. "People all over the world come to see *me*," she said, dismissing his remark. "I've helped many rid themselves of terrible habits through past-life regression."

Past-life regression. He'd heard that term before. "You used to practice on Abby, didn't you?"

Maeve buttoned her left sleeve. "She was kind enough to be my first patient."

"More like experiment—"

"It's thanks to Abigail I was able to push my potential. I could send people's minds and souls back centuries to observe their past lives. It was then I realized how powerful the mind truly is. I could, say, alter one's consciousness. Just like that"—she snapped her fingers—"their perception could be entirely skewed. That method proved handy in helping take care of some bad people. Oh, not to worry—they deserved it." Seán flinched at the indifference in her voice. "And all I've ever had to do was force them to see whatever it is I wanted them to see."

A sudden tautness assaulted his insides. *No. She couldn't have. This entire time . . .*

Slowly, she rose from the ground. "I made you see your dear

Abby weeks ago, right here. I made you look into her eyes whenever you looked into mine. I made you smell her."

He was going to be sick.

"I made you stay."

No! "You bitch."

"It was rather easy. Some whispers here and there . . . Your mind is *very* malleable. Have you completely forgotten everything Abigail taught you about protecting your energy field?"

"You're a complete psychopath, you know that?"

"I kept you here until this very night," she went on. "The most powerful night of the year, so I could call upon my ancestors to break the protection spell Abigail cast long ago."

And he was the key to reversing it. "So you could find her. But why? Why are you desperate to find her?" His eyes grew wide at the realization that all this time, Mckenna was still out there, alone. Nowhere to be found. Did she want her, too? "And where's *my daughter*?" he said through gritted teeth.

"I won't lie, I don't ken at this very moment, but I trust she won't be hard to find." Her fingers grazed the stone pendant dangling low on her chest. "And now, thanks to my lovely ritual, Abigail won't be either."

"Why did you need me for your sick ritual?" he spat.

"As the Wise One's flesh and blood, and Abigail's one love, you have unique ties to them, and therefore you're the only one who could break their magical bond."

Seán's legs acted of their own accord—he leapt for her, taking her down to the ground, his hands wrapped around her long neck.

She smirked. "Oh, do you care for another round?"

His fingers squeezed tighter. "You disgust me."

She let out a half-laugh, half-cough. "You won't do it," she choked.

His face grew hot, and his entire body shook with rage. He couldn't let her go—he *wouldn't*. She had humiliated him. Humiliated Andre. She was going to hurt Mckenna, Abby . . . And who knew what the devil else she had planned. He had wasted enough time. He wanted her gone.

He wanted to see the light leave her eyes.

A vein popped beneath his thumb, and he watched the blood rush to her head.

Andre hurried towards the struggle. In the distance, he spotted a flickering flame in the centre of a smaller stone circle within a large outer one. In the heart of the smaller circle were two figures, rolling around in the grass . . . half-naked? He squinted, unsure whether he was interrupting something or witnessing a murder. He inched closer, ever so quietly.

Both his jaw and his duffel bag dropped.

Seán was straddled on top of a woman as pale as snow, his hands wrapped around her bony neck. She was wearing a thin, loose-fitting frock, and Seán nothing but a pair of jeans.

Shirtless. Why was he shirtless?

"Seán!"

His partner's head lifted towards him. "Andre?" he shouted in disbelief, his voice trembling. His body was trembling too, copiously. But his hands, still seizing the woman, were unmoving.

"Seán, wh-what are you doing?"

"Don't come any closer, Andre! She's dangerous."

"I don't know what's going on, but you need to stop!"

"She's a lunatic. She wants our daughter—she wants Abby. I'm going to finish this . . ."

Andre took a step closer. "You're not *finishing* anything, Seán. Let's talk about this, before you do something you regret." He watched as the love of his life was literally squeezing the life out of someone. "Please, I don't want to lose you again. You'll end up in jail for this. Let her go, and we'll find Mckenna together."

Tears streamed down Seán's face as he shook his head fervently. "I w-won't let her run."

"Just . . . just loosen your grip, okay?" Andre said gently, feeling déjà vu. He'd been in this position before with clients, talking them down from doing something detrimental. "I'll tie up her wrists. I think I have a tie wrap in here . . ." He bent down and dove into his duffel, rummaging through his belongings.

The woman gasped violently for air.

"Seán! Wait, I said I'm looking . . ."

"H-h-help," the woman rasped.

His eyes bulging, Seán shouted, "SHUT UP!"

Andre lunged, seizing Seán's waist and rolling him over to the woman's side.

"Andre—no!"

DALRY, NORTH AYRSHIRE, SCOTLAND
1572

Elizabeth Dunlop was afraid for her cow, Bonnie-Jean. She'd been looking unwell for days and hadn't produced milk in weeks.

"A bit of exercise might work wonders for you," *And I could use it too*, she thought, tenderly stroking the cow's chin. She led Bonnie-Jean out of the barn and up the winding road towards the gardens of Monkcastle, taking in the scent of burnt peat and the musty aroma of wet leaves. There was a common grazing by the old castle, where she often walked her cattle and sheep; it served a dual purpose—a leisurely stroll through the village to exchange greetings with neighbours, and an opportunity for her animals to revel in the attention they never failed to receive.

"Bessie, m'dear!" shouted Ms. Wilson from her front porch, a rake in hand. It was thanks to her that Bessie awoke every morning at the crack of dawn to wafts of freshly baked bread; it'd become a great comfort of hers. "It's a dreich day, what are you doing out and about?"

"Good day, Ms. Wilson. I find a stroll after a rain refreshes the soul."

Ms. Wilson tilted her head in a proud motherly manner. "Always a creative thinker, our Bessie." She glanced up and down the road, and leaned on her rake. "How's the bairn doing? And poor Andrew?"

"It's very kind of you to ask, Ms. Wilson. I'm afraid they're still unwell, as is Bonnie-Jean."

The truth was Bessie was not afraid for her husband, and the reason for this was much too preposterous to voice aloud, let alone burden an old lady with. Mere weeks prior to today, Bessie was in labour when a strange and striking woman, small in stature but grand in presence, strode into her bedroom. "Might I trouble you for a drink, ma'am?" she'd asked.

Bessie found it quite eccentric for a stranger to be barging into her home unannounced, demanding a drink whilst she suffered through labour, but she obliged nonetheless. The woman thanked her, and uttered parting words that haunted her to this day: "Bessie, your bairn will die, but your husband will be mended of his sickness."

Before Bessie could ask how she knew her name and how she'd come to know such a dreadful thing, the woman left without another word. Bessie had since tried to come to terms with the impending death of her one and only bairn, which she knew in her heart and soul would be any day now.

"Are you quite alright, Bessie?"

Bessie looked up at a concerned-looking Ms. Wilson. She'd let her mind wander for too long; she must've looked like a loon. "My apologies, Ms. Wilson. I've much on my mind. I fear I didn't catch your words."

"Of course, m'dear. I said the stroll will help old Bonnie-Jean. And I shall pray for your family."

"Thank you, Ms. Wilson. You are most generous." With a gentle wave, Bessie continued her promenade, Bonnie-Jean at her side, fighting to keep the tears behind her eyes from escaping.

The abandoned castle was ensconced within a thicket of trees, its surrounding gardens more alive than the castle had been in decades, with leaves of deep red, burnt orange, and golden yellow covering the ground like a rich tapestry. For a moment she slowed herself to admire the thistles, wild roses, and meadowsweets, no longer in full bloom but not yet wilted from the autumn wind. As she cupped a pink rose in her hand, so prim and perfect, unbeknownst to its impending death, she could not contain her sorrow any longer. The moment her knees hit the ground, she wept and wept.

Bessie would soon lose almost everything she loved.

She didn't know how long she was there, crying into her palms. Minutes—or perhaps hours—later, the clouds parted, and a light shone through a dyke nestled deep within the gardens. Bessie shielded her eyes with her hands, and as she lowered them, a man appeared before her, emerging from the cove. Her first impression was that he looked severe, perhaps because he was dressed spiffily in a clean shirt and trousers, but his five o'clock shadow and caramel-coloured eyes softened his presence.

Wherever did he come from? Had he heard her crying?

"Good day," the man said in a thickly, resonant voice. It was one of authority, confidence.

Bessie shot up from the ground and instinctively placed a hand on Bonnie-Jean's neck. She hesitated before returning the greeting. "Good day."

"Why do you weep, my dear Elizabeth?"

He knew her name. "How do you—?"

"It matters not. I am here to guide you."

It was strange because in that moment, Bessie felt as though it really didn't matter how he came to know her name, or what he meant by *here to guide you*. She should have disgorged question after question, but instead, like a churchgoer in a confession booth, she unburdened herself of her worries—how her cow and sheep were ill, and it would soon become impossible to make ends meet; how her bairn and husband were sickly; how a stranger predicted that while her husband would recover, her newborn would die; how she was ashamed that she wished her husband would die in her bairn's stead.

"A terrible plague is sweeping across the land, and so 'tis true your bairn will die. I'm afraid Bonnie-Jean will, too, as will two of your sheep."

Bessie let the tears fall until there were none left to shed. "Wh-who are you?"

"My name is Thomas Reid. You can call me Thom." And with that, the man named Thom turned around and ducked into the same small cove from whence he came.

"Wait!" Bessie followed but stopped at the threshold, for it was much too narrow to squeeze into.

She peered inside. It was empty.

GLASGOW, SCOTLAND
NOVEMBER 1991

"Thom!" Mckenna O'Dwyer shouted, snapping out of her dream. She stared up at Nissa and Cillian's equally flummoxed expressions, then rubbed at her eyes. Where had she been just then? And where was she now?

Sunlight beamed in through the hotel window, cascading over the pearl-white comforter. Squinting, she looked around until everything snapped back into focus. Two double beds, classic mahogany furniture, and a view of the haunting Glasgow Necropolis, a Victorian-era cemetery that loomed over the end of the street, dominating the entire hillside.

Right. She, Nissa, and Cillian had checked into a bed and breakfast when they arrived in Scotland two days ago on an Isle of Man ferry.

"Who's Thom?" Nissa said, raising an eyebrow.

Mckenna breathed a sigh of relief; simply having Nissa nearby was enough to calm her. Nissa tucked a loose pink strand behind her ear, a habit she had whenever she was overly concerned, Mckenna noticed. Her pixie haircut had grown out, and her mostly dirty-blond hair now fell just above her shoulders. Time had certainly passed quickly since that day in the schoolyard, when Mckenna had sent her wren companion flying into Nissa's bully's head.

"I'm . . . not sure," Mckenna muttered, running a hand through her auburn curls.

Cillian's brow furrowed in concern. "Are you alright, lass? You were crying. A lot."

How many more times am I gonna wake up crying? "Yeah, I'm fine," she muttered meekly, sagging back against the headboard.

Cillian placed his hand on hers, but she jerked it back. "I said I'm fine."

He retreated. "Sorry, I was just—"

"You know what?" Nissa said, giving Cillian a firm pat on the shoulder. "Do you think you can grab some tea in the breakfast room? I think that'll do her some good."

Feeling Cillian's eyes on her, Mckenna fixed her gaze on the landscape painting of a mountainside town hanging on the wall opposite her. The colours were muted, dull.

"Okay, spill," Nissa said as the door snapped shut behind Cillian. She leaped onto the bed and grasped Mckenna's hands.

Mckenna hung her head. "I had another dream. It felt so real. I . . ." She trailed off, doing her damnedest to cling to the images before they faded away.

"Maybe it was. Describe it to me."

"It was about me . . . as Elizabeth Dunlop. The witch who predicted the Scottish Scrolls." She went on to describe the scene in detail, enjoying Nissa's *oohs* and *ahs* along the way. "And then, he just disappeared through the cove thingy . . ."

"So weird. This sounds like it happened before she knew she was a witch."

"Exactly. It's crazy, Nissa. I feel like I know her, you know?"

"Well, she *was* you."

It seemed like forever ago that Maeve, the High Priestess who'd been hunting her, told her she was the very witch who predicted the Scottish Scrolls . . .

"You, as Bessie, envisioned a utopia. Peace and harmony on Earth. The natural world thriving."

"At the cost of billions of lives!"

"Not lives, dear—souls. Oh, you've still so much to learn.

I've forgotten how young you are. But I've faith in you; you'll soon ken that this is the only path. Tell me, which is the real evil: preserving the natural world, or allowing those who will cause its destruction to continue to have their place here on Earth?"

"Who are we talking about?" Cillian chimed in as he entered, balancing a tray of three steaming mugs of tea.

"No one," Mckenna said quickly. Cillian looked askance, as though it would help distinguish her lies from the truth.

She'd exchanged few words with Cillian since their departure for Scotland. Needless to say, the ferry ride had been awkward. The truth was, she couldn't bring herself to trust him again; he flat-out lied about being a mystic practitioner who had known her true identity from the start, and who'd supposedly been sent to help her find her mother.

Despite the complexities of their relationship, he had, in a sense, saved her life—journeying all the way to the Isle of Man to warn her about the High Priestess . . . helping her locate her mother . . . rekindling her understanding of the magic she, as a Wise One, possessed. Her mind drifted to the way he'd placed his hand on her heart, reminding her of the centuries of magic inside of her.

Still, he would not tell her who sent him to "protect" her on her quest to find her mother. And she simply didn't care for any more secrets.

Seán watched Maeve fight for breath, then turned to stare into his partner's eyes. "Andre, I'm telling you. We can't let her get away—she manipulated me! I promise, I'll explain everything."

Andre huffed. "Okay, I'll hold her down." As he stepped towards Maeve, a sudden violent wind hit them like a hurricane, pressing both their bodies against the ground.

Maeve was muttering under her breath, looking as determined as ever.

"Seán, is she . . . ?"

"Jaysus, she is. Take my hand! Hurry," Seán shouted over the gale, feeling for Andre's hand.

Maeve was on her feet, her arms extended on both sides, her gaze fixed upon the sky. A current of air, fiercer now, hurled them backwards, causing Seán to collide with one of the boulders within the inner circle.

"Seán!"

"I'm okay! We need to get to her," Seán shouted, rubbing at his shoulder blade.

With a nod, Andre crouched low to the ground, battling against the raging winds. He summoned every ounce of his strength to make his way towards her. *Push . . . harder . . .*

A tempest had formed around them, originating from the outer stone circle. The winds twisted and swirled, gradually closing in. The air turned ice cold and nearly unbreathable. Andre struggled for each breath as both oxygen levels and temperatures plummeted. She had conjured a tornado, and he was in its death zone.

Just a little . . . farther . . .

A warlike cry erupted from him, causing Maeve to break concentration. As she looked down at Andre, the tornado ceased, and its residual winds ran their course. Andre seized the moment and lunged for her ankles.

She tumbled to the ground, and he pounced, pinning her down, his fingers tangled in the chain around her neck. "Make it stop, Maeve!"

"Now, why would I do that?" As if puffing out a birthday candle, she blew a gentle breath across his face.

He was sent flying several feet into the air before landing beside a shivering Seán. They lay there until the winds dwindled, and the still night finally returned.

Andre's eyes darted around the stone circle, pain coursing through his entire body. "She's gone. I'm sorry, Seán. I couldn't stop her."

Seán flinched as he made to sit up against the stone boulder, then placed a hand on Andre's leg. "That's alright, luv. You're a hero. *My* hero."

Andre's heart fluttered. "And you're an idiot."

"I do not deny these allegations," Seán said, his hands up in surrender.

"I did manage this, though. Not sure if it'll help." Andre nudged Seán's hand and slipped something pointed into his palm.

Seán's eyes grew wide. "Oh, luv. This is good. This is very good."

II

A GHOST, AGAIN

Mckenna admired the way Nissa could pack down three blueberry scones in one sitting.

"No more detours, Casanova," Nissa said in the midst of scarfing down her last bite. "We go straight to Oog." She'd insisted that morning they discuss their plan over breakfast, surely an effort to ease the tension between Mckenna and Cillian. It was quite the spread: fruits, yogurt, pastries, cereal, and scones, of course—Nissa's new favourite breakfast, midday snack, and evening dessert.

Mckenna nudged Nissa's elbow. "Uig."

"Ueeg."

"No, it's like, U-ig."

"I agree, let's head there straightaway," Cillian said, surprising them both. Normally, he seized every opportunity to play tour guide. "The Isle of Skye's a long way."

Mckenna split her scone open and smeared blackberry jam on it like it deserved to be punished. "How long?"

Cillian eyed her scone, looking afraid for its life. "Erm, well, it's about two hundred kilometres from here—"

"Speak American, please," Mckenna spat. Her scone was now drowning in jam.

"About a hundred and twenty miles? I reckon if we leave tomorrow morning and drive nonstop—"

"Better believe it."

"—we should get there by early afternoon."

"Sounds good to me."

Nissa looked from Mckenna to Cillian, then clapped her hands together. "Glad that's decided! Cillian, how about you get us a car rental? We'll meet you back here for some dinner and make it an early night."

Mckenna's gaze briefly flicked in his direction, and in that moment, a sharp pang of sadness washed over her. It wasn't her own emotion but his; as she locked eyes with him, she delved into his energy field, her heart sinking with each passing second.

No, she ordered herself. This has to stop. Before her empathic abilities could overwhelm her, she suppressed Cillian's emotions, burying them deep in what she called "the barracks of her mind"—a coping mechanism she'd devised to contain foreign feelings, those that didn't originate from within. It was the only way she knew to preserve her sanity, or at least a semblance of it.

Who the hell cares what he's feeling? Sorry or not, remorseful or not, he didn't warrant her sympathy, let alone her empathy. Lately, she'd adopted an unusually icy demeanor, a deliberate effort to shield herself from experiencing whatever emotions he was harbouring. The lines between her own feelings and his had blurred, making it nearly impossible to differentiate them.

And so far, being an asshole had proven effective . . . as long as she avoided eye contact with him.

Mckenna happily allowed Nissa to escort her through downtown Glasgow for the entire day, grateful to have a friend who knew exactly what her soul needed: a few hours of purposeless meandering to distract her from, well, everything. Since Samhain, she'd discovered that she was a Wise One—across her various lifetimes, she had incarnated as a witch, endowing her with innate abilities spanning centuries. She also discovered that one of these incarnations was Elizabeth Dunlop—the very witch who had prophesized her destiny as "the last living Wise One," fated to save the natural world by "expiring" billions of souls on Earth. In addition to this burden, she learned that a High Priestess had been relentlessly pursuing her and her mother's powers to fulfill Dunlop's sixteenth-century prophecy. And finally, her mother was hidden away in a town called Uig on the Isle of Skye.

It was easy to fall for Glasgow, reminding Mckenna of Boston in how its bustling energy belied its quaint charm. A fascinating blend of old and new, the city's rich history was evident from some of the Victorian architecture and cobblestone roads. As they explored the city centre, Mckenna admired the eclectic mix of big stores and small shops, each one luring them with its unique offerings. The air was thick with the aroma of fresh-baked goods wafting out of bakeries, tempting them to indulge despite their dwindling funds. And amidst it all, coffee shops, restaurants, and bars sprang up seemingly out of nowhere, each one ready to offer a taste of Glasgow.

"Tell me those are not freshly made donuts," Nissa squealed as they passed a yellow storefront with the most glorious display of donuts Mckenna had ever seen. Each was drizzled with thick, coloured glaze and sprinkled with a variety of chunky chocolate toppings. "Also, are you planning on avoiding Cillian until we find your mom?"

"Thought you'd slip that in, did ya?"

The answer to Nissa's question, of course, was yes, but it wouldn't be easy. How did it make sense that all she yearned for was to be close to him when, A—he was a liar; and B—she knew virtually nothing about him? The real him, the mystic practitioner, as he referred to himself. What did that even mean? Was he self-taught, or did he possess inherent abilities, too?

She shrugged as they rounded the street corner and found themselves back in front of the hotel. "He's frustrating. I'm not sure what to think. But I still . . . you know . . ."

"Like him?"

Mckenna grunted. "Why, though? I hate him."

"Because he's hot, dingus."

"Dingus, really?"

"And he calls you lass. 'Oh, lass . . . I have a sexy Irish accent . . .'"

"Ew, my dad has, like, the same accent, stop!" Mckenna whined, giving Nissa a punch on the arm. "Also, I'd like to think I'm not that shallow."

Nissa snort-laughed back. "For real, I think it's just because there's an undeniable connection—these things, you can't predict or control them. I assume that's why you're keeping him around?"

Mckenna sighed. Nissa was right, and it was annoying as hell. "You think he's too old?"

Nissa raised an eyebrow. "Aren't you, like, ancient?"

"True. Age is but a number, really," she said in a terrible British accent, waving a hand in mid-air like an aristocrat.

"But no. I'm pretty sure John was at least ten years older than Brigit."

"Oh, yeah, a hundred percent."

"And they're great together!" Nissa released more snort-laughs, making Mckenna double over. The two stood there chuckling for several minutes, recalling the memory of Brigit shouting at John about apricots.

Finally relieved of the giggles, Mckenna stared out into the distance; the Glasgow Necropolis looked both eerie and beautiful at dusk. She'd been admiring it from her room since they arrived, and last night she could've sworn she saw the faint outline of a spectral figure gliding up and down the same row of tombstones. Even all the way from her room, it looked lost, lonely, and purposeless, not unlike how Mckenna felt for most of her life.

"No," Nissa said, watching her.

"What?"

"You're not taking a stroll around the creepy cemetery. It's already pretty dark out."

Mckenna looked down at her watch, shocked to see it was only 4:15. "So what? It's not creepy, it's . . . peaceful."

"And full of ghosts, who are just begging for a weirdo like you to talk to."

She was counting on it. "Nissa, it's fine, I won't be long. I promise, I'll be back for dinner."

The truth was, she hated how terrified she was of ghosts. It made her feel like a complete impostor, this supposed all-powerful Wise One—some sort of bridge to all of existence, according to Abby—who secretly slept with a night light. How would she ever tap into her true potential if she couldn't even confront the occasional dead person? It was high time she faced her fears head-on. Admittedly, Petronella might have chased her down and given her a thorough flogging until she was nearly knocked out, but to be fair, she had been grievously wronged. All poor Petronella had needed in the end was a heartfelt apology and some closure, both of which Mckenna had provided as a reincarnation of Petronella's former mistress (and, frankly, deserter)—the infamous witch of Kilkenny, Dame Alice Kyteler.

Sighing, Nissa shook a finger at her. "I'm coming to get you if you're not home in thirty minutes."

With a thumbs up and a "You got it, dude!" (Michelle Tanner style), she crossed the road and turned onto Castle Street. It had been a beat since she was fully alone with her thoughts; from cruising to Dublin with John and Brigit—their honorary grandparents—to road-tripping with Nissa and Cillian, to training with Esme, to bunking with Nissa and her grandmother, Arethusa, to reuniting with Cillian at the faery bridge, she'd scarcely been in her own company.

"Ouch!" she yelped when her knee collided with a low stone wall that ran along the bottom of the hill. Rubbing the sore spot, her eyes travelled upwards and widened at the sight of an exquisitely crafted terracotta monument of a sharply arched doorway, with ornamental columns and detailed mouldings fit for an earl's dwelling. Had it not been for the charcoal stone barrier that stood in place of the opening, she would have thought it a portal to a neighbouring land. You never know, she thought, her fingertips grazing the damp stone, half expecting the solid wall to turn to jelly.

Nope, it's just a monument.

Was she losing her grip on reality? Given everything that had transpired lately, she found it increasingly difficult to discern what was possible and what wasn't. Magic felt surprisingly tangible, more rooted in the world than she could ever have imagined. It was as if it lingered just within her grasp, a feeling that had intensified since her seventeenth birthday, and particularly after her lessons with Esme in Ballycastle. Each time she stepped outdoors, she sensed it—in a muddy path, in the sway of trees, in the presence of a wilting flower. In retrospect, she recognized that she had always been attuned to the presence of magic; it simply revealed itself in less refined forms, like her deep appreciation for the crisp autumn air and her enduring fascination with the night sky.

In the past month, however, her awareness was magnified; she could almost hear the wind whispering secrets, could sometimes spot the shadows of elemental creatures stepping in and out of their respective realms. And most certainly, she could feel the energy radiating from all living beings—at times much too strongly . . . In fact, since she hopped on the ferry to Scotland, she couldn't shake the feeling she was being carefully watched. She'd kept looking up stupidly, as if a falcon would swoop down at any moment and throw her overboard.

She'd felt it here in Glasgow, too.

I need to learn how to protect my energy field, she told herself as she walked the paved path up the hill, passing Gothic spires, weathered tombstones, and memorial statues. The Necropolis was huge—she'd read on a plaque somewhere that fifty thousand burials had taken place here, and the grounds had something like thirty-five hundred tombs. She'd always loved graveyards, which wasn't something she usually cared to admit. Besides Wednesday

Addams, what sort of weirdo liked to hang around a field of corpses? But she'd never seen it that way—even before she knew a soul didn't simply die with its host, but lived on for many, many lives.

She gave her body a good shake, vowing to herself not to think about her past lives, Bessie Dunlop's prophecy, and the Scottish Scrolls tonight. Instead, she opted to admire the various tombstones, stopping every so often to take them in.

She gravitated towards a small stone plaque lying flat on the ground, the name and year covered by moss and dirt, and sat in front of it. If she truly wanted to open herself up to the spirit world, she had to make centring and grounding herself second nature. She longed to feel that same connectedness to the Earth she'd felt under the Harvest Moon at the delegates' cocktail party in Belfast, and when she'd sensed the presence of that melancholic ghost, the wandering Grey Lady, amongst the tunnel of warped birch trees. From what she understood, the spirit plane was not far from their own. Esme had explained that spirits had to have lowered their vibration significantly to be seen in the physical plane, and their low-energy state was typically tied to some unfinished business. Equally, if she mastered how to raise her own vibration, through the simple practice of centring, grounding, and clearing her chakras—energy centres—she could just imagine what other planes and dimensions she could access.

Centre and ground. Placing her hand on the spot below her navel—also her sacral chakra, where her centre was, for that was where she felt her emotions the strongest—she closed her eyes and inhaled for three Mississippis, then let out a long exhale. Unburdening herself the only way she knew how, she let her worries melt into a heap of grotesque, murky liquid, which she pictured pouring out of a medieval goblet (the dramatic image seemed to work for her).

Feeling a weight being lifted, she let out another long, drawn-out breath. Like Esme taught her, she imagined herself as a tree, roots sprouting from the soles of her shoes—it was much too cold out to be barefoot—and into the grassy hill. She was the very earth she stood on, as well as the Earth she lived on; her core was its core. She was here for a purpose, and as the top of her head grazed the clouds above her, she knew her place. Not as the wondrous tree she embodied in this transcendent moment, but as an ancient soul who would change the course of history.

The wind picked up, as though in acknowledgement of her truth, a truth she was no longer afraid to embrace, and she opened her eyes. Her senses heightened, she intuited that each tombstone held its own vibration—some high, perhaps visited frequently, and others much lower, possibly neglected for years or unseen in the shadow of some of the more extravagant designs. Which probably wouldn't sit well with any spirits that returned to visit their graves . . .

As the thought entered her mind, the hairs along her neck prickled. There was someone here. An entity—maybe the one she'd spotted gliding about.

Don't be afraid. This is what you wanted. She rose from the ground and turned her head slowly, praying it wasn't another vendetta-driven ghost. It would take some time to get over Petro-nella, even if she had eventually gone to the light.

The spectral figure of an elderly woman stood before her. She had short, stark white hair, waves of wrinkles along her forehead, and hooded eyes, the dark bags beneath them telling Mckenna she'd suffered greatly before her death.

"Good evening, d-dear," the spirit said in a motherly cadence, her Scottish accent much heavier than any Mckenna had yet heard.

"Hello," was all Mckenna could think to reply.

The spirit grazed the tombstone, staring at it in admiration. Mckenna followed her gaze—the name read Lily Williams.

"Is that—is that you?"

The spirit's vacant eyes travelled from the stone to Mckenna. "Mm? Oh, no . . . b-but close, I suppose. Me name is L-Lilias Adie. That is a b-beautiful thought, however. Thank you, d-dear."

Mckenna was unsure what she meant by this and whether she

should press on, but her curiosity got the better of her. "What do you mean by that?"

Lilias smiled a sad smile. "I'm n-not as worthy as that," she replied, her chin lifted towards the grave.

"Why not?"

"They believed me a w-witch, and witches don't g-get proper burials."

Mckenna swallowed, and her heart sank into the depths of her stomach. "Do you want to tell me what happened?"

Lilias drifted closer, and it was a test of Mckenna's resolve to not back away. "A n-neighbour of m-mine had a wee bit much to d-drink one night. I don't ken why, but she told everyone I was coming after her." As she spoke, the image of a very alive Lilias being seized by the arms and dragged out of her home materialized before Mckenna, like a hologram. "I've no idea w-what I c-could have done to anger her," she continued. "I was t-taken to the local m-minister of Torryburn, in Fife. There, I was accused of p-practicing witchcraft and s-sleeping with the devil." Her voice trembled on the words witchcraft and devil. The holographic Lilias faded into an image of a church, where Lilias was shackled like an animal to a rusty iron ring on the edge of the altar, as though it was designed for such an occasion. "The church forced a confession out of me—I-I had no ch-choice. I wanted the pain to stop. They sentenced me to b-burn at the stake, but . . . I refused to suffer such a d-death."

Poof. The hologram vanished, leaving only mist hanging between them. Mckenna hesitated before gently whispering, "You ended your life before . . . didn't you?" Lilias turned away, and Mckenna took that to mean she did. "Do you know what happened to your body?"

"I-I'm not certain, really . . ." She looked at the tomb with longing, stroking its engravings like she would a dear pet.

Mckenna swallowed, keeping the lump in her throat down. Lilias didn't need her tears—she needed hope. She needed to rest. "What if we find a spot just for you, Lilias? Would you like that?"

Lilias's small mouth stretched into a sweet, toothless smile. "I should like that very much."

"Lass, who're you talking to?"

Mckenna spun around, and there Cillian stood, with what looked like a brand-new black suede jacket rippling in the wind behind him.

"What are you doing here?" she said, a bit more defensively than she intended.

"Nissa was worried."

Her insides danced a little. *I was worried* was what he meant. "I'm fine. I don't need a babysitter."

"I never thought you did."

She scoffed. "Are you sure about that, because you literally popped into my life out of nowhere to do just that."

"I was following orders."

Orders? "What the hell, Cillian, could you be any vaguer?" This was such bullshit. Crossing her arms over her chest, she turned back to Lilias.

She was gone.

Great.

His footsteps approached her from behind. "I vowed to help you find your mum, lass. And I vowed to keep silent. It was all for a grander purpose. What would you have had me do?"

"Tell me what's going on, not lead me to believe you're some perfect stranger."

"Perfect, eh?"

"Don't . . ."

"I'm sorry. I wish I could have told you the truth from the very beginning."

She wanted to stalk off, leave him there among the dead, pondering his mistakes. Instead, she turned around to face him. "I did think it pretty convenient, running into you and suddenly having a way to Northern Ireland. Nissa thought it was just someone being nice. Like John and Brigit. Yeah, right . . ."

"Actually, John and Brigit were sent to you by the fae folk. To help get you closer to finding your mum."

"How do you know that?"

Cillian said nothing.

"More secrets," she mumbled, and turned away. Her eyes were drawn to a towering sandstone column that rose up from among the graves, mere feet away. At the top of the column stood a statue of a man, clutching a Bible in his right hand. The details of the statue were impressive, from the folds of the figure's gown to the intricate etchings on the cover of the sacred text. She squinted—the base of the column revealed the man was John Knox (c. 1513–1572), and he was a former Scottish minister who played a key role in establishing the Church of Scotland.

As she stared into its stony eyes, a tremor coursed through her body. The longer her gaze lingered, the more certain she became that this was not a man she would have wanted to cross paths with. His eyes seemed to follow her, unblinking and relentless, as if daring her to challenge his authority. Her mind conjured up vivid images of the time period the statue represented—a time of harsh judgment and cruel punishments. She could almost feel the weight of those ancient beliefs pressing down on her, suffocating her.

Cillian took a step forward and grabbed her hand, transporting her back to the present moment. Her skin burned at his touch.

"I know because of a seer. Her name's Pravadi."

Mckenna peered down at their hands, loosely entwined. A seer. Is that how he knew there was a High Priestess after her? "Okay . . . So, John and Brigit were sent by the faeries. Were they, like, even aware of what was going on?" She'd hate to think their encounter was inauthentic.

He looked as though he was fighting back a laugh. "Of course. They were completely themselves; they just got a sort of nudge from the fae . . . . The good people can be persuasive. Some whispers here and there, and it'll just seem like an inner voice."

"The good people?"

"Oh, yeah, it's just a superstition, I suppose. It's said they like to be called that."

"Okay," she said again, trying to keep her voice steady.

"And why do the fae want me to find my mom so badly?" The answer to her question came to her before Cillian could weigh in. During their brief astral encounter, Abby said something about Mckenna being the bridge between worlds, between all of existence, to be more specific. She didn't know what that meant, and she wasn't sure if she could trust Cillian with this yet. She pulled her hand back.

It seemed he could sense her trepidation, because rather than respond, he took a step towards her. "Lass, is there something you're not telling me? Back at the faery bridge, you fainted, but it seemed like . . ."

I was astral projecting, Mckenna thought. She hadn't yet disclosed her little astral chat with the High Priestess—Maeve. Or the fact that Mckenna was a reincarnation of Bessie Dunlop, who predicted the Scottish Scrolls . . . and who was destined in this lifetime to bring peace to the natural world by banishing billions of souls. Or did he already know all of that? Esme's voice echoed in her head as she recalled the prophecy: *As twin flames rekindle and the last living Wise One unites with her creator, billions of souls shall expire upon this Earth. Peace shall be restored to the natural world, and all beings shall exist in perfect harmony.*

"Were you astral travelling? Did you see someone other than your mum that night?" Cillian said.

"Yes," she finally said, against her better judgment. Why did he make her so weak? "The High Priestess."

She could have sworn she heard Cillian gulp. "You . . . you saw the High Priestess?"

Mckenna nodded.

"What did she say?"

Her eyes fell to the ground, and she hugged herself.

He closed any bit of distance left between them. "I can help you. And you can trust me—I'm on your side."

His body was much too close for her to think clearly. The wind picked up again, and the solemn silence was interrupted by the rustling of leaves.

She lifted her gaze. His eyes were more green than grey today.

Could she trust him?

Gently, he lifted her hands and entwined his fingers with hers. "You have to know, Mckenna, I will do anything and everything to protect you. And if there are things I'm not telling you right now, I promise, I have a good reason. I want to go back to being us again. D'you reckon we can?"

For the first time since arriving in Glasgow, she let her guard down. A rush of emotions wrapped her around like a wool blanket, prickly and comforting all at once; she felt his fear of losing her, his need to help her, his desire to be with her.

She wanted to say, I'll think about it, but she still didn't forgive him for lying. He would have to do a lot more than declare false promises to get her to trust him again.

"Take me to my mother. And I'll think about it," she said, then let their hands drop between them.

A slight smile curved his lips. "I'll take what I can get."

"Good," she said with a nod, and gave him a once-over. "New jacket?"

"Sort of," he said, flipping up his collar like The Fonz. "At a thrift shop on Byres Road. It's getting colder out, and your cute leather jacket won't cut it. I got you and Nissa a pair also . . . and some scarves and gloves," he confessed, his cheeks reddening.

"You didn't."

"Relax, they were a steal. And I knew you wouldn't let me if I asked. Swallow your pride, will you?"

Cillian Hayes breathed in deeply, letting the delicate fragrance of juniper and lavender take over his senses. It was a scent that he had come to intimately associate with Mckenna.

As they walked in silence back to the bed and breakfast, he wondered what the High Priestess had told her. Could she possess an understanding of the prophecy? The Scottish Scrolls? The Priestess's ties to Mckenna's mother?

Cillian yearned to rebuild the trust between them. He longed for her to see beyond the surface, to grasp the essence of his mission. To understand that preventing the reincarnation of billions of souls was not an evil act but an act of compassion, sparing humanity from the perils of a ruined world. It was an act of mercy.

That day at Kylemore Abbey, the white horse had revealed to Mckenna the planet's future if the prophecy remained unfulfilled. She'd seen for herself that Earth was hurtling towards a grim fate, and would become uninhabitable. With time, he would make her understand that the High Priestess's plan—while executed immorally—was the only way to save the natural world.

But they didn't need the Priestess. They would succeed without her. Maeve was dangerous and unpredictable, and there was no telling what she would do with Mckenna and her mother once she was finished with them.

Cillian felt an unwavering determination rise inside of him. He had to make Mckenna see.

III

THE DOE, THE APE, AND THE WOLF

Mckenna insisted they leave at dawn the next morning. She didn't want to waste another day *not* being with her mother. With every passing second, her mind was conjuring up more and more questions, some falling into the realm of just plain ridiculous (such as, was levitation off the table?). She needed answers.

Nissa was all for getting an early start, and Cillian didn't dare argue. Mckenna had to admit, she liked being the one in control . . . though having the upper hand wasn't enough to keep her anxiety at bay. What if Abby didn't like her, the person she had become? What if they didn't share a mother-daughter connection at all? Or worse, what if Abby wasn't the person Esme made her out to be? Even Seán, when he was recounting his memories of her back in Andre's study, made her sound like some sort of goddess.

Nissa must have sensed Mckenna's angst because she threw

her a reassuring smile from the passenger seat of their rental, a yellow Vauxhall Astra.

"Don't think the yellow is conspicuous enough," Mckenna had said upon setting eyes on it in the B&B parking lot—or *car park*, as they said in the UK.

"It was all they had available for over a week, and, erm, I wasn't sure how long we'd need it for."

Good point. Mckenna didn't have a clue either—and would Cillian leave once she found her mom? Following their graveyard chitchat, she'd had a strong sense he wasn't planning on going anywhere any time soon.

It seemed unnatural for such a buzzing city to be so eerily quiet, though unsurprising at this dreadful time of day because no one in their right mind would voluntarily wake up so early that the sky was still as dark as tar. But even the murky, noiseless atmosphere had a comfort to it. She couldn't quite pinpoint what exactly it was about Glasgow that warmed her. Perhaps it was simply because Scotland was her mother's homeland— and Bessie's.

They drove under a pleasant drizzle out of Scotland's biggest city, and she stared with longing back at the urban landscape that faded into the misty air. She wished she could have had the chance to speak to Lilias again. Her heart ached for her—a lost soul whose body was God knows where . . . and with no place of rest. If Cillian hadn't spooked her (ironically), she might've been able to help her.

Ahead, the road stretched past a town on the outskirts of the city, granting them glimpses of its hidden treasures—colourful buildings, rolling hills in the backdrop, and a castle dominating the town's skyline.

Somewhere along the way, the entrancing trickles of a waterway met Mckenna's ears. "Is this the same river that runs through part of Glasgow?" Mckenna wondered aloud as it came into view, gracefully meandering through the town. The drizzling turned into a heavier, harmonic drumming, and the river surged onwards in satisfaction.

Cillian responded by opening the glove compartment in front of Nissa, which held napkins from a place called Costa Coffee and a stained—likely from said coffee—crinkly map. Cillian unfolded bits of it before declaring, "Yep! It's the River Clyde. We just passed Dumbarton. Cool, one of my old classmates from Trinity, Jack, is from there."

"Tell Jack it seemed pretty," Mckenna said as the town called Dumbarton was quickly replaced by thick, towering pine trees.

Cillian laughed, and Mckenna and Nissa wrinkled their foreheads at him. "Just a funny story Jack told me about a whisky warehouse around here. Ballentine, I believe."

"And?" Nissa prodded.

"They used to get robbed quite often by the townspeople, so they placed guard dogs around the property. That wasn't enough to stop a, erm, 'thirsty' Scot," he said, using air quotes.

"Lured the dogs with meat, didn't they?" Mckenna said, amused.

"Basically," Cillian said. "The Ballentine workers had had enough, so they replaced the dogs with geese, which were much more aggressive—*and* shrill—and called them the Scotch Watch. Can you imagine all those horrid honking noises the townspeople had to endure every time a trespasser attempted to outsmart them?"

Maybe it was fatigue from the zero hours she'd slept last night, but the thought of a gaggle of geese scaring off whisky thieves made Mckenna completely lose her composure. She fell into a fit of giggles, and Nissa and Cillian quickly joined in. She didn't know how long they'd been laughing, gasping for air, when Nissa suddenly shouted, "STOP!"

Before Mckenna could see what prompted Nissa's outburst, the car swerved in the rain at a forty-five-degree angle and into a large enough creature for the car to come to a screeching halt. There was a sharp, painful cry.

"Are you alright?" Cillian shouted, his head darting frantically from Mckenna to Nissa. He had his arm in front of Nissa like a protective shield.

"Oh my God," Mckenna breathed, flipping her hair out of her eyes.

"Oh my God," Nissa repeated, unbuckling her seatbelt and throwing open her passenger-side door. She stumbled out, then took a tumble onto the wet ground.

"Nissa!" Mckenna pushed open her own door and ran around to Nissa's side, the rain pounding around them. Cillian followed, lifting Nissa off the ground and settling her into her seat.

"I'm okay . . . just a little dizzy," Nissa said. "The deer—did we kill it?"

"Did you hit your head on the dash?" Mckenna said, checking her friend's forehead for any sign of injury.

"No . . . maybe . . . I don't know. I'm okay. Please, the deer, Kenna—"

"We'll find help, just relax," Cillian said.

Nissa gestured wildly towards the doe. "She's gonna die!"

Mckenna lifted her eyes to the creature. It took everything she had not to burst into tears. Judging by its small size, it must have been a young deer or a doe; its torso was covered in blood, and its eyes were fluttering wildly, as if it was trying to keep from passing out.

"We have to do something!" Mckenna yelled, in a much higher octave than she meant to. *What can I do?* she thought repeatedly, glancing back at Nissa to make sure she was conscious; Nissa gave an elaborate thumbs up.

Cover it. Mckenna ripped off her jacket and draped it over the deer's wound. "It's—it's gonna die. It's gonna . . ." She watched helplessly as the rain streamed down its little body, blood dripping onto the pavement.

Cillian came around to her side, and placed an arm around her shoulders. "Lass, you're in shock. We need to get you and Nissa to an emergency."

"I'm fine, okay? We need to save it!" She had no idea why she was shouting so loudly, or whether what she was saying made any sense. She just knew her insides were burning with pain— and this creature couldn't die like this.

The doe's eyes stopped fluttering and settled heavily on her own. Its brown irises glistened, its unwavering gaze seemingly yearning to communicate.

"I think . . . I think it wants to tell me something," she whispered, her throat dry from the adrenaline.

"Try listening," Cillian said.

"What?"

"As a Wise One, you have the ability to communicate with animals."

Mckenna gaped back, as though he'd said a unicorn had just trotted by.

"You haven't even begun to tap into a fraction of what you're capable of."

Mckenna was at a total loss for words. She'd certainly formed a connection with the wren, but that just . . . happened. She couldn't even begin to explain the logic or magic behind it. "I wouldn't even know where to start. How? What do I do?"

He shook his head. "I'm not exactly sure. Try to centre yourself."

She nodded and closed her eyes, then placed her hand on her sacral chakra. *Breathe in and out.* In her mind, she tipped over her trusty goblet—of fears, uncertainties—and focused solely on the sound of the now-thrashing rain.

"Good," Cillian said softly, placing her hand gently over the doe's neck. "Open your eyes."

When her eyes met the doe's, something extraordinary happened: a thin, jelly-like string sprang out of the doe's forehead—precisely where her third eye was located—twisting up and down like a roller coaster and leaving behind traces of silver dust, until it hit the centre of Mckenna's forehead. In the seconds that followed, the doe's mind and body melded with her own. Mckenna clutched her stomach and let out an agonizing yelp; she was frightened and cold, and every muscle in her body was searing with pain. Cillian's hand rested on the nape of her neck, offering solace, his faint words of encouragement mingling with the patter of rain. Her vision turned hazy, as though a grey cloud had passed in front of it, and a whirl of images flooded her mind. She witnessed a family of deer and graceful does prancing amidst thick forest foliage. The doe's brothers and sisters leaped over babbling streams and through lush undergrowth. The image the faded into a peaceful lakeside village with a backdrop of majestic mountains.

There, along the dock, a sign read: *Luss.*

Bring me, the deer implored. The thought floated in her mind so faintly, she nearly let it go by.

Mckenna snapped out of her vision, and, as if she'd just ducked out of a tunnel, Cillian's worried voice went from muffled to sharp.

"We have to bring her to Luss. It's . . . a village," Mckenna said, panting as though she'd run a mile.

Cillian's grey eyes bore into her. "Are you sure?"

"Yes."

"Okay," Cillian said with a nod. "We'll have to carefully lift her into the back seat. Can you grab her by the head, and I'll grab her by the legs?"

"I think so." Mckenna cradled the doe's head and neck while Cillian carefully elevated her hind legs.

"On three—one, two, three!"

Together, they lifted the doe's flimsy body off the ground and stepped towards the backseat, where the door was still open. While the creature wasn't as heavy as Mckenna expected, it was quite the struggle to wiggle her in. After several attempts, they managed to lie her down.

Once she was secured, Mckenna's eyes flickered to the front passenger seat—Nissa was totally knocked out.

"If Nissa's got a concussion, we need to keep her awake," Cillian said.

"Is that really a thing?"

"Not sure, only ever seen it on the telly. Can you squeeze in beside her up front?"

With a curt nod, Mckenna ran over to Nissa's side. "Nissa.

Nissa!" she shouted, shaking her by her small shoulders. "Wake up. We have to save the deer, remember?"

"Save . . . the deer?" Nissa mumbled, wiping away the saliva dripping from the corner of her mouth. "Was I . . . asleep?"

"You were knocked out. You probably have a concussion, so you need to stay awake, okay?"

"Okay, okay."

Mckenna slid in beside her and grabbed the map from her lap. Gently, she closed the car door, leaving hardly an inch of space between her hip and the handle.

"You both good?" said Cillian, settling back in the driver's seat.

"We're good, just go! Luss is just north of here," she added, spotting the village on the map at the edge of Loch Lomond.

Cillian hit the gas, zooming past more forest, until the faintest outline of a mountain peak rose up over the trees. As they drove, the trees became sparser, and another, much larger body of water came into view. It must be Loch Lomond, darkened by the silhouette of the vast mountains, where Scotland's rural landscape began.

"Beautiful, isn't it?" Cillian whispered.

Mckenna was eager to witness the vista in the sunlight. Were these larger than the mountains—or *bens*—she'd seen in Connemara and at Lough Tay?

The sound of Nissa's snores made Mckenna start. "Nissa!"

She jerked awake. "I'm here, I'm here . . ."

Behind them, the doe let out a pitchy whimper. It was the most horrible noise Mckenna had ever heard.

"Cillian, can you go any faster?" Mckenna snapped.

"I'm trying to avoid skidding in the rain—"

"You're fine, step on it." She could feel the doe's body shutting down. They needed to get there, fast.

The car accelerated. Minutes passed until a sign indicated Luss was six miles away.

"See? The Scots use miles," she said before she could stop herself.

Without removing his eyes from the road, he smirked. She

grinned back, despite the horror this moment imbued. "I'll get us there on time, I promise," he said.

Around fifteen minutes later, Cillian turned them sharply right into Luss village, coming to a stop in front of a tiny home that looked to be on the brink of a garden gnome infestation.

"Now what?" Cillian said breathlessly beside her.

I have no freakin' idea.

"Oi! Would you turn those beams off, lad?" a man shouted from the gnome house. "You're off your head, the sun isn't even up yet!"

Mckenna stepped out of the car. "We need a vet, please! We hit a deer, and my friend—"

"Christ, not another deer . . ." He stomped over to the neighbour's house, slippers and all, and rapped thrice on the crimson door. A thin middle-aged woman appeared on the threshold, her austere expression a stark contrast to her head full of purple curlers.

"Another deer?" Mckenna heard her say. The gruffness in her voice reminded her of her dads' tough-as-nails travel agent, Dina.

"These young folk brought her in," the man said, pointing to their car. "Can you treat her?"

"Of course I can! Was having a rather pleasant dream, though." She stepped down to the road and began waving her hands frantically at Mckenna and Cillian. "Bring her in!" she shouted, apparently caring little about waking up the entire neighbourhood.

"The deer or my friend . . . ?"

"Your friend's injured too?

Cillian climbed out of the car. "A concussion, we think!" Mckenna wondered how much longer their cacophony of shouts would persist.

"Oh, dear . . ." The woman with the purple curlers, whom she gathered was the vet, crossed the road to a home where vines covered most of its façade, her navy velvet nightgown brushing over the cement, while Mckenna followed closely at her heel.

The vet knocked urgently on the door. A boy, no older than ten, answered.

"Get your dad, David. Go on, he's got a patient," she said. The boy rubbed at his eyes and nodded, and seconds later, a stocky man with wire-rimmed glasses was at the door.

"Was there a road accident?" the man asked, concerned but calm all the same.

"A girl's hit her head. No visible injuries—possible concussion."

Mckenna watched anxiously as the vet and the man with the glasses, whom she gathered was the town doctor, vanished into each of their homes and reappeared with two stretchers, one for Nissa and one for the deer. In perfect synchronicity, the two medical professionals steadily lifted the injured onto their respective beds.

"You, lad—help me roll the deer in," the woman said to Cillian, who quickly obliged.

Mckenna instinctively hovered over Nissa, following her stretcher inside the doctor's home. She stepped directly into what looked to be the entire house, with the kitchen, living room and dining nook sharing a single space, a shaggy burnt-orange rug the only thing dividing up the area.

"Have a seat while I tend to your wee friend. My wife will fetch you some tea," the doctor said before wheeling Nissa into a room tucked away down the narrow hallway. As she surveyed her surroundings, Mckenna's gaze settled on the inviting sight of a honey-brown leather sofa, its worn texture promising a spot where she could sink comfortably into the cushion.

"Will she be okay?" she called out, but the doctor had already closed the door behind him. Feeling utterly helpless, she got up and began pacing around the coffee table. Typical of Nissa to make out like she was perfectly fine while she suffered a head injury. There may not have been any blood, but what if she had internal bleeding? Having no clue whether that even made any sense (she avoided *M*A*S*H* each time her dads watched the reruns), she shook the thought away.

She could really use that tea right about now.

As though in answer to her prayers, the doctor's wife, she gathered, appeared in front of her, wearing a white-knit sweater, a neat bun rolled atop her head. "Mornin'," she greeted Mckenna cheerfully.

Mckenna forced her lips to mutter a "Good morning, ma'am," even though she firmly believed morning had not properly arrived.

"Call me Mrs. Wood," she said while putting on a copper kettle. "Oh, and don't worry your wee head, your friend's okay—just needs a rest," she added, seeing Mckenna's panicked expression.

Mckenna released a breath as deep as a meditating monk's. "Thank goodness." Her gaze drifted out the window to the tranquil expanse of the dark loch, the mountains in clearer view under the gentle orange hues cast by the rising sun. "It must be so peaceful. Living here."

"It's all we could hope for. Where are you from?"

"America. A small town outside of Boston."

"Ah, so you're used to being solitary?"

"Sort of. Not like this, though."

"You've got a thing for mountains," Mrs. Wood remarked, her voice accompanied by the comforting whistle of the kettle. Coming around the kitchen counter, Mrs. Wood placed a pink teacup adorned with a gold rim on the coffee table. "We only drink Earl Grey here."

"That's perfect," Mckenna said, lifting it to her lips and savouring the faintest hint of citrus on her tongue.

Mrs. Wood sat down beside her. "How did you know to come to Luss?"

Mckenna gulped down more tea than she intended, the liquid burning hot on her palate. "Um, I . . . the accident happened nearby, and this was the closest village." Not such a deviation from the truth.

Mrs. Wood nodded in quiet observation, watching Mckenna as she sipped the rest of her tea, the passing minutes stretching into a languid rhythm. "Looks like you're all done. I'll get you another." Before she knew it, Mckenna's cup was scooped out of her hand, and Mrs. Wood was bustling back to the kitchen to fetch her more tea. But as Mrs. Wood gingerly lifted the kettle, instead of pouring she gently rested it back down, her eyes fixed on the inside of Mckenna's cup.

"Is something wrong?" Mckenna asked, a little shaken at the perplexed look on Mrs. Wood's face.

"It's nothing. It's . . . peculiar."

"Peculiar?"

"I read tea leaves, see," Mrs. Wood said. Mckenna waited. "Tell me, what do you reckon this looks like?" Crossing the room, she placed the teacup in Mckenna's hands.

Mckenna examined the black sunken leaves, at first seeing nothing but a blob with holes for eyes, but spinning it around and around, two images then became clear.

"I think I see an ape. And if I turn it this way, it looks like . . . a wolf?"

"My thoughts exactly." Mrs. Wood sat down beside her and folded her arms over her thighs—surely a precursor to the deliverance of dire news. "An ape is quite rare. It warns of a secret enemy."

Secret enemy? The High Priestess wasn't so much a secret anymore.

"As for the wolf—"

"I suppose it's not synonymous with sunshine and rainbows?"

Mrs. Wood offered a small, sympathetic smile. "I'm afraid not. A wolf usually means a false friend."

Yep. Just what a girl with trust issues wants to hear.

Before Mckenna could ask her to elaborate, there was a knock at the door. Mrs. Wood gave her one last thoughtful look before she answered with a "My, aren't we a busy household today!"

Cillian was standing in the doorway, his normally smooth, ashen skin spotted red from sweat. He removed a dark strand of hair from his face as he said breathlessly, "The doe's alive. She'll be alright."

Mckenna shot up from the couch, the teacup slipping from

her grasp and shattering to bits at her feet. "Oh my gosh, I'm *so* sorry." She bent to pick up the pieces, but Mrs. Wood put an arm out in front of her.

"Leave it—there could be small shards, I'll have to hoover it. And not to worry, my lad breaks a cup a week . . . that one's lasted longer than most."

"Why don't we get out of your way for a bit," said Cillian. "Mckenna, do you fancy a walk?"

Her heart did a little hop at the sound of her name, which he so rarely used. "Sure." He leaned lightly aside for her to walk past, their shoulders brushing. Muttering one last "Sorry!" to Mrs. Wood, she stepped out onto the quiet street, all thoughts of the dreaded tea leaves escaping her upon setting her eyes on the sun rising above Loch Lomond, fighting its way through the gravel-coloured clouds. The rain had now ceased, the water rippled gently under the sun's scrutiny, and the once-shadowy hills bordering the lake sparkled a golden-green that felt unique to the Scottish landscape. There was a familiarity to it. All of it. Like she'd been here before, though she surely hadn't—at least not in this lifetime. A sudden warmth crept over her body.

"This place . . ." she began.

"Luss?"

"Yes, but no. Scotland. It feels like home. I can't explain it." She hugged herself, even though she felt toastier than she had in a long while.

"There's a song about Loch Lomond." His eyes glinted, as if in search of a memory.

"What's it called?"

"*The Loch Lomond Song*," he said with a smirk.

She let out something between a laugh and a snort. "Go on."

"What? Sing it?"

"Yes, please," she teased, nudging him in the elbow.

He laughed, but humoured her all the same. He began singing in a soft, euphonious voice, the lyrics painting a beautiful picture of the bonnie banks and braes of Loch Lomond, but it quickly turned melancholic at the mention of two individuals taking separate roads to Scotland—one pleading for his friend to take *the high road* while he took *the low road*.

Mckenna didn't know why, but her eyes welled with tears.

"Was my performance that noteworthy? And here I was, scarlet for myself," he said with a chuckle, putting an arm around her shoulders.

"You were alright," she said, hugging herself tighter, acutely aware of his hand so close to her cheek. "What's the song about?"

"I think it has to do with the Battle of Culloden, which was incited by Charles Edward Stewart in 1746—or Bonnie Prince Charlie, as the Highlanders liked to call him. See, they wanted a Scottish king back on the throne, so Prince Charlie led a revolt against the British. But they lost—*badly*. Following that, loads of Scottish soldiers were imprisoned within an English castle, near the border of Scotland. *The Loch Lomond Song* tells the story of two soldiers, one of whom was executed, and the other set free."

"He sacrificed himself," Mckenna said slowly, thinking of the chorus. "He knew that by taking 'the high road,' his friend would live, and if he took 'the low road,' he would die."

Cillian nodded, adding, "His soul didn't die, though; the low road still led him home to Scotland."

No wonder her heart ached. "How do you know about this?"

"I mean, I studied history, and the Battle of Culloden's rather infamous—"

"No, I mean the song."

Cillian appeared taken off guard. "A friend. Very proud Scot." He gently turned her towards him, his hands resting on her shoulders. "I would do the same for you—you know that, right?"

It was hard to focus on his words with him standing so close. His skin gave out a kind of cedar and pink-pepper blend that suddenly became all-consuming. "Do the same?" she repeated stupidly.

He tucked a strand of damp hair behind her ear. "Sacrifice myself if it meant you would live."

Her knees nearly buckled. Before meeting Nissa, it seemed like she pushed away everyone she met. No one paid any mind to her, and if they did, it was only to throw her a snarky comment or a look of disdain, partly due to her social awkwardness and partly because of the nature of her upbringing, having two dads. She'd always sensed people disliked her immediately, and perhaps that was because she didn't like herself yet. She didn't *know* herself yet, and what kind of vibe did that give off?

Until she knew who she was and what she was meant to do, and until she had reason to fully trust him again, she couldn't forgive Cillian. She knew that was where this conversation was headed.

She pulled back. "Cillian, I can't—"

"Your wee friend is awake!" Mrs. Wood's voice carried over to them. Mckenna and Cillian spun around to see her poking her head out of her living-room window. "Oh, sorry. Hope I'm not interrupting anything."

Cillian watched Mckenna race inside the doctor's home to be by Nissa's side. Shoving his hands into his pockets, he turned to face the sunrise. Before his brain could register what he was doing, he picked up where he left off, humming *The Loch Lomond Song* under his breath. The first time he heard it was after one of his early practical sessions with the High Priestess. She'd just taught him how to ground, centre, and connect with the element of his choosing—earth. Then, she'd regressed him, talking him into a trance state, where he travelled to one of his past lives in 1776 as a Scottish soldier who died in the Battle of Culloden. Even then he believed in fighting for his people, for a greater cause.

It seemed his very soul was rebellious in nature.

Upon learning of his soul's past, he was surprised at first; he'd always felt intrinsically tied to Ireland, and only Ireland. But Scotland, he quickly discovered, called to him too, in a different way. There was a wildness to it, an inimitable, untamed beauty in its rugged mountains. The way they intertwined with glens, lochs, and rivers unapologetically . . .

The High Priestess had been good to him. She'd showed him everything he knew, but he was done with her and her militant methods. He would do this *his* way, with Mckenna by his side— soon enough. He was slowly winning Mckenna back, he could feel it. And once she saw reason, together, they would save the natural world.

"Is she going to recover quickly?" Mckenna said, stroking the doe's nose with Nissa by her side, holding her hand. The doe lay on the vet's operating table looking restful yet aware. Mckenna had a sense she was fighting to stay awake.

"She'll be good as new in a few days," the vet said, opening up the blinds and letting the sunlight pour in. "They recover fast, these creatures. A wonder, aren't they?"

The doe's earth-brown irises glistened, piercing Mckenna's as though, once again, trying to communicate a message. Mckenna leaned into Nissa's ear. "Niss, can you lure the vet out of here for a sec?"

Nissa asked no questions. "Um, Mrs. . . . doctor, can I trouble you for a glass of water?"

"No trouble at all, dear," said the vet, and the two disappeared from the room.

Mckenna waited until the door was closed before centring herself. In minutes, the jelly-like string sprang from the doe's forehead and into hers, melding their thoughts and leaving behind a trail of shimmering silver dust.

Thank you, Wise One, the doe's dulcet voice echoed in her mind. *We've been waiting for you.*

Who? She leaned in closer. *Who's been waiting for me?*

The animal kingdom. You are our only hope.

What do you mean—?

The vet burst into the room. "Sorry, dear, this poor creature needs her pain reliever and a good long rest. Off you go!"

IV

MISGAUN MEDB

Seán led Andre to the inn he'd been staying at—a handsome three-storey cottage, whose owners clearly had an affinity for flowers and hummingbirds. They entered his single room and sat on the lily-print bedspread, and he recounted all the events that had unfolded since leaving their home in Abredonia Woods, leading up to this very night.

Andre rubbed at his head. "So, you're saying Maeve could *hypnotize* people?"

"I don't know what to call it. She can get into your head and manipulate what you see."

"And she made you . . . do some sort of sex magic." Andre's voice was raw, the word *sex* a mere whisper.

Seán sighed, then buried his face in his hands. "She also . . . made me say things. A spell. I felt trapped, Andre. Like I was in a trance."

"What about the other times you were together?"

"I was seeing Abby the whole time. And even when I knew I should leave, that I should go find Mckenna, I was pulled back in. It was like I was aware of what I was doing, but I couldn't do anything about it. I think she was making old feelings surface somehow, and I was acting like . . . the old Seán."

"The one who had feelings for Abby," Andre said, looking away.

Seán shot up from the bed. "Yes, *had*. Past tense. Are you still angry about that?"

"About the fact that you still loved her when you parted ways? That you never told me *she* left *you*, and she did it to protect our daughter? It's kind of a huge thing to get past, Seán."

"You're right, luv. I should've told you. I just didn't want you to think I was still hung up on her." He paused, unsure how to phrase something he'd never verbalized. "I was afraid if I told you how I fall in love, that gender has nothing to do with it, you'd think I'd have a wandering eye or something. Which, now I'm saying it out loud, I realize is bonkers."

"That *is* bonkers. It's not like I would've thought you'd hit on everything with a pulse, Seán. It just means you love a person for who they are. And that's beautiful. That's not at all why I'm angry. I'm angry because you lied to me."

Seán placed his hand over his. "I'm so sorry for lying. When I met you, I just didn't think it would matter because you were everything I needed."

"What about Abby?"

"I loved Abby once, but I don't feel that way anymore. Even if I know she's alive."

Andre pulled his hand back. "You might feel differently when you see her."

"Andre . . ."

"You know we need to find her, right? She might be easier to locate than Mckenna, who's probably always on the move. Being as persistent as she is, I bet she's close to finding her by now. That is, if they're not already together."

"No way Abby would have kept that from me. No, let's focus on finding Mckenna."

"And how do we do that?"

Seán pointed at Andre's hand. He was still clutching the necklace he'd yanked off of Maeve's neck in their brawl. "Abby gifted Maeve that necklace over seventeen years ago. That's no ordinary stone." He reached out, grazing the pointed edge, cold to the touch. "We need a map."

As Maeve strolled away from the stone circle, her frock draping over her, she couldn't help but think how smoothly the ritual had gone. Of course, it hadn't been without its challenges. She hadn't foreseen the unexpected arrival of Mckenna's American father. Was he ever the essence of dark and handsome, that one.

She focused on putting one foot in front of the other. Her body trembled from head to toe, possibly at the thought of Andre's flawless jawline, but mostly due to her weakened condition. It had been years since she had summoned that kind of magic, calling upon the sylphs—the air elementals. The consequences would have to be addressed later. After all, what harm could one more favour do? From the very outset of her practice, she had always been captivated by the air element; it was a wonder, something people breathed without a second thought, yet simultaneously, it possessed the power to obliterate an entire region within minutes.

Following tonight's Samhain ritual, the long-standing protection spell cast by Abigail was finally shattered. Now, Maeve could locate Abigail without any magical barriers. Satisfied, Maeve instinctively reached up to touch the meticulously chiseled stone that always hung around her neck.

She froze. *No*, she thought, her fingers searching her bare, wet collarbone.

It can't be.

It must have slipped off during the scuffle. What if Seán got his hands on it? That sly, insufferable dobber. He'd always been an obstacle from the very beginning. Maeve could never quite comprehend why Abigail was so enamored with him. If they possessed the stone, locating their daughter would become possible, and it wouldn't be long before they'd reunite with Abigail. Maeve was sure she'd do everything within her power to safeguard them and keep them concealed, wherever they might be. Astral projection was out of the question—travelling to a person, regardless of their location, was a rare feat, signifying a profound connection between souls. Maeve had never managed to achieve it.

Perhaps Seán and Andre were still lying in the stone circle, recovering from her tornado. She had to get to them . . . she had to run . . . she needed . . .

Chest heaving, her knees buckled, and in one swift motion her body crashed to the ground.

Mckenna stared blankly out the passenger side window, her mind consumed by the doe's cryptic words. What could she possibly have meant by saying that Mckenna was the sole hope for the animal kingdom? Was the doe, like the High Priestess, foreseeing Mckenna fulfilling Elizabeth Dunlop's prophecy to rescue the natural world? And if the prophecy was not fulfilled, would all animals endure suffering in the apocalyptic world that the white horse, Eachna, had revealed to her at Kylemore Abbey? What a harrowing vision it had been—the decaying trees, lifeless oceans, and the suffocating smog . . .

"I have such a headache," Nissa whined, her short legs completely stretched out on the back seat. Mckenna had propped her head atop her new vintage jacket, courtesy of Cillian. "I'm not comfortable."

"I know, Nissa, but you have to rest. Doctor's orders," Mckenna said sternly.

"But it's bumpy."

Mckenna turned her torso diagonally to face her. "Did you take your pain med?"

"I don't like pills. I'll live."

"It's a pain reliever, Nissa. Take it, please. I can feel your head pounding." Mckenna pressed her index fingers against her temples, and as she did, something erupted inside her chest—a latent fear of Nissa's, buried somewhere beneath the positivity she normally exuberated. Fear of becoming like her father, the infamous Simon Fage, the drug lord who smuggled dirty money into the Isle of Man, killed Nissa's mother, and set out to finish his own daughter off, too. Nissa's grandmother, Arethusa, wasn't explicit, but Mckenna was sure he was also an addict on top of it all.

The whole thing sounded like an Al Pacino film.

Mckenna stretched her arm back and laid a hand on Nissa's knee. "The answer is no, by the way. That's never going to happen. You don't have to take it if you don't want, but I'll be here if you do."

Nissa sneered, then smiled widely. "I forgot you can do that."

"Annoying, isn't it?" Cillian said, his eyebrow raised in mock annoyance. Mckenna hit him on the arm, conscious of the fact that Nissa might be watching, but the latter's head was inside her backpack, reaching for the small bottle of pain relievers Dr. Wood had prescribed. "Fine, just one," she muttered, swallowing it with a gulp of water. She fluffed her jacket, rested her head on it, and closed her eyes.

It took all of three minutes for her soft snores to follow. As though he'd been waiting for Nissa to slip into sleep, Cillian slid his hand from the gear shift to hers. She let their fingers tangle, even though his touch sent so many shockwaves up her arm that she felt she might electrocute him.

They drove in silence for the next hour, and Mckenna didn't mind one bit. She could cruise through this country for the rest of her life, revelling in its calm, dark lochs, mercurial skies, and sparkling green mountains. Present company and all.

"Why are you exiting? We have to continue on the A82," Mckenna whispered as the car veered right onto a smaller road.

"When I told the veterinarian we were going to Skye," Cillian began in hushed tones, "she basically called me an arse if I didn't stop here, even for two minutes. It's literally on the way."

"I'd really rather keep going—"

"That's what I told her. But then she showed me pictures and . . ." He trailed off, as though his breath had been taken away, and Mckenna knew why.

They'd pulled up in a valley that went on for miles and miles, and she felt like she'd been swallowed by a Van Gough painting. She hardly even noticed Cillian coming around to her side, opening her door, and holding out his hand, which she took.

The air smelled like fresh mint tea and damp moss. Before them stood three sky-piercing mountains of Eden-green, with rocky peaks she was suddenly itching to climb. A shimmering brook spiraled down in the grassy fields a few feet away. She wondered if sprites or water nymphs swam in its ripples, remembering the "hopping fish" she'd seen in Niamh's realm, and other elementals Esme mentioned dwelled close to their physical plane.

"Should we wake Nissa?" Mckenna asked. *She would love this.* They both turned to peek over their shoulders—Nissa's eyelids were fluttering like mad in her dream state, and a trail of drool was dripping down the corner of her mouth.

They chuckled and brought their gazes back to the three mountains, flowing into one another like humps on a camel's back. The phrase "attached at the hip" sprung to mind when she stared at their collective formation—they stood separately, but remained a part of a single entity.

"Where are we again?" Mckenna said.

"Glencoe. The vet told me, 'Be sure to see the Three Sisters.' I guess they're these."

"They definitely are," she breathed. She took a step back, peering down the valley, and suddenly, her body turned ice-cold. "Whoa."

"What is it, lass?" He stepped forward, placing a hand on the small of her back. "You felt something?"

"Yeah, I'm . . . f-frozen," she said, her teeth chattering.

He cupped both her hands, lifting them to his lips, then blew warmth over her fingers. "Hmm . . . you don't actually feel cold. Better?"

Yes, she wanted to say, but not because it did anything to warm her up.

"You're shivering. C'mon, let's get you inside. I'll blast the heat." His brow furrowed with concern, he led her to the car, and they sped back down the A82, towards the Isle of Skye. Oddly, the cold began to ebb as soon as they drove away.

She longed to absorb the beauty of every loch and highland, but her eyelids grew heavier with each passing mile. And for the first time in a long while, she drifted into a dreamless sleep.

The sound of a jeering crowd jolted Mckenna awake. On either side of a narrow black canal that divided the village in two, old stone homes and shops were adorned with red, yellow, and blue trim. The canal seemed to stretch endlessly into the distance, its end nowhere in sight. Beyond the concrete footbridge—the connecting point—and down the symmetrical staircases leading to the water's edge, a boisterous crowd had gathered. They shouted and waved their fists in the air, while a few held signs with messages like *Nessie doesn't eat rubbish!* and *No more fishing!*

"What the hell?" Mckenna muttered, rubbing her eyes. As they inched closer, the crowd's chants perforated the car windows: "Keep your mess . . . from Loch Ness! Keep your mess . . . from Loch Ness! Keep your mess . . ."

Cillian swore. "I think I took a wrong turn." He pointed at a sign that read *Welcome to Fort Augustus* in block letters.

Mckenna peered down at the map on her lap, smiling at the heart Nissa had drawn around Uig. "Sorry . . . hang on." Yawning, she ran her index finger over the route they'd taken from Glencoe and swiftly spotted where he'd accidentally deviated. "No big deal, you missed the left turn onto the A87. We can follow—"

"Shhh!" Nissa hissed, sticking her head between the two front seats. They fell silent, watching her listen fixedly to the angry mob, who hadn't changed their tune.

"What are you—?"

Nissa jumped out of the car, slamming the door behind her. They watched, amazed, as she worked the crowd, demanding to know from villager after villager what this was all about.

"I'll just park," Cillian said, gesturing for Mckenna to join Nissa while he found a spot.

"And what about you, ma'am? Have you ever seen it?" Mckenna heard Nissa ask a stout, middle-aged woman.

"Not me, no. Me daughter-in-law has! She swears it, she does."

"Nissa . . . ?" Mckenna hissed, waving her over. "What's happening?"

"This is the famous Loch Ness! Where the sea monster lives."

Naturally, Mckenna had heard of the legendary Loch Ness monster. When she was little, Seán used to retell famous tales of its sightings. "And?"

"Well," Nissa said, "there's been tons of pollution in the lake, and they're saying it's waste from fish-feed, fishermen dumping their garbage—or *rubbish*—in the water, and, like, nets that end up sinking to the bottom. Stuff like that."

"Makes sense," Mckenna and Cillian said in unison, his sudden appearance causing her a brief start.

"I just want to stay a little longer, if that's . . ." She stopped to peer over Mckenna's shoulder, and Mckenna turned around. A white van with *BBC Scotland News* plastered across its side doors pulled up, and a three-person crew consisting of a camerawoman, boom operator, and reporter leaped out like the A-Team.

"Who's the leader here?" said a woman Mckenna gathered was the reporter. Tall, with tight, strawberry-blond curls and eyebrows as arched as a drawbridge, she was sporting an important-looking red blazer with large gold buttons.

"I am!" a young man shouted, making his way to the front of the crowd. Mckenna immediately liked his poised, self-assured vibe.

"Hit record now," the reporter said urgently to the camerawoman, but with an underlying calm that undoubtedly came from experience. "What's your name, sir?"

"Macleod. Logan, ma'am." He removed his sporty shades to reveal a set of deep brown, expressive eyes.

"Mr. Macleod, what is this all about?"

"We get a fair bit of boat traffic 'round here, all thanks to our friendly neighbourhood monster." Mckenna chuckled, his Scottish lilt carrying through his words. "Tourists are keen on searching for Nessie, and fishermen, well, they're all hoping to cross Loch Ness off their list. We've had our water tested, and it's not in a bonnie state. There are more pollutants these days than we've ever seen, and there's a lack of vegetation, you see."

"What do you think is the solution?"

"BAN FISHING!" Nissa's soprano voice cried out, and as Mckenna scanned the crowd, she spotted wisps of blond and pink highlights drifting towards Logan's side.

The crowd responded to Nissa's enthusiasm by chanting, "Ban fishing in Loch Ness!"

"And what's your name?" the reporter asked, holding her microphone up to Nissa's nose.

"Nissa Febland!"

"I detect an American accent, Ms. Febland. Are you visiting?"

"Yes, my friends and I are passing through on our way to the Isle of Skye. And I'm glad we did!" She nodded to Logan, as if to say, "Take it away," then stepped aside and raced towards Mckenna and Cillian.

"Did you see me?" she squealed.

"I did!" Mckenna said, giving her a high-five.

"That was exhilarating."

"You're a natural, Niss."

"Maybe you should consider a career in politics," Cillian said, looking impressed.

"No offence, but *your kind* take way too long to get stuff done," Nissa retorted, bouncing away. "Which way's the car?"

Cillian pointed towards a pharmacy at the end of the block and let out a hearty laugh. "Can't argue with that! Politicians aren't exactly known for taking rapid action. 'Your kind . . . '"

As they strolled on, passing by a pub, a fish and chips shop, and a Nessie gift shop, he kept his gaze fixed on the ground. A weight settled in Mckenna's chest, and she felt the ache of longing in his eyes. She sensed that he was remembering. "This was you once, wasn't it?" She nodded towards Nissa, who appeared entirely at ease.

His attention seemed half in the present, half in the past. "It was."

"What happened?"

"I thought I could make change if I became part of the system—a politician."

Mckenna couldn't help herself. "Was that around the same time you started practicing magic?" She'd had a burning desire to ask since Samhain.

He paused. Had she thrown him off guard? "Yeah, I suppose it was. I've always felt a strong connection to the earth, so I took an interest in elemental magic."

"Elemental magic," she repeated, as though saying the words aloud would help her understand.

"Yeah. We each have an element we're drawn to more than others. If you take the time to cultivate a relationship with it, you can learn to work together."

She leaned in. "What kinds of things can you do with earth?"

"Well, we're part of the earth, so grounding becomes second nature. And when we're grounded, our focus grows tenfold. By building a solid foundation within ourselves, we're completely supported."

"Does that make it easier to work with other elements? Like, they sort of tag along?"

"You could say that."

"What about gravity?" Mckenna wondered.

Cillian smiled. "Ah, yes. Well, gravity is actually drawing matter directly towards the Earth's core."

"Right . . ."

"If you're wondering if such a thing can be manipulated—"

"Mhm."

"I believe it can."

Awesome. "Can you?"

He laughed. "Can I defy gravity? Levitate and such?" She nodded. "Not sure I'll ever have that kind of power. It's interesting, though . . . I've always thought we owe that kind of advanced magic to the creation of stone circles, and mysterious phenomena like Stonehenge."

Wheels were turning in Mckenna's head. It struck her as logical that the Neolithic people had a deeper connection to the elements. "I get that. Nature was all they had," she responded. She hungered for a deeper understanding, to put her abilities to more use than simply talking to birds and deer, absorbing people's emotions, and sporadically slamming doors, which she'd only done once; it had happened after a fleeting vision of Seán's past, where he'd tucked Abby's goodbye note into his wallet. Mckenna had been so determined to find it that she accidentally swung open her dads' bedroom door when she approached it.

"You want to try, don't you?" said Cillian.

"So badly."

"It's difficult, but maybe together—"

"I'd like that," she said eagerly. "How did you learn all this? You must have had some sort of mentor?" Esme's kind, oval face appeared in her mind, and she wondered when she would ever see her again.

Cillian cleared his throat. "Yep. By now, I'm sure I can teach you a few things." He winked, nudging her hand with his knuckles.

"Um, guys?" Nissa called out from the pharmacy parking lot. "Where did you say you were parked?"

"Right there . . ." Cillian said, his eyebrows raised. Mckenna's eyes darted around in search of their yellow hatchback. It was nowhere in sight.

Cillian held up his index finger as if to say "be right back," and entered the pharmacy; he returned moments later, all colour drained from his face. "They towed it."

"Who towed it?" Nissa and Mckenna barked back, as though Cillian had done it himself.

"I'm such an eejit . . ." Cillian put a hand to his forehead. "I parked in the delivery zone. The trucks couldn't unload the inventory."

Mckenna sighed in annoyance. "We were here barely thirty minutes! So unlucky."

"Let's go pick it up, then," Nissa said, folding her arms over her chest. "Where is it?"

Cillian held up a ripped piece of paper. "The manager gave me an address, but, er . . ."

"But *what*?"

He sighed. "He said the tow trucks don't go directly to the yard, so he can't say when it'll be there."

If Mckenna were a dragon, smoke would be puffing out of her nostrils right now. "What does *that* mean?"

"We've got to check in the morning."

"Jesus Christ—"

"Swearing, Kenna."

"I'm *pissed*, Nissa. I wanted to be in Uig *today*."

Nissa shook her head. "This is all my fault."

"It's not. Don't worry," Mckenna said softly, resolving that she should be more patient with her best friend who'd just suffered a concussion.

"If it's anyone's fault, it's mine," Cillian said, nodding his head towards a threatening sign suspended from a nearby pole. The sign bore the words *REGISTERED DELIVERY VEHICLES ONLY* in bold red letters. Below it was a miniature illustration of a tow truck.

"To be fair, that's a really tiny drawing," Nissa offered.

Mckenna held in a sigh. "What do we do now?"

"He recommends staying at the Cluanie Inn. It's about a half-hour from here in Inverness-shire. The car yard's around there—and it's towards Skye, so we could be worse off."

Mckenna grunted. "Fine. How do we get there?" she asked wearily as an old man emerged from the pharmacy, bundled up in a blue and green tartan scarf, a rolled-up wool hat, and a coat twice his size. She peered into his azure eyes, resting in a bed of tiny wrinkles. He had to be at least eighty.

"The manager's offered to drive us," Cillian said with a shrug.

"Apologies for the mix-up!" the manager said, his voice surprisingly booming. "I was on lunch when the lorry arrived, and me nephew was watching over the shop. He's a right stickler for them rules, that lad. Takes after his stubborn mother, he does . . ."

"It's okay! It's so nice of you to drive us, mister," Nissa said.

"Lewis, please, Lewis."

They trailed behind Lewis as he climbed into his rusty grey coupe. Mckenna and Cillian wedged themselves into the backseat, shuffling aside a heap of assorted items. Meanwhile, Nissa took the front seat, volunteering to act as his co-pilot, offering to assist in reading the signs.

"Oh, that's kind, lassie, but me vision's twenty-twenty! I've never been lost a day in me life. Well, except the one time in Inverness when I took a wrong turn and found meself in a sheep pasture."

Mckenna, Cillian, and Nissa chuckled.

"What brings you three to Fort Augustus? Visiting our Nessie?" He winked.

"We were driving through, headed to the Isle of Skye," Cillian said.

"Aye, Skye. No place like it."

Mckenna smiled, letting the excitement around the place name envelop her. She looked up to meet Lewis's small eyes squinting at her in the rear-view mirror. "I bet you've got some Scottish in you!" he said, surprising her.

"Oh, uh, yeah. Half." She stumbled over her words, as though she'd just realized it, too. "How'd you know?"

"Fair skin, reddish hair, freckles." She couldn't argue with that. "Fae where?"

Fae where? "Sorry, I don't understand."

Chuckling, he said slowly, "Which part of Scotland?"

"Oh! My mom's from Aberdeen."

"Off the western coast! Never been meself, but Aberdeenshire is bursting with castles, they say. Loads of history in those parts, but nothing quite compares to the beauty of the Highlands," he remarked, gesturing to the brooding mountains above. They felt charged with magic—the ancient kind, born from land once honoured, blessed by the Mother Goddess herself. Mckenna gave him an enthusiastic nod, unable to imagine a more breathtaking experience than being surrounded by these majestic peaks.

By the time he'd poked into each of their origins, how they'd met (to which they had each mumbled something incoherent) and what it was like to live in America, the car eased to a stop in front of the only building in the remote wilderness: a plain white stuccoed inn. It seemed rather unassuming against the majestic backdrop, but it had an air of belonging, as if it had weathered time, witnessed wars, and hidden its fair share of secrets.

"You're doing that thing, Kenna," Nissa whispered, twisting her neck to face her.

"What thing?"

Nissa made her eyes wide. "That 'Spidey Sense' tingle. Any *you-know-whats* you sense we should be worrying about?"

Mckenna took *you-know-whats* to mean ghosts. Laughing, she shook her head and turned to Lewis, who, thankfully, wasn't listening. "What if they don't have any rooms left? There's nothing else around here . . ."

Lewis waved off her concern with the casual confidence of a small-town Scotsman. "Don't fash yourself! I doubt it's full. And if you're truly that unlucky, there's a camping site near Loch Shiel. You'll be just fine," he reassured her, noticing Mckenna's worried look. "Enjoy yourselves. In Scotland, it's no curse to find yourself off course!"

Expressing their sincere thanks, Mckenna, Nissa, and Cillian hopped out of the car and waved their goodbyes as he drove off.

What a nice person, Mckenna thought. Perhaps there *was* hope for humanity. "Come on," she said, "let's get something to eat inside. I can feel both your stomachs rumbling."

V

THE CAILLEACH

Once Seán and Andre realized they could uncover Mckenona's whereabouts using Maeve's stone necklace, they fled the inn in a frenzy; surely, Maeve had noticed it missing by now. Seán couldn't help but relish the thought of the witch's reaction if she could see her beloved necklace around his neck.

As they wheeled their carry-ons through the revolving doors of Heathrow Airport, Seán immediately sought out a map stand.

"Information desk!" Seán said a bit too loudly, pointing to a semi-circular desk near the taxi kiosk and bustling over. Andre followed.

"Excuse me, may we have a map, please?" Andre asked the blonde woman working the counter.

She lowered her rectangular glasses and flashed him a smile that was a notch above friendly. "Hello. Certainly! That'll be one pound."

"*One pound*—?" Seán started.

"Thanks," Andre said, then looking sideways at Seán.

Sighing, Sean fished a coin out of his pocket, and slipped it to the clerk. "Last one."

When they stepped aside, map in hand, Andre swore. "Damn, this is only England."

"We need all of the UK," Seán said, aware he was stating the obvious. "We've no idea where she could be looking for Abby. Could be Northern Ireland, where we lived . . . or Aberdeen, Scotland, where she was born . . . or *anywhere* in Scotland, really—"

"I know all of this, Seán." Andre sighed, then approached the clerk. "Sorry, me again."

"No trouble at all," the woman said, leaning forward. "Do you need directions?"

"Not quite. I'm wondering if we can swap this for a larger map."

She cocked an eyebrow. "A larger map?"

"Yeah, see, we're feeling adventurous and, uh, we can't decide if we want to head to Scotland next, or—"

"Oh, well, Edinburgh's worth a visit, that's for sure . . ."

His impatience rising, Seán stepped in front of Andre, waving the map of England in her face. "Thanks for your suggestions, but can you please just give my boyfriend and me a fecking map of the whole bloody United Kingdom?"

She winced at the word *boyfriend*. "Oh. Fine." She dug into a bottom drawer, and placed a thicker map on the counter. "Two pounds."

"You had to say 'boyfriend'? I was working her," Andre said as he followed Seán to a seating area by the baggage check-ins.

"You're easy on the eyes, luv, but you weren't getting her there fast enough." Seán settled into a black faux-leather chair, then spread out the map on the seat beside him.

"Well?" Andre said.

"Well, what?"

"Do it," Andre whispered, looking around for any eavesdroppers.

"You say that as if I've taken lessons in this or something. You're the academic, you do it."

"Yes, my law degree definitely covered ancient stones and their magical properties. You must have seen Abby do this before?"

Seán thought back to when he and Abby lived in their quaint apartment above her shop in Ballycastle. A memory fluttered into his mind that felt as old as the rock dangling against his chest—of finding his back-then wife and her strange friends, Maeve and Esme, sitting in a circle on the creaky wooden floors, surrounded by coarse salt and five white candles:

"Ancient stone of divine power, find my true love in this hour," *Abby, Esme, and Maeve chanted.*

"Will you be up soon, Abby?" Seán called as he climbed halfway down the steps to the shop.

"Won't be long, mo chridhe, we're in the middle of something," Abby called back, her gaze never lifting from the map flattened at their feet.

Seán peered down at them. "What are you doing now, summoning Elvis? Never mind, forget I asked . . ."

"Shh!" Maeve hissed. "We're trying to focus."

"We're searching for Maeve's one true love," Abby said in a sing-song voice.

He watched from above as the three young women held hands, and Maeve dangled a stone over a map of Scotland.

Seán let out a deliberately long sigh. "Well, I'm off to bed. So glad you ladies are in for the weekend . . . again. Just lovely." And he stomped back upstairs, ignoring their sudden fit of giggles.

"Are you saying we need to get some salt and candles?" Andre said in disbelief after Seán recounted his story.

"No, no. Abby's always said those things—the candles, salt, moon water—they're just tools. What's important is intention. It's all about intention."

"Okay. How do we make ourselves . . . intentional?"

Seán slipped off Maeve's necklace, suspended it over the map, and held out his other hand. Andre took it.

"Ancient stone of divine power . . ." Seán began.

"We look like complete lunatics."

"Doesn't matter, does it?"

Andre sucked in a breath. "No, it doesn't."

"Find our daughter in this hour," Seán continued.

"Ancient stone of divine power . . ." they both said in unison, disregarding the passersby that shot disapproving glances their way.

"It's gonna get dark soon," Nissa said after a hearty pub lunch— chicken pot pie with a side of mushy peas, and sticky toffee pudding for dessert—in the inn's cozy dining room, which pulled out all the Scottish stops with its red and green tartan wallpaper, rustic wooden tables, and Scottish paraphernalia hanging over the fireplace. Both Mckenna and Nissa politely declined to sample the haggis, Scotland's signature dish, which Mckenna had learned was made of sheep insides, minced with spices and onions.

"Don't knock it 'til you try it," their waitress had said, getting Cillian to give in. ("I rather enjoyed that!")

"Erm, bad news," Cillian said, leading Mckenna and Nissa outside to meet the nippy air.

"We're not coming out so you could have a smoke, are we?" Mckenna sneered.

Cillian shook his head. "Afraid not. Also, I'm trying to quit, if you must know."

"Uh-huh."

"Anyway," he continued, "there are no rooms available . . ."

"We're going camping!" Nissa said, hopping up and down like a child at Toys "R" Us.

Mckenna grunted. "Can't we ask them to call us a cab to another inn?"

Cillian chuckled. "Look around—this is *the* inn. The one inn to rule them all."

"Hilarious."

"Camping it is!" Nissa said, looking excited. "I, for one, as an orphaned, underprivileged youth, have never been. I've always been envious of those Girl Scouts."

"Really, Niss? Playing the poor foster kid card."

"It's not often I get to," she said, poking Mckenna's nose.

Mckenna hugged herself tight. "It's *freezing*. Can't you bribe them, Cillian?"

"I'm an honest man," Cillian said, making her scowl. "And I tried . . . It's alright! We'll keep close," he added with a grin.

While Cillian fetched the kindling, Mckenna and Nissa pitched their tent, which had been supplied by the campsite. Surrounded by the snowy peaks of five majestic mountains, they gazed out over the serene expanse of Loch Duich. Its glassy surface made it resemble more of a tranquil pool than a typical lake.

"What are you thinking?" Nissa asked, inhaling the sleeping bag as she tossed it into the tent; there was only one available at this short notice, but fortunately, it was fit for a family of five.

"Did you just sniff the sleeping bag?" Mckenna said, watching her.

"I want to be sure it's clean!"

"Girl Scouts don't sniff their sleeping bags."

Nissa stuck her tongue out.

"We have no choice either way," Cillian said, returning with a bundle of kindling in his arms, which he began placing haphazardly in the firepit.

Mckenna bent to her knees beside him. "The fire will never light like that." She grabbed a handful of dry twigs and stuck them strategically upright around the base of the logs, forming a kind of tipi. "This has to catch first, then it'll slowly light the logs." Extending her hand, she beckoned for Cillian's lighter, then deftly ignited a cluster of twigs. With gentle breaths, she guided the flickering flame towards the remaining kindling, coaxing it to life.

As mesmerized as their Stone Age ancestors, they watched as the twigs caught quickly and trickled onto the nearest log.

"Show-off," Cillian muttered.

She grinned in satisfaction. "My dads took me camping *a lot*."

"Lucky," Nissa said, tossing a twig in the fire.

"Why were you so reluctant to come, then?" Cillian asked.

"Well, their idea of camping is renting a yurt with a private bathroom and a grill."

Cillian laughed. "That's quite glamorous."

"I think you spoke too soon, Kenna," Nissa said, hovering over the now-fireless pit.

"Man, I thought it caught," Mckenna said, moving and poking the kindling around with a stick. "The kindling's burnt up now. The logs must be damp." She groaned. Even without marshmallows, she was eagerly looking forward to the simple pleasure of warming her hands and toes. That was the best part of camping, after all.

"Kenna, what if you used . . . you know?"

Cillian snapped his head in Nissa's direction. "Brilliant—"

"Do you think she can—?"

Mckenna stood up. "What are you two mumbling about?"

"Try lighting the fire," Cillian said, tugging her back down. His hand, black from soot, was cold and clammy. Despite her frosty fingers, they warmed instantly at his touch.

"I can't do that. It seems advanced."

"Have you tried?" Nissa asked, sitting beside her.

"I mean, no."

"Maybe fire is your element," Cillian encouraged. "Do you feel especially drawn to it?"

Mckenna had thought about it back at Luss, when Cillian revealed his element was earth; the truth was, she couldn't for the life of her choose just one element. She felt the same connectedness with trees as she did the many lochs they'd driven by, and a flickering flame brought her as much comfort as a light breeze.

"I'm not sure. How would I even do this?"

"I can't really tell you. Try attuning yourself to the elements."

And then it dawned on her—elementals. Esme mentioned them once before: *An elemental is a spiritual being connected with one of the four elements of the Earth.* Faeries and gnomes were earth elementals, sylphs were air, undines water, and salamanders fire. Perhaps if she asked for their help . . .

Mckenna sat staring stupidly at the wet logs before her. *Hey, there, uh, salamanders. Can you please help me light this fire?*

Nothing. Not a single flicker of a flame.

"Try closing your eyes, Kenna," Nissa whispered. "I know that helps you focus."

Mckenna tightly squeezed her eyelids shut, as if the pressure alone could somehow make a difference. *Please help me light this fire.*

Zilch. "It's not happening."

Cillian placed a hand on her shoulder. "You don't believe you can do it."

"Yeah, no, not really," she admitted. "The only time I've ever made anything happen is by accident. When I'm like really mad, or something. I once shut a book with my mind . . . and burst open a door."

"That's not true, lass—not every instance was an accident. What about communicating with the doe?"

"I mean, I was scared out of my mind that she would die. There was definitely pressure there."

"That's the proof, you see," Cillian said, "that your magic flows from your emotions. If you're not sensing that urgency right now, then summon your anger. Get mad, and be purposeful about it. You were able to do those things, in those very moments, because you wanted nothing more."

Get mad. That was easy. She contemplated how different her life might have been if her dads had been honest about who she was when she was a child. All those years spent feeling incomplete, as if nothing and no one could fill that void, not even her dads . . . She loved them and missed them more than words could convey, but she couldn't help but harbour resentment towards them for standing idly by as their weird kid grew into an even weirder teen, never quite fitting in and having no inkling why. And now, here she found herself, feeling just as distant from Abby as ever. Nissa had suffered a concussion, a young deer nearly died, tea leaves had ominously foretold she'd be stabbed in the back—yet another unwelcome prophecy—and to make matters more perplexing, Cillian smelled *really* good, and she didn't know what the hell to do about it.

Her temples began to pound, or scream, more like. She half-expected the sides of her head to split open from the pressure.

This was the moment. It was now. She opened her eyes, and muttered under her breath, "Salamanders—I invoke thee."

She didn't know where the verbiage came from, but she knew they were the right words. Her third eye revealed a small, lizard-like being, blood-red with black polka dots. The creature may have been small but its energy was large, imposing, nearly palpable. Its head tilted into a sort of bow, and extended its slim, slithering tongue towards the firepit.

That was all it took for the logs to burst into perfect flames. *Whoa.*

"Whoa," Nissa agreed.

"Lass, that was incredible!" Cillian wrapped his arms around Mckenna, sending a jolt of electricity through her as his right hand lingered beneath her curls.

"How did you do it, Kenna? Did you whisper something?"

Mckenna searched the ground for the salamander, but it was gone.

Gazing in awe into the orange flames, she whispered, "I . . . got angry."

They sat around the restless fire for some time, the flames refusing to settle even for a moment. Cillian confessed his life-long dream of someday being Dublin's Green party leader, while the girls shared their experience of staying with Nissa's grandmother, Arethusa, and how they had connected with the fae folk. Nissa was even brave enough to recount the tragic story of her parents.

"Your father thought you were a changeling?" Cillian said. "That's incredibly superstitious, even for me."

"Well, he seemed to think that's what was bringing him such bad luck."

Cillian nodded in understanding. "They say blood's thicker than water, but blood isn't everything. Your real family is who you choose," he offered. Mckenna gazed at the flames flickering in his eyes. It sounded as though he was speaking from personal experience.

"Where's your family?" Nissa asked.

Cillian kicked a log deeper into the fire. "My parents are back in Dublin—they live on the south side, across the bridge."

"No siblings?"

Mckenna gave Nissa a curt shake of her head, warning her not to pry. She recalled the somber expression on his face when he had shared a memory of his brother during the delegates' cocktail party in Belfast, under the Harvest Moon.

"A brother," was all he said. "I think I'm going to turn in. If we want to get to Uig quickly, we should head to the car yard first thing in the morning."

"Agreed," Mckenna said. "You coming, Nissa?"

"Nah, I'm gonna stay out just a little bit longer. The fire's still so alive," she added, flames dancing in her eyes.

Mckenna smiled. "And it will be all night."

"How do you know?" Nissa asked.

"Because I conjured it," she said with pride. It was the first time since learning about her abilities that she actually felt a semblance of being in control. She knew how to do something, and it wasn't as difficult as she had thought. Esme had taught her to ground and centre herself, to become one with the earth, but Cillian had shown her that it was okay to use her raw emotions, which she had always considered a weakness until now. It felt good to channel her anger rather than suppress it. Really good.

Cillian stepped aside to make room for Mckenna to crawl into the tent, and followed her inside. It was spacious enough for each of them to have a corner, but they only had two blankets to share among the three of them, along with one extra-large sleeping bag, which lay open on the ground as their sole cushioned surface. "You and Nissa could share one," he said, seeing her eye the two blankets.

"Oh, whatever. I mean, we could kind of spread them out among the three of us." She didn't want to give the impression that she *wanted* to snuggle under a blanket with him, but she also didn't want to come off as a prude who refused to share a blanket with a guy.

"Which corner would you like?"

"The one facing east," she said enigmatically.

"What?"

"I'm kidding."

He chuckled. "Right." He gestured to the open space, and she took the centre, reasoning that it might be less awkward for Nissa if she slept beside her rather than Cillian. Or at least, that's what she told herself.

He lay down beside her and spread the blanket over them, maintaining just the right amount of distance so they weren't too close nor too far apart.

He turned to face her. "How did it feel?"

"What?" She could smell the firewood scent on his hair.

"Starting the fire." His tone was filled with admiration.

Mckenna's smile held a hint of a secret. "Amazing."

"How'd you do it?"

She hesitated. "I . . . I spoke to the salamanders."

Cillian's eyes went wide. "You what? How?"

"I don't know. I knew all I had to do was ask. Why, is that, like, weird?"

He gave a short laugh. "You could say that." When Mckenna frowned, he went on, "Usually, it takes years of practice to connect and forge a bond with the elementals. It's high-level magic . . . They don't show up for just anyone. And it also makes me wonder," his eyes sparkled with curiosity, "if you could step into their plane as easily as you can call them into ours."

"I've actually, um, done that."

"You have?" he said incredulously, propping himself up on his elbow.

She mirrored his pose, tangling her curls in her fingers. "Yeah, back in the Inagh Valley. Remember when I came back without my shoes? Well, I left them in the faery realm. Niamh's idea of a practical joke, I think."

"Who's Niamh?"

She explained how she had followed the twinkling lights to a thicket near the lake and discovered herself in what seemed like a storybook forest. There, the grass felt as soft as feathers beneath her toes, and sprites glided through the streams. It was in this enchanting place that Niamh, a beautiful fae, had disclosed that once upon a time, humans communicated through thoughts and did so freely with other realms.

"And then she said that because of this transparency, the fear of death didn't exist." She could understand the allure of such an idea. Ghosts were currently shrouded in mystery, which made them unsettling. However, if it were possible to peer into the afterlife at any moment, essentially bridging the gap between their realm and ours, the dread arising from the unknown would vanish. The world would become an open and authentic place, where people could truly witness everything it had to offer. There would be no conflicts sparked by differing beliefs, no triviality that so often clung to everyday human existence. Mundanity would give way to the transcendental and the supernatural, becoming the new norm.

"Fascinating. That's . . ." Cillian trailed off, as if his very breath had been stolen. He looked at her as if she'd descended a spiral staircase dressed in a sparkling silver gown and glass slippers. She'd always disliked the story of Cinderella; the prince's feelings for her were infatuation, not love. What else would drive a man to search every home in the region based on one silly dance? However, in that moment, Cillian's gaze, filled with raw intensity and awe, hinted that he would do the same for her.

"Hi," she said under her breath.

"Hi," he whispered, inching his face closer.

His eyes travelled down to her lips. She bit her lower lip,

as if it would grant her the courage she needed to move hers closer, as well.

ZIP.

"Coming through!" Nissa announced, stumbling into the tent and landing face-first between them. "You're right, Kenna, that fire is-a-*blazing*."

Not anymore, Mckenna thought, scooching over to make room for Nissa. She forced a yawn. "I'm exhausted. G'night, guys." She turned onto her side, hoping the sound of her shallow breaths and pounding heart didn't carry.

"*Dùisg*," a soft voice crooned in Mckenna's ear. *Wake up.*

She gasped at the horrifying figure standing over her but was silenced as the thing's wrinkled, withered hand covered her mouth. The figure appeared to be an elderly woman with long, knotted white hair that cascaded around her pale blue complexion. In the centre of her forehead rested a single eye, dark and glistening like black granite. She wore a worn-out blue and green tartan cloak that hung loosely from her shoulders.

"*Trobhad*," she hummed. *Come here.*

Mckenna could have protested. She could have awakened Nissa and Cillian, then pushed the woman out of the tent. But a part of her yearned to follow her. A part of her remained unafraid of the woman's cyclops appearance and grotesque complexion. A part of her trusted that she would be safe with her.

She followed the old woman out to the lakeside, where she beckoned Mckenna to sit facing a range of mountains. *"Beautiful, aren't they?"*

Mckenna was surprised that such a silvery voice could reside within such a horrid-looking creature.

"Very," was all Mckenna could manage to say under the circumstances.

"Do you know of their tale?"

She shook her head. *"Can't say that I do."*

"*Long, long ago, a local chieftain had seven lasses. The two youngest were dearly loved by a pair of Irish princes—brothers, in fact. The other five sisters were, aye, fuelled with envy, for they longed to be loved just the same. The chieftain only wished for their happiness, so, he struck a deal with the Irish princes: They could wed his daughters if, and only if, they returned to Ireland and brought their five elder brothers back to Kintail to wed his five daughters. Sadly, the two princes were ensnared in a terrible storm while sailing back to Ireland, and never made it.*"

"*What happened to the five sisters?*"

"*They waited and waited, and when the brothers still hadn't returned, they beseeched the Grey Magician of Coire Dhunnid to preserve their beauty.*"

"*And did he?*"

In response, the old woman stared at the mountain range before them. The *five* mountains.

"*Oh.*"

The old woman nodded. "*Precisely. 'Tis the price one pays for fighting the natural law.*"

"*But they didn't know,*" Mckenna sympathized, staring across the loch. "*They just wanted to be loved.*"

"*Aye, mayhaps. But there are many ways of getting the outcome one's heart desires.*" Mckenna had the sense the woman was no longer referring to the five sisters. "*Had they not given in to fear, they might've had another chance at love.*"

"*Fear of what?*"

"*Of aging. Of solitude. Of dying alone.*" The old woman leaned in close, near enough for Mckenna to see her reflection in her glistening black eye. It was like staring into the abyss on a new moon night. "*We all have darkness within us.*" The words sent goosebumps up Mckenna's arms and legs. "*We're neither born with it, nor is it thrust upon us. We tip the scales. We forge our own path.*"

"*Funny, I could swear some people are born evil.*" She thought of Nissa's father, Simon Fage; of the High Priestess; and of herself . . . prophesized to cause the death of billions of souls. A reincarnation of the maleficent Alice Kyteler.

"No one is born inherently good or evil, lassie. We bide in duality—we possess both shadow and light. Without shadow, finding the light would be that much more challenging, aye?"

"I'm not sure what you mean."

"Balance, Wise One. Balance."

Mckenna gasped. How did she know she was a Wise One? *"Who are you?"*

"Just an old crone," she said with a grin and began to walk towards the water, as still as the night itself. *"I must go now. Winter is near."*

"Careful, you'll—"

The old woman moved with an otherworldly grace, her steps defying nature as she glided effortlessly above the water's surface. Slowly, she turned to face Mckenna. The wrinkles around her eyes, nose, and chin tightened, and her bluish skin brightened to a coconut white; from root to tips, her once snowy hair glistened into a brilliant blonde, and her single black eye split into two emerald ones, as vibrant as the hills of Ireland.

Mckenna stood with her mouth agape. *"How . . . ?"*

"The eye reveals only a fraction of its true sight, for 'tis bound by the confines of our own minds." And with that, the old-crone-now-goddess tossed her tartan cloak at Mckenna's feet, revealing a long white robe. She walked on, stepping lightly towards the Five Sisters of Kintail and leaving behind small ripples in her wake.

"I thought I heard you out here," Nissa called out, jogging up beside her.

Mckenna put a hand to her chest. "You scared the living crap out of me."

Nissa yawned, pointing at the cloak on the ground. Her tired expression demanded an explanation.

"You wouldn't believe me if I told you."

"I think we're past that, Kenna."

Mckenna laughed. "True."

"So," Nissa said, folding her arms over her chest. "You gonna tell me who you were talking to and what in the world language you were speaking?"

The following morning, Mckenna, Nissa, and Cillian were met with a brisk wind that no longer carried with it the lingering touch of fall. *Winter definitely is near*, Mckenna thought, handing over her camping gear to the attendant, an acne-faced teen who looked like he'd rather be swimming in the deep, mysterious waters of Loch Ness than be working here.

"Nice cloak?" Cillian remarked, his hand outstretched in a "care to explain" gesture.

"Mckenna's quite the Scotswoman now!" Nissa said in a terrible Scottish accent.

Cillian cocked an eyebrow.

"I'll tell you about it on the ride to Skye," Mckenna said. Nissa wasn't just referring to the tartan; last night, Nissa described Mckenna's words as throaty and, to her, sounding like complete gibberish but somehow musical.

"Might've been Scottish Gaelic," Mckenna had suggested to Nissa. "Maybe past-life knowledge?"

"Your dad didn't teach you?" Nissa had asked.

"Not unless you count a couple of swear words and the *Happy Birthday* song," she'd replied. "But that was in Irish Gaelic, which my dad says is way different."

Once they had retrieved their car at the yard, where a stout, ginger-haired woman guided them out of the lot, they were back on the main road, Loch Duich to their left, and the Five Sisters of Kintail steadily fading from view. Funnily enough, the second sister looked as if it had a pair of eyes near the peak, gawking at her. *Did it just wink at me?*

"Look!" Nissa shouted, pointing ahead at a medieval castle at the end of a centuries-old stone footbridge. The castle was tall and boxy, with low stone walls keeping it safely tucked into the small isle on which it stood.

"Oh wow, it's here!" Cillian said.

The girls spun their heads towards him. "What's here?"

"That's got to be Eilean Donan Castle. I reckon it's one of the most visited castles in Scotland. I've always wanted to see it."

No kidding. It wasn't just the castle that was breathtaking; it was its location—perched in the most commanding position at the centre of the loch, shielded by an endless range of mountains. How could the landscape in this country shift so dramatically from one moment to the next?

Nissa let out a dreamy sigh. "It looks so *old*."

"It is," Cillian said. "Like, from the twelve hundreds. It was destroyed in the Jacobite rising—the one that led to the Battle of Culloden, remember?" he added when Mckenna tilted her head. "They restored it and opened it for visitors in the '30s, I think."

"It's beautiful," Mckenna and Nissa said in unison. *What isn't in Scotland?* Mckenna thought. "You know everything, huh?"

His cheeks reddened. "Everyone knows about Eilean Donan Castle."

"Uh-huh."

"So, where am I headed, co-pilot?" he said, looking into the rear-view mirror at Nissa, who had officially been elected the map bearer.

"Continue on the A87, and we'll be crossing Loch Alsh over to Kyleakin—did I say that right? Then woohoo, we're in the Isle of Skye! And I really have to pee."

"Why didn't you go before we left, Niss?"

"I didn't have to go when we left . . ."

It was a relatively short drive over the bridge, so Mckenna made a conscious effort to savour the incredibly dramatic views, which, until now, she believed only existed in one's imagination. As the road meandered through an endless expanse of mountains and lochs, she wondered just how many of both Scotland possessed.

As soon as they reached the isle, they slowed down in search of a restroom, no longer able to ignore Nissa's incessant bouncing in the back seat. "I'll go in the woods, I don't care!" she yelped as the car came to a full stop, and she hurried out and disappeared into a thicket of trees.

Mckenna leaned back in her seat, closed her eyes, and let go of a long breath.

"Something wrong, lass?"

"No, I . . . I just feel how close my mom is."

He squeezed her hand. She opened her eyes, knowing he was staring into hers, and jumped in her seat.

Someone stood just a foot away from their car in the dead centre of the road, hands in his pockets, and a lightness in his eyes that had nothing to do with their sky-blue hue. He couldn't have been much older than Mckenna, with wavy chestnut-brown hair that gleamed golden in spots, and light freckles scattered across his boyish face.

"Who the hell . . ." In an instant her heart doubled its rhythm, while her chest felt as if it had cracked down the middle. She glanced sideways at Cillian, who looked like he'd seen a ghost. *Please don't be a very lifelike ghost.* "Cillian? Who is that?"

Without a word, Cillian pushed open his driver's-side door, then slammed it, causing Mckenna to jolt at the impact. She rolled down her window as Cillian approached. "Mathis." She watched as his usually composed demeanor faltered, a visible tremor in his composure that she'd never witnessed before.

"Brother," Mathis replied.

VI

REUNITED

Simon spent the entire day on his fishing boat, and all he had to show for it were two of the tiniest brown trout he'd ever seen—barely enough to stretch through the weekend. His luck had deserted him a long time ago, but this . . . this was bleak, even by his standards.

Dragging his meager catch to his secluded cabin, a faint rustling stopped him in his tracks.

Please let it be the stag. Please, please, please . . .

He lowered his cooler to the ground, careful not to make a sound, and turned slowly. There, some hundred metres distant, was the stag that could potentially ensure his survival through the coming winter. It was beautiful, boasting a robust build and standing tall, its proud antlers reaching far above Simon's head. Although that wasn't saying much.

And Simon was going to kill it. Luckily—for once—he had

his rifle slung across his back; he'd made the last-minute decision to grab it that morning, in case it came in handy.

As if the stag had tuned into his thoughts, its head pivoted sharply towards Simon's position.

"Oi, you great brute," Simon whispered. "I won't hurt you . . ."

The stag held him in contemplation briefly before bounding away.

Simon let out a yell of frustration that reverberated among the trees, and in a surge of unfiltered anger, he kicked his cooler. It toppled, and along with the ice and bait, his catches spilled out, cascading into the nearby brook. "Nooooo!" But the water had already carried his dinner downstream.

This was a joke. His entire life was one cruel joke. Thoughts of his fruitless journey back to the cabin, supperless, painted his existence as a dark comedy.

When he spotted the rolled-up newspaper on his doorstep, he thanked no one in particular that at least one local paper made it to the middle of nowhere. It was his only link to the outside world, after all.

Tossing the cooler aside, he grabbed the paper and spat on the ground before entering; his father had done this ever since Simon was a lad to ward off evil spirits and bad luck. Loads of good that brought him, but it couldn't hurt.

He pushed the door in—unlocked, of course, as there was nothing to steal except a worn cot and an empty miniature freezer, both retrieved from a nearby rubbish tip. He passed by every so often in hopes someone was chucking out a perfectly functional stove; he did all of his cooking and tea-warming in the hearth, like he was living in the ruddy eighteen hundreds.

He lit a fire and settled on the floor, accompanied by *The Oban Times*. Its coverage confined to the West Highlands and Islands of Scotland, it rarely held groundbreaking news. But it passed the time and gave him the illusion that he wasn't in complete isolation.

"'*Highlands witness surge in tourism*' . . . just what everybody needs . . . '*Salmon season has come to an end*' . . . thanks for stating the obvious . . . '*Protestors call for a fishing ban in Loch Ness* . . ."

Simon rolled his eyes at the photo. *Ridiculous. Protesting people's bloody meals. Should be illegal. Bunch of stupid hippies . . .*

He squinted at the caption beneath a photo of the protesters: *Logan Macleod (left) leads efforts to ban fishing in Loch Ness, supported by American tourist Nissa Febland (right).*

Simon blinked. Had he read that correctly? He read it again. And again. She looked to be the right age. Even had Annie's nose. And *his* eyes, which made him sick to his stomach.

Could it be her—the changeling whose arrival marked the onset of his unending rotten luck? He blamed the fae. Since her birth, his world had unraveled—his business, his marriage—like dominoes falling. She was no daughter of his. Her soul was swapped for a faerie's, he never doubted it. It happened to one of his old flatmates, who'd claimed he'd even witnessed them flying over their newborn's crib, giggling madly. These creatures were not the stuff of fluffy faery tales; they were malicious, spiteful beings.

Could the girl really be in Scotland? If this was her, she was in the West Highlands, no less.

Something inside of Simon flared like lightning. It was a sensation he hadn't had in seventeen years.

The feeling that his luck was about to take a turn.

"I think we're here," Andre said to Seán as he pulled into the pebbly driveway of a countryside inn as mystical-looking as the woman who occupied it. It was a converted cottage, three stories high, each level boasting a wide bay window on the right-hand side. The inn sat at the foot of a hill, its hundred-year-old stone façade half covered in ivy, and two chimneys sticking out of opposite ends of a red clay-tiled roof. As if that ensemble weren't adorable enough, the windows, of which there were many, were dressed in lilac shutters that looked to be freshly painted.

"This is it," Seán said, looking from the spot he had circled on the map of the Isle of Skye, courtesy of Maeve's stone, to the sign perched on the lawn that read *Rowan House*. After the stone had pinpointed the Isle of Skye at Heathrow Airport, they flew to Inverness and, once again, dowsed with Maeve's stone on a detailed map of the Isle of Skye—this time inside a bathroom stall.

Andre pulled on the handbrake, relieved he'd managed to make it, collision-free, driving on the opposite side of the very narrow, very snaky road. "Wow. Cozy."

"Very Abby," Seán whispered, warmth in his words.

Andre examined his partner's face. "It's okay to be nervous. You haven't seen her in—"

"Seventeen years."

The front door opened, and Andre nearly gasped. It had to be Abigail; she was the spitting image of Mckenna—or, rather, his daughter was the spitting image of her. Her complexion, fair and luminous, boasted a gentle dusting of freckles, like tiny constellations. Her auburn curls swayed in the wind, a few strands sweeping across her face. With a gentle gesture, she brushed them aside, revealing a set of amber eyes that seemed to hold both her heart and soul in them at once.

"Seán," she called from across the lawn. Her voice was like velvet. It was the kind of voice that could transport you, hug you, lull you into a satisfying sleep.

Seán stepped out of the car, and Andre watched from the driver's seat as his partner was tugged by an invisible rope towards his first love. Seán stepped towards her and wrapped his arms around her.

She began to cry, as did he. Andre expected nothing less. There was so much hanging over them, so much they had suffered. This was normal. Completely normal.

Right?

After the longest minute Andre had ever experienced, Seán pulled away, roughly wiped away his tears, and gestured for

Andre to join him. He did, not so much with reluctance but with caution, feeling like an intruder with every stride.

"Abby, I'd love for you to meet Andre."

Her smile was warm and her eyes full of kindness, but Andre couldn't help seeing the sadness behind her gaze. Forcing a smile, he allowed himself to be pulled into an embrace.

Mckenna flung open the car door and swiftly joined Cillian's side, while Nissa emerged from the edge of the woods. "Who's the hunk?" she said, leaning into Mckenna's ear.

"Cillian's brother."

"He's not my brother," Cillian spat, holding Mathis's gaze. "What the hell are you doing here, Mathis?" Mckenna had never heard him speak with such disdain.

"Um, thinking maybe we move this conversation to the *side* of the road . . ." Nissa said.

Ignoring Nissa, Mathis took a step forward. "I've been searching for you." He was softer-spoken than Cillian, possibly due to his British accent, and his voice carried an intriguing rasp. Mckenna made a mental note to ask him why they didn't share the same Irish accent. Didn't they grow up together?

"It's been four years," Cillian seethed. "Why now? How'd you find me?"

"We need to talk."

"Not in the mood. Catch you in another four years." Cillian turned on his heel and grabbed Mckenna's hand. "Let's go."

"Brother, if you could just let me explain—"

"Don't call me that."

"Cillian . . ."

"C'mon," Cillian urged, tugging Mckenna towards the car. Shrugging, she and Nissa exchanged equally perplexed glances and gave Mathis the same awkward wave before returning to the car. Back in her seat, Mckenna stared at Mathis, unable to shake the feeling that there was something familiar about him.

In a swift and overwhelming surge, sorrow overcame her, and she was suddenly burdened by a cascade of unresolved emotions—Mathis's and Cillian's intertwined. The pain she felt radiating from Mathis, the heaviness of his loss, and the profound sorrow over parting ways with Cillian weighed heavily on her heart, on *his* heart. She yearned to bridge the divide, to share this with Cillian. "Cillian, listen . . ."

With an abrupt press on the gas pedal, Cillian swerved past Mathis, leaving him behind as he sped off.

"Cillian!" Mckenna shouted.

"He's fine," he said quickly, without so much as glancing in the rear-view mirror.

"Cillian," Mckenna said again. "He's hurting too, I felt it—"

"Don't care."

She sighed. "Can you please tell us what happened?"

With a sigh of reluctance, he began. "After my parents had me, my mum had three miscarriages." Mckenna instantly felt a stab to her heart. "They wanted to give me a sibling so badly, and I begged them for a brother. They decided to adopt, and there he was—Mathis Oder. A sweet, well-behaved, orphaned toddler from West London. He was the perfect little brother, dropped right from the heavens, my mum would say; we played rough, but we were inseparable. Then, at sixteen, he just left. 'Dear Mum, Dad, and bro—I'm sorry I have to say goodbye this way, but I must return to where I belong. Thank you for giving me a home all these years. I love you all.' And that was that." Cillian stared ahead, seemingly in a daze.

"What did he mean by where he belonged?" Mckenna asked.

"I don't know. Back to West London? I didn't bother to look. Clearly, he didn't want to be found."

"Why don't you let him explain?" Nissa offered quietly. "He seemed genuine."

"Because someone who chucks their family away with a note doesn't deserve a second chance."

Mckenna stiffened.

"Oh, I'm sorry. That's not what I—your mother is a totally different situation."

"Is it, though? And you forget I also ditched my dads with a shitty note." Guilt coursed through her. "We both had our reasons. Maybe Mathis does, too."

The car quickly filled with silence, until Cillian said, "I don't know where I'm going, by the way. What happened to the map?"

"Oh man, it might've fallen out of my pocket on my peepee break," Nissa said, springing from the back seat and practically climbing over Mckenna to rummage through the glove compartment. "We're good, here's another!" She pulled back, map now in hand, looking eager to continue navigating again. "Michael J. Fox!" Nissa shouted excitedly, her fingers snapping to indicate she'd remembered something.

"Excuse me?" Mckenna said, cocking an eyebrow.

"Mathis *totally* looks like him, right?"

The trio zipped through the single-track roads ("How is this a two-way?") along the moody backdrop of the crags and cliffs that made up the Isle of Skye. She hadn't been this taken aback by scenery since entering the Inagh Valley back in Ireland; but here, the landscape wasn't of lush green fields and rolling hills. No, this ancient landscape was unruly, rugged, haunting.

"Stop!" Mckenna shouted as they weaved through a familiar valley of misty mountains, sparkling pools of water dotted along its green and stony shell. This was it—the very spot she'd astral travelled to on Samhain, where she'd spoken to her mother for the first time. "It was here. Where I astral travelled to her."

Cillian began pulling over on a stretch of wildly swaying grass on the side of the road, and the car barely came to a complete stop before Mckenna stepped out and dashed down the valley. Her senses were met with the fragrance of wild berries and exotic florals, and the familiar sound of rushing water.

"Kenna, are you sure?" Nissa shouted from the car.

"I'm sure!"

And there she stood—this time in physical form—as radiant as she had been a few nights prior, standing tall and glowing like a single star in the night sky. Her birth mother. The woman whose powers she shared, whose waves ran as wild as her own, whose entire being was the missing piece to the broken life she'd been living all these years.

"Swan."

"Mom." A lump rose in her throat, and her eyes swarmed with tears. She hadn't known whether she would ever be comfortable calling her *Mom* once they'd met in person, but the word slipped from her mouth as though it had done so millions of times before.

She broke into a run. Abby did too. They fell into each other's arms, neither giving the other the space to breathe. It was not an embrace between two faraway strangers but a fierce one, overflowing with the weight of seventeen years of heartbreak. In this moment, mother and daughter—*the Wise One and her creator*, her *twin flame*, as the prophecy foretold—were finally reunited.

"And who is this charming wee companion of yours shedding tears . . . of joy, I hope?" Abby's voice had a warm, velvety texture that made Mckenna wish she could fall asleep listening to it for the rest of her life.

Nissa was jogging towards them, her face buried in her hands, Cillian at her heel. "I'm sorry! I'm just so happy . . ."

"That's Nissa," Mckenna said, smiling widely. "She's my best friend."

At this, Nissa began blubbering.

"And the brooding lad?" Abby whispered, nodding towards Cillian, who mumbled something about it being an honour to meet Mckenna's mum.

"That's Cillian. He's, uh, a friend."

"I see." Mckenna admired her mother's ability to not appear judgmental while sizing someone up. "Shall we head home?" Abby said, beaming.

"We shall," said Mckenna, linking her arm with hers.

Seán's heart skipped a beat when he spotted them entering through the inn's front garden from the living room window. He'd nearly forgotten how much Mckenna resembled her mother. Wild, natural curls cascading down her back, heart-shaped lips, and a latent hardness behind her eyes that meant hurt—and stubbornness—lingered there. To his surprise, his daughter was not alone; she was accompanied by a small, wide-eyed girl and a dark-haired boy, whose tallness and handsomeness he immediately distrusted.

He looked over at Andre. His lips were subtly quivering, the way they did whenever all of his emotions were surfacing at once. Seán grabbed his hand, and together they stepped outside and walked down the porch steps.

"Dads!" Mckenna shouted, sprinting towards them and jumping them both at once. They each caught one of her legs. "I'm so sorry—"

"*We're* sorry—"

"Stop that, Andre, it's entirely my fault. All of it . . ."

They went on like this for about five minutes before Seán and Andre let her go, and Seán smacked her lightly in the back of the head. She rubbed the spot, as if surprised he had restrained himself from punishing her first thing.

Seán folded his arms over his chest. "Are you mental?"

Andre stepped forward, towering over her. "Don't you ever, EVER take off like that again."

"I said I was sorry! And I won't. I promise." When their huffing dissolved into threatening *You better not!* expressions, she asked, "So, when did you guys get here? And, um, where *is* here?"

"It's an inn I've been staying at for . . . oh, a while," Abby said, appearing beside Mckenna. "I help run it—the owners are the most wonderful people. But it's just us! I'm watching over the place while they're away on holiday for the winter."

"And we're grateful to be here," Andre said to her, then turned back to Mckenna. "We got here a day ago."

"How did you find me . . . and Mom?"

Seán and Andre exchanged knowing looks, Seán stroking Maeve's stone in his pocket. Andre cleared his throat. "How about we explain over some lunch? You must be starving."

"Yeah, swan, I whipped up some boxty." Seán winked.

Right on cue, Mckenna's stomach rumbled. "Yes, definitely. But first, I'd like to introduce you to my friends." As though waiting to be announced, the girl scurried to Mckenna's side, leaving the boy fending for himself down the garden path.

Seán's heart warmed. "Friends?"

"Yes," Mckenna said with an eye-roll. "*Friends*. Rare, I know. This is Nissa."

"It's an honour to meet Mckenna's gay dads. I mean dads! I mean parents, like, in general. So, *so* nice to meet you."

"Likewise," Andre said, holding out his hand. She wrapped both her hands around his and shook it with vigor, then took Seán's and did the same.

"I like this one," Seán said, wagging his finger at her, and he meant it. He leaned over to meet her eyes. "Thank you for sticking with our kid."

The girl's eyes sparkled, then she giddily skipped away and up the front steps. "See you guys inside!" She reminded him a touch of Abby in the way she carried herself—an air of lightness, innocence, and congeniality that was rare to come by. Abby quietly followed her inside.

"Mckenna," Andre interjected, "who's the scared-looking fellow lingering behind that plant, pretending not to see us?"

"That's my friend Cillian," she said quickly.

Seán lifted an eyebrow. "Friend, you said?"

"Yes, *friend*, I said."

"Then why does he look like he'd rather be shearing sheep than meeting us?" Seán pressed on, arms crossed over his chest.

Mckenna looked over her shoulder. The man-boy Cillian was closely examining a thin but thriving tree like it was an alien species. As though sensing he was being watched, Cillian lifted his eyes towards the lot of them, and walked over with a stride that was about as confident as an acrobat tightrope walking for the very first time.

"Sorry, eucalyptus, erm, fascinates me," he said.

Mckenna snorted, then cleared her throat. "Cillian, these are my dads, Seán and Andre."

"It's a pleasure, sirs," he said with a respectful nod, his hand extended out to them. Seán's gaze travelled from his buffed brown boots to his tousled dark hair. Meeting the parents and he hadn't even bothered to comb it. Classic bad boy—and worst of all, the preppy kind, with those Italian leather boots. Likely never suffered honest, hard work a day in his life . . .

Mckenna cleared her throat again, this time more deliberately, giving her best *don't be jerks* look.

"I'm Andre, it's nice to meet you." Andre elbowed Seán in the ribs.

"Seán," Seán said in an unnaturally deep voice. "Pleasure."

"Is lunch ready?" Mckenna asked shrilly.

Andre responded by cupping her face. "Right this way."

Mckenna hung back, letting Andre and Cillian file in first, and tapped Seán on the arm. "Dad? What was it like? Seeing Mom after so long."

The truth was, Seán wasn't sure how to put into words what he had felt. When his eyes met Abby's, her entire face lit up with glee. Her smile had always been contagious. So, he smiled back, despite the melange of befuddled feelings he had for her. Andre had been watching them the whole time from a distance, even as tears ran down her beautiful face and stung his own eyes, too. Admittedly, as they neared Skye, he had been afraid of old feelings resurfacing, but none did. There were no lingering romantic emotions whatsoever, which he had later confided to Andre.

"You're more handsome than I imagined," Abby had said after pulling Andre into a hug. Seán distinctly remembered seeing his partner's shoulders drop in relief.

"And you're as alluring as I knew you would be," Andre had replied. Such a class act, his partner was. Perhaps he was being naïve, but from then, it was like any tension that might've existed evaporated, for the love they shared for their one daughter was greater than any jealousy or past resentment.

Grinning at the recent memory, Seán placed a hand on his daughter's shoulder. "It was like seeing an old friend."

In the mere ten minutes that Mckenna had been in her mother's presence, she could already attest that the inn had Abby written all over it. It was both bright and warm all the way through: Wooden chimes not unlike the ones in her old witchy shop in Ballycastle—now Esme's—tinkled in welcome as they entered; facing the front door, a violet and cream-coloured Persian rug ran up a flight of forest green stairs, which twisted and turned at least two more stories; the entrance flowed directly into the kitchen, furnished with old but sturdy-looking birch cupboards, with flat round knobs, each hand-painted a different pastel design, and a grey stone countertop that was clearly made for chopping.

"I've already claimed the kitchen," Seán said mid-way through the tour.

The lengthiest part of the counter extended outward to face the wide, open living area, which looked like Scotland itself birthed it: two plaid armchairs—the exact blue and white of the nation's flag, as Abby pointed out—sat across from a navy three-seater sofa; mismatched side tables were positioned here and there, somehow tastefully, and a coffee table that looked to be a refurbished cedar trunk was centred on the maize-yellow rug, quite a nice complementary hue to the dark furniture. Like most older homes, the focal point of the space was the hearth, where a fire roared under the mantel.

Mckenna looked around at the potted plants that occupied every available ledge, tabletop, and corner. "I love it," she breathed, overcome by a sudden unfamiliar feeling of serenity. "Oh, and I think I spot your nook, Dad," she added to Andre, her gaze flying over to the large bay window, where a wooden desk looked out onto the distant snowy peaks.

"Already claimed it," Andre said with a wink.

Lunch was the most awkward gathering Mckenna had ever been a part of, counting the disastrous dinner with the delegates in Belfast. There was so much she wanted to say to her mother, but not here. She was desperate for some one-on-one time.

"The food's wonderful, Seán, thank you," Abby said, breaking the silence. Her melodious Scottish accent was like a warm hug. "You were always quite the chef!"

"Yes, it's delicious," Cillian muttered nervously beside her.

"It's Mckenna's favourite," Seán said. "Isn't it, swan?"

"Why do you call her swan?" Nissa asked.

"Ever heard of the story of *The Children of Lir*?"

Nissa shook her head.

"Ah, well, if you don't mind a bit of storytelling . . ."

"Not at all!" Nissa said excitedly, leaning in.

Mckenna leaned back in her chair. "Here we go . . ."

"In the days of old Ireland," Seán began, his voice taking on that familiar storytelling lilt, dropping an octave and drenched in a touch of the dramatic, "there reigned King Lir, the sovereign of the sea. By his side was the enchanting Eva, who graced him with four children: a son Aodh, a daughter Fionnula, and twin lads, Fiachra and Conn. Fate took Eva from them after the children were born, and the king yearned for a motherly presence in their lives." He paused, locking eyes with Mckenna. "So, he wed Eva's sister, Aoife, a woman of wondrous and mystical powers."

Nissa giggled. "I can see why you liked this story, Kenna."

"Mmm, hold that thought," Mckenna said with a chuckle.

"Right," Seán agreed. "Aoife, with her heart tainted by jealousy, grew resentful of the king's affection for his children. Crafty as they come, she was. One day, she lured the children to the water's edge and wove a spell that transformed them into swans. For nine hundred long years, they would dwell in this form: three hundred on the tranquil waters of Lough Derravaragh, three hundred more on the Straits of Moyle, and the final three hundred on the shores of the Isle of Inish Glora."

Nissa gasped.

"But ah, a spell can always be broken," Seán continued, playing off her reaction. He was loving every minute of this. "This enchantment held a secret: it would break when the sound of a bell met St. Patrick's arrival. However, Aoife had missed one crucial detail: she hadn't taken away the children's voices. So, day by day, they sang their swan songs, and in time, they were able to communicate their plight to their father. Outraged, King Lir banished Aoife into the mist. She was gone forever."

Nissa stood and clapped. "I *love* that—"

"Although saddened by his children's fate . . ." Seán carried on, interrupting Nissa's praise.

She slowly sat back down. "Oh, there's more!"

"Lir spent his days by the lake, listening to his children's swan songs. They journeyed to the Straits of Moyle, fought through storms, and found their way to a tranquil lake on the Isle of Inish Glora. There, they spent their last three hundred years. When at last the bell rang, they were guided to a holy man named Caomhog, who cared for them during their final years. Yet, as fate would have it, a man claiming to be the king of Connacht strutted in one day, wanting to claim the 'legendary and mystical swans with beautiful singing voices.' Just as he was about to grab hold of them, another bell rang out, and a mist appeared . . . ."

"What happened?" Nissa shouted. Mckenna threw her head back, laughing, loving her friend's childlike reaction.

"They turned back into the children they once were," Mckenna finished.

"And," Andre chimed in, knowing the story well, "the king of Connacht fled like a coward!"

"Ah, a happy ending. Thank goodness," Nissa said, leaning back in her chair.

"Not exactly," Andre said. "When the children turned into their human forms, they began to age rapidly. Before they died,

Caomhog christened them in order for their legend and names to live on forever."

"Just a bit of Catholic fear for good measure—*be christened and you'll be saved*," Seán said. "Was going to leave that bit out, luv."

"Wow. That's a devastating story," Nissa said. "I wish it ended when the new wife got banished."

"You and me both," Abby said with a smile.

"It is rather devastating, isn't it?" Seán agreed. "Even so, it was our Mckenna's favourite story as a child."

Nissa turned to her. "Morbid from the start, huh?"

"You know it," Mckenna said through a mouthful of soda bread.

Cillian snickered beside her. She'd nearly forgotten he was there.

"Did you know Mckenna also means 'daughter of Aodg'?" Abby said. "King Lir's eldest son."

"I don't think I even knew that," Mckenna said.

"Aren't you glad I ask questions?" Nissa said. "Oh, Kenna, where would you be without me?"

"Probably still in that horrid motel off the highway," Mckenna hissed in her ear, making her nearly choke on her water. Out of the corner of her eye, Mckenna caught Abby beaming.

"So," Seán said loudly. "How *did* you girls meet?"

Nissa took the reins, explaining their encounter at school ("Kenna got her whole class to sign my recycling bin petition!"); how Mckenna and a bird saved her from a bully in the school-yard; their run-in in their neighbourhood woods ("Oh my gosh, it was like we'd known each other *forever* . . ."); how, coinciden-tally, Mckenna had been the one to find Nissa's missing bracelet; and, lastly, their journey from Boston to Ireland, with the gra-cious assistance of their honorary grandparents, John and Brigit, who—by yet another serendipitous coincidence—happened to be travelling to Ireland via an ocean liner. "And then we met Cillian, who had a bunch of important delegate meetings across Ireland, so we tagged along until Belfast . . ."

Abby chuckled into her glass. "These are not coincidences, my bonnie lasses. These are synchronicities."

Mckenna was about to ask what that meant when Seán banged his fist on the table. "Belfast! As in Northern Ireland? You girls must have screws loose up there." He pointed at his temple. "Have you *any* idea what's going on in the North right now?"

"This is no joke, Mckenna," Andre said in his sternest voice, which never failed to frighten Mckenna as a child. "Shootings and bombings and—"

"We didn't know at the time!"

"It's true, we didn't! Not until John told us—"

"Nissa!" Mckenna pleaded, shouting *shut up* with her eyes.

"You *knew* and you went ANYWAY?" Seán bellowed. "and you, lad . . ." He shook a finger at Cillian.

"I was trying to find Mom!" Mckenna interjected before he could scold Cillian. "I found her note in your wallet, so—"

"Note?" Abby said softly, turning to Seán. "*My* note?"

"Let's, erm—maybe another time . . ." Seán mumbled. "Right now, I'd like to lock my daughter up in a bloody tower."

"We were fine, Dad. We didn't run into any of that sort of trouble at all."

"And you've no idea how lucky you were for it," he shot back.

Andre nodded, his lips pursed.

"Your dads are right," Abby said, her tender voice trimming the tension. "I *love* that you were willing to scour the world for me, swan, but you could've ended up seriously hurt."

Although she would have done it all over again, Mckenna nodded, then bit her lip to refrain from asking, *Why didn't you scour the world for me?*

"What about *you*?" Seán said a little too loudly, turning his attention to Cillian.

Cillian straightened up. "We met in Dublin, sir. See, I'm a youth delegate, and I was bound for Belfast for a conference. Given the current situation, I knew Mckenna and Nissa would not be able to get to Ballycastle on their own. I only wanted to offer a safe ride there."

"To two teenage girls." It was not a question.

Please don't tell them you knew who I was the whole time, Mckenna pleaded in her mind.

"Erm, yes, well," Cillian responded. "They're quite more, erm, mature than teenagers . . . I thought they were older, actually. And I just turned twenty-one, really—"

"And you two," Seán barked at the girls. "Another reckless act! Thought it was safe to jump in a car with a complete stranger?"

At this, Mckenna and Nissa looked down at their plates.

"In our defence," Nissa uttered feebly, "we had a code word." At the thought of their super-secret code word *nincompoop*—in the event of Cillian proving to be a serial killer or human trafficker—Mckenna had to hold her breath to keep from bursting out laughing.

As if Nissa hadn't spoken, Seán rounded on Cillian. "How do we know to trust you, lad? Why are you still here, anyway? What are you—?"

"Cillian was sent to protect me," Mckenna found herself declaring; she couldn't lie to her family any longer. Silence fell around the table, and all heads turned towards her.

"By whom?" Andre said in a tone that suggested he had no patience for any bullshit.

Cillian's face contorted with an overwhelming sense of guilt, his eyes downcast in shame. "No one did."

What? Mckenna's jaw tightened. "What do you mean? You said . . ."

"When I got wind of the High Priestess's scheme to locate you and your mum, with the aim of harnessing both your powers to fulfill the Scottish Scrolls, I knew I had to track you down."

"Why? You didn't even know me." Mckenna was hyper-aware of everyone's eyes on them.

"I knew once she succeeded, she'd essentially have no use for you. I couldn't bear that burden on my conscience, so I made it my mission to find you and . . . watch over you. As I got to know you, I found myself wanting to continue to watch over you."

Why would he lie about such a thing? Something was off. Mckenna didn't buy it. "Wait, if no one sent you, then how *did* you know the High Priestess?"

Cillian hesitated. "Remember when I told you I was a mystic practitioner? She's the one who took me under her wing. She trained me."

Her chest felt as though Irish giant Fionn MacCool had sat on it.

"Oh, lad," Abby muttered, burying her face in her hands.

Seán slammed his hand on the table. "I don't even know where to start. YOU!" he roared at Cillian. "How dare you! That woman, Maeve, is as mad as a hatter. Abby," he said gravely. "We have to stop her! After what she did to Andre and me—"

"Wait," Mckenna interjected. "What did she do?"

"We'll tell you, Mckenna," Andre said, "but I think we should hear one disturbing story at a time."

"Lass—" Cillian breathed in Mckenna's ear.

"You should leave," she snapped.

Without a word, Cillian gave a curt, awkward nod around the table, then walked briskly out the front door.

"Does the boy have a place to stay?" Abby said, her brow scrunched up in concern.

"Man," Seán corrected. "Full-blown adult."

"I don't care," Mckenna said, fuelled with anger. "I agree with Dad. Mom, I think you should start from the beginning. Tell us everything."

Abby took a long gulp of her lemon water, setting it down in front of her. She started by recounting what Esme had already told Mckenna in Ballycastle: the origins of it all, with the faeries revealing to young Abby, Esme, and Maeve that they were special children. Their purpose was to convey a message to the world regarding the existence of the fae and other beings, as well as the state of the world if humanity failed to become more conscious and caring towards their planet. They had also revealed to her that she, Abby, was an incarnated elemental—a faery.

"Maeve wished to lead her own path. She was right radical,

wanting to set fire to oil companies, cast curses on right-wing government reps . . . It was a bit *ower* much. I thought a bit of distance might be best. That's when I took a wee trip to England, and we crossed paths," she nodded at Seán. "Maeve seemed to have settled down a bit at first. We remained close friends; when Seán and I got married and moved to Ballycastle, her and Esme would visit quite frequently."

"That they did," Seán said with a tinge of annoyance.

"And we began to mend our burned bridges . . . until I got pregnant. When I found out, I told them about a visit I had from the faery queen. She said I was giving birth to the last living Wise One, and she would be very powerful. She would be the key to our cause. The bridge between all of existence."

Mckenna nodded. "That's what you told me the other night on Samhain. When I astral projected to you."

"You astral projected?" Seán said, his eyes bulging from their sockets.

"Do you know what it means?" Mckenna pressed on. "Being the bridge to all of existence?" The weight of this declaration had been haunting her.

"I have my theories," Abby said thoughtfully, "but I never got to find out. And so, Maeve became obsessed with the idea of the Wise One and the utopia the faeries spoke of. Day after day, she plunged into research and stumbled upon Elizabeth Dunlop's prophecy from the sixteenth century: *As twin flames rekindle and the last living Wise One unites with her creator, billions of souls shall expire upon this Earth. Peace shall be restored to the natural world, and all beings shall exist in perfect harmony.* Maeve put two and two together and grew relentless; she forced me into a hypnosis session to extract more past wisdom, then discovered my bairn was a reincarnation of Elizabeth Dunlop. It was at that moment she also managed to uncover the Scottish Scrolls, the roadmap to saving the natural world. Through you."

"By '*billions of souls shall expire*' . . ." Nissa started.

"Mckenna and I are living proof that reincarnation exists," Abby declared. "If Maeve succeeds, billions of souls will never have the chance to incarnate on Earth again, meaning they would never fulfill their soul's purpose."

Mckenna wasn't following. "Meaning . . . ?"

"Humanity would never evolve as it was intended to. Death is meant to be a transformation, a leap into the next phase of our experience. Billions of souls trapped in a single, unevolved form for eternity, unable to return to Earth and ensnared in our atmosphere, would be . . . catastrophic."

The wind whistled, filling the silence. Mckenna's thoughts drifted to Petronella, trapped in her spectral form, then to the universe, imagining it stuffed with resentful spirits who were powerless to move on. She conjured an image of a sea of angry floating heads, bouncing aimlessly in the darkness.

"Mom . . . Esme told me this was supposed to happen this year, on the Winter Solstice. Is that true?"

"Only according to Maeve's seer friend, whom she met shortly after Seán and I moved to Ballycastle. Maeve claims she's never been wrong."

Pravadi. Cillian had mentioned her at the Necropolis . . . Her blood boiled at the mere thought of him.

"Listen," Andre began, "we have to stop this . . . this witch, who we *barely* escaped. The good news is we have her magic stone, which means we're safe from being found for now. But it's only a matter of time before she finds another way to locate us, right?"

"You say *witch* like it's a bad thing," Mckenna said, unable to stop herself.

Her dads looked at her crossly. Seán winced.

"You're spot on, Andre," Abby affirmed. "If I ken her well, she's already on the hunt for a replacement stone. I've got this place protected, so there'll be no arguments; you're all staying put with me. As for your *friend*, Cillian, there's a guest house just down the road. I'll be setting up another layer of protection spells around this whole area pronto." Mckenna was ready to protest, but Abby silenced her with a look. "I understand he's done you wrong, but the truth is, he's in grave danger if he goes off on his own. Maeve's likely none too pleased with him, and who knows what she's got in store for him. I can sympathize with the charms of Maeve," Abby admitted, her regretful eyes revealing her own past experiences. "And let's not forget, with him wandering the streets unprotected, Maeve might just pick up his trail through astral projection if they've got a strong enough connection. That means she'd soon figure out where we are too. It's vital that we stick together, swan."

Knowing she would have no say in the matter, Mckenna nodded in agreement.

"As for our Mckenna," she carried on, her gaze sweeping the room, "she's got a lot to learn, and that means we've got some training to do. She's still to fully tap into her true power." Abby's eyes sparkled with a sense of pride. "Being the last of the Wise Ones, swan, you've got to grasp the full extent of your gifts. It's your birthright."

Mckenna's arm hairs flew on end, goosebumps cascading down to her knees. *Finally, someone who gets it.*

Seán cleared his throat. "Abby, can I speak with you in private?"

"Dad, *don't*. No more shielding me from this—from who I am. I'm ready. And I want to learn *e-ver-y-thing* there is to know," she annunciated.

A long moment passed before Seán and Andre nodded, then laced their fingers together. And Mckenna could feel how terrified her dads truly were.

VII
THE TWELVE BEINGS OF ELFAME

Following Cillian's Irish exit (literally and figuratively), Abby went after him. By her account, Cillian had been sulking in the yellow rental car, but his demeanor brightened considerably when she insisted he stay at the MacDonald Guest House, just a third of a mile down the road, under her protection enchantment.

Mckenna couldn't fathom why, but her body shivered involuntarily at the mere mention of MacDonald, her skin feeling as if it had been touched by a chilling frost.

"What's up?" Nissa asked, catching Mckenna's sudden jolt. She placed her hand on Mckenna's forearm. "Your skin is ice cold!"

"I know. I have no freakin' clue why," Mckenna said before her body temperature swiftly returned to normal. *Strange.*

Abby showed Mckenna and Nissa to their adjoining rooms ("Yay! I'll try not to barge in unannounced, Kenna") and welcomed them to borrow her clothes. While Mckenna appreciated the kind offer, she couldn't shake the feeling of being somewhat of an intruder. Her mother was still a stranger to her, and vice versa, and now she was raiding her closet?

"No need to be bashful, lasses," Abby encouraged, noting Mckenna's hesitant look. "Scotland can get awfully chilly, so feel free to help yourselves! I've got plenty of snug sweaters to spare. Half of these I haven't even worn in the six years I've been here."

Mckenna wondered, even amidst the constant need to uproot and remain hidden, if there was ever a place that truly felt like home for Abby. "Where else have you lived?"

Abby let out a breath that told Mckenna she'd been just about everywhere. "Galloway, Perthshire, Fife, Inverness-shire, the Isle of Lewis, Ullapool . . . and, oh, way up north in Orkney."

Wow. Mckenna hadn't heard of any such places. "That sounds exhausting," she blurted.

Her mother released a timid chuckle. "It was the only way to . . ." *Stay safe, duh.* Mckenna wanted to face-palm her forehead. "I might've been by myself, but I was never feeling lonesome. I had the company of the most breathtaking natural spots on this planet," Abby mused.

Mckenna's heart weighed heavily at the thought of her mother on the run for seventeen years.

"I'd take literally anywhere in Scotland over one of my foster homes." Nissa's voice echoed from behind a tower of clothes she'd piled in her arms.

Abby flashed a bright smile. "Great choices! I see you're not afraid of some colour."

It was true—each of the garments Nissa had plucked out was more vibrant than the last, while Mckenna had opted for simpler, frill-free, and darker-toned pieces. As the yin to her yang, she couldn't be more unsurprised. Smiling as only Nissa's short legs peeked out from beneath the stack of clothes, she remarked, "Nissa's not afraid of anything."

Once the girls had folded away their 'new' sweaters and bottoms ("I'll pick up some knickers and bras for you in town tomorrow"), they followed Abby downstairs, across the kitchen and living area, and through the back door.

"Shouldn't we grab our coats?" Nissa said.

"No need!" Abby sang.

Abby was right. The slap-you-in-the-face draft Mckenna expected never came. Instead, the air felt warm and carried the earthy, fresh scent of post-rainfall, giving her the toastiest of feelings. The inn was connected to a greenhouse—above them, a glass dome comprised of triangular panes fit together like an effortless jigsaw puzzle. Lit by the afternoon sun, the space, about the size of the living room, was filled with an exquisite array of the most exotic plants Mckenna had ever encountered, including in her biology textbook. Rows upon rows of potted herbs had grown lush enough to season a meal every night for an entire year.

"I *love* greenhouses," Nissa squealed, already skipping down the aisles. "I've only ever read about them, though."

As Mckenna strolled among the plants, she rubbed the various leaves, occasionally giving them a sniff. "This one smells, uh, interesting." It was a bitter, musky scent, with notes of berries and . . . marijuana?

"That there's mugwort. A bit pungent," Abby said, wiggling her nose like Samantha in *Bewitched*. "Great for divination, amongst other things."

"And this one?"

"Anise Hyssop, or *Agastache foeniculum*. A phenomenal healing herb!"

Abby proceeded to highlight the assortment of strangely named herbs, eliciting snickers from Mckenna and Nissa at names like snakeroot, lady's slipper, and devil's shoestring. Mckenna eagerly looked forward to her upcoming sessions in this space, where she could delve deep into the world of herbs and potion-making.

"This one is so pretty!" said Nissa, singling out a perky purple-petalled plant.

Abby chuckled. "Spiderwort. It opens the heart chakra,

and"—she cupped her hand over one side of her mouth—"makes for a very powerful love potion."

Nissa bounced her eyebrows up and down suggestively, then tossed a knowing glance Mckenna's way.

Hoping to hide her flushed cheeks, Mckenna crouched down to examine a plant with tiny bell-shaped flowers of striking magenta, their delicate beauty juxtaposed with glossy black berries gracefully nestled among the branches.

"Don't touch that!" Abby ordered. "That's poisonous."

"What is it?" Why would such a plant even be here, casually soaking in some sun next to a pot of rosemary, was what she wanted to say.

"It's called *atropa belladonna*, or deadly nightshade. If you ingest it, as the name implies, it's deadly. But even touching it can be harmful." She gestured towards a pair of red rubber gloves hanging on one of the thicker branches.

"Sorry."

After being introduced to a series of intricately named plants, Mckenna politely excused herself, feeling her anxiety mounting as her face, neck, and chest suddenly flushed with heat. She hurriedly crossed the empty living room, dashed to her bedroom, and collapsed face-first onto her comforter.

In addition to not truly knowing her own mother, she was also completely clueless about this magical herb stuff, and her inexperience was glaringly evident. She must already be a disappointment to Abby, whose flawless expertise was as daunting as it was admirable. Here she was, supposedly an all-powerful witch, yet she had little control over her abilities and, fair to say, *nil* understanding of magic. How could she ever gather enough knowledge to face off against the High Priestess?

Shake it off. She rolled onto her back, her eyes darting around the room for a distraction. Lo and behold, there it was—the finest distraction of all: books.

Her body practically teleported to the thin bookcase in the corner of the room, equipped with oldies but goodies, like *The Strange Case of Dr. Jekyll and Mr. Hyde*, *Jane Eyre*, the entire boxset of *The Chronicles of Narnia, The Great Gatsby, Wuthering Heights, Great Expectations, Treasure Island* . . . nothing she hadn't read before.

Yes! Her eyes landed on her all-time favourite book—a book that most people she knew absolutely despised: *The Catcher in the Rye*. Mckenna couldn't quite explain why, but somehow this messy, melancholic story provided her with comfort. Perhaps it was because of how relatable Holden Caulfield's isolation felt, or how his scattered yet honest thoughts resonated, even if his perspective was skewed. Yes, he was rough around the edges and far from eloquent, but he remained unapologetically himself, refusing to conform to the game everyone else seemed to be playing. To him, the rules of life were illogical, and Mckenna couldn't help but agree.

She cracked open the book and began to read, a smile forming at the strangeness of the opening line, which essentially shunned the reader. As she turned page after page, the familiarity of the words embraced her in the way she needed at that moment.

Finally, her eyelids succumbed to the utter exhaustion that had been steadily building for weeks.

Elizabeth Dunlop spent her days mourning the loss of her bairn, and to compound her sorrow, Bonnie-Jean and two of her sheep had also perished.

Just as Thom predicted.

One rainy afternoon, after she had shed her fair share of tears into her woolen blanket, she elected to wander outside. It was damp and chilly, hence no one would be out in this kind of weather, and she needed to breathe air that was not confined within these four walls.

She found herself at the stone castle, in front of the dyke where Thom appeared days ago, or was it weeks? The days folded into one another like bread dough. This time, she didn't need to shed tears for Thom to appear; mere seconds after she arrived at the cove, he stood before her.

"You've returned," Thom said.

"Everything you predicted has come to pass."

"And so it has. My dear Elizabeth, would you allow me to show you something?"

Had she not been numbed by the anguish of her loss, she would have declined. Alas, she was not of sound mind, and she responded with a nod.

"Do not fear what you are about to see," Thom said cryptically, leading her a pace forward. Before her, the cove unveiled twelve of the most exquisite beings she had ever laid eyes on. They stood tall, their hair cascading in shimmering waves of silver, rose-gold, and brilliant red, their angular features softened by compassionate gazes.

"Hello, Elizabeth," said the tallest, most beautiful of the lot. "Thom has told us about you."

"I-I can't imagine why. What could he have to say about *me*?"

"That you are special, Wise One," she replied. And in that moment, Bessie believed her. "We wish to extend an invitation to you, to our enchanting home."

There was a cadence in her voice that spread instant calm to Bessie's bones, that made her troubles seem trifling and the world not as bleak. Although tempted to accept, Bessie did not respond. Prompted by her better judgment, she instead asked, "Who are you?"

"Does it matter?" asked the handsomest of the men. "How do you feel in our presence?"

The truth was she felt as though she could float above a mountaintop with little effort. "I feel light and . . . at ease."

All twelve individuals smiled. Or rather, their eyes did, for their lips appeared to be at rest. "Come with us."

She wanted to. Oh, did she ever. But what if this was a trick? Could she endure any more heartache? "No, thank you," she finally stated, stepping back, and at once the twelve beings disappeared, the cove empty once more.

Bessie turned to Thom. "Who were those people?"

"Ah, people, they were not. They are the good neighbours that dwell in the Court of Elfame, and they want you to go with them."

"I see no reason to go with them."

"My dear Elizabeth," Thom said, approaching her. "They want to bestow you with the gift of Second Sight."

"I-I don't understand."

"You are a gifted soul, Elizabeth. Are you curious to unearth these gifts?"

She stared into the eyes of the man who predicted the death of her bairn, two sheep, and her beloved Bonnie-Jean. She should be angry with him—she should detest this strange, watchful man with every fibre of her being. And yet . . .

"Aye. I am," she heard herself say.

Every afternoon following this second encounter, Bessie met Thom at the cove near the castle. They would roam the grounds, and he would point out the flora and fauna, lecture her on their medicinal properties, and test her knowledge. Within days, they were making use of them, concocting herbal blends that miraculously got her sickly lamb to eat again, caused her own stomach-aches to subside, and utterly banished her husband's headaches.

Soon, word spread around town that Bessie could heal wounds and mend sicknesses. Some would come to her for good luck charms she would fashion using stones and leaves from nature; others would shamelessly beg for her aid in solving matters that, frankly, seemed unsolvable.

"I wish I could do more," she would say to Thom nearly every day as the sun set behind the bonnie braes.

"You can," Thom replied.

"How?"

"Allow the Elfame beings to bestow upon you the gift of Second Sight. Consider the number of villagers you could aid. With this ability, you would be capable of forewarning them of danger, of guiding them on the right path."

She had indeed been contemplating it. "Thom . . . there's something I don't understand. Why me?" The thought had been gnawing at her. Why was she so special? Why did she deserve such a gift?

"Lizbeth . . ." The way Thom uttered this new and endearing name for her bequeathed a sense of protectiveness not even her husband could provide. "Do you remember when you were lying in childbed, and a stout woman came to your door to ask for a drink?"

"Aye," she said, chuckling at its absurdity. "I remember that very well."

"That was the Queen of Elfame."

Bessie gasped.

"She was drawn to your spirit, good nature, and deep-seeded gifts. She paid me a visit afterwards," he revealed.

"Why?" was all Bessie could muster.

"She implored me to guide you on the path of your soul's true purpose."

Mckenna awoke gasping for air, her mother's cool, steady hand on her sweaty arm. Hopping between the present and *very* distant past was starting to take its toll.

Abby's eyebrows furrowed in concern. "You were talking in your sleep, swan." *Figures.* "Bad dream?"

"Not exactly," Mckenna admitted. "I was . . . remembering."

"Oh?"

"I've been having dreams—or memories, I guess—of Elizabeth Dunlop. And whenever I go back to sleep, it continues from where I left off. It's like I'm watching a movie, except I feel everything that she's feeling." And it was exhausting.

Abby gave Mckenna's arm an affectionate squeeze. "Well, Elizabeth is you, and you her."

"Yeah, and I know how her story ends." At the mere recollection of her birthday nightmare, in which she, as Bessie, faced the stake and flames, her skin grew warm, and her chest constricted. The shouting mob and troll-like man's mad laughter echoed in her mind.

"I'm afraid tens of thousands of innocent lives across Europe met the same grim fate," Abby said heavily. "In Scotland alone, historians reckon around three thousand executions happened, mainly women."

Mckenna's heart sank into her gut. "That's horrible." An understatement. It was unthinkable. "But why?"

"Why women, or why Scotland?"

"Both."

Abby looked thoughtful. "Well, what right did a woman have being so brilliant? So outspoken? So skilled? So talented? So beautiful? If she so much as ventured a bit beyond the societal bounds, she'd be marked as a witch."

The deep-seated hurt from living lifetime after lifetime as this very witch or alongside such women fizzled like a cauldron about to brim over. If Mckenna allowed herself to fully experience it, all the pain, the needless suffering, the death, she would shatter. And she couldn't afford that, especially not in front of her mother, who had clearly mastered the art of controlling her empathic abilities. How was she always so composed?

Before her proverbial cauldron of emotions could bubble over, she placed a lid on it, swallowing the lump in her throat. "And why Scotland?"

Abby scrutinized her, like she was piercing her armour. "There are a few reasons. First off, Scotland went through a radical Protestant Reformation, and with that came a great fear of the devil—and, aye, what is a witch if not a servant of Satan?" Her mother smirked. Mckenna rolled her eyes. "We've King James VI of Scotland to blame for it all, and a daft ship captain by the name of Donald Macdonald." Mckenna chortled at the name. "His name isn't the nutty part . . . Donald Macdonald and his crew were hired by King James to fetch his bride, Princess Anne of Denmark, but the ship took ages to return. Not wanting to get in trouble with the king, he blamed the stormy journey on witches; they'd cursed the ship, he claimed. The rumour was he'd simply gotten a wee bit greedy hunting for gold.

"This incident—a fable, really—led King James to carry out the first-ever witch trials in Scotland, turning into the biggest witch hunt in British history. They came to be called the North Berwick trials."

"Wait, that sounds familiar . . ." Mckenna searched her brain. Of course, she'd seen it flipping through Mr. Heathley's history textbook: a black and white sketch of four women begging at the foot of King James, circa 1590.

"You might've heard of the trials, they're infamous. King James got himself obsessed," Abby went on, "even putting out a book called *Daemonologie*, a grand treatise on witchcraft and the devil's craft, with many of his notions backed by verses from the Bible."

Mckenna's inner cauldron sizzled again, threatening to blow off the lid she'd snapped on. "That must've created so much fear." She hated this. No wonder the word *witch* was still associated with devil worshippers.

"The legal system didn't help." Mckenna leaned in close, equally captivated and disturbed. "Courts were ruthless when it came to those suspected of witchcraft."

"Wasn't it like that everywhere?"

"Not quite. In England, accused witches were at least given a trial—by two judges, if I mind right. They'd scrutinize the evidence, and a jury would decide the verdict. Not that it made the accusations any fairer," she added with a hint of sorrow. "But in Scotland, an alleged witch was often pressured into confessing by the local gentry or clergy . . ." *Like Petronella*, Mckenna thought, wondering whether Ireland's witch trials were tried in the same unjust manner. ". . . then that confession was sent off to the government, who'd then decide the punishment."

"Execution," Mckenna whispered.

Abby nodded.

Mckenna was suddenly reminded of the time Seán sat them down in Andre's study; he'd said Abby was a *mystic*. "Is that why you call yourself a *mystic* instead of a *witch*? And Cillian, he told me he was a mystic practitioner."

"Maeve, Esme, and I preferred *mystic*, aye. We were *feart*, I suppose, to call ourselves witches. Afraid," she clarified, seeing Mckenna's perplexed expression.

"But it's the twentieth century! You shouldn't be."

Abby's eyes twinkled. "You're absolutely right, swan."

For a moment, they sat in quietude, their concealed secrets hanging in the air.

"Mom." Once again, the word rolled easily off the tongue. "There's something about Scotland. It feels so . . ." She couldn't explain it, but there was magic *everywhere* here, and it was magnetic.

Abby's face glowed. "Scotland is," she sighed, hand on her heart, "magic. It's in the bens, in the deep, dark lochs, in the mist . . ."

"It's overwhelming," Mckenna said, and she meant it.

"Aye, it is. It's a debt we owe to our forebears: the Picts, Britons, Celts, Vikings, and Anglo-Saxons. They're the ones who wove power into the land, seeking answers beyond the veil of what we call 'reality.' The tales, the herbal craft, and the faery lore we've embraced, it's all because of their inquisitiveness— their love for the land that nourished them, welcomed them. Thankfully, they handed down their wisdom. We're at heart storytellers, are we not?"

A warmth spread across Mckenna's body. "So, everything we know about healing, divination, alchemy and herbalism . . . ?"

"All them."

Mckenna was aware that her soul was old, but she was beginning to think it was ancient. As her mother spoke, images flickered in her mind like memories—gathering plants, crafting shelter, and sharing tales. Her thoughts drifted to Newgrange and how magnificently strange it was; how its roof-box was aligned perfectly with the sunrise on the winter solstice; how that soaring sensation overcame her, as though her spirit wanted to ascend and settle amongst the stars; and how shortly after, the chamber filled with sparkling spheres of light.

"Come, I want to show you something," Abby said, squeezing both her hands and lifting her off the bed. "I've got an extra pair of wellies if you need them."

Trying not to look too perplexed as to what *wellies* were, she muttered a "No, I'm good," and slipped on a fresh pair of wool socks that were tucked in her nightstand, no doubt stealthily stocked by Abby. Ordinarily, being forced to function before dawn would annoy her to no end, but after a twelve-hour or so slumber, she was well-rested and eager to finally enjoy some one-on-one time with her mom.

C'mon, you wimp, we're alone now. Ask her.

"Uh, Mom?" she whispered, tiptoeing behind her downstairs and following her to the entrance. "I've been meaning to ask you something. And, well, I'm not sure how to . . ." She trailed off as Abby vanished into the coat closet and reappeared with a flashlight and Mckenna's new old jacket—a green coat lined with faux fur that Cillian had picked up at the thrift shop in Glasgow.

"You're wondering why, with all the magic within our reach, I couldn't find a way to keep us together."

Just as she'd felt with Esme in Ballycastle, Mckenna was beginning to wonder if her thoughts were written on her forehead. "How did you know?"

"Because I ask myself that very question every day."

There was nothing more for her mother to say. Despite Abby's poised exterior, her heart was shattered into pieces. Mckenna could sense its fragments scattered like shards from a fallen glass vase. Had Abby not departed seventeen years ago, the High Priestess would have gone to great lengths to exert complete hypnotic control over both Abby and Mckenna, using their collective magic to prevent billions of souls from reincarnating. Mckenna envisioned a childhood spent on the run, in constant fear of becoming a prisoner of her own mind. Who would she be today without the stability she had grown up with? Without her loving home? Without both her dads?

In the end, everything unfolded exactly as it was meant to. She believed that now. She was blessed with three parents, and though her previous definition of normalcy might not align with what most considered normal, this new normal felt the most . . . well, normal.

Fighting to keep the tears down, she took her mother's hand, squeezing it hard. Abby reciprocated, their non-verbal, intuitive or psychic—whatever—understanding a testament to their empathic powers. Or, simply, a testament to the inborn connection between mother and daughter.

Moments later, Abby twisted the doorknob quietly, then pulled her gently towards a dirt trail that zig-zagged into the dark woods, their only source of light the beam from Abby's flashlight.

In silence they walked, hand in hand, like two halves of a whole. Like twin flames.

As twin flames rekindle and the last living Wise One unites with her creator, billions of souls shall expire upon this Earth. Peace shall be restored to the natural world, and all beings shall exist in perfect harmony.

Twin flames rekindling. The Wise One uniting with her creator. Was she fulfilling the prophecy without knowing it?

"We're here," Abby said, pulling Mckenna out of her swirling thoughts.

They stopped some feet away from a tree, modest in size but brilliant in just about every other way. Its delicate autumn foliage hung on for dear life, and its branches bore clusters of bright red berries that looked about ready to be stuffed into a pie crust. That wasn't the most captivating feature, though; for one, the trunk was encircled by dozens of miniature stones, and for another, every single branch was adorned in ribbons and strings of all colours, lengths, and textures. It was a mess—and a beautiful one.

Her mother offered up the explanation before she could ask. "This is a rowan tree. The ancient Celts have been planting them for eons. A rowan is thought to be the Tree of Life."

"The one in Norse mythology?" Mckenna asked, remembering the book Andre had gifted her for her twelfth birthday, full of gorgeous illustrations of Norse tales and ancient runes.

"Aye. The legend goes that Thor, the God of Thunder, was once saved by a rowan tree. He near got swept all the way to the Underworld by a river's wild current, but a rowan tree bent down just enough for him to clutch onto."

"Those are some strong branches."

"And it had loads of uses! It's said their wood was used to craft boats, walking sticks, and even amulets for protection."

"And the ribbons . . . ?"

"Each ribbon represents a wish from a visitor," she said, stepping around the tree and brushing her slender fingers over some dangling ribbons.

"A wish to who?" Mckenna asked, but answered her own question when the tree suddenly flooded with specks of light—blue, yellow, green and white—darting between each leaf, branch, and berry. *The fae.* "These ribbons are for the faeries, aren't they?" Mckenna said breathlessly. Their glow-in-the-dark dance was as mesmerizing as it was at the faery bridge on the Isle of Man.

Abby nodded. "And they don't appear for just anyone, swan" Abby said brightly, extending her arms towards the sky and tilting her head back, as if to welcome them.

"You see them too?" *Stupid question. She's an incarnated faery, duh.*

"The fae and I have been well-acquainted since I was a young lass, but even so, the odds are, if you come across a rowan tree, they're around—whether you can see them or not! See, rowan trees are sacred in Scotland. You'd never want to chop one down."

Mckenna stared in awe at the tiny creatures, silently thanking them for revealing themselves to her.

A chirpy voice responded in her mind. *Happy to! We need you, Wise One.*

Mckenna's body jolted in surprise. Right, they were telepathic; she seized the opportunity to respond. *Why? And can you please tell me what it means to be the bridge?* she thought just as the specks gradually faded into the first of the morning's rays. Mckenna was reminded of the famous Beatles' song *Lucy in the Sky with Diamonds* as the gradient grey sky lightened with streaks of marmalade. "Where did they go?"

"Through the tree and back to their realm."

"Is the tree a kind of . . . portal?"

"Doorway, more like. Rowan trees, mounds, faery pools, and mushroom rings can all serve as doorways."

She remembered Esme mentioning other-realm doorways. "Can humans go through it?"

Abby hesitated. "By invite only."

"A faery lured me into a bush once, in the Inagh Valley, and I ended up in her realm." Mckenna sniggered, aware of how outrageous she sounded.

Abby gasped. "What an honour! She must have had a very important message for you."

She did. The faery, Niamh, had nudged Mckenna towards Griffin's Bar, where, thanks to a lovely—and chatty—waitress, they discovered the Isle of Man emblem and the Latin motto etched on Nissa's bracelet.

"Is there a way to access the faery realm at any time?" Mckenna wondered.

"Wouldn't that be nice?" Abby said dreamily. "To wander freely in and out of other realms . . . If there is a way, I've yet to uncover it. But who's to say we cannot? Limitations are not but a construct to make us forget our true potential."

A pretty big, bold statement to muse on before a cup of coffee, Mckenna thought. She mulled over her words until Abby clapped her hands together, startling two tiny birds perched on the rowan's lowest-hanging branch. "Fancy a bit of breakfast?"

VIII

RISE ABOVE, RAIN BELOW

Mckenna couldn't wait to show Nissa the faery tree. She would likely set up camp beneath it, given the chance.

A maelstrom of Mckenna's favourite morning aromas met her and Abby's senses the moment they crossed the threshold. Seán was zooming around the kitchen, whipping up a full breakfast spread, while Andre set the round table for five. The thought of Cillian totally alone, upset about his brother and shunned by the person he'd come all this way for, formed knots in her stomach. The complex nautical kind.

"Good morning," said Andre and Seán together, looking chirpy and less sombre than the day prior. The latter came around the table balancing a tray of poached eggs, stir-fried mushrooms, and sausage—or *bangers*—on one hand and a bowl of oatmeal and blueberries on the other.

"Mmm, smells amazing," Mckenna moaned, pouring herself a tall black coffee. "Mom, would you like some, or are you a tea person like Esme?"

"Goddess, no . . . not in the morning. Coffee for me, and loads of milk, please! Thank you, swan," she said, taking a seat.

Mckenna filled her cup with three-quarters coffee and one-quarter milk, then joined her at the table. "What's with the mushrooms, Dad? Seems a little intrusive at 8:00 a.m."

Abby chuckled. "It's pretty standard for a Scottish breakfast. You remembered." She gazed across the kitchen at Seán, her bright eyes filled with fond memories.

Mckenna stared from Seán to Abby to Andre, who spilled coffee all over the countertop while pouring his cup. She instantly regretted her choice of the word *intrusive*.

Seán handed him a dish towel and cleared his throat. "Not to worry, the American stuff is coming." The sizzling sound of freshly poured batter positively screamed pancakes. "Where were you two off to this morning, anyway?" he added not so coolly, ogling Abby like she'd just conjured an invisible goblin.

"Throwing fireballs, of course," Mckenna said before she could stop herself.

Abby let out a hearty laugh as she served Mckenna a spoonful of mushrooms before Mckenna could refuse them. "We had a bonnie walk up to the faery tree."

A noise escaped Seán that sounded like a cross between a grunt and a snort. "Fancied some alone time?"

"Naturally," Andre said quickly, throwing Mckenna a subtle, reassuring smile by the kitchen sink. "I'm making more coffee, who's having a second cup?"

Mckenna and Abby raised their arms, then exchanged amused looks.

"I've been thinking, lads," Abby said, "Mckenna's got loads to catch up on. I was hoping to nab her for the day."

"For what?" Seán said, stopping mid pancake flip. Andre caught it before it hit the countertop. "Very James Bond . . ."

"It's high time Mckenna gets a proper training, or she'll never get a grip on her abilities."

Seán dropped the spatula into the pan with a clatter. "Abby—"

"*Seán.* If we're to stop Maeve, we need to work together. She *will* come for us, and Mckenna needs to be ready."

Mckenna gulped.

"Once Maeve gets a hold of her stone again . . ."

Andre held his hands up. "Hang on, hang on. *We* have the stone."

"Mom mentioned a replacement stone, though, yesterday—right?"

"Aye," Abby said. "The stone's cut from a rock in County Sligo, in the northwest of Ireland. They call it Misgaun Medb, and it holds ancient mystical powers. It can attune its magnetic field to whatever the holder seeks. I ken how Maeve's mind works—she's likely journeying there to chip off another piece. And once she's got it, she'll have no trouble finding us."

"What about astral projection? Sorry, I was eavesdropping," Nissa said from the doorway. Mckenna smiled, glad she was up to speed. "Can she find us that way?"

"Mom said she has our area protected. Right?" Mckenna asked, trying not to wince at the taste of mushroom and coffee in her mouth.

"You're a canny one, Nissa, that's some fine magical thinking! But don't you worry, we're under a powerful protection enchantment—thanks to Esme," Abby added, tapping Mckenna's arm. "She was always a master of shield spells; I learned from the best." Mckenna's heart swelled with gratitude for Esme. "We're safe for the time being."

"How long do you think we have?" Seán asked.

"Finding the stone is not an easy task. It's up at the top of Knocknarea Mountain, at least a thousand feet high. It could take months . . . but with her determination, it could be weeks."

"Which is why I need to be trained now, Dads. Please," Mckenna pleaded, and their collective sigh told her they'd finally given in.

Cillian's absence that morning caused Mckenna's stomach to churn like butter, except the mass sitting heavy in her stomach was that of unequivocal guilt—even though there was *zero* reason whatsoever she should feel guilty. Ever since he'd revealed the High Priestess had been his mentor, her trust for him had vaporized into a puff of smoke, like from one of his vile cigarettes. If he was lying about that, what else was he lying about?

"You look distracted," Abby remarked as they strolled through the dramatic landscape known as the Quiraing. With mist looming overhead, they trekked from the car park down a boggy path amidst a rugged, hilly terrain, boasting Scotland's signature green; it was not a rich emerald like Ireland's, but a complex blend of mosses, with golden hues that shimmered through the blades of grass as though brush-stroked by Monet.

They walked and walked, the ground's moisture seeping through to her socks. Mckenna instantly regretted not asking Abby for a pair of rain boots.

"Next time you'll be glad to have my pair of wellies," Abby said, shaking her head at Mckenna's muddy Converse sneakers, then lowering her hands in a *ta-da* motion to her perfectly impermeable plum-coloured rain boots.

"Oh, that's what wellies are!"

Minutes passed, and though her legs grew weary, she still managed to appreciate the jutting cliffs, bumpy hills, and glittering pools. Engrossed in her surroundings, she wondered whether anyone lucky enough to have been in this enchanting place dared refute that magic existed.

After an hour's hike, they reached a viewpoint overlooking the dark, swaying sea, and a floating isle far off in the distance told her this wasn't the westernmost edge of Scotland at all. She wished she could explore every inch of this country, soaking in the sunsets over the myriad lochs, climbing each ben, and hopping to every island, devil-may-care. Her heart lifted at the thought of being a nomad, of relishing all that nature had to offer.

She closed her eyes, listening for whispers from the landscape. In response, the whistling wind dwindled, making way for a distant burbling of water. Pulled out of her meditation, she peered around the cliffside in search of the source; farther to her left, a waterfall cascaded confidently down into the depths. Her lips parted in awe at its perfection, at how easily it flowed from one element to the next. *This is it*, she thought. *This is the most beautiful place on Earth. Is there anything more magical?*

Her gaze wandered along the cliffside, stopping at an odd-looking formation. "That looks just like a kilt!"

There was no mistaking it—the cliffside, which looked like it was made of the same basalt columns as the Giant's Causeway, except reddish in colour, fanned out like the flair of a Scottish kilt right into the sandstone base, the most striking feature being its contrasting tartan-like pattern.

Abby laughed. "You're right. We call this wonder Kilt Rock."

"Is there some kind of cool Scottish legend behind it?" Perhaps there was a giant walking around Skye who'd lost his kilt, she wondered, grinning at her musings.

"Hmm . . ." Abby lifted her dainty fingers to the air and moved them like she was playing invisible piano keys. Mckenna noticed she did this when she was pondering her words. "I don't think so. Although, some have claimed that when the winds really whip through, there's an eerie sound that comes from it. A bit like a bagpiper."

Chuckling, they carried on with their hike. Before she could ask where they were going next and when the magic training was going to begin, Abby pointed up at two massive jagged stones, their ruggedness etched by time and the elements; Mckenna's first impression was that they didn't at all fit the landscape— rather, they appeared as if they had been placed there like statues. Oddly, the taller one resembled the weathered visage of an old man, while the stout one looked like its companion.

"This is your first lesson. You'll blend your energy with these rocks and listen closely for their message."

This sounded totally ridiculous to her. "Um, yeah, I don't think I can do that."

Abby tilted her head in the way Andre did whenever Mckenna was being snarky or self-deprecating. "You're an empath, swan. That doesn't just mean being able to sense when someone's feeling sad, happy, or angry. It means you've got the power to temporarily sync your vibration with what's around you."

Mckenna recalled Esme's explanation about how all beings vibrated at different frequencies. That was why Petronella had been able to touch her; the sadness, hurt, and anger she had been clinging to had caused her frequency to drop to that of a human, allowing her to manifest on the physical plane.

"I'll give it a try," Mckenna said, knowing Esme would have called her out then and there for not sounding more confident. *You'll try or you will?* she'd have said.

Wishing she'd made more of an effort in her P.E. class, she climbed up the hill and, panting, finally reached the base of the lower rock formation. With one more step to go, she stretched her arms out to make contact with it.

It was as though she'd hit an invisible wall; what felt like a literal wave of sadness crashed into her. She fell to the ground and lay there, unmoving, on the bumpy surface.

"Are you alright, swan?"

"I'm okay!"

Why did she feel so heavy . . . so melancholic? She stared up at the two stones, standing side by side. *Why are you so sad?*

She squeezed her eyes shut in pursuit of the answer, and imagined peering through her third eye. Almost instantly, a spark of indigo materialized in the darkness; it began to swirl and grow, typhoon-like, until it flashed into a fleeting mental image of a thickset, hairy creature, with bulging eyes and a full head of brown coiled hair. He was both ugly and adorable, kind of like those neon-haired troll dolls she collected as a child.

The creature beamed, and her heart nearly burst. A flood of imagery rushed within her psyche . . . of an old man who saved him from drowning . . . of them fishing together and hiking through the woods . . . of that same old man losing his wife to illness, and dying of a broken heart as a result . . . and finally, of the creature chiselling two rocks in their memory.

Mckenna's eyelids fluttered, adjusting to the sunlight, which was now so strong she found herself missing the cloudy grey sky. Abby was standing beside her, her hand outstretched. Mckenna grasped it and recounted what she'd seen.

"The wee beastie's a brownie, a bit like a household fae keen on staying busy with chores. He was sending you his memories."

"How? Is he . . . here?"

"A part of him is, no doubt. His soul's tied to this very place, and he must've felt you were worthy of hearing his tale."

"How do I know if what I saw was true?"

"Well, you seem to think it's more conceivable that your mind cooked up such a heart-wrenching tale . . . Perhaps your talent lies in writing stories!" She gave a slight smile, then whispered, "And, just so you ken, this rock is known as the Old Man of Storr."

Mckenna couldn't have known that, and Abby was right— she certainly hadn't made it up.

After a promenade through the Quiraing loop, now Mckenna's favourite place in Scotland, Abby steered Mckenna back towards the car. The cold November winds were kicking in, but the sun was strong as ever. She unfurled the scarf Abby had wrapped around her as they headed out, and let it hang loosely over her coat.

"The weather's temperamental here, isn't it?" Abby said.

"Very," Mckenna huffed, unsure if she was hot or cold.

"You can get four seasons in a day here, I swear it. Though, November rarely feels this warm!"

In response, Mckenna shielded her eyes from the sun. Abby stopped in her tracks, and turned to her.

"What is it?"

"What's your favourite weather, swan?"

Mckenna laughed, wondering why this question couldn't wait until afternoon tea. "I like when it's mostly cloudy, like after a rainfall, but not too grey either. And there'll be the slightest hint that the sun is about to peep out."

Abby smiled. "Me too." Looking around, she sat cross-legged on the spot, then tapped the ground in front of her.

Mckenna followed suit. "What are we doing?"

"We're going to summon some rain."

Mckenna's heartbeat quickened. *Yes! Finally, some real magic.* "What do I do?"

Abby laid her hands flat on the ground, and Mckenna did the same. "Do you feel that?"

Mckenna felt the cold earth beneath her palms pulsating, like a small beating heart. Her fingertips began to vibrate. "I do."

Abby let in a long breath, then closed her eyes. "First, let us centre and ground."

Thanks to Esme's teachings, she'd nailed this by now. Picturing her quintessential goblet of murky liquid—a symbol for her burdens—she tipped it over in her mind's eye. The familiar warmth in her sacral chakra told her she was centred now.

And now, ground.

She imagined roots sprouting from her feet and piercing the earth; they spread and coiled and twisted into one another, as though she'd been planted here for centuries.

"Wonderful, Esme taught you well. Just a few more moments," Abby said serenely, her eyes remaining closed.

A flash of light as bright as high beams made Mckenna start. Her eyes flew open, and she saw a cluster of floating light forms, similar to the orbs she'd seen at Newgrange . . . but not quite. She distinctly remembered how feather-like those made her feel, like she could soar past the tomb's domed ceiling; how their sparkling particles were bright and uplifting all the way through. Though these looked similar, perhaps more greenish, they made her skin crawl. On the outside, their luminescence was vying desperately for attention, but at their core, they felt denser.

What are you? she thought.

WHOOSH. Almost instantly, they merged into one large form, taking on a human-like shape. Something told her to retreat, to scream and warn her mother there was an unidentified ethereal humanoid gawking at her. Instead, she sat there like a victim of sleep paralysis, unsure whether she was physically incapable of moving or utterly frozen from fear.

Please go away, she pleaded.

The humanoid-shaped cluster suddenly dropped, hovering inches from her nose.

No. Stop!

In one swift motion, the thing hit her square in the chest.

Fighting for breath, she thought the worst had happened: Had she been possessed? Would she be eaten from the inside out by whatever had nested in her? She thought of the film *Alien* and wanted to vomit.

"Are you alright?" Abby said, her eyes open now. "Your eyes were fluttering heavily a moment ago. I thought you were having a vision, which can happen during meditation. Did you glimpse something?"

Had she seen none of this? How could she not have sensed the entity?

"The weirdest thing just . . ."

Mckenna's breath caught in her throat as a deep, gruff voice commanded in her mind, *Say nothing.*

The voice appeared to tap into her deepest fears, whispering dreadful possibilities. Images flashed before her eyes, depicting her loved ones shrouded in black smoke, their eyes devoid of any emotion. They resembled empty vessels, like robotic servants. Was this the fate they threatened if she dared to speak up?

Gulping audibly, Mckenna said, "No visions, I think I-I fell asleep and . . . started dreaming. That's never happened before while meditating." *You are the worst actress.*

"Dreaming of what?"

"I, um, don't remember."

Abby was suddenly full of concern. "We could end our lesson here if you've had enough for the day, swan. I'm sensing a touch of unease."

Empath, right. "I'm totally fine, I promise. I *really* want to keep learning." It was true. And perhaps what had occurred *was* merely a dream—or waking nightmare.

Abby gave her a once-over. "Alright, then." Mckenna let out a short sigh of relief. "Now, think of your intent: rain."

Relaxing her gaze, Mckenna did just that, until a rustling sound snapped her back into focus. Abby held a stick of incense in one hand and a match in the other.

Mckenna eyed her mother's shoulder bag curiously. "Do you always carry around incense?"

"Shouldn't every witch?"

Mckenna smiled at the word *witch*, a term that now made her feel entirely at home.

Abby lit the incense stick. "Next, picture the smoke as vapour rising. Soon, you'll begin to see it transform."

"I just see smoke . . . and smell sandalwood."

"Patience. Keep your eyes on the smoke, and repeat after me: *èirich thar, uisge gu h-ìosal.*"

"What does that mean?"

"It's Scots Gaelic for 'rise above, rain below.'"

Mckenna did her best not to butcher the words.

"Good. Again . . . *èirich thar, uisge gu h-ìosal.*"

"*Èirich thar, uisge gu h-ìosal,*" she chanted, and as she repeated the mantra, her nose caught whiffs of steam, like she'd stepped out of a long, hot shower. And then the smoke turned to vapour. *It's working.*

As they chanted, Mckenna thought of only one thing: rain. The vapour continued to rise, but the clouds hanging above their heads seldom moved or changed. She waited for the power to surge through her like it did at the campfire, but no such sensation came. Growing impatient, she thought of the salamanders, how easy it was to communicate with them, to get them to do what she wanted.

Cillian's words rang in her ears. *Get mad.*

That she could do. It was easy to become *infuriated* at the thought of Cillian lying all this time about his connection to the High Priestess. It was easy to feel *pissed off* at how he'd so effortlessly pretended not to know exactly who Mckenna was, even though he claims his intentions were altruistic. It was easy to be *enraged* at the way he'd stuck by her and gotten her and Nissa here safely, and how much worse his deceit felt because of it.

Her heart pounding and her jaw clenched, she closed her eyes, imagining the sylphs—the air elementals—hopping from cloud to cloud.

Sylphs, I invoke thee, she thought firmly.

A laughter so faint it was nearly inaudible reached her ears, and there was an immediate downpour.

She looked up in disbelief. "We did it! I can't believe it." Lifting her arms into the air, her anger washed away with the rain. *This* was power. *This* was magic.

And it was exhilarating.

Her mother, on the other hand, appeared far from exhilarated. In fact, she looked to be the exact opposite. "What did you do, Mckenna?"

Mckenna licked the rainwater off her lips. "I—what do you mean?" She hadn't known Abby long, but the look of severity on her face and the shock in her voice told her she was not pleased.

Without a word, Abby abruptly rose from the ground and stalked away.

"Where are you going?" Mckenna yelled after her, her words muffled by the heavy rain.

"We're leaving."

Mckenna didn't dare argue. Back in the car, Abby turned the ignition on, paused, then turned it off again. "Have you the faintest idea what you've done?" she snapped, turning to face her.

"I summoned the rain, like we wanted."

"You took a shortcut. You invoked a nature spirit you haven't formed a bond with yet."

"I mean, I felt their energy around me. Does that count?"

"Building a bond with an elemental takes time, it does. You cannot just demand a favour. And even once you've formed that bond, you don't snap your fingers and—"

"Okay, fine. I won't do it again. What's the big deal?"

"Swan," Abby said slowly. "Did you agree to give them anything in return?"

She shook her head. "I didn't agree to anything."

"I'm afraid you did. You signed a blank cheque, so to speak."

"Are you saying I owe the sylphs? I thought elementals were there to help." She should've known calling the elementals was too easy, too good to be true.

"Elementals have a duty, you ken? They nurture our environment, keeping the ecosystem in balance. And while on occasion, elementals lend humans a hand in times of trouble, like how the fae on the Isle of Man let you tap into their magic to find me, their purpose is not to be at our beck and call. Altering the weather on a whim, whether it's a bit of rain or sun, it's our own will, not theirs."

So, that was how she'd been able to astral travel to her mom back on the Isle of Man. Cillian had begged her to return to Ballycastle, convinced that astral travelling directly to Abby would only work if she attempted it in a place sacred to her. But something had told Mckenna that the faery bridge was all the magic she needed, and she'd been right.

"What's the difference if we do it your way, with the incense spell, or if we ask?"

"Every time we seek their help, we're diverting them from far more important tasks. My method, as you say, might take longer, but it carries the fewest consequences and is also much more short-lived." She motioned towards the window—the rain had given way to thunder, showing no sign of letting up anytime soon. "I also believe, with practice, your magic will manifest quicker than mine, perhaps even quicker than invoking an elemental."

"What kind of consequences?"

Abby hesitated. "They vary," she said cryptically.

How could Mckenna be so thoughtless, so stupidly naïve? Was she truly that self-centered and hungry for power, to the extent that she had already forgotten Esme's first lesson at the Giant's Causeway? Esme had taught her about cause and effect, the intricate cycle of nature, and the interconnectedness of all things. She explained that when people cut down trees, the creatures relying on them would die, and in turn, humans would suffer from oxygen depletion. Nature would respond to human actions. The vital lesson Mckenna had absorbed—apparently not fully—was to honour and respect nature, recognizing its potential to retaliate. She also learned the importance of maintaining balance and carefully considering her actions.

Mckenna's face flushed. "I get it now, and I should've known. I'm sorry."

Abby's eyes narrowed, then fixed on her like she had Superman's laser vision. "I'm sorry, too. I should've spoken about this sooner, but I had no idea you'd be so advanced."

A fusion of guilt and pride simmered in Mckenna's stomach. "What do I do now?

"We wait out the storm."

"And what about the sylphs? How will I know when they need me?"

"You just will," was all she said.

On the silent ride home, all Mckenna could think of was how little she understood magic. What was the best way to forge a connection with the elementals? When did the rules apply, and as a Wise One, was she an exception to them? Considering the fate of the natural world relied on her, it was not totally unreasonable to think so.

She yearned to tell Cillian about this afternoon. He'd been all for her summoning the salamanders. Amazed, actually. Would he feel the same way after learning of the consequences?

"Kenna!" Nissa's squeal greeted Mckenna and Abby as they entered, looking like they'd climbed out of Loch Ness. The scent of freshly baked bread wafted to her nose, and her stomach groaned. "Crazy storm, huh?" Nissa said while playfully shaping a ball of dough, flour clinging to her nose.

Mckenna cleared her throat. "Yeah, nuts. Mmm, you guys making soda bread?"

Seán popped up from behind the counter. "'Course! She's a natural baker, this one."

Nissa was all teeth.

"Back so soon?" Andre said from the armchair, his nose buried in a book with a pen tucked behind his ear. Mckenna started, still adjusting to the open floor plan. "How was your training?"

Mckenna looked round at Abby, who smiled reassuringly. "We have a natural here, as well." Abby winked.

Mckenna sighed in relief, and joined her dad on the armchair. "Always working, huh, even when you're not working," Mckenna teased, giving him a kiss on the cheek.

"Well, I'm technically on sabbatical, so I'm taking advantage of the extra time I have to finally finish my research paper."

"The one on negligence in the youth justice system you started, like, three years ago?"

"Four, actually."

"That's embarrassing, luv," Seán called from the kitchen. He poked his head inside the oven. "Needs to be more golden, I think, Nissa."

"Yeah, totally. Almost done the pie crust here!"

"You're a dream. Swan, why don't you ever bake with me?"

"Did you want to swap me for her, Dad?"

"Maybe for a month or so," he said, nudging Nissa on the elbow. She threw her head back and burst out laughing.

"Mckenna," said Andre in her ear, cupping her elbow. "Cillian's here to see you."

Her heartbeat quickened. She should refuse to see him. She should leave him there waiting, restless and alone. She should tell Andre to tell him to leave and never come back. He deserved nothing more.

Instead, she nodded and said, "Where is he?"

He bookmarked his page and closed the book gently, like it was made of glass. "The greenhouse. Really into gardening, that fellow."

Seán could see why his daughter connected so effortlessly with Nissa. The girl was an absolute delight. After their second loaf was placed in the oven, she offered to clear up their mess, literally shooing Seán, Andre, and Abby away. It was "her pleasure," she'd said. And she'd meant it—unlike most people who tossed it around, like something they ought to say, right up there with "Things are great" and "It's good to see you!"

What he couldn't understand, however, was Mckenna's infatuation with that Cillian fellow. He seemed downright dodgy to him. A youth delegate who appeared out of nowhere, ensnared the affections of a teenage girl (whether Mckenna acknowledged it or not), only to later confess he'd known her enemy all along and had prior knowledge of Elizabeth Dunlop's prophecy, which was his motive for seeking her out.

No. Just no. He knew Abby had her whys and wherefores to keep him close, but there was no good reason to allow him near his daughter.

"Abby, a word?" he said, stopping her in the hallway upstairs. She'd emerged from the bathroom, wrapped up in a plush lilac robe, her wet locks somehow as vivacious as the day they'd met.

She nodded, slipping her hands into her robe pockets.

"This Cillian—I don't trust him. I wish you'd discussed it with me first, having him stay a stone's throw away."

"I don't trust him either, Seán, which is why I wanted him where I could see him," she said coolly. "But if it's any consolation, I can feel how deeply he cares for Mckenna."

Her calm demeanor had always been equally frustrating and admirable. "You can, can you?"

"I'm an empath, remember?"

Here we go. "Well, I'm a father, and I don't like him."

Her smile told him she understood. "There's no telling what the lad would do if he wanders off. I ken it's a lot to ask, but I need you to trust me."

He was about to protest when a glint of violet she'd been

fiddling with in her pocket caught his eye. "Is that what I think it is?"

She looked down at her right hand and retrieved the hackmanite stone he'd gifted her when he'd found out she was pregnant. There it sat in her palm, an exquisite pale violet, with pink undertones befitting a unicorn's tail. He'd found its colour composition extraordinary, for it glowed in the darkness but dulled in the sunlight.

"*Hackmanite is rare,*" she'd said in disbelief. "*Wherever did you find this?*"

"*I picked it up in a funny-looking shop in Finland during my summer abroad. The shopkeeper told me it was imported from Greenland, and it was the last one in stock. Thought I'd lost it until recently, but turns out all this time it was still in my old suitcase, stuffed inside a filthy pair of socks. Anyway, when I first laid eyes on it, I remember thinking, 'This is the weirdest, most beautiful thing I've ever seen—it has to be magic.' So, when it resurfaced, I knew without question it was meant for you.*"

Abby's voice, though scarcely above a whisper, transported him back to the present. "I never go anywhere without it."

He thought of her heartbreaking goodbye letter, how it had been folded up in his wallet since he'd read its mortifying, heartbreaking words all those years ago. He'd told Andre he'd forgotten about it, and perhaps he'd convinced himself he had, but the truth of it was that the letter was, and would forever be, etched in his memory.

"Abby," he breathed, his hands closing around hers. "I've missed you."

He knew he'd said something wrong the moment the words escaped him. When she didn't respond and instead stared past him, he whipped around, and the stone dropped between them with a blunt *thump*.

Andre was standing at the end of the hallway, his expression crestfallen. "Oven rang," he uttered before pacing back to the main stairwell, and up to the third floor.

Mckenna spotted Cillian bent over a lifeless plant, sporting purple polka-dot gardening gloves as he turned the earth. She patted her hair down in an effort to reduce the frizz. "I think the cold got to that one already."

He stopped mid-potting but didn't look up. "He might be okay. Can't say the same for them," he said, nodding to five dead (by Mckenna's standards) plants lined up by his feet. "I found them outside, fighting for life."

"You think you can save them?"

He shrugged. "Got to try."

"And what are these?"

"Marjoram, fennel, chives, rosemary, thyme . . ." He placed the near-lifeless thyme plant carefully in a box filled with earth, nestling it inside.

"Cillian. Why aren't you looking at me?"

A long sigh escaped him. "I'm ashamed."

Good. "Well, you should be. You lied. Twice now."

He closed his eyes, his head hanging over his knees. "I know." Silence.

"Well, why are you here—to tend to chives? Are you even sorry?" she prodded. *He* was the one who came to see *her*.

"What does it matter? You won't ever trust me again. And you shouldn't."

"Well, gee, thanks for deciding that for me. Good talk." She spun around and reached for the doorknob, until the touch of his hand over hers rooted her to the spot. A rush of emotions, his emotions, of fear, of guilt, of passion, of affection, washed over her.

"Of course I'm sorry," he whispered, his breath in her ear. Shivers surged through her arms and neck, sending a tingling sensation rippling through her entire body.

She turned to face him, their noses inches apart, and strained with all her might to expel his emotions, which only left her feeling queasy. "Then why didn't you tell me from the start who you were? That you trained with the High Priestess? That you had heard of Dunlop's prophecy? That you set out to find me on your own?"

Do not throw up. Do not throw up. Do not throw up.

He took a step back and threw up his arms. "Right, how did you think that was going to go? 'Hello there, you don't know me, but there's this mad priestess who's looking for you and your mum so she can fulfill a prophecy involving stopping the reincarnation of billions of souls on the planet. Oh, and I'm Cillian, by the way.'"

Mckenna rolled her eyes. "Cry me a freakin' river, Cillian, you had *tons* of opportunities to come clean." The queasiness subsided, quickly replaced by anger.

"I would've lost you!" he shouted, his voice cracking. "Want to hear the truth? For real?" He took a step towards her; he was so close she could see his irises fade from grey to green. "I don't care that I lied. Because I'm here. With you. So, what does that make me?"

Back to queasy. "That's really messed up, Cillian," she whispered. He meant it—he'd have lied all over again if it meant . . .

Before she could attempt to rationalize his actions, she found herself pressing her lips to his.

IX

THE MIDNIGHT RITUAL

It took every ounce of self-control Andre had to remain in his room for the rest of the afternoon, resisting the tempting allure of Seán and Nissa's Guinness stew. *Damn him.*

No, Andre would not surrender . . . because he had a point to make: He was pissed off.

Was he aware his anger might be misplaced? Entirely. His frustration wasn't directed at anyone in particular, but rather at the situation itself. For all he knew, he might have misinterpreted what he'd seen. Seán and Abby, they were innocent in all of this . . . Abby had made the painful sacrifice of distancing herself from her daughter and husband to ensure their safety, and as for Seán, he had simply moved on, found love again, and raised Mckenna the best way he knew how.

Seán and Abby had unresolved matters between them—that was abundantly clear. They hadn't had the chance to mend old wounds, find peace in their shared past. They were torn apart by a deranged individual, only to be thrust back together almost two decades later.

Andre contemplated joining them downstairs for dinner, but what would he say? *Seán, you need to figure out how you feel about Abby before we go back to being . . . us?*

That was exactly what he said when Seán entered their room that evening.

"I know," Seán replied, sitting at the foot of the bed, staring up at the popcorn ceiling.

Andre, who was curled up with his back to the door, swung his legs off the bed, and sat for several minutes gazing at the branches swaying outside the window before making his way to one of the spare bedrooms.

Seán couldn't continue pretending that sleep was an option any longer. He'd tried every conceivable position, shifting his body in a complete circle at least four times since getting into bed.

When he'd told Mckenna that reuniting with Abby again felt like seeing an old friend, he'd meant it. He attributed his momentary lapse to that stone; it had unearthed long-buried, beautiful memories.

Perhaps that was all this was.

Whatever his feelings for her may be, Andre was right—Seán needed to find out once and for all what he and Abby were to one another. He owed Andre that. He owed himself that.

Tea. Some fresh chamomile from the greenhouse. That'd knock him right out.

The stairs creaked beneath his feet on his way downstairs, where an earthy, lemony scent hit his nose. Was Nissa down here whipping up a snack?

Seán jumped at the sight of a shadow in the entryway. Instinctively, he snatched up a wooden vase on the end table near the banister, stepping lightly.

"Don't move!" he hissed as he charged at the figure and pinned it against the front door, hanging the vase threateningly in the air.

"Seán! It's me," Abby hissed back, placing a firm hand on his chest and giving him a nudge. He flipped the switch behind her and there she was, wearing an uncharacteristic scowl and, oddly, about six scarlet sachets, each hanging from a string around her décolleté.

"Abby, what the hell are you doing? It's midnight, for Christ's sake."

"I could say the same for you."

"Fancied some chamomile."

"Tossing and turning?"

He nodded, unsurprised she remembered it was his go-to sleeping draught, then flicked one of the sachets. "What are those for?"

She grasped it protectively. "I'm placing these at every door and window. They're a rosemary, dill, and basil blend."

"So that the house permanently smells like salmon seasoning?"

She smirked, then said playfully, "Don't be a *gype*, Seán." He grimaced, remembering the Scots word for *idiot* well. "I'm placing the sachets by the doors and windows. I want to be absolutely certain she cannot astral project in this house, even when she can find us with the stone."

"Ah, this is the added layer of protection you were referring to. Do basic ingredients like these actually work?"

"Aye, the simplest things found in nature can often be the most effective."

Such an Abby thing to say. "Alright, she might not be able to spy through astral projection, or whatever you call it, but once she's got the stone, won't she just pop in here *for real*?"

"We can surely expect a visit shortly after." Seán heaved a heavy sigh, and she added reassuringly, "But we ken her next move—that's a good thing. We'll plan for her arrival. I just need to think of the perfect trap she won't see coming."

"She's got a seer friend, hasn't she?" Seán said, skeptical.

"She does, but even seers are limited in what their third eye can access. We need to be subtle and keep our plan between us."

Seán admired her optimism and tactical mind—he always

had—but his patience was wearing thin. "We can't just kill her then? She nearly killed me and Andre."

"We're not killers," she said firmly. "How is Andre doing with . . . all of this?"

"He's coping. Erm, Abby. We need to talk."

"I agree," she said softly, brushing past him and placing a sachet on the hanging plant above the arched entrance window.

Come out and say it, he urged himself, following her to the bay window in the living room, by Andre's desk. "I realized the other night how—how much I've missed you."

She paused, fiddling with the sachet in her hands, then placed it on the windowsill. "I've missed you, too."

"Can you look at me?"

When she finally did, he was not prepared to face her tearful eyes.

"Come here," he said quietly, and when she did, he took her in his arms. Her scent was the same it had always been—a fusion of honey and wildflowers, much like the sweet, unpredictable person she was.

She pulled away gently, brushing her tears from her freckled cheeks. "I'm sorry, I'm overwhelmed. It's been so long, and I have missed you, of course, but I'm not the same person I was. You love our old life together, our memories . . . but you don't love me, Seán. I ken you love Andre, and he loves you and Mckenna more than anything." She placed both her hands on her heart. "I feel it so strongly. Honestly, I haven't met someone so pure of heart in a long time."

Andre was the epitome of good. He knew that. "Andre is one of a kind. And I love him more than I could . . ." *More than I could say*. As he uttered the words, tears stung his eyes, and before he knew it, he was weeping like a widow. Abby motioned for him to sit in the armchair and began rubbing his back in circular motions. "This is embarrassing," he blurted, his face in his hands. But he knew she understood, she always did. He didn't have to say a thing for her to know he'd misread his sentiments; indeed, he'd been afraid he might still have romantic feelings towards her, but not because he missed being with her—because he missed what they once had. He was finally mourning the biggest loss of his life, something buried deep within before now.

Who he loved unequivocally, unconditionally, unquestionably, was Andre. And that would never change, even with the former love of his life standing before him, and now entangled in their lives. He didn't want that to change, either; she was Mckenna's mother. She was family.

"I want you in our lives, Abby," he muttered through his tears.

Her eyes glistening, she nodded several times, cupping his face with her warm hands. "I'm not going anywhere. I promise."

As tired as he was, Seán didn't go up to his bedroom that night. He found himself lying next to Andre in the guest bedroom, his arm wrapped around his torso, listening to his long, peaceful breaths. "I'm with you," he whispered in his ear. "Always."

He hadn't expected Andre to hear, let alone respond, but within seconds Andre's hand was on his, squeezing his fingers in a manner that said he, too, would never let go.

X

Earth, Air, Fire and Water

"Spill your guts," Nissa rasped after she and Mckenna cleared the breakfast table the following morning. Mckenna flinched at the phrase, once uttered in her nightmares by the troll-like man who'd dragged her—as Bessie—to her death.

"Shhh," Mckenna said, nodding over to her dads. In that moment, Seán and Andre were the picture-perfect couple, stretched out on either end of the couch facing one another, their legs intertwined. Andre had his self-editing face on, violently marking a document with a pen the colour of spilled blood, and Seán was lightly sketching in his pad, looking impressed with himself.

"That's it," Andre said, slamming his hand on the intimidating pile of papers that, undoubtedly, was his dreaded thesis. "I'm going to need a computer. I need to rework this whole section. It's awful. And my goal is to send it off for publishing by Christmas, so I need to get moving."

"You can do it, luv," Seán said, waving a supportive fist in the air. "The same goes for me. My boss is being gracious letting me work from here, but if I don't fax him my progress every week, I'll be slaughtered along with this stout pig." He held up his sketchpad to reveal a big-eyed pig peering through a cage that hardly accommodated his spiral tail.

"You're illustrating a children's book about a pig that's about to be slaughtered?" Mckenna asked.

"Indeed," he replied. "It's a ballsy move by the author, I know. The idea is to not sugar-coat where meat comes from. Will probably get banned, honestly."

"I hope not!" Nissa said, coming around to the living room. "I think kids should understand where their food comes from."

"I quite agree," Abby sang, emerging from the greenhouse. She placed her muddy gloves carefully on the bench by the door, along with her sky-blue wool hat.

"I hope it's okay to say that I just *love* your accent, Abigail," Nissa said. "It's so calming."

Abby's cheeks flushed. "That's right lovely, Nissa!"

"Don't be fooled," Seán chimed in. "She's toning it down. Some dialects from Aberdeen are incomprehensible."

Abby rolled her eyes. "Oh, *get tae,* Seán."

"See?" Seán said, pointing at her accusingly.

Mckenna laughed. "What does *get tae* mean?"

"Get lost," her mom said with a grin.

"What other words do Aberdonians say?" Nissa asked.

"Well . . . I'll call a wee girl like you a *quiney*, which is kind of like *lass*. And rather than, '*How are you*,' in my dialect I'll say, '*Fitlike?*' And a common response is, '*Nay bad, who's yourself?*'—to which many perplexed non-Aberdonians might respond, '*I'm me!*' It's particular, isn't it?"

"It's weird, is what it is," Seán said.

The room erupted in laughter. Abby gave Seán a light smack in the back of his head, then took a seat at the table. "Thanks for cleaning up, *quineys*. Swan, how's Cillian doing at the MacDonald House?"

Once again, it was as though a cold front hit Mckenna in the face. She shivered, rubbing her arms.

"Again?" Nissa said, looking worried. "What's the trigger?"

"I'm not sure, but it first happened at Glencoe—we stopped on our drive, but you were asleep." Glencoe was the mountain range known as the Three Sisters, where Cillian pulled in on the way to Skye. She remembered feeling a sudden cold draft, like she was momentarily caught in a blizzard.

"Hmm," Abby began, looking fascinated. "What do you know of the MacDonald clan, swan?"

Mckenna shrugged. "Do the MacDonalds have something to do with Glencoe?"

"Aye, they do. I believe you were experiencing the residual energy of the Glencoe Massacre."

"The what?" Mckenna and Nissa said in unison.

"Here we go," Seán called from the couch.

"Speak for yourself," Andre said, finally looking up from his paper. "I, for one, love a good history lesson."

"It was mid-February in 1692. To cut a long story short, when King James II was replaced on the English and Scottish thrones by William III in 1689, many Scottish clans remained loyal to him. The government persuaded all clan chiefs to swear allegiance to William III before January 1, 1692."

"And the MacDonalds didn't," Mckenna gathered.

"They did, a wee bit late. As punishment, Campbell of Glenlyon led a group of some hundred and twenty-eight soldiers to Glencoe Village. They lodged with the MacDonalds, and one early morning, they turned on their hosts, taking the lives of thirty-eight of them."

A stab of pain hit Mckenna in the chest. "That's horrible," she whispered, her hand on her heart. No wonder she felt like she was about to catch hypothermia each time their name came up.

"Wow," Nissa said. "The Campbells betrayed their trust!"

"Hence the feud that will never end," Seán said as Andre tore a page from his thesis in half, and buried his face in his hands. "Abby, before Andre sets his book on fire, is there anywhere we can buy a computer 'round here, or is civilization too distant here in Uig?"

"Not sure the smugness is warranted, Dad," Mckenna said, trying to detach herself from the horrific story she'd just heard. "Our hometown doesn't even have a RadioShack."

"There's Portree," Abby said. "I don't ken if they've got an electronics shop, but it's worth a look. Oh, and it's a bonnie wee town! It used to be a nineteenth-century fishing village. You lasses should go there as well. Take a break from all this madness."

Mckenna and Nissa gave each other an enthusiastic nod. Some leisure time with Nissa sounded perfect right about now.

Andre tossed his terrifying stack of papers on the coffee table and clapped his hands.

Seán closed his sketchbook lightly. "I'll take that to mean we're off to find a computer."

Portree was as Abby described: charming. Seán parked Abby's blue Ford Fiesta on the harbourfront, where cliffs bordered buildings of bright pink, blue, green, and yellow, the reflections of which sparkled below in the calm waters. Blanketing the sheltered harbour stood grassy and rocky hills, quietly stunning and unpretentious, which Mckenna was quickly learning was the Scottish way.

The foursome spent the first thirty minutes or so exploring, walking past old-looking banks, ornate churches, and a heap of cafes, restaurants, and gift shops. Nissa kept snapping pretend photos of Seán and Andre as they held hands ahead of them, making Mckenna positively glow from the inside out. She didn't care that passersby stopped to gawk at her dads, some unable to keep themselves from sneering. This was still the most fulfilled she'd felt since taking over John and Brigit's cruise cabin.

"So," Andre began, emerging from a tiny café and handing Mckenna and Nissa a hot chocolate. "I called our neighbour, Mrs. Claiborne, this morning to let her know we'd be gone a while due to a 'family emergency' and to collect our mail in the meantime. She kept me on the phone a while, the gossip that she is, and word on the street is a girl in town's been reported missing." He lowered his gaze to Nissa.

Nissa choked, then yelled, "Haaa!" as she fanned out her burnt tongue. "I'm surprised my foster family bothered to report it."

Andre looked sympathetic. "It's a small town, and your new school would have also been concerned. Which reminds me, Mckenna, I also told your principle there's been a family emergency in Ireland, so we're overseas indefinitely. It poses fewer questions since you're half Irish. Now, Nissa, if you'll allow Seán and I to contact your foster family, we could let them know you came of your own free will because you'd heard of Mckenna's family emergency, or something along those lines . . ."

"So they don't think we snatched you," Seán added.

Nissa suddenly took an interest in a falcon-sized seagull perched on one of the docks. "I can give you their number, I guess . . . but even if you had kidnapped me, they wouldn't care." She laughed, the bitterness in her tone not at all Nissa-like.

Mckenna didn't like the idea of getting her horrible foster family involved. "What if they force her back home?"

Uncertainty flickered across Seán and Andre's faces. "We don't want you to worry about that," the former said.

Andre placed a hand on Nissa's shoulder. "We promise to do our best."

The subject was dropped, and they took to sipping their hot beverages as they sauntered past the eclectic range of shops, most devoted to arts and crafts and outdoor gear.

"We might have to go to the mainland, luv," Seán said, grimacing at a store devoted entirely to fish bait.

"Hang on," Andre said, then disappeared into one of the outerwear boutiques. He emerged moments later, looking hopeful but wary. "The cashier said if we head towards the high school, south of the town centre, there's a small electronics shop past the schoolyard. And if they're closed, he gave me the owner's home address. He said, 'Just knock twice and tell him Clyde sent you.' I'm not sure what to think of that."

"Small towns," Seán said with a nod. "Let's do it."

"You guys go ahead. We'll roam," Mckenna said. After establishing a meeting place and time, Andre gave Mckenna a kiss on the cheek, then led Seán across the street.

"Don't get too distracted, lovebirds!" Nissa shouted. Mckenna giggled, loving every minute of Nissa's adoration. "Your dads are amazing, Kenna."

Her cheeks warmed. "I know." Mckenna wanted badly to tell Nissa about Cillian. All Nissa knew was he had "dropped in" and they'd spoken, then he left suddenly after Seán called Mckenna in for dinner.

"Niss, I've been *dying* to tell you—"

"Tell me everything right this second."

Mckenna's chest fluttered. "'Kay, so he was out in the greenhouse potting a plant . . ." Mckenna began, but was interrupted by Nissa's gasp—they'd walked past a small shop with a sign that read *RARE BOOKS*. Nissa turned her sad eyes to Mckenna, pleading with her like a child who'd spotted an ice-cream truck.

Mckenna sighed. "Obviously, we'll go in, but will you be too distracted by the pretty books to hear my story?"

"No, no, I promise!"

The harmonic clang of wind chimes greeted them like a warm applause as they stepped into the shop, which was probably no bigger than Andre's study back home. Every square inch of the place was covered in books; in addition to the floor-to-ceiling shelves, piles upon piles of ragged copies and vintage editions were stacked daringly high atop an eclectic assortment of Persian rugs. It was such a bazaar, Mckenna almost didn't notice the small elderly man hunched on a stool in the corner of the room, the lower half of his face obscured by *The Catcher in the Rye*. Mckenna let out a low chuckle.

"What?" whispered Nissa, who looked like a pirate who'd struck gold. Her eyes grew so big at the surrounding treasure, Mckenna thought they were going to pop out of their sockets.

"Nothing, I was reading that book the other night," she said, nodding in the shopkeeper's direction.

Nissa smiled. "That's a sign. There's something in here for you."

Chuckling again, Mckenna trailed behind her friend as they scanned the floor stacks and shelves in silence. Until—

"So, I kissed Cillian."

Nissa stopped in her tracks, making Mckenna ram into her elbow.

"Ouch! Geez, Nissa . . ."

"I need to know every detail!" Nissa shrieked.

"Shhh!" Mckenna hissed, glancing over at the shopkeeper, who hadn't so much as flinched.

She recounted every word she and Cillian had exchanged, up until their impromptu kiss, which was weirdly fuelled by anger—or passion, according to Nissa. Just thinking about it made Mckenna feel concurrently ashamed and exhilarated.

"Basically," Nissa began, "he doesn't give a flyin' hoot that he lied—"

"You can say *shit*, you know."

"—because if it meant being close to you and protecting you, then so be it?" Man, that sounded horrible. "How do you feel about this? Can we ever really trust him again?" Nissa said at lightning speed.

Mckenna grinned at the word *we*. "I don't know. When he's next to me, I can feel his . . ." She paused. *It's not love.* ". . . affection towards me. That he wants to protect me, help me with this whole prophetic destiny thing."

"Mhm."

"Like, it should be as simple as, 'You're a liar—get out of my face.' But this stupid empathic ability and annoying, strong-as-hell pull I feel towards him is just . . . UGH," she groaned, picking up a random book to distract herself.

"Yeah, except love is never simple, is it?"

"I don't . . ." Mckenna started to say, then sighed. And in that moment, Cillian's words surfaced: *Love is love, right?*

he'd said when she let slip in Kilkenny she had two dads. In this instance, if this were even love, what would that mean? That love could be cruel?

Nissa poked the book in Mckenna's hand. "Whatcha got there?"

"Oh," Mckenna murmured. Peering down, she couldn't believe what she'd haphazardly swiped. The cover illustrated a woman in a forested area, a stream running behind her; she was bent beside a fire pit, her right hand pouring water from a clay pitcher into a matching bowl, which she held with her left. The book was entitled *Earth, Air, Fire, & Water: More Techniques of Natural Magic*, written by Scott Cunningham.

"Interesting," Mckenna whispered.

"Didn't I say there would be something in here for you?"

That night, Mckenna sat upright in bed, *Earth, Air, Fire & Water* open against her knees. She'd never seen a book devoted to magic before. Who was Scott Cunningham? Was he a witch with inherent abilities or a practitioner, like Cillian?

She flipped over to the first page. One of the author's dedications was to the witches of Salem, Massachusetts. Mckenna breathed out an anxious sigh, unable to fathom what those witches, and non-witches, no doubt, went through so close to her hometown. She read on, learning in the preface that the book's central theme highlighted the fragility of our planet amidst human turmoil, while emphasizing the responsible approach of magicians who work with the earth and its elements—without abusing it.

This was what Cillian had been saying all along . . . and Abby, just yesterday, about leaving the elementals be. Her mother's words of warning rang in her ears: *. . . their purpose is not to be at our beck and call.*

She gulped. She'd already invoked the salamanders back at the campfire with Cillian and Nissa, and recently, sylphs. It just didn't seem fair that someday, at any given time, she would have to pay for it. She was a powerful witch, a Wise One, with centuries of magical knowledge and abilities. How was she expected to channel it all? Surely, it couldn't all be about grounding and centring. There had to be more to it.

Her mother had hinted at the importance of establishing a rapport with the elementals. Perhaps by doing so, they would be willing to assist her without consequence—and she could finally unleash real magic.

She wanted nothing more.

Three light taps on the door jolted her back to the present. Abby stood at the threshold, looking whimsical in a star-printed white cotton nightgown. "Can I come in?"

"Of course," Mckenna said, placing the book on her nightstand.

Abby's eyes fell on it as she crossed the room. "Ah, I haven't read that one yet. *Earth Magic* was brilliant, though."

"Really? You've read Scott Cunningham?"

She nodded fervently, then said grandly, "His approach to magic is simple and pure."

"What do you mean?

"He recognizes that it's all around us, and we can tap into it at any time."

Could've fooled me, Mckenna thought, but instead forced a smile. If she wanted to learn more about her abilities, now seemed like the perfect time to ask. "Mom," she began as Abby lifted the blanket over Mckenna's chest, like she was a little girl. All those years she'd missed with moments like these, she didn't mind a bit.

"What is it, swan?"

She had been longing to confide in her about the magic she'd encountered, beyond her empathic talents: how she could keenly sense the presence of spirits; how she effortlessly closed a textbook as well as her dad's bedroom door with just her thoughts; and the extraordinary connections she'd forged with a deer and a bird. What if she had been misusing her gifts all this time?

Mckenna didn't know how long she rambled for, but when she finally stopped, she realized she might've said it in one breath.

Abby tilted her head and gazed at her daughter as if seeing her for the first time. "You can communicate with animals . . . that's *marvellous*." Mckenna sighed with relief. "That wee wren guided you to John and Brigit, all the way to Ireland, then to Esme in Northern Ireland! Unbelievable. But, you ken, when you're in tune with your soul's calling, synchronicities happen—effortlessly. And that's pure magic, swan."

"You've mentioned synchronicities before," Mckenna recalled.

"Aye, when things start happening that seem like pure coincidences at first, they're oftentimes meaningful occurrences brought to us by the divine."

"Like meeting Nissa. It was meant to be." There was no doubt in Mckenna's mind.

Abby beamed. Mckenna noticed that her smile never failed to reach her eyes.

"I have another question. And I don't mean for this to sound harsh. I just don't think I fully understand . . ."

"Go ahead, swan."

"Would you say humans are, well, harming the planet every day? That our habits are poison?"

Abby took a long breath. "Not everybody. Many are working hard to make things better."

"Not enough of us, though, right?"

Abby wrinkled her brow. "What are you getting at?"

"The whole '*billions of souls shall expire upon this Earth*' *thing*' . . . I mean, is it so terrible if our souls don't reincarnate? I know you said we need to in order to evolve, but I have a hard time understanding what the point is of coming back to a planet that we're slowly destroying."

Abby responded slowly and deliberately. "It's not for us to decide when a soul is called to Earth. As some souls depart, others step into their place, and so it goes on. You see, every soul has a role in the evolution of the planet and each other. How can that happen if, say, half the souls in our universe were to vanish? We're not saving Mother Nature by taking a piece of it away—because at our very core, we are nature; you ken that, which is why grounding feels so natural to you." She was spot on—sending roots from her feet deep into the earth felt like a natural extension of herself now. "We'd be harming the Earth in a much more real way than Maeve might think."

"But I've seen what the world will be like." Mckenna vividly recounted the vision of the apocalypse she had witnessed at Kylemore Abbey: the desolate trees, the stagnant and murky lake, the dead fish, and the thick shroud of smog that enveloped it all.

Fear flashed in Abby's eyes. "I've heard of the legend of the white horse, but be cannie. Visions can be deceiving."

"Why would Eachna show me something so horrible if it wasn't a warning?"

"I don't ken, swan, maybe we're not meant to understand just yet. You've got to grasp that destiny's never etched in stone. Remember when I spoke to your astral self about it on Samhain?" Mckenna nodded, listening closely. "What you saw may never become our reality. Don't forget, the fae have their own foresights and predictions—that the two of us, you and I, would be the bridge between realms, and that someday, we'd all coexist in harmony."

Mckenna remembered Esme's words well: *There is a reason your mother incarnated as a human in this lifetime. She was meant to give birth to you—to "the last living Wise One". The fae said that together you would act as the bridge between realms, and we would all come to live on the same vibration and communicate freely.*

"Even so, there *is* a possibility that Eachna's vision could come true," Mckenna said, still unconvinced. "Am I supposed to do nothing? We don't even know what the hell the faeries' prediction means. You *were* a faery—can't you just ask them?"

Abby moved a curl away from Mckenna's face. "I've tried, but the fae don't meddle more than they think they should, even though I was once one of their own. The answer will come when it's meant to."

Mckenna half laughed, half scoffed. "And in the meantime?"

"In the meantime, we must accept that humans will make mistakes and need to learn from them. Over time, our reality will shift. We're here on this planet to learn lessons, and with each rebirth, our soul grows, and as a result, we vibrate at a higher frequency; we become more self-aware and draw closer to our higher selves, our very essence. Until then, all we can do as individuals and as a species is strive for that reality, even if it feels distant. However long it may take. Are you with me, swan?"

Mckenna couldn't affirm that just yet. "How do we move towards a higher frequency?"

"By expressing our love and gratitude for Mother Nature, by following our passions and enthusiasm, and by listening, always, to what's in here." She placed her hand on Mckenna's heart.

Mckenna mulled over her mother's words for the better part of the night. She grasped the idea, yet it also eluded her understanding. What if permitting humans to err simply proved ineffective? What if their time was running out? The prophecy suggested that stopping the cycle of soul reincarnation would preserve the natural world.

And she was finding that concept increasingly difficult to ignore.

XI

THE EXCEPTION

The following day, Mckenna awoke with a strong determination to harness her abilities, beginning with mastering her telekinesis. Following a hearty full-Irish breakfast, whipped up by Nissa and Seán, she tried her hand at meditation, then spent a solid two hours in the greenhouse concentrating intensely on a watering can. It hadn't so much as vibrated.

When Abby came out to check on her, she begged for her help.

"Swan, I promise to pass on my knowledge, but I don't possess such gifts. That's something you'll need to discover on your own. Just like anything else you've picked up, it starts with grounding, centring, and connecting—"

"With the earth, yeah, I get it," Mckenna said impatiently.

Her mother raised her eyebrow at her. "It's crucial that you stay grounded, Mckenna. Otherwise, you'll lose your way."

At those words, Mckenna excused herself to get a drink of water but stopped short when she opened the back door to Cillian and Seán watching BBC Scotland News intently. When had Cillian come in?

"Looking cozy, lads!" Abby sang, then kissed Mckenna on the forehead before crossing the living room, her gaze lingering on Cillian a little longer than usual. Abby was hard to read, but Mckenna had the distinct feeling she was sizing him up. "I'm off to the market. Does anyone fancy anything?"

Neither Cillian nor Seán seemed to have heard or seen her. As Abby slipped out the front door, shrugging, Seán turned up the volume:

"Yesterday, a bomb detonated in Saint Albans City Centre in Hertfordshire, England, killing two IRA members," reported the journalist. "The explosive incident occurred prematurely, near Barclays Bank. Authorities are currently working on the theory that the intended target of the suspects may have been the tour bus affiliated with The Blues and Royals military band, who were performing at a nearby venue."

"Christ," Seán muttered.

"Serves them right," Cillian said.

"If that blast had happened just a few minutes later, it would've killed nearly three hundred folks who were leaving the concert!" said a distressed-looking witness.

Mckenna cupped her mouth in disbelief. How could such evil exist?

"When will it all stop?" Seán said, shaking his head.

"When both sides agree to disagree," Cillian responded, running his hand through his hair.

"Like that'll happen. You're in politics," Sean said, his tone tinged with disapproval. "What would you do?"

Mckenna wasn't certain if her dad was testing Cillian, but she understood Cillian well enough to know he held a deep passion for this subject. Test or no test, she knew he would respond truthfully.

"That's a tricky one, Mr. O'Dwyer. I might come across as a tad idealistic for a politician. I do wish for a united Ireland, and being from the South, like yourself, it's hard for me to align with loyalists who still seek Crown rule. Both sides have done terrible things. While the IRA may be republican, they've also engaged in acts of terrorism."

Seán nodded, rubbing his chin. "There is no easy solution, is there?"

"Afraid not. There'd need to be a declaration of a ceasefire all around."

"Both sides will have to reckon with the actions of their own people."

Cillian nodded slowly. "You'd be amazed at how willing people are to move forward and make amends, even when they haven't truly forgiven themselves."

Mckenna looked from her dad to Cillian, who she supposed was no longer talking about loyalists and republicans. "Cillian, our lesson?" she said, stepping in front of the TV.

"Are you mad?" Seán barked. "Get out of the way!"

"In a minute, promise," Cillian said to her softly, throwing her the subtlest of winks. Mckenna walked over to Seán's side and ruffled his hair in a thank-you-for-giving-Cillian-a-chance gesture; from what her "Spidey Sense" could tell, for the first time since he'd met Cillian, Seán's sentiments were not centred around suspicion and contempt, but something resembling respect.

"I'll be outside when you're done with your hot date," she said, feigning jealousy.

Not five minutes later, Cillian joined Mckenna in the greenhouse. Mckenna—jaw clenched and eyes bulging—was once again trying to will the stupid watering can to move.

"Am I, erm, welcome here?" Cillian asked hopefully, squinting.

"I haven't decided yet," she said, finally ceasing her focus.

"I respect that." He stepped around her in a circle. "You look like you're having some trouble."

"I am. I can't move the goddam watering can. I tried the whole Zen thing, and it's not happening." She was suddenly hyper-aware of his eyes on her bare shoulder; she'd deliberately gone with a red boat-necked sweater that slipped down her arm, for a "subtle sexy look"—Nissa's suggestion ("You don't wanna look frumpy!").

"That's because you're a passionate person," he said, a glint in his eye. "You've got to use that."

Mckenna's entire body tingled mercilessly. "If you think *you're* making it easier to focus . . ."

He flashed a wicked grin. "Want to give it a go?"

"Cillian, I *just* said—"

"I meant practicing your telekinesis," he said with a chuckle, then raised his hands in surrender. "I'm keeping my distance. Try moving the watering can again."

"I tried. It hates me. I don't know what to do differently."

"I do. But you may not like my advice."

Mckenna knew what he was going to say, even without tapping into her empathic abilities. "What, air elementals? I thought of that, but my mom is totally against invoking them. She got super pissed yesterday when I used them to summon the storm."

"That was *your* storm?"

Mckenna nodded, feeling her cheeks flush.

"Why's that, though? Wouldn't they want to help?"

"That's what I said! Apparently, it means I'll owe them."

Cillian's expression was dubious. "Elementals aren't dark beings. They're neutral, which means whatever they ask of you isn't likely to be unreasonable."

"Maybe. But what if it is? My mom knows her stuff. I should trust her advice." And yet all she wanted was to be convinced otherwise; being able to speak directly with the elementals awoke something dormant in her, a power that'd been in a deep slumber for ages. Maybe lifetimes.

"Listen, lass," he whispered, glancing over his shoulder. "I've no doubt your mum's right—when it comes to us normal folk. But you, you're the last living Wise One, and I just can't see how the same rules apply to you. What if you're *meant* to invoke the elementals to help harness your abilities?"

Cillian had affirmed what crossed her mind after her mom

explained the possible dire consequences of her actions. What if she was the exception?

"You've got to do what feels right. She can't disagree with that, can she?"

He had a point. Plus, the salamanders hadn't come for her yet—perhaps they never would. And wasn't her mom and Esme always going on about listening to her intuition? Abby had just encouraged her to follow her enthusiasm, listen to her heart.

"So, you think I should invoke the sylphs?"

"It's completely up to you, lass. But do mind the sylphs— they're the most powerful of the elementals; your thunderstorm was a real spectacle. They're also the ones closest to us humans, you see, because, well, they're all around us." He waved his hand around the room.

She nodded and, for the umpteenth time, focused on the watering can. Closing her eyes, she inhaled and exhaled slowly, and just as she had done back at the Old Man of Storr, opening her heart to the energy of the atmosphere around her. A cool breeze caressed her skin, causing her arm hairs to stand on end. Through her third eye, she could make out dainty silhouettes seemingly sculpted by the very air itself. They appeared wispy and drape-like, yet Mckenna could sense the immense power radiating from them, an almost palpable force.

Hello, she greeted them.

The sylphs gracefully danced in her presence, and the gentle draft that had encircled her skin warmed. In an instant, it was as if she'd been transported to a tropical paradise. She embraced this enchanting sensation as their literal warm greeting.

This is it. Now or never.

"Sylphs," she uttered. "I invoke thee."

The watering can didn't merely tip over—it flew across the room in one swift motion.

"You did it!"

Without warning, she found herself lifted off the ground, twirling in the air as Cillian's arms supported her. She clung onto his shoulders, letting out a joyful yelp as he spun her around, faster and faster, the world around them becoming a dizzying blur.

"Put me down!" she shouted through a fit of giggles.

"You're sure you want me to?" he said, gazing up at her.

"Mhm," she murmured. He lowered her gently to her feet so the two were nose to nose, and her heart hammered in her ears, "The Tell-Tale Heart" style.

He grasped her hand and placed it on his heart. "What do you feel right now?" he whispered.

She tried to keep her hand from trembling as his chest rose and fell; beneath her palm, his heart thumped as ferociously as hers. He smelled like an odd but intoxicating blend of sage, mint, and a touch of tobacco.

"I feel . . . like you should stop smoking."

Cillian laughed in spite of himself. "Try again." His eyes locked with hers in a way she'd only ever witnessed in melodramas.

"I feel like you understand me. And you'd do anything for me."

"Ah, you get it now," he breathed, lifting a hand to her cheek.

Her pulse thundered. "And that you're a bad influence."

"I am, am I?"

"You are."

"And what can I do to convince you otherwise?"

"Just kiss me."

He didn't waste a millisecond. His hands rose to the back of her head, tangled beneath her curls. He held her tightly against him, as if he wouldn't—couldn't—take the risk of letting her go. She surrendered, letting his hands travel down to her neck, and leaned into him harder, feeling the electrifying warmth of his lips and body coursing through her all the way to her toes.

They remained in this in-between state, where neither time nor space was present, until the afternoon sun's rays illuminating the greenhouse indicated it was well past their usual lunchtime.

"My dad's gonna call me in to eat, like, any minute now," she said, pressing her hands to his chest in attempt to separate them. "He gets cranky if the food gets cold."

"Fine," he breathed in her ear. "Only because he frightens me." He kissed her hand.

Laughing at his Gomez Addams-like behaviour, she finally pushed away, then crossed the room before he could change her mind. The watering can was sprawled on the ground near the spiderwort, the love plant. *Won't need you*, she thought cheekily, bending to pick it up. She'd nearly forgotten why she'd been here all morning.

"Cillian," she said, stroking the aluminum handle. "What do you think of the prophecy?"

He hung his head back and let out a long breath. "Honestly?"

She nodded.

"It's not unidealistic."

"Because fewer people equals less damage to the planet over time?"

"Sadly, yes."

"Do you think that's . . . a good thing?"

Cillian seemed to be in search of the right words. "I mean, it's the utilitarian, greater-good theory, isn't it?"

"And it's not genocide? Preventing souls from reincarnating . . ."

Cillian looked as though she'd slapped him across the face. "*Genocide*? Do you really think I'd be okay with something like that?"

She'd offended him. "Of course not, Cillian." She took a step towards him. "I just wonder—"

"Listen, I'm not endorsing the High Priestess's methods—she's mad, to be sure—but if you think about it, are her intentions entirely mad? Who'd want to return to a ruined planet, anyway? In the end, it's the preservation of the natural world that's on the line."

"Yeah, that's where I feel lines are blurred. Eachna's vision . . . it was horrifying. Everything was destroyed. *Everything*. What sort of world would we be coming back to?"

"Exactly. And, well, what if Eachna sent you that vision because you're the one person who can change it?"

Weeks went by, and before Mckenna knew it, they were well into December. By now she'd fallen heavily into a routine that, as abnormal as it was, felt just normal enough to give her a semblance of an ordinary existence. Early mornings were dedicated to lessons from Abby, who was adamant about teaching spell-casting using only nature, Scott Cunningham style. They'd covered lunar rituals, household charms, growing a mystical garden, room cleansing, finding lost objects (she'd successfully performed a spell that located Abby's pendulum, which the neighbour's cat, Lennox, had buried under the porch), and next, they were moving on to protection spells. She couldn't wait to learn how Abby had cast such a complex seventeen-year-long spell, wherein she could only be found by those she was protecting. *Ingenious.*

"And next week, we'll delve into potions and mystical recipes, something your father can surely lend a hand with," she said, raising her voice to reach Seán's ears.

Mckenna's jaw dropped. She turned to her dad, who was doing all he could to avert his eyes. "Daaaaaad, what is she talking about?"

Andre raised an eyebrow. "Yeah, Seán—what is she talking about?"

"No idea. She's daft."

"Come on, Seán . . ." Abby said in a sing-song voice. "There're no secrets here!"

Seán huffed, making a sound in between a sigh and his throat clearing. "Your mum might've made me help her with some 'magical recipes'"—he used air quotes—"and I innocently obliged because it's just cooking, is all."

"With intention," Abby added.

During their "family lunch" (Nissa's words), Andre announced everything around Nissa's "disappearance" had been taken care of. He'd informed her foster family that he found her with his daughter, and she was in safe hands. As Nissa suspected, they didn't appear perturbed; her foster father grunted an "I'll let the cops know she's fine," and that was that. Since she was still technically under their care, his word was enough for the police to drop the case. "A bit frightening how quickly they let that go," Andre said, shaking his head.

After devouring Seán's homemade chocolate pudding, Mckenna and Nissa ventured out to explore the surroundings, including a visit to the faery tree. Nissa had her own special routine going, continuing a tradition she started back on the Isle of Man with her grandmother, Arethusa. Each day around noon, Nissa would leave offerings beneath the rowan tree. Encircling its trunk were now silver coins, strawberries drenched in honey, chocolate milk, and an assortment of glistening rocks and pebbles. "I remember my grandmother saying they adored shiny objects!"

In the evenings, after Abby's lessons, Cillian would rendezvous with Mckenna in the greenhouse, where he'd assist her in honing her abilities and engage in other . . . activities.

"You're supposed to be helping me tap . . . into my . . . intuition," Mckenna said in between kisses, standing over a mugwort plant. "Why the mugwort?"

"Mugwort," Cillian said, his breath in her ear, "opens the third eye chakra. It's used in elixirs to help us dig into our deepest thoughts and tap into our psychic capabilities."

Mckenna tried desperately to absorb what he was saying. "Mhm. And how does one use mugwort?"

"You could use it during any kind of divination," he whispered, nibbling her earlobe, "like reading tarot. Or when you need answers, you can stuff it under your pillow to inspire messages or to try dreamwalking—projecting into someone else's dream." When Mckenna's eyes widened, he added, "I know, it's very invasive. Supposedly, dreamwalking allows for one to speak to another's subconscious while they're in their most vulnerable state. But I've never heard of anyone who could dreamwalk. I, for one, think it's a myth."

Despite her tingling body, Mckenna pulled back. "Dreamwalking."

"What about it?"

"I've done it before."

He finally put more than a foot of distance between them. "You have?"

"Yeah. With you." She recounted the time she'd visited Cillian in a dream while staying at Arethusa's; the two had parted on not-so-great terms at the party on faery hill in Belfast, and she'd regretted it. "You were telling me to come back, but I thought it was just a dream."

He let out a small laugh, then laced his fingers with hers. "It wasn't. It all makes sense now. I think that's what made me come find you at the faery bridge."

The sentiment filled her heart and stomach with flutters of warmth, but her mind quickly trailed off; she'd done this without the help of a spell or herb. What else could she achieve without implementing any practical magical techniques?

How powerful was she, truly?

"Now, rub this upon his chest every eve—it be eucalyptus oil. That should aid his breathing," Bessie said softly, holding out a glass vial.

Mrs. McDougall nodded gratefully. "I thank you, Bessie. You're a heavenly creature!"

After Thom's assistance and guidance over these past few weeks, news had circulated throughout the town that Bessie possessed a gift for healing. Each morning, a queue of neighbours, or more accurately, customers, formed outside her door, willing to swap whatever they could spare in exchange for her miraculous care. By weaving clever words infused with virtuous intentions, she'd helped fulfill wishes, crafted herbal blends that mended wounds, lifted people's spirits, and soothed their troubled minds with the warmth of her hands. She also assisted farmers in comprehending their animals' needs and, on certain occasions, guided those in dire need of change towards a new path by simply listening to her innermost thoughts. Bessie never sought anything in return, yet her community, appreciative of her gifts, expressed their gratitude through modest offerings of food, clothing, and livestock.

"Thom, I'm ready," Bessie said with fervour back at the cove, staring up at the twinkling sky. It had been a quiet day, spent mostly in the kitchen testing various ingredients to help steady Mrs. Vass's chronic trembling hands. Bessie's husband was once again gallivanting around town, though truth be told, she found solace in the solitude, allowing her to contemplate the offer presented by the Elfame beings. Ever since she had embraced her healing talents, he hadn't engaged her in much conversation.

Smiling brightly, Thom said, "I agree," and led her inside the mysterious dike. This time, Bessie stepped forward without hesitation.

A rush of cold wind whipped her hair back, and the ground beneath her feet vanished. It felt as though she were plummeting from the very peak of Ben Nevis, with the world spinning wildly around her until the soles of her feet touched down on a soft, mossy surface.

As notes of juniper and lavender, her favourite herbal blend, wafted into her nose, she surveyed the lush forest into which she had descended. It was evident that she'd arrived in a place far removed from her own world. The area abounded with trees broader than her entire kitchen, and the earth was adorned with exotic and captivating plants she yearned to get to know better; sparkling streams wound through the undergrowth, and the sky . . . Oh, how she longed to gaze upon such a sky every day until her last breath. It remained mist-free, quite unlike Dalry, and was as serene as a blue lace agate crystal.

Before her stood the same twelve beautiful beings Thom had introduced her to not too long ago. She hugged herself, even though the air felt more temperate here, and met each of their eyes.

Welcome to our home, the one with short, wispy rose-gold

hair said, though her lips remained unmoved. Something about her instantly lifted Bessie's spirits.

They were telepathic, she recalled. She needn't waste time with pleasantries. In her mind, she responded, *Good Elfame beings, I am prepared to receive the gift of Second Sight.*

And so we shall grant it unto you, the male fae replied. *We have awaited your arrival a long time, dear Wise One.*

Excitement surged through her. She nodded, then instinctively bowed her head. With the gentlest of touches, the fae with the rose-gold hair placed both her thumbs at the centre of Bessie's forehead.

A brief *zap*, like a static shock, surged into Bessie's head, followed by a tingling sensation. Images flickered before her—faces of those she knew, faces of total strangers, places she recognized, places she'd never set foot in. When Bessie finally blinked open her eyes, her vision was as clear as the Elfame sky.

"Thank you," she whispered, feeling more herself than ever before.

Bessie was in a joyful mood that evening, as she no longer solely possessed the ability to heal—she could now also prevent harm from befalling her loved ones and neighbours. She could forewarn them about any impending heartbreak, suffering, or illness and offer solace to their anxious minds by assuring them that, in time, everything would indeed be alright.

As keen as she was to explore her newly bestowed gift, she found herself with a great deal to accomplish before the village fair on the morrow, an annual event eagerly anticipated by all of Dalry. The town square would be aglow with torches, abound with quaint wooden stalls showcasing a myriad of homemade wares, ranging from fragrant soaps to savoury chutneys and the most exquisite desserts (Bessie had already secured a few servings of Mrs. Brown's famous flummery). The evening would conclude with traditional Scottish music and theatrical performances, some of which might extend beyond one's capacity to fully enjoy without indulging in spirits.

Every year, Bessie and her husband filled their stall with home-made Caboc, a locally beloved double-cream cheese. But in Bonnie-Jean's absence, and in light of recent events, Bessie packed her stall that evening with healing herbal teas and blends, skin-soothing ointments, vials of what she fittingly named *mood-boosting juice*, and a spice fusion that ignited passion (which she could proudly say was tried and tested). Unsurprisingly, these sold nearly as quickly as Mrs. Brown's flummery.

The night passed in a whirlwind. The town square teemed with visitors from nearby towns, and throughout the evening, her stall consistently boasted the longest queue. She handed yet another customer one of her mood-boosting juices, accompanied by a sachet of dried herbs and rose petals—her signature soothe-your-soul bath blend.

"It appears your table has garnered much favour among the folk," said a familiar voice.

Bessie looked up to find a grinning Thom inspecting her spice fusion. "*Ignite the passion you desire with but a modest sprinkling upon yours and your true love's cherished dish!*" he read aloud. "How quickly does this take effect?"

Bessie blushed. "Erm, once the dish has been eaten by both parties," she said, vying to keep her tone even and professional.

"By both parties? How romantic."

She burst into giggles, snatching the sachet from his hand. At the touch of his hand, her skin sparked, and a current zipped through her arm, down to her legs. She fell to her knees, feeling suddenly hundreds of pounds heavier, as though her body was weighed down by the fate of every townsperson. The gasps, murmurs, and yelps around her turned faint, until she could hear nothing but her own breath heaving.

The words escaped her lips before she could register them:

"As twin flames rekindle and the last living Wise One unites with her creator, billions of souls shall expire upon this Earth. Peace shall be restored to the natural world, and all beings shall exist in perfect harmony."

Gasps and shouts ensued from the crowd. She could hardly see what was in front of her. *What's happening to me?* she thought, clutching her stomach, now swirling with nausea. She began to dry heave—she was most certainly going to be sick.

"What are you on about, lassie?" a nearby villager said, their voice barely audible.

"Is this an act?"

"She's a witch!"

"Shut up! That there's Bessie Dunlop, the healer."

"*Our* Bessie—"

"She's a miracle worker, she is. Write this down, you boggin bampots!"

Bessie was no longer in control. It was as though the words had been trapped within a concealed chamber of her mind, patiently awaiting the ideal moment to break free.

There was more:

"Her soul's beginning, she need discover
A darkness within she'll ken e'ermore
But 'tis the horse's vision of Earth Mother
That lights her path to days of yore."

There was an uproar.

"It sounds like a prophecy!" a shrill voice shouted.

"I've written it down on a scroll!" another man announced importantly.

"Lizbeth, are you alright?" Thom said in her ear, cradling her head.

"I feel . . . weak."

Silently, Thom scooped her up from the cobblestones and carried her into the hospice tent. There, he placed her gently atop a bundle of blankets. "Shall I call for the medic?"

"No. I just need a rest." He nodded, lifting the thickest wool blanket to her chin. "Thank you, Thom."

"No need," he whispered, stroking her forehead with the back of his hand.

"Thom?"

"Yes?"

"Have you got some parchment?"

His eyes flitted to the small table, where the medic had left his belongings, including a quill and scroll. "Yes. Is there more?"

Nodding, she sat upright, readying herself to spew out another passage:

"The boldest fae flees from our neighbour land
Her charge, the Wise One, and she the key
Whence the ancient passage tomb stands
United their magic, and so shall it be."

Mckenna jolted awake in a fit of short, frantic breaths.

The connecting door between her and Nissa's room burst open. "Kenna! I heard . . . are you hyperventilating?"

"Pen. Paper," Mckenna said, vaulting out of bed and pulling open the drawers of her nightstand.

Nissa followed suit, raiding the bookshelves, no questions asked. "Here!" she tossed a pen across the room.

Mckenna snatched it out of the air and began to scribble across her arm.

"You finally dreamt of them, didn't you? The Scottish Scrolls?"

Mckenna's eyes lingered on the last word scrawled on her skin before she glanced up at Nissa from across the room, and nodded.

XII

A Secret Meeting

It was still pitch black out when Mckenna and Nissa tiptoed down to the kitchen and got the coffee brewing.

"Read it again," Nissa whispered.

"Her soul's beginning, she need discover . . ."

"Wait—can you please transfer this very sacred text onto actual paper before it smudges?"

"Good idea." Mckenna searched the top drawers. "Got it," she said, waving a yellow pad in the air as Nissa poured their cups of coffee.

"Okay, read it again," Nissa said, fetching the milk and placing their steaming cups on the table. Mckenna watched as Nissa dumped three teaspoons of sugar in her very pale coffee.

"That looks disgusting."

Nissa swallowed. "I could say the same for that cup of tar you're drinking. Yuk."

"No, see, this is me drinking actual coffee."

"Agree to disagree. Now, read it again."

"Her soul's beginning, she need discover . . ."

"Okay, do we even know what that means?"

"Not really. And I'm really not liking the sound of *A darkness within she'll ken e'ermore.*" Mckenna was well aware of her own inner darkness. Now she had a goddam prophecy to confirm it.

"'Ken' means 'know', right? So . . . knowing the darkness within. I mean, we all have a smidge of a dark side, don't we?"

"Not you." Nissa's cheeks flushed. "It's this part that freaks me out: the *horse's vision of Earth Mother*. It must be referring to the vision Eachna gave me—you know, of the destruction of the natural world."

"Yeah, not a fan. What do you think *lights her path to days of yore* means?"

Mckenna didn't want to admit it, but she held a firm suspicion that it implied such a catastrophic global event would rewind the world to a simpler era, one marked by a smaller population and reduced pollution, when nature flourished more than humanity.

"Not sure," she lied, aware that Nissa could sense her lack of disapproval. "As for the second Scroll—*The boldest fae flees from our neighbour land*—I have a better idea. Esme told me the faery realm is closest to ours, so the 'neighbour land' has to be the faery realm. And 'the boldest fae' must be my mother. She *is* an incarnated faery."

Nissa's eyes widened. "*Her charge, the Wise One, and she the key.* Of course! You're her charge—the one she came back as a human for. And well, we know your mom is the key to, um . . ."

"To helping me stop souls from reincarnating," Mckenna said. "*As twin flames rekindle and the last living Wise One unites with her creator, billions of souls shall expire upon this Earth. Peace shall be restored to the natural world, and all beings shall exist in perfect harmony.*"

"Man. That's heavy."

Silence fell. Suddenly, the dull sound of water droplets hitting the sink became so overwhelmingly intrusive, her head began to throb.

Mckenna stood up. "I need a break."

As Bessie, she had been a source of help and kindness to many. She considered herself a virtuous person, a *good* witch. Yet, why would such a good witch predict something this dreadful? What if following the guidance from the Scottish Scrolls was the only hope for the planet's survival? She wished there was a way to be certain.

There *was* a way. Only, it could also be a death wish.

"Still not feeling well, swan?" Seán repeated for the third time that week, while Abby, for what felt like the thirtieth time, had her hand pressed against Mckenna's forehead.

"Hmm. You don't feel warm."

"I don't think I have fever. I just feel stuffy and tired, and my throat's all scratchy." Mckenna let out a hopefully convincing cough before saying, "I think I need another rest day, Mom. Sorry, I know we're behind schedule on potion making . . ." Truthfully, she'd been excited to delve into potion making, but there was a more critical matter at hand.

Abby's face glowed. "Apologizing for being sick is daft. We'll resume our lessons next week. I'll fetch you more of my special tea."

"And I don't want to see Cillian coming up here, d'you understand?"

"Ew, Dad, please!"

"Okay, Seán, let's let her have a rest." Gripping his shoulders, Abby steered him out the door, blowing Mckenna a kiss on the way out.

Mckenna breathed a sigh of relief. All week, she'd been stuck in an ongoing mental struggle, trying hard to make herself believe that if she genuinely wanted to understand the prophecy's implications—its pros and cons, what was at stake, and the potential consequences—she had to go through with what she was about to do.

Her only option was to talk to the High Priestess.

She reached for *Earth, Air, Fire, & Water* on her nightstand, then flipped open the book to the page where she had tucked away a mugwort leaf earlier that day before carefully placing it inside her pillowcase. Inhaling deeply, she closed her eyes.

Breathe in, and out. In and out. Centre.

Clear. She focused on her chakras, clearing each one as she emptied her medieval goblet, releasing any blockages it held.

Ground. In her mind's eye, roots sprouted from the soles of her feet, reaching out to meet those of the mighty oak trees in the yard, their long-standing surly roots entwining with hers.

"Allow me into Maeve's dreams," she declared with conviction.

The sound of the wind rustling and rain drumming against the window quickly faded. It was the strangest sensation; she could feel herself falling into a deep sleep, except she remained acutely aware of it, much like in a lucid dream. Then came the peculiar, familiar feeling of her body vibrating, a phenomenon that always accompanied her astral projections. This time, the tugging was unrelenting. She didn't resist as she once had, allowing her ethereal body to be swept up by the unseen forces around her, trusting that her soul would not lead her astray.

She soared upwards, breaking through the ceiling and emerging into the vast expanse of the starry sky. On this plane, neither time nor fear held sway, existing only as distant memories, which had been left behind with her slumbering physical body.

The dream landscape unfolded, and there she stood on a swaying houseboat, floating serenely down a narrow river. The scene appeared distorted, as if she were peering through a fisheye lens.

The High Priestess stood at the stern, leaning over the rail. When she turned around, it didn't take Mckenna long to realize that this dream wasn't merely a creation of Maeve's subconscious; Maeve's state within the dream mirrored her reality, a tireless journey in search of the mystical stone, Misgaun Medb. The weariness of her prolonged trek weighed heavily on her, evident in the dark rings around her eyes. Her once immaculate, white-blonde hair was now carelessly tied in a haphazard French braid. As Mckenna sensed Maeve's emotions, she could feel the palpable frustration radiating from her; the High Priestess was not just weak—she was downright pissed off, perturbed by the relentless pursuit. But the moment she saw Mckenna, her entire face brightened.

"Dreamwalking already?" Her voice was as icy as Mckenna remembered it. "To what do I owe the pleasure?"

Unsure of how long she could endure this dream state, she got straight to the point. "We need to talk."

"I'd like nothing more."

"Tell me about the prophecy," Mckenna demanded.

Maeve smiled. "It's simple. You and Abigail hold the power to halt the reincarnation of billions of souls, and in turn, it'll save the natural world."

"And what will happen if we don't?"

"I don't need to tell you that. You've seen it yourself."

Mckenna was hoping for a different response. She'd been haunted by Eachna's horrifying vision since she'd seen it. "My mom thinks differently."

"Evidently," Maeve spat.

"She says we *need* souls to come back to Earth—to help it evolve. To work towards raising our vibrations and—"

"Unity consciousness?" She scoffed. *What the hell is unity consciousness?* "That's a bonnie notion, isn't it? Abigail was always an idealist . . . Even if that were a possibility, it wouldn't happen for centuries! In the meantime, Mother Gaia's unique creation will wither away. My seer kens it. The white horse kens it. And you ken it, too."

Mckenna fully expected the High Priestess to try to sway her, but her words only reinforced what Mckenna already suspected: Maeve's sole ambition was to protect and preserve Gaia's creation, no matter what the cost.

Maeve awaited the Wise One's response, surprised not only by the girl's astonishing abilities but also by her audacity in appearing in her dreams, in her very subconscious. She felt both intruded upon and flattered . . . and hopeful. Was there a small part of her that understood what was at stake?

"And Cillian . . . you trained him," the girl said, her voice unsteady. *So, he told her that much.* She would tread carefully, not reveal too much.

"I took him under my wing, aye."

"Did he share your views on the prophecy?"

She hesitated. "Not all of them. We've gone our separate ways, as you must ken."

"Why?"

Mindful of the Wise One's empathic abilities, she kept as close to the truth as possible. "He didn't agree with my methods."

The girl scrutinized her. "You feel betrayed."

Maeve said nothing.

"But he doesn't think you're wrong. About following the Scrolls, saving the natural world."

"I'm not wrong, Wise One. The sooner you realize that, the sooner we could save this planet from ruin." She took a step towards Mckenna's figure. "I'm not the villain here. I never was."

"You were going to kidnap my mom and me and force us to use our magic against our will!"

"Maybe against my better judgment, but in times of dire need, Wise One, desperate times call for desperate measures. You've witnessed it yourself—how could you turn a blind eye to such a dreadful fate?"

The girl clenched her jaw. *She's torn.* "The world needs you, Mckenna." Maeve softened her expression, as did the girl at the sound of her name.

"I'm—I'm not a killer."

"And I wouldn't dare to make you one. We're not taking lives here; we're rescuing billions of souls from a fate where they'd return to a world doomed by natural disasters. From sweltering heat. From starvation and homelessness. From breathing air that'll soon be toxic."

Lightning lit the night sky, exposing Maeve's simmering anger. "I'll think about it," Mckenna finally said.

"Think quickly. I'll be in touch."

"Or what?"

Maeve smiled. "May the best witch win."

As the Wise One's dream form dissolved before her, she wondered whether her timing was intentional.

Maeve peered into the murky depths. So, that protégé of hers was not entirely useless after all. He was swaying her, like he'd promised. Being young and impressionable, there's still a chance the Wise One could change sides. Abigail, on the other hand, will pose more of a challenge. She was much too obsessed with unity consciousness; it would take a miracle for her to willingly fulfill the prophecy.

"Marvelous," Maeve thought irritably. She was lucid dreaming, fully conscious within her dream. Returning to an unconscious sleep would prove difficult now. Her thoughts drifted to the upcoming morning and the miles yet to be covered. However, the satisfaction of finally reaching Misgaun Medb was worth the effort; it was the ancient stone from which Abigail had carved her dowsing necklace so long ago. In her mind's eye, the stone faintly glowed, hinting at the magnificent powers it held. She could sense its proximity. It was close, so close she could almost feel it.

Soon enough, Maeve would pinpoint Mckenna's location, as well as her loved ones, surely sheltered beneath Abigail's protective enchantments. This situation, in fact, simplified Maeve's mission. Should the Wise One resist cooperation, Maeve would not shy away from leveraging anyone necessary. Given the girl's immaturity and self-importance, a touch of pressure would unquestionably nudge her towards fulfilling the crucial Scroll at the passage tomb.

The next morning, Mckenna needed to be alone with her thoughts. As she lay in bed, she replayed the High Priestess's words in her mind.

There was no winning. No good outcome. No obvious solution. Did she trust the future she'd seen with her own eyes, or did she trust her mother, who held an optimism and hope for humanity Mckenna didn't quite share?

If only she could somehow speak to Bessie, or to Thom, who appeared to be some sort of all-knowing guide. From her last Bessie dream—or flashback, whatever they were—it seemed he might have also been a past love. She wondered if there was a way to dreamwalk into the past.

"Mckenna," Andre called, tapping thrice on the bedroom door.

"Yeah? Uh, I'm still not feeling good . . ."

"Why don't you get dressed and come downstairs? There's someone here to see you. I'll put on some tea."

She frowned. Hadn't she told Cillian not to come by today? Kicking off the duvet, she flipped her hair upside down, attempting to make the curls fall into place, threw on one of her mom's heaviest wool sweaters, and headed downstairs.

But it wasn't Cillian. She felt a twang of disappointment but smiled all the same at the sight of Mathis, Cillian's brother, standing at the front door. "Mathis, hey. You found us."

He grinned back, moving a sandy-golden strand away from his forehead. "I found this after your car sped off . . ." He pulled a roadmap out of his coat pocket, with Nissa's heart drawn around Uig—right, Nissa had lost it after her bathroom break in the woods. "I've been searching the area for some time and finally spotted Cillian coming this way the other day. I hope it's alright I've come." His words carried an air of refinement that came across as off-puttingly formal.

"I mean, it's alright with me. I'll go call Cillian—"

"Hang on." His fingers grazed her wrist, and her skin zapped. She laughed, pulling away. "Static," they both said in unison, then chuckled awkwardly. He slipped his hands in his coat pockets, as though for safe measure. "Erm, I was hoping you might speak with him alone first. I trust he'll listen to you . . ."

"Sure. I'll talk to him."

Cillian was not content, to say the least, when he discovered why Mckenna summoned him to the greenhouse. It took quite a bit of persuasion—no thanks to her frumpy appearance today—and lots of "But he's your brother!" until he finally agreed to listen to what Mathis had to say.

Mckenna poked her head through the back door. "*Psst,*" she hissed, making Mathis jump up from his seat at the kitchen table. "You can come out now."

He grinned in thanks and followed her out into the greenhouse to face his brother, who was sitting with his arms crossed on the wooden bench, looking as indignant as a child who'd just had their yo-yo snatched away. "I'll leave you two alone to talk," Mckenna said, but Cillian pulled her down beside him.

"Stay. I want you here."

She looked from Cillian to Mathis, who gave a curt nod, then shifted his eyes to the watering can sitting near the lemon balms. Was she imagining it, or was he avoiding her eyes? She sat beside Cillian and took his hand.

"I'm not who you think I am," Mathis said, like he'd been holding this information hostage for years.

"Obviously not," Cillian snapped.

Mathis shook his head. "That's not what I meant. I . . ." he trailed off, shuffling his feet. Mckenna's chest sat heavy; this wasn't easy for him. Mathis's heart ached for his brother, for leaving him all those years ago, for making him believe he'd abandoned him. But there was more.

"Spit it out, *bro.*"

Mckenna squeezed his hand. "Give him a chance, Cillian."

For a fleeting moment, Mathis's gaze met hers, and in that

instant, a soft blue glow suffused the outer layer of his skin. *What the . . . ?*

"This is going to sound unbelievable, so please, bear with me," Mathis said.

"Sure, whatever." Cillian made no effort to shield the skepticism in his voice. Had he not seen what she'd just seen?

"Cillian, I had no choice but to leave you and Mum and Dad."

"Right. MI6 phone you in for a mission, did they?"

"Anything I say may appear implausible . . . but here it is." Mathis released a long breath. "I'm an Arcturian."

XIII

NEXUS

Mckenna had no clue what an Arcturian was. He could have just admitted to being a platypus, for all she knew. She turned to Cillian, who scoffed. "What the hell's an Arcturian?"

"We are part of the Galactic Council—a group of high-vibrational entities who help maintain peace in the universe."

Mckenna's jaw dropped.

"Yeah, and I'm a fire-breathing dragon," Cillian mocked, "but only when the sun goes down."

"It's true," Mathis said earnestly. "Some assignments are larger, some smaller. Our objective is to help humans 'level up,' so to speak. Collectively, to raise the vibrations of humankind. To—"

"Achieve unity consciousness," Mckenna found herself saying.

Both Mathis and Cillian gawked at her like she'd just levitated. "Yes, precisely," Mathis said. "How did you—?"

"My mom," she lied.

Cillian sneered. "No offence to your mum, but I've heard of this so-called unity consciousness. It's complete rubbish."

"Please," Mathis continued softly. "Allow me to finish. I have been sent to this plane numerous times throughout the centuries for various assignments. Most recently, my existence was Mathis Oder, your younger adopted brother. My purpose was to help guide you, but it was getting increasingly difficult to sustain my frequency. I stayed beyond my allotted time, and maintaining my physical form became impossible."

"You sound like a mental patient, Mathis."

Mathis sighed. "Read my aura, Cillian. It's a kind of blue you've never come across before, isn't it?"

It was true. When Mckenna tuned into his energy field, his aura radiated an extraordinary shade of blue, as if it existed beyond the conventional spectrum of colours.

Cillian's eyes lingered for a moment on Mathis's aura, then snapped out of focus. "Say I believed any of this, tell me—you were to guide me to do what?"

Hesitating, Mathis shot Mckenna a brief glance. "To ensure you did not lose your way."

Cillian sprang to his feet, nostrils flaring. "Excuse me?" he hissed, inches away from Mathis's face.

Mckenna's gaze flitted from brother to brother. "Cillian, calm down."

Mathis didn't flinch. "You have a tendency to be swayed, brother."

Knowing that would hit a nerve, Mckenna rose to her feet and planted her body between them, pressing Cillian's chest gently back.

"You were sent to keep me in check, were you?" Cillian said. "Well, I turned out fine. Not an evil conqueror. Mission accomplished."

Mathis sighed, the hurt in his eyes making Mckenna's heart feel brittle. "Give me another chance. I returned *for you*."

Cillian hesitated. "See, why don't I believe a word of that?"

"Um, sorry," Mckenna chimed in. "I have a question about the whole Arcturian thing. Does that mean you're from, like another planet?"

"Yes and no. Arcturians live on Arcturus, which humans perceive as a star in the Northern Hemisphere, when in reality, it exists within the realm of the fifth dimension. That being said, while our physical presence may be anchored there, our spirit has the capability to journey to other planes and dimensions."

"Gotcha," Mckenna said, as though he'd merely revealed he was Canadian. She felt as though the magical world she was getting acquainted with had collided with the *Star Trek* universe. "Lots more questions, but carry on."

Cillian's laugh was bitter. "So, you *are* a spy . . . except when you're assigned to be a gullible human's brother. Then you're just a scammer."

Mathis shook his head. "You do not quite grasp the challenging position I was in. I manifest as a human when it is needed, yes. But you must know, leaving you was never my intention. I returned the moment I could to ensure you were okay. And, well," he leaned in, "things are beginning to get a bit complicated." He whispered this last part, but Mckenna heard every word. Mathis glanced in her direction, his gaze not lingering more than a half a second, then whispered something in Cillian's ear.

Cillian's jaw clenched. "*You* don't understand, Mathis. You're sitting up there with your Council or whatever, judging everything we do, but you've *no feckin' clue* what it's like to be human, why we make the decisions we make."

"You are absolutely right; I do not fully grasp it. That is why I'm here, to attempt to understand and, in doing so, help you see—"

"There it is. Your opinion is always the righteous one, isn't it?"

"Okay, that's enough, children!" Mckenna shouted. "I don't know what the hell's going on, and it's pissing me off. Either *spill*, or get out of here—both of you. You can come back when you've worked it out."

Nissa burst through the greenhouse door, making each of them jolt. "Dinner's ready! Oh, hi again," she added to Mathis, her cheeks flushing.

He gave a partial bow, like he hailed from a different century, then looked round at Cillian. "I'll go."

Mckenna could tell from Nissa's confused but flattered expression that she was thinking the same thing: chivalry must not be dead.

"Kenna, why don't we invite Mathis to stay for dinner? Seán and I made *way* too much stew."

"He can't," Cillian said quickly. "He's vegetarian."

"Well, lucky for Mathis, I've been vegetarian for about a month now, so us veg heads have a meatless portion."

Mckenna held back a laugh. *Veg head?*

I know, I'm hilarious.

Mckenna froze, as did Nissa. What had just happened?

"Alright, there?" Cillian said. "You both look like you've kicked a faery hill."

This is weird, Mckenna thought.

I'm freaking out, Nissa's voice echoed back.

"It's nothing," Mckenna said quickly. "I, uh, need to let my dads know to add a place setting." *We'll talk about this later*, Mckenna thought as loudly as she could.

Mckenna was starting to get used to awkward dinners. While Seán, Andre, Mckenna and Nissa tried to process what Mathis was, Abby was in awe, soaking it all in.

"And while you're on assignment, you're entirely human, aye?"

Mathis nodded. "I am, yes. Until I can no longer hold my frequency. It usually feels like . . . an uncontrollable trembling, I suppose, followed by difficulty breathing. Though, I try not to let it get to that point."

"Fascinating," Abby said, wide-eyed.

"Are you considered an alien?" Nissa blurted out. Everyone turned their heads towards her. "What?"

Mathis chuckled. "No, we Arcturians are not aliens. We

are beings from the fifth dimension, a higher plane of existence beyond our conventional three-dimensional reality."

Curiosity lit up Nissa's eyes. "What's it like?"

"Well," Mathis continued, "for one, time is perceived differently, and there is a greater understanding of interconnectedness."

Abby's expression showed that all her hopes and beliefs had been confirmed. "Tell me, is it true Arcturians had ties with Atlantis?"

Mathis nodded, swallowing a mouthful of stew. "Absolutely. The Atlanteans were an extremely advanced civilization for a reason. What is most astonishing is when we arrived, they did not fear us; they welcomed us with open arms, and for centuries, we co-existed harmoniously. During this time, we imparted our wisdom on advanced technology and instructed them in harnessing the power of the universe."

Mckenna couldn't help but think of Mr. Heathley, her history teacher, who would be jumping for joy if he were here. He'd been trying to convince his students of the existence of otherworldly beings since day one. Everyone had always thought him a complete wacko, but alas.

"How does one harness the power of the universe?" Andre asked, leaning in.

"In many ways, mostly through nature. For instance, and this may sound implausible, the whole of Atlantis was powered by crystals."

"Crystals?" Seán said, eyebrows raised. "Like, proper rocks."

Mathis grinned. "Holding a crystal enables the holder to connect with the universe's energy, somewhat like fine-tuning a radio to a clear signal. In the process, it enhances the natural electromagnetic fields within our bodies and surroundings. Oh, humanity has yet to fully explore the potential of crystals."

"I *love* crystals," Nissa squealed, topping up Mathis's water glass. "And that makes sense to me. They're pretty for a reason, aren't they?" Mathis tilted his head, his brow furrowed in interest. "It's their way of grabbing our attention," Nissa clarified.

"They want us to covet them. We just don't see what's beneath their outer layer. Yet."

Without trying, Nissa understood the complexities of ancient magic.

"That's lovely, dear," Abby said. "I think you're right!"

"Why aren't we using crystals to harness energy now?" Mckenna wondered. "Seems like the answer to pretty much everything."

Mathis looked round the table. "Humans are indeed reawakening to the potential of crystal powers, but they have a considerable journey ahead to reach the same level of mastery as the Atlanteans."

Abby nodded, looking pensive. "That's understandable. Are you free to tell us where the Atlantean civilization has gone?"

One of the world's greatest mysteries. Mckenna had been wondering the same thing.

"And where Atlantis was located," Andre slipped in, the history buff that he was.

Mathis hesitated. "I know it's terribly boring of me, but the lost city of Atlantis must remain a mystery at this time in human history. As for where they've gone, all I can say is they've gone off world."

"Abandoned ship," Seán deduced.

"So to speak," Mathis said.

"Probably anticipated the destruction of the planet," Mckenna said before she could stop herself. Abby shot her a look that fell somewhere between concern and disapproval.

"Speaking of . . ." Seán said. When the ruin of the natural world became a regular topic segue, there was cause for alarm. "Abby's found a spell to stop Maeve once and for all. Prepping it will take a fortnight."

Mckenna nearly choked on her beef cube. *Fourteen days . . .* "The winter solstice. That's when Pravadi predicted we would, you know . . ."

"When the prophecy would come true. Aye," Abby said, "I ken the irony. The winter solstice marks the juncture where days start to lengthen, symbolizing the gradual return of light and the sun's rebirth. There's no better time to cast a transformation spell."

"A transformation spell," Mckenna repeated. "How will that stop her?"

Abby took a breath. "I've suspected since she first started studying hypnosis, becoming obsessed with the prophecy, that she was . . . how can I put this? Afflicted. I cannot quite put it into words, but I sensed something off. It was as if I was watching her lose a piece of herself, and I've always believed it to be some unseen force. One that clung to her." Mckenna shuddered at the thought that such evil could exist, veiled in between worlds. "That's why I reckon the best way to stop her is by banishing part of her consciousness to another plane of existence. It'll be a fair bit complicated, to say the least, but if it works, she'll revert to being the old Maeve, before she was consumed by the euphoric vision of the prophecy."

To Mckenna's surprise, Nissa said, "Is that really the best we can do?"

"That's what I said," Seán muttered in agreement.

Abby looked considerately at Nissa. "My *quiney*, regardless of what someone's done, causing harm is not the solution. Seán, Andre, and I have had our fair share of discussions on this, and it's the best course we've got."

Mckenna didn't have a good feeling about this. "But, Mom, aren't we walking right into a trap? She wants us together on the winter solstice, too. What if it doesn't work? Shouldn't we consider getting rid of her for good?"

"We are *not* murderers," Abby declared firmly, raising her voice. Mckenna had never witnessed her display of anger before.

Silence swept over the dinner table. Mckenna glanced at Cillian, who hadn't said a word since they'd sat down, staring down at his plate and scooping up the last of his stew. Nissa looked thoughtful, and Andre kept watching Mathis from the corner of his eye.

"I was thinking," Mckenna began, about to address Mathis across the table, but the latter stood up suddenly.

"I must be off."

Seriously?

"So soon?" Nissa said.

Mckenna wasn't ready for him to leave just yet. "You should stay with us." He had answers, and he was holding back—she could feel it. Perhaps he was the key to understanding what the future held for the planet, what Mckenna was meant to do about it.

At last, Cillian spoke. "I don't think that's a good idea."

"For once, my brother and I agree," Mathis said, already making his way to the door.

Abby stood up. "Nonsense, Mathis. Seán and Nissa slaved over the dessert!"

"Chocolate trifle," Nissa said proudly. Seán gave the air a chef's kiss.

Mckenna nodded enthusiastically, though she didn't have to; Abby's tone suggested there was no room for negotiation. Her mom had this *je ne sais quoi* way of being authoritative without being commanding. It was downright impressive.

"Only if it's alright with Cillian," Mathis said, looking over at his brother.

Cillian sighed. Mckenna kicked him in the shoe. "Sure. You're all very kind," he said in his best politician voice, but he gave Mckenna a sideways look that suggested he was far from pleased.

Cillian excused himself after dessert. Mckenna sensed he wanted to be alone, and after the bomb his brother had just dropped, she didn't blame him one bit. Mathis was also quick to excuse himself, claiming his human form was still adjusting to Earth's atmosphere. Seán took the liberty of escorting him to one of the guest bedrooms—on the third floor, down the hall, farthest away from the girls' rooms—and Abby went off to work on the transformation spell. Yearning to talk to Nissa alone, Mckenna suggested they pay the faery tree a visit. It was now lit up with flashing pink holiday lights.

"What the hell was that earlier, do you think?" Mckenna said when they'd settled comfortably beneath the faery tree, a thick wool throw over their legs to ward off the December chill.

"The whole fifth-dimensional being thing? Yeah, no, that's a lot."

"No. I mean, yes, that's a lot. I meant in the greenhouse, Niss. We heard each other's *thoughts*, right?"

Nissa hit her forehead with her palm. "*Yes*, it was weird! I have no idea what that was."

Mckenna had a thought. "Remember Niamh, the faery from the Inagh Valley I told you about?"

"Hard to forget. Yeah, she said humans once communicated telepathically."

"Exactly. I'm thinking because I'm starting to, you know, develop my abilities, my ancient magic is kicking in. Like, I'm able to harness powers I had in my previous lives."

"That makes sense! Maybe we should tell your parents."

"Can we not right now? There's so much going on. I would rather try understanding it a little more on my own first. Things are weird enough as they are."

They sat in comfortable silence for some time. She wished she could simply sit and meditate, like Nissa seemed to be doing, but Mathis's sudden presence was nagging at her like a persistent toothache. And what had he whispered to Cillian that had got him so upset?

"Niss, what do you think Mathis's angle is?"

"Angle? I'm not sure he has an angle. He seems to be here to make things right with Cillian."

Mckenna bit the inside of her cheek. "I dunno. He seems off to me." She thought immediately of her bad-news tea leaves. *A wolf usually means a false friend.*

"He is off. He's not from here," Nissa offered.

"I don't mean that. I feel like he's hiding something. And . . ."

"What, Kenna?"

"He won't look at me."

"What do you mean?"

"I mean, he literally won't look at me. It's like he's avoiding my eyes."

"Are you sure? I didn't notice . . ."

"Yeah, I could see why," Mckenna said, shoving her friend playfully.

"He's so dreamy it *hurts*," Nissa shouted, her word echoing among the trees.

She wasn't wrong, Mckenna thought. Anyone could see how attractive he was, with his swishy, sandy-blond hair, well-define cheekbones, and dimpled smile. Mckenna was never one for blue eyes—she much preferred Cillian's mysterious blend of grey and green—but she couldn't deny the captivating, crystal-clear allure of his blue gaze.

They fell into their famous fit of giggles, until the cold was too much to bear, then headed back inside for tea.

Night after night, Mckenna dreamt of Bessie. Often, the visions were brief, a mere snippet of her life in Dalry, usually involving concocting an elixir or telling a villager's fortune. But no matter how short the dream, it was always vivid enough to make Mckenna feel as though she was living two lives simultaneously.

"Hold my hand, Mr. Aitken," Bessie said, her left hand outstretched and her right cupping a satin cloth sachet filled with her handmade runestones.

"Aye, aye, but I must admit, Bessie, I don't believe in any of this supernatural haver. My wife insisted . . ."

Chuckling heartily, Bessie grabbed his hand, shook the bag of runes, and closed her eyes. "Your wife is wise."

As she uttered *wife*, an image of Mrs. Aitken's lifeless body appeared before her third eye; she was lying on the forest floor, her head resting in a pool of her own blood. Nearby was a sharp rock that was undoubtedly the cause of such a fatal blow.

In a state of shock, Bessie yanked her hand back from Mr. Aitken's grasp.

"You're as white as a sheet, Bessie. Should I be worried?" he asked with a nervous laugh.

"Of course not, Mr. Aitken. It seems I've come down with a sore head from concentrating so hard. I'm truly sorry. Could we meet again on the morrow?"

Mr. Aitken nodded politely before leaving, though Bessie could sense his angst.

Poor Mrs. Aitken was headed for an untimely, sorrowful death—and soon. She had to caution her. She could not simply allow her to carry on and . . .

What would she think? What would the town think? Bessie was a healer, and thus far, had only ever used her gift of Second Sight for gentle guidance. She had offered counsel, to be sure, but nothing more than wee nudges towards improving their health or current trying situation. Nothing remotely as grave, as pressing as this.

She would be persecuted. Tried for witchcraft—and everyone kenned how that sentence ended. Bessie's gifts were a well-kept secret in this town, and she was eternally grateful for it; her neighbours trusted her guidance, had come to rely on her remedies. But something as grim as predicting one's death? They would only come to fear her.

No, she would not tell her, but she would check in on Mrs. Aitken on the morrow, for afternoon tea.

The following day was a dreadful day—on the verge of rain, but never giving in to its urges, with howling winds and a wet kind of cold that burrowed into one's bones. Regardless of the dreadful weather, Bessie promised herself she would check in on Mrs. Aitken.

Bundled up in layer upon layer of cloth, her legs fought against the wind, all the way up the hilly road to the Aitken's house.

"It's Bessie!" she shouted, rapping vigorously on the front door.

No response.

"Mr. and Mrs. Aitken?"

Her heart beating out of her chest, she knocked again, louder still. Perhaps they were in the cookroom, unable to hear through the winds, she thought, her ear now pressed against the door. *Aye, that must be* . . .

The sound of Mr. Aitken's wailing confirmed her very worst fear. She was too late.

Mckenna awoke with a single thought: *I'm a killer.*

How could Bessie have kept that vision to herself for an entire day? That poor, innocent woman died because Bessie was too afraid the town would turn on her. Had it been Mckenna today, in 1991, she would have said something straightaway.

At least, she'd like to think she would. She *had* kept her big magical secret from Nissa, at first . . . and witnessed the end of the world without telling a soul. Was she just as much of a bad person in *this* life as she was in 1576—and in 1324, as the horrible Alice Kyteler?

Her mom kept going on about how everything was a choice, and no one was inherently good or bad. What would helping halt the reincarnation of billions of souls make her? Was she screwing with the natural order of things, or saving the planet?

Nothing truly felt right or wrong. She was on the precipice of altering the state of the world—shouldn't she be leaning towards one side over the other? Clearly, she lacked pertinent information. She imagined this was what Andre often felt on the job when his clients failed to disclose the full story. And even so, no matter what they'd done, he had to set his opinion aside and let the evidence, or lack thereof, speak for itself.

The digital clock on her nightstand was flashing 6:07 a.m. Surely, Andre was already awake, typing away at his thesis. And sure enough, when she headed downstairs, there he was, his face scrunched up in concentration.

"You're up early!" Andre chirped brightly from behind his desk.

"You look chipper."

"I'm making great progress, and I'm enjoying my new work-station. I love coming here while it's dark and watching the sun rise over the mountains."

"Valid," she said groggily. They certainly didn't have such stunning views back home.

"I made another pot of coffee."

Mckenna yawned. "How long have you been up?"

He glanced at the clock hanging over the mantel. "About two hours now. I'm really making a dent in this . . ."

She gave him a thumbs up—that was all the enthusiasm she could muster this early in the morning—dragged her feet to the French press, filled a mug to the brim, and joined him in his nook.

"Dad?"

He stopped typing, leaned back in his chair, and folded his hands together. "What's up?"

"You started as a defence attorney, right?"

"I sure did," he said with a nod.

"Why did you become an immigration lawyer?"

He let out a long breath, gathering his thoughts. "I wasn't happy with who I was becoming." Mckenna sat down, and leaned into his explanation. "The job often entailed defending criminals, and after a while, I was tired of how it was making me feel. I wanted to use my powers for good," he said with a smile, adding, "It's not easy for people to come to this country, especially visible minorities. That's who I wanted to help."

Mckenna smiled. She'd met several of Andre's clients over the years, and every single one of them was worthy of entry into the U.S.—each was either brilliant in their field, in the midst of escaping unlivable conditions at home, or simply wanting a fresh start, like Seán.

"Totally. But wasn't part of being a defence lawyer also negotiating a fair sentence?"

"Yes," Andre replied slowly. "That's an important part of it."

"And how do you know what's fair?"

"Well, every situation is different. If it was a petty theft, for instance, but I could see the defendant was struggling with addiction, I'd try to keep them out of jail and negotiate community service and mandatory psychotherapy sessions in their sentence. All I could do was use my better judgment. It's rarely black and white, guilty or innocent. There are usually circumstances attached."

"That makes sense. Did it feel like no matter which decision you made, you lost? Like reducing a real douchebag's sentence—"

"Language, Mckenna."

"Sorry. It's just . . . how do you know what's right?"

"Yes, in those cases—and there were many—it didn't feel so good. I did what I was hired to do and tried my best to be objective. I looked at the bigger picture, which was that this person was a human being and it was their right to retain counsel."

Nodding, she took a large gulp of coffee. *The bigger picture.* Which was the bigger picture here—the greater good? Souls or Mother Nature?

"Is there something you'd like to talk about?" When she didn't respond, he added, "What are you questioning?"

Andre was good at making you want to open up without being the least bit pushy, but she didn't like the intonation in his tone; there was a hint of worry there, fear of what she was casting doubt on.

"There's so much I don't understand about my past lives, and who I am in this life," she diverted. "And I sometimes wonder if I deserve this much power."

Andre rolled his chair over to her, gently placed her coffee cup on his desk, and held both her hands. "You, Mckenna O'Dwyer, are the most deserving person I know."

Mckenna let Andre's words stew while she took a walk to nowhere in particular. With it always being a full house these days, it was difficult to be alone with her racing thoughts. Shouldn't her decision be simple? Was she losing her mind, thinking of siding with a fanatic like Maeve—who her very knowledgeable and experienced witch of a mother was convinced had been afflicted by an evil, unseen force?

It was so dark and misty out that it was impossible to discern the time, so when the sun emerged from behind the distant mountains, she was thrown, but took it as a much-needed sign that her darkened mood would not last.

The sound of a very long, very loud "*Moooooooo!*" made her whip around. Standing in the middle of the road, grazing her ear was what appeared to be a cow, though much hairier all over, her shaggy brown fur and wild '80s fringe a little reminiscent of a sheepdog, except with small ivory horns sticking out of her head.

"Hey, cutie," she said in an uncharacteristically sweet voice, her pitch rising several levels. Only animals could turn her into this. "You lost?"

She could swear the hairy cow nodded, her beady eyes pleading for help. Mckenna locked eyes with her and centred, hoping to spark that same connection she'd had with the doe near Luss. Her eyes shut tight, she waited for the silver, jelly-like string to extract from her third eye.

"*Moooooooo!*"

"Alright, then." She scanned the area, looking for a nearby farm. There appeared to be nothing for miles. "Come with me, Crazy Bangs. Let's explore."

Crazy Bangs followed her off the road and across the field, which hit a small incline, then dropped slightly to reveal a farmstead surrounded by a handful of hairy cows grazing the golden grass.

"This look familiar?" she asked her new companion, who was already traipsing down the hill to join her fold.

Thanks, friend, a raspy female voice murmured in her head. Aha! She knew she'd understood her. *Anytime.*

"Nutmeg! Knew you'd run off again," an elderly man shouted, giving Mckenna an exuberant wave. "Thank you, lass! This one lives for adventure, she does."

Mckenna chuckled, somewhat taken aback by how heavy his Scottish accent was, and with a wave of her hand replied, "Not a problem! Nutmeg is a treat."

"Care to come in for a tea? Me wife's just made some blueberry scones, and I'll tell you, there's nothing like them." He said this last part in an urgent whisper, like he'd let slip something top secret.

"How could I say no to that?"

Mckenna followed him down to his home, a modest-sized stone building, with bright red accents around the doors and windows, warped roof shingles, and dangerously crooked wooden steps leading to the front door. The interior was just as old-school as the exterior, with both furnishings and finishings that looked like they hadn't been updated for a good five decades, at least, and smaller-than-normal appliances that would have Seán in a tizzy every time he wanted to bake a loaf of bread. Though the man's wife, a petite woman who looked like Lucy Ricardo in her hairnet and apron, seemed to be managing quite well as she zipped around the small kitchen.

"Another wanderer?" she said.

"It's Nutmeg who's the wanderer, Catriona."

"Don't give me that tone, she's your *harry coo*, Alastair."

"*Harry coo?*" Mckenna repeated.

"What us highlanders call a *hairy cow*," she replied with a smile. There was something so adorable about this; she couldn't wait to tell Nissa. "Sit, dear. I'll put a kettle on. What's your name?"

"Mckenna."

"What brings you about?"

"Uh, my mom. I'm visiting from America."

"Aye, the accent says it all. Who's your mam, dear?"

"Abigail Douglas. She's staying over at the inn."

They exchanged perplexed looks. "No inn I can think of nearby," Alastair said. "Must be new."

Mckenna shrugged, uncertain how long the inn had been around. The trio sat in silence, somewhat awkwardly, until the kettle whistled.

"Sugar?" Catriona said, placing a cup of tea in front of her.

"No, thanks." Mckenna traced the teacup's floral rim with her index finger. "My friend Nissa would love your vintage teacup."

Catriona's laugh was high and hearty. "Vintage! Strange you say that, I just picked that one up brand-new at the market. Me cousin hand-paints them. Go on, take it home with you when you're done."

"Oh, no, that's alright. They must be pricey."

Both Alastair and Catriona eyed her like she'd proclaimed she had a fear of plants. "Not at all, dear," Catriona said. "Take is as a thank-you for bringing our Nutmeg back safely."

Mckenna peered outside the window, wondering whether there were predators in the area. "Do you have wolves nearby or something?"

"Wolves! Hardly. There hasn't been a wolf in Scotland in, oh, over two hundred years now?"

"Wow, how come?"

"We hunted them to extinction," Alastair said. "Killing our livestock, they were."

"That doesn't seem natural," Mckenna said before she could filter her thoughts. They gaped at her like she was the Mad Hatter.

Alastair furrowed his brow. "How are us farmers to make a living?"

Gulping down the rest of her tea, Mckenna nodded frantically. "Mhm, you're right. Definitely. Sorry," Mckenna said, even though all she could think was that the food chain they'd just tampered with would definitely come to bite them in the ass one day.

There was a loud clatter as Catriona reached for something on an upper shelf, slipping on her hand-made step stool. Mckenna instinctively rose to steady her, but was too far away to reach her in time. With her hands outstretched, she watched as Catriona didn't fall as gravity would dictate but instead rocked forward and quickly regained her balance, as if someone had given her a gentle shove.

Did I just do that? And so effortlessly, like it was the most natural thing in the world. She thought of Cillian theorizing how gravity could be manipulated, owing to phenomenon like Stonehenge, and how he didn't think he'd ever have that kind of power . . .

Catriona and her husband exchanged looks of horror. They'd noticed she'd done something. "Um, I should go!" Mckenna shouted. "Thanks again."

"I knew there was something off with you, lass. Are you some kind of *witch*?"

Still clutching the teacup, Mckenna dashed out the door, across the field, past the fold of *harry coos*, and back up the road. Panting, she walked the rest of the way back to the inn.

She must have alarmed whoever was awake by now by bursting through the door of the inn, Kramer style.

As though she'd never left, the main floor was still empty, save for Andre, hunched over his computer. "Goodness, Mckenna, where's the fire?"

"Sorry," she huffed.

"Unlike you to go for a run. Thought you were taking a long walk?"

"I did. I sprinted back, is all."

He raised an eyebrow, then looked down at his leather wristwatch. "You call ten minutes a long walk? And where d'you get that teacup?" he added as she set it down on the console.

As she made to hang up her coat, she fumbled and missed the hook. "Ten minutes? What are you talking about?" Her coat was sprawled at her feet; she stepped over it to take a closer look at the time on the stove. It read 7:00 a.m. How was that possible? She'd left at ten to seven. It'd taken nearly ten minutes to find

Nutmeg wandering about. She must've been in that weird house for at least fifteen . . .

What in the world had just happened?

"Maybe you stepped into another dimension?" Nissa suggested after Mckenna dragged her to the very spot where she'd run into Nutmeg, teacup still in hand. Except this time, there was no farmstead in the distance, no *harry coos*—just an abandoned house.

Nissa grabbed the teacup. "Well, whatever happened, thanks for bringing me back a souvenir."

"Don't mention it," Mckenna said in a daze. "Wait a minute, can I see that?" Mckenna yanked the teacup from her grasp and flipped it over. The date read 1951.

"Hello?" Nissa's fingers snapped in front of her face. "What is it?"

"Catriona said this teacup was brand new. Niss, I think I travelled in time . . . or like you said, I stepped into another dimension."

Nissa's eyes nearly fell out of their sockets. "Did the house look a little like that one?" She pointed to the abandoned house, which, upon closer examination, did appear to be the same size and have the same stonework.

"Yeah, I think that was it."

"Okay, *now* can we talk to your mom? Things are getting hella weird around here."

Mckenna wanted to tell Abby what had happened. Being the super witch that she was, she likely had an explanation. But she'd been preoccupied day and night with crafting the perfect spell to banish part of the High Priestess's consciousness, and she looked permanently worn out, like she was shouldering the weight of the world—which she was. Mckenna had no desire to exacerbate her burden any further.

"It's fine. I don't want to worry her. Nothing bad happened, right?"

"Not this time, no. But who knows where you could end up next time!"

True. She could have easily been transported into the Middle Ages amid a wild boar hunt.

"I think it had something to do with this place," Mckenna rationed. "Not *me* necessarily."

"As in that spot in particular is extra magical, like some kind of vortex?"

"Exactly. My abilities were also super heightened there. I was able to communicate with Nutmeg easily, and I stopped Catriona from falling just by thinking about it. I didn't have to summon an elemental or anything."

Nissa folded her arms over her chest. "I thought you stopped doing that, Kenna. *You* said your mom said those abilities are inherent, so you don't need to invoke the elementals. You just need to keep practicing—"

"I know, I know, relax. I'm saying it was weirdly easy, that's all." Nissa could always detect a lie or half-truth, so she swiftly changed the subject, saying she had a headache and could use a soak in the tub. It wasn't a bad idea; basking in her mom's home-made bath salts seemed the perfect natural calming agent right about now.

It was easy to see why her mom was keen on baths—her aroma-therapy salt blend was exquisite, a word Mckenna customarily reserved for Seán's Baileys Irish cream cheesecake. Her muscles relaxed in the toasty water, her skin tingling pleasantly, and she quietly breathed in the woody, herbal aroma of rosemary and chamomile.

She'd had every intention of reading *Earth, Air, Fire & Water*, but she must've only been two pages in before her eyelids grew too heavy to focus on the words in front of her. Laying the book down to rest on the tub's step, she leaned back onto the bath pillow and exhaled.

Don't dwell on anything, she urged herself, in no mood to descend into her usual tumult of parasitic dark thoughts, as she did whenever she was alone these days. She was envious of how effortless her mother made meditation look each time she spotted her sitting on the floor in front of the fireplace at any given time of day, or out in the greenhouse before sunset. She wanted more than anything to achieve that same sense of calm. To some-what—at least temporarily—ease her worries, or gain *some* kind of clarity, or as her mother so often preached, "cultivate that deeper sense of self-awareness."

But the more she tried not to dwell on the Scrolls, the High Priestess, Bessie, Mathis, and her debt to the elementals, the more her chest felt like a balloon being overinflated, ready to burst at any moment.

This bath wasn't working. Not even a little bit.

Maybe rather than try *not* to focus on her (various) issues, she should face them head on. Perhaps she should stealthily check on the High Priestess's progress in finding the stone; judging by the last visit she'd paid her, she was probably very close . . .

Maeve would surely sense her presence, as she always had. She wondered if there was another way, without astral projecting. A way to view her, undetected. Almost like a vision.

And then it dawned on her—she'd nearly forgotten she'd had a vision once before, of her mother's tragic departure note being folded into Seán's wallet. And she, as Bessie, was given the gift of Second Sight. Perhaps in this lifetime, she could still wield it.

Her third eye was her psychic centre. Why not test its limits? It was worth a try.

With her eyelids shut tight, she made as if she was seeing through the centre of her forehead, forcing her eyes to roll upwards inside her head. It was merely a void at first, like staring into a darkened pit, but then a small opening formed, like a hole tearing through a sheet of fabric.

This is new.

The opening gradually grew, until it was large enough for her to step inside; not knowing whether her body was still lying in the bathtub or whether she'd just been transported somewhere else, she stepped over the threshold.

On the other side was the High Priestess, lying in a tent, her body wrapped up in a thick sleeping bag. Mckenna couldn't tell where she was, but the mossy, floral scents reminded her of . . .

Of Scotland. She was in Scotland.

As Mckenna inched closer to get a better look at her neck, from which she'd bet anything dangled her newly acquired stone necklace, she caught a glimpse of a subtle glow emanating from her head. Three green orb-like lights hovered above her—the very same orbs that entered Mckenna's chest while meditating with her mother at the Quiraing during their first lesson.

She put out her hand, and in one swift motion the lights merged into a single shape. This time, she could see every detail of the humanoid's spine-chilling appearance: Its scaly purple skin was unlike anything she'd ever seen, with an odd sheen to it that didn't quite match its coarseness. Its eyes were the most striking feature—large, luminous green globes that blazed like freshly brewed poison, and pupils slit like a cat's.

The ugly thing stood behind the High Priestess, its warped, four-fingered hands cupped around her head. Just when Mckenna was questioning whether the entity could see her, it abruptly swivelled its head in her direction. "You shouldn't be here," it said, its screeching, unearthly voice as cringy as nails on a chalkboard.

She gulped. "What are you doing to her?"

"Ensuring she does not stray."

"Stray from what?"

Laughing, it replied, "From the path we set her on."

The path they set her on? Was her mom right? Were these the dark entities that had been messing with Maeve's head since she discovered the prophecy? "You're brainwashing her."

The thing let out a horrific sound resembling a scoff. "You humans think you are the centre of the universe. You think you are the key to making this planet great, when in actuality, the Earth would thrive without your interference."

"Sounds like you're the one who's interfering. You've been

planting these crazy ideas in her head, haven't you? You made her like this. How many others do you do this to on a daily basis?" Including herself, she thought. All this time, while she weighed the pros and cons of going through with the prophecy, of being responsible for halting the reincarnation of billions of souls, was she being influenced by these assholes?

"I don't plant ideas, I nurture them. *She* is the one who became intrigued by the utopia of the fae's prediction, wherein all beings lived on the same frequency, the same plane of existence—of communicating freely like we once did." There was longing in its voice, but it was far from romantic. "*She* is the one who discovered Bessie Dunlop's prophecy, in connection with the fae's prediction. We simply kept her in line."

"Who's *we*? Who are you?" she shouted.

The thing's arms dropped by its sides, almost robotically, and it turned its unsightly humanoid body towards her. "You are asking too many questions. Leave now. You have interrupted my work enough."

"Maeve!" Mckenna shouted, hoping to snap her out of her state, but the entity was quick to retaliate. What must have been Maeve's chisel levitated from the ground and was aimed directly at her. Fleeing the tent in a panic, she found herself in a thicket of Scottish pines, praying the black hole would swallow her up, fast.

It was nowhere in sight.

She glanced behind her—the chisel was hurtling towards her at full speed. She dodged it, thinking stupidly that learning how to avoid targets would have been a hell of a useful lesson to have in her training, but with every narrow escape it would come back around like a boomerang.

And this is how I'm gonna die. Think, think, think . . .

Something smooth appeared in the palm of her hands. She opened it, and there sat the stone Arethusa gifted her when she and Nissa departed from her home. "*Black onyx. It absorbs negativity and helps the bearer resist negative influences. Think of it as a shield of sorts,*" Arethusa's voice echoed in her head.

In the blink of an eye, the opening reappeared. She could

scarcely make it out in the darkness, hovering a hundred or so yards away. *Yes! Thank you, Arethusa.* Despite not knowing whether any of this was real or not, she'd never run so fast in her life. Whatever plane this was, she had a distinct feeling if she were to die here, she would die for real.

The opening was almost within reach now. Just a few . . . more . . . feet . . .

As something cold and sharp grazed her cheek, she instinctively brushed her fingers against the wound, feeling the warmth of blood. Her eyes travelled upwards—the thing stood barring the black hole, the knife now hovering threateningly above it.

She was stuck. Cornered, with nowhere to escape to . . .

Except chances were, she was not *physically* here. If she could find a way in, she could find a way out. Perhaps this was wishful thinking, perhaps she was losing her mind, but something inside of her incited her to close her eyes and declare aloud, "My soul is free. My soul is free. My soul is free."

Mckenna cautiously opened her eyes. The humanoid still stood in front of the opening, but he looked to be utterly frozen. Suddenly, the chisel clattered to the ground with a metallic thud. She let out a gasp of relief, and the next moment, found herself back in the bathtub, her skin shrivelling from soaking much too long in the now lukewarm water.

"Whoa."

XIV

THE WOLF UNVEILED

That night, Mckenna spoke of the bath incident to no one. Nissa would panic until she cracked, her dads . . . she wouldn't go there, and her mom would think something was seriously wrong with her—most likely reprimand her for exploring magic she knew nothing about.

Was she on the same dark path as Maeve, being influenced by those scaly, ugly beings, with no way of stopping it?

Mckenna sat up on her bed, gazing beyond the window. Light snow fell gracefully against the distant mountains, painting the landscape in a tranquil symphony of white and earthy tones.

She had to tell her mom that Maeve had the stone. That meant she'd discovered their location by now and was headed here . . .

Knock. Knock. Knock.

Mckenna jumped. "Come in."

Abby entered, her hair clipped up, curls cascading around her face, and dark circles casting shadows under her eyes. "Can we have a wee chat?" she said sweetly, taking a seat on the bed.

"Over the past few weeks, I've not been around as much as I'd have liked. I'm so sorry—"

"Oh, Mom, that's okay. I know you've been working day and night on Maeve's spell."

Abby placed a warm hand on Mckenna's leg. "Still, I'm not the best at sharing my attention—your father would agree, I'm sure. When I'm focused and preoccupied, I tend to get . . . consumed. I've let your lessons slip, and I don't want our trust to slip away too." She gave Mckenna a knowing look, as if expecting her to confess something. "I ken you've been anxious, and even more so after the other night. I hoped my bath salt blend would help, but . . ." Mckenna gulped. Of course her mom could sense her angst. "You can tell me anything, swan."

Mckenna took a deep breath. She had to tell her.

"Please don't be mad," Mckenna pleaded before recounting what she'd seen in the bath. When she finished, she felt both relieved and afraid to be scolded. Perhaps she should tell her about the green orbs that struck her chest during their first outdoor lesson and Nutmeg the *harry coo* some other time.

Abby seemed to be caught somewhere between relief and concern. "Thank you for telling me. I've never encountered such beings, but it confirms what I believed about Maeve all along. Her mind is being toyed with."

"And, Mom . . . she has the stone."

Abby nodded. "I felt it the moment she placed it around her neck." Mckenna should've guessed it wasn't news to her. "The spell is nearly done. I'll be ready for her."

"You can't think you'll do this all on your own . . . ?"

"You'll stay as far away from Maeve as possible, do you understand? Trust me," she added, though Mckenna couldn't shake the feeling she was in way over her head.

When news spread that the High Priestess had secured the stone and was en route, the atmosphere in the inn was bleak, to say the least. Abby, ever the optimist, worked diligently to buoy everyone's spirits, assuring them they still had days, at least—the return trek from the stone's hidden location to a town or main road would span around seven days, a journey she vividly remembered from the time she embarked on it with Esme, all those years ago.

"We're just supposed to sit around and wait for her to blast through that door?" Seán said during breakfast the following morning.

"I've got it under control, Seán," Abby asserted.

"Still so cryptic, after all these years. You ought to include us in your plan—"

"Dad," Mckenna interjected, "we need to trust her." She exchanged a nod with her mother, who beamed back at her.

Over the next few days, Cillian and Mathis seemed to be mending fences. When Mathis wasn't out for a walk with Cillian or hanging around at his guest house, he was holed up like a recluse in his room, and at dinner, he would barely utter two words.

Mckenna didn't trust him one bit. He was holding something back, she knew he was, and it didn't help that he would scurry away like a woodland critter whenever she approached him. She'd been seeing a lot less of Cillian these days, too, with him being whisked away by Mathis at any given moment. She wasn't jealous, per se. Just suspicious.

Seán and Andre cornered Mckenna one afternoon to ask what she thought about moving to Scotland. "We need a bit of good news around here. What do you think of moving to Edinburgh?" Seán said brightly. "Andre's old professor's been in touch, and it sounds like there's going to be an open lecturer position at Edinburgh Law School for the spring term. Plus, it's somewhere we can start over, be close to your mum too."

Andre's face spread into a wide grin. He looked more excited than he had about work in a long time.

The thought of living closer to Abby elated her, as did the idea of staying in Scotland. She'd felt more at home here than she ever did in Massachusetts. "I think that'd be kind of amazing," she replied. "But . . . what about Nissa?"

"Did you think you could get rid of me that easy?" Nissa

said, emerging from the hallway, and squishing her small body between Seán and Andre. "Mind if you share your family with me a little while longer?"

Despite the impending doom that hung in the air, Mckenna could have been floating on a cloud in that moment. Fighting back tears, she said, "Niss, we're already your family."

Her bright blue eyes glistening, Nissa gave her a playful shove.

"We're glad you feel that way," Andre said, "because . . ." Without warning, he and Seán threw themselves to their knees. Shooting one another a giddy, knowing look, they each grabbed hold of one of Nissa's hands.

"Nissa Febland," Seán began.

"Will you allow us to formally adopt you?" Andre asked.

Nissa gasped in the most delightful and jovial way, yanking her hands out of their grasp to cover her gaping mouth. As she lowered her hands back into Seán and Andre's palms, she said with utmost sincerity, "I would be honoured."

Her heart ready to burst, Mckenna darted towards them and threw herself into a group hug she'd only ever seen on *Full House*. "How did you do it?" Mckenna asked, pulling back slightly.

"Turns out your dad's a big fat liar," Seán said, pinching Andre's cheek.

"Am *not*," Andre shot back, narrowing his eyes at Seán. "I called the agency in charge of Nissa's file, and they were ecstatic she would be out of the foster system; the sad truth is, teens almost never get adopted."

"Don't beat around the bush, luv—what did you tell them?"

"The truth . . . mostly. That I'm Nissa's best friend's father and would love nothing more than to welcome her into our family."

Seán cleared his throat, adding, "And that you're happily married to a librarian named Cindy."

Mckenna and Nissa burst out laughing.

"Hey, hey, it worked, didn't it? They would've shut us down immediately if I had told them we were in a same-sex relationship."

Seán swore under his breath, just as the greenhouse door swung open. "Did she say yes?" Abby sang.

"She said yes!" Seán shouted, throwing Nissa over his shoulders.

Abby rested both hands on her chest, tears rolling down her cheeks.

Bessie's home was surrounded. Half the town, along with dozens of neighbouring townspeople who'd attended the fair, including some nobles who had come to trust Bessie in her counsel, were gathered in support of her, fighting off a group of court-ordered men.

"Madam Elizabeth Dunlop," a pitchy, self-important voice bellowed outside her door. "By order of the High Court of Judiciary, you are hereby accused of sorcery, witchcraft, and incantation, with invocation of spirits of the devil, continuing in familiarity with them at all such times as you thought expedient, dealing with charms, and abusing the people with devilish craft of sorcery aforesaid."

"SHE'S DONE NO SUCH THING, YOU BOGGIN' BAMPOT!" one neighbour shouted.

Bessie and Thom sat in front of the hearth, staring into the wild flames.

"I am deeply sorry about your husband, Lizbeth. His actions are unforgivable."

Bessie's laugh was bitter. "Would you have stayed betrothed to me, amid all of this?"

"You know the answer to that."

Even with the utter chaos outside of these walls, Bessie's stomach fluttered with warmth. "You must ken, Thom, I am grateful to you."

His soft brown eyes were imbued with self-loathing. "Why? Had I not sought you out in that cove, you would have been—"

"Unfulfilled," she finished. She held his gaze, leaning into him, until a banging on the door caused her to jerk back.

"Mrs. Dunlop! The court demands you come out *at once* . . ."

"I feel utterly helpless," Thom uttered, his breath reaching her ear.

"You've been gallant, Thom. There is no more you can do. I am prepared to meet my fate."

"Won't you reconsider—?"

"Running off to Elfame would be but an escape. They will only respond vengefully, by seeking out others like me."

Thom shook his head stubbornly. "This is not the manner it was meant to be."

"But it is," Bessie said, as sure of herself as her cattle-healing elixir. She placed a hand on his cheek. "I was meant to see what I saw. And I am meant to die for it."

"Please, come with me."

"I do not belong in Elfame, Thom—"

"Not Elfame. Somewhere else."

Bessie cocked her head. "Thom, is there something . . . ?"

The front door was blasted open, and five men in black robes and white perukes poured in. Thom stood up as they seized her arms. "Unhand her!"

Bessie's eyes implored him to let her go. *It's alright*, she mouthed. *I love you.*

I'll find you again, he mouthed back, and watched as Bessie was dragged away to her ill fate.

Mckenna awoke with a tear-stained face, the morning sun peeking through a small crack in her blackout curtains. She knew only too well the tragedy that unfolded after Bessie was hauled out of her home; she remembered her seventeenth-birthday nightmare like it was yesterday.

She banished the image from her thoughts, unwilling to relive the most awful, inhumane, and excruciatingly painful moment of all of her lives.

Thomas Reid. He'd been the love of *that* life. Her chest sat heavy and yet empty all at once, the loss from lifetimes ago lingering like it had never left.

And now I'm up, she thought, heaving a heavy sigh. She kicked off her blanket and headed downstairs, Scott Cunningham's book tucked under her arm. Perhaps some good old fashioned magical wisdom by the fire would help cure her melancholic soul.

The fire was already crackling away when she stepped into the living room.

"Mathis," she said, not doing well to shield the irritation in her voice. He was doing some reading of his own in Andre's armchair. He looked younger, and oddly human.

Mathis shot to his feet. "I apologize. I thought everyone would be asleep for a while."

"That's okay, you can stay. I was just coming to get a drink of water."

Mathis gestured to the book under her arm, grinning shyly. "Please don't leave on my account. I was thinking of going for an early morning walk anyway."

Mckenna blocked his path. "I insist," she said firmly, "make yourself comfortable." In that fleeting moment, the air between them thickened.

"How kind of you," he finally acquiesced.

"Splendid," she replied, trying not to sound overly mocking. "I'll make some coffee."

Mathis carried on reading, and once the coffee was ready, she did the same, her back turned towards him on the adjacent couch. Though she wasn't sure what point she was making, she was adamant on making it.

They read in silence for a stretch, neither daring to admit their discomfort, until Mathis broke the silence. "How are you enjoying that?"

Caught by surprise, she replied hoarsely, "It's great." She took a gulp of coffee. "Informative."

"I imagine your magic must have improved greatly since being under your mother's wing."

Tired of twisting her neck, she turned to face him. "I guess. I'm not so sure. I still feel like I have no idea what I'm doing."

Without looking up, he replied, "Not to resort to a cliché, but practice truly is paramount. You already possess all the knowledge you need."

"You sound like my mother."

"It's true. Your abilities stem from your past incarnations. You know, meditating can help you remember."

He flipped a page. She nodded, thinking of her and Cillian's sessions. "I've never been great at meditating, but Cillian's helped a lot."

A shadow of concern crossed his face. "I am sure you're aware Cillian's mentor was not an ethical one, not like Abigail. If I may, I do caution you when it comes to heeding his advice."

"You may *not*, actually. And you don't have to be so formal with me, Mathis. Drop the nice guy act."

He closed the book on his lap, leaning forward. *"The nice guy act?* I assure you, I'm not putting on a charade."

"Who even talks like that? *A charade,*" she mocked, mimicking his dapper British accent. As anger swelled within her, Mathis's armchair slid across the living room, coming to an abrupt halt right in front of her. She'd hardly registered what she'd done when she fumed, "Look, Mathis, why don't you tell me what your angle really is? You obviously can't stay on this plane or dimension or whatever for too long, so why did you come back?"

He leaned in closer. "Do you really think me a threat? I thought you wanted me here, for Cillian and me to find a truce."

She was suddenly terribly aware of how loudly she was breathing. "I did. I do . . . I don't know what to think. There's something not right about you showing up here. And I have good instincts."

"Without question. Though, not when it comes to my brother."

"What does *that* mean?"

Mathis hesitated, staring at his feet. Mckenna wasn't having this. She raised his chin up so that her eyes pierced his. "Say it."

This time, he didn't avert his gaze; she tried not to get entranced by it. "Cillian's heart is in the right place—it always has been. But he's not to be trusted."

"I do trust Cillian," she stated, though not without a hint of reservation.

"I appreciate that you trust him. My brother's intentions are good. Righteous, even. He wants what is best for you, for the world—he truly does. However . . ."

"However?"

"He is sorely misguided."

"Man, you Brits really have trouble spitting things out."

"He has been in the service of the High Priestess since you met him. She is the one who sent him to you."

Her mind and body froze, and she suddenly felt cold, like she'd slipped through a sheet of ice and sank into its chilling depths. "No. Th-that's not true." She hated that she couldn't stop her voice from trembling. "She was his mentor at first, but he tracked me down when he found out about her scheme."

"Mckenna, he was complicit."

"He was . . . playing me?" *No. It couldn't be.*

"I failed my first assignment. My purpose was to guide young Cillian, to divert him from the path that would lead to the High Priestess, but alas, it made no difference. Still, he fell under her influence. I've returned to make amends and to caution you, Lizbeth, that his influence has set you on a dark course."

"What did you just call me?"

"Mckenna," he said quickly, running a hand through his hair. "Naturally, I know of the prophecy, of your soul's past. It was a mere slip-up."

She was on her feet now, looming over him. "We've met before, haven't we?"

He sprang to his feet too, as though it would redeem him in some way. "I, erm, I'm not certain what you mean."

And then it hit her. "Wait." She reached for a pen and sticky note on the end table, then proceeded to unscramble the letters in his name:

MATHIS ODER

THOMAS REID

It was an anagram.

"You were Thomas Reid."

Nodding slowly, he whispered, "I was."

"I dreamt of us last night. We were in love."

"I regret it. As your guide, that was not supposed to happen."

"My guide?"

"Yes. I was your guide in your lifetime as Elizabeth, however—"

"You broke the Council's rules, didn't you?"

His sigh carried a sense of embarrassment, shame. "I knew that in another life—in this life—yours and Cillian's paths would cross. I had to see you again, before . . ."

"Before the prophecy came true. Before I'd trap billions of souls in limbo or whatever, and he'd help me do it."

Mathis reached for her hand, but she pulled it away.

"Don't. You and your brother, you're both liars. I don't know what they teach you up in space school, but coming to Earth to manipulate a Wise One, *the* Wise One, having her fall for you, then showing up centuries later just to completely ignore her, then dropping the biggest goddam truth bomb possibly ever— not cool."

"Mckenna, I'm sorry."

"Go to hell, Mathis. Or whatever the equivalent of that is for you."

She stormed out through the back door, then broke into a run. And like a chaotic jazz symphony, wherein the notes didn't feel the least bit melodious, the pieces finally reached a crescendo;

it all came together: Cillian successfully led her to complete each and every task on the first Scroll. How could she have been so stupid? So naïve?

Her soul's beginning, she need discover—this had to be about Newgrange. What she'd felt in that tomb . . . her soul soaring, belonging, perhaps to that very time and place. She remembered he supposedly had a delegate meeting in the Boyne Valley. He was the one who'd suggested a tour while he "subjected himself to hours of fruitless small talk". Unbelievable.

A darkness within she'll ken e'ermore. Alice Kyteler. Discovering Mckenna was once the cruelest woman in Ireland proved, if anything, she had a darkness inside of her that most people didn't. Cillian brought her to Kilkenny—for a "conference," he'd said.

But 'tis the horse's vision of Earth Mother
That lights her path to days of yore

What else could this be other than the vision Eachna shared with her at the lake at Kylemore Abbey? Another one of Cillian's "meetings."

This was so carefully curated. It disgusted her.

She was a goddam puppet.

Her legs carried her down towards Cillian's guest house. The moment she spotted his hideous yellow rental car in the front lot, something inside of her burst. Her right hand was suddenly raised in front of her, her palm pointed towards the bumper.

CRASH.

Thousands of pieces of glass flew to the ground and into the wind, leaving nothing but a large gaping hole in place of the rear window. She screamed, not in shock or fear, but in pure, unadulterated anger.

She hadn't even seen Cillian emerge from the guesthouse, but suddenly, he was standing in front of her. "*What the hell?*" he bellowed.

Mckenna wasted no time. "YOU LIAR!" It was her voice that shook the nearby trees, not the wind. "You were working for her all along. You *manipulated* me, Cillian! Mathis is right. You're *really* messed up."

"Mathis? Wait, he told you this?"

"What does it matter who told me? It's the truth, isn't it?"

"Lass, you have to let me expl—"

"*Don't* call me that."

"Listen—please, *please*, listen to me. You yourself are questioning all of it, aren't you? You're wondering if Maeve's mad at all, right? I did too. I believed in what she was doing, and I still do. But I didn't lie to you about that."

"You deliberately took me to those places, Cillian." She kept her voice eerily steady. "You lied about everything else."

"In the end, I left her! I came after her to save you *from* her."

"You knew Eachna would rise this year from the lake—every seven years," she continued. "You *knew* you had to take me to Newgrange . . . *'Her soul's beginnings she need discover.'* Because it all ends there, doesn't it?" she said, realizing it as the words left her lips. *Whence the ancient passage tomb stands, united their magic, and so shall it be.*

He was visibly shaking. "Mckenna, you and I both know it's for the greater good. I would never intentionally hurt you."

"You knew Maeve would. Before you knew me, you hopped on her screwed-up bandwagon and worked me *good*. Once I found my mom, you were gonna let her have me, like I was nothing," she spat. "You were gonna let her hypnotize us to use our powers and fulfill the prophecy."

"I'm sorry about how this started." His voice cracked. "But our world, whether you like it or not, is headed for destruction. Do I regret partnering with a mad woman? Yes. But I wouldn't have known about the prophecy and how to save the natural world if I hadn't met the High Priestess. And I wouldn't have met you. This was all meant to happen, don't you see?" He reached out to touch her, but she held her hand up in front of her.

"Oh, I see everything super clearly. I see you're a liar. And the world's biggest coward." A wolf, to be more precise. A false friend.

Wolves. That was the crux of it all. Eliminating wolves might provide a temporary boost to livestock, but in the long run, it would surely disrupt the delicate balance of nature. It was akin to erasing souls; a fleeting benefit for nature, but what then? How would the world adapt and progress? Abby had been right from the start. How had Mckenna allowed herself to be swayed into considering the prophecy a viable option? She grew increasingly convinced that she, too, had fallen victim to those grotesque humanoids who had tampered with her mind. All along, a sinister darkness had been infiltrating her very bones, permeating her thoughts.

"Does it help if I say I don't care about any of it anymore? I just want you." She could feel his heart tearing, weeping. "I'm in love with you, Mckenna."

"I love you too," she heard herself say. She hated herself for it, but it was true. "But I can't trust you. I should never have trusted you."

Despite the ache in her heart and sarsen stones sitting in her chest, she turned on her heel and sprinted for the inn. She needed to get away from Cillian before she gave in, like she always did, and wanted nothing more than to confide in Nissa.

"Nissa!" she shouted while dashing up the inn stairs, then burst into Nissa's bedroom. Her bed was unmade, which was unlike her. After checking every bedroom, she made her way back down to the landing.

"Nissa!" she called, checking every bedroom, until she reached the landing at the bottom of the stairs. Where *was* she?

"Swan, there you are," Seán said from behind the stove, an already-dressed Andre sipping coffee at the kitchen counter. "Been out for a walk with Nissa? Can't find Mathis anywhere either."

"No." She hesitated. "I was, um, alone. And I'm not sure Mathis is coming back." She'd certainly made him feel unwelcome. Before Seán could ask, Mckenna said, "You haven't seen Nissa? I was just gonna check the faery tree."

"She's not there," Abby said, coming through the front door. "I didn't see her come downstairs this morning, and there was no old coffee sitting in the French press, so I went looking for her."

Mckenna looked around at their worried faces. Like her, they were thinking the worst.

XV

A FAE AND A FELON

Nissa woke up with her hands tied tightly behind her back, sprawled atop a stone bridge, the sound of water rushing below. She was staring into the ice-blue eyes of a man she didn't recognize; he had dusty-blond hair and an unkempt goatee she'd only ever seen on old film villains.

She felt lightheaded. Had she been knocked out? "Wh-what's going on?"

The man smiled. "I finally found you, *ducky*," he said in a funny British accent.

Ducky? Only her grandmother, Arethusa, called her that. "Who are you?" She wiggled her hands behind her, her skin searing from the rope. "Why are you doing this? I don't have money—"

The man let out a shrill laugh. "Not the sharpest one, are you? Just as stupid as your mum."

Her heart sank into her gut. *Oh no. It couldn't be.* "You're my . . . you're my . . . ?"

"Dear ol' dad, that's right," said Simon Fage. The wanted drug lord. The man who killed her mother. The lunatic who wanted her dead. "I've been looking for you ever since that old hag shipped you off to America."

Don't show him you're scared. "How did you find me?"

Simon pulled a rolled-up newspaper from his back pocket and held it up in front of her. There Nissa was, in *The Oban Times* amongst the Loch Ness protestors. Below the photo, the caption read: *Logan Macleod (left) leads efforts to ban fishing in Loch Ness, supported by American tourist Nissa Febland (right).*

"Wish you were more careful, now, don't you?"

Nissa gulped.

"It was easy to track you down after that, *ducky.*" Hearing him call her Arethusa's affectionate nickname made her entire body squirm. "You and your friends are twits. You left a trail of breadcrumbs, you did. Even the bird at the car yard knew you were headed to Skye. You must be a talker, like your bloody nan," he spat, hatred etched across his thin face. "Both from the same lot, there's no question—faery folk. I never wanted you, and I was right not to; my life started to crumble to bits the *second* you came home from the hospital."

Arethusa warned her that her father thought her soul had been swapped for a faery's, and that was what he believed brought him so much bad luck—Simon's once-loyal men betraying him, the sudden loss of the fortune he'd built, a mole within his organization.

"I'm not a changeling," she stated, keeping her voice strong. "You're a rotten person, and you got what you deserved."

"SHUT IT! I know what you are."

"You're delusional. You need some serious help."

"Watch yourself . . ."

Psst! a girlish, preppy voice called in her ear. Nissa looked frantically around the wooded area. Had the voice been inside her head?

You're not alone. We're here for you—and we thank you for visiting us every day! We very much enjoyed the honey.

Oh my gosh, are you the fae? I've been wanting to speak with you for so long!

The voice giggled, and a different, male one replied. *We are. You're one of us, you know.*

A changeling?

More giggles. *Of course not! We didn't have to do any swapping. You left Elfame all on your own, but you won't be remembering that, of course. That was part of the bargain you made to live a human life.*

Her heart soared. She was a fae once too, like Abigail. *Bargain? I don't understand.*

You will, the first voice replied giddily. *And don't let this puny man frighten you! You were the boldest, bravest fae of our land, Nissa. That's never left you.*

Despite the horrifying circumstances, she smiled.

Seán, Andre, Abby, and Mckenna held hands around the kitchen table, a quirky map of the Isle of Skye lying flat on top, with odd-named places and cartoon illustrations marking various spots. Maeve's necklace was laced between Abby's fingers as she dowsed, swinging the stone over each region. She swept it over the inn first, slowly letting the stone drift around Uig without missing so much as a parkette.

Andre eyed the map with skepticism. "Is this really the only map you have, Abigail?"

"It is, and it never lets me down."

Mckenna's patience was wearing thin. "Come *on*," she shouted, banging her fist on the tabletop.

"You've got to be calmer, swan, or it won't work," Abby said.

Andre squeezed Mckenna's hand. "It's true, we've got this. We just need to focus."

"Yeah, your dad's a pro dowser now," Seán said with a short laugh, but his voice was trembling. Mckenna looked up; he was staring at the map intensely, tears swimming in his eyes. She couldn't think of a time she'd seen him this afraid.

A few moments passed. Nothing.

"I think I need to do it," Mckenna declared. "Please," she added desperately.

Abby nodded, and dropped the necklace into Mckenna's palm. Mckenna began again around the inn, letting it hover over the trail to the faery tree, around the woods, and then back down . . . further south . . . then further west, until the stone affixed to a spot on the map with the Gaelic words *Beul-Ath nan Tri Allt* stamped over a small winged creature peeping below a stone bridge.

"The Ford of the Three Burns," Abby proclaimed. "That's at least thirty minutes from here."

Seán darted for the door. "Not if I'm driving."

Mckenna threw the necklace around her neck. "Let's go."

Simon Fage held his pistol to Nissa's head.

Buy time! As much as you can, the male fae squealed.

Mustering up every ounce of courage her small body could hold, she said, "You're really going to shoot your own daughter? Isn't that a little soap-opera dramatic?"

"I said shut it, girl."

"If you're willing to go to jail for this, that's your prerogative. But for someone who's complained all I've done is give you bad juju, I wouldn't let my death make things worse for you, too."

"That's where you're wrong, ducky. Your death will be my resurgence."

"Okay there, Captain Hook—whatever crappy luck you ran into, you brought it upon yourself. You never wanted me, I get it. I got in the way of you and my mother's Bonnie and Clyde fantasy. But she *did* want me. More than she wanted you." His nostrils flared, and for the first time, he looked vulnerable, anxious, like a boy who'd been told there was no Santa Claus. Like someone who'd realized he'd been lying to himself for half his life. "And you couldn't bear it, could you?"

She's said seven words too many.

Simon pressed the pistol against her forehead. "Keep talking, changeling. I dare you."

She shut her eyes tightly, her heart thudding so hard she could feel it in her ears. With every passing second, her mind raced with events from the past few months, of finally feeling like she had a sister, like she had a family who loved her. Who wanted her. She could only pray this would not be the end, that she would not meet her fate at the hands of a psychopath. After the enchanting journey she'd been on, she'd hoped for a much more meaningful death than this.

As she held her breath, the world around her faded, leaving only the chilling sensation of the metal against her skin.

Mckenna and her three parents peered through the trees at the goateed nutcase who held a gun against Nissa's head. She lay sprawled across a stone footbridge with a stream flowing beneath, her hands bound behind her back.

"Who the hell is this lunatic?" Seán hissed.

In that moment, Mckenna knew. "That's her biological father, Simon Fage. I'll explain later—we have to do something *right now*."

"We," Seán began, pointing at the lot of them, "aren't doing a thing. But we," he gestured to himself, Andre, and Abby, "are. Stay here and don't move. I mean it," he ordered when Mckenna opened her mouth to protest.

The second Seán stepped out of the woods, Simon pivoted, pointing the gun directly at Seán's chest. As Mckenna instinctively took a step forward, Andre barred her with his arm, mouthing, *Shush*.

Seán threw his hands in the air. "Calm down, calm down, I'm not armed. But I wouldn't do that if I were you," he said coolly, slowly stepping onto the footbridge.

"And why not?"

"You've no idea how many witnesses you've got, mate."

Simon's eyes darted around the trees. "I don't see no one."

"Andre, luv, don't move, but show our friend here that you're around."

Andre cuckooed, feigning a bird call.

"See? Let the girl go."

Simon laughed. "I don't know who you are, or why you think you've got the upper hand, but guess what, *mate*? I'm the one with the gun." He cocked it, and Seán dove up the bridge as the shot fired.

He hit the ground.

"SEÁN!" Abby and Andre screamed.

"DAD!" As Mckenna made to sprint to him, Andre grabbed her arm, then threw her a definitive don't-you-dare-move look before running to his aid, Abby by his side.

Simon shifted his aim between Andre and Abby. "Who've we here, the bloody Brady Bunch? Ah, ah, ah, I wouldn't move another muscle."

Mckenna was left paralyzed, transfixed by the horrific sight unfolding before her: Andre's blood-soaked hands were pressed against Seán's abdomen, and Abby's entire body was trembling with terror. Mckenna could feel all of it; her fear was not of Simon, nor even of dying, but of losing the family that had only just been returned to her. That had filled her heart more in these past months than the entirety of the last seventeen years. Mckenna had come to look up to her mother as a source of strength and reassurance, but seeing her so vulnerable, defenceless, made Mckenna more frightened than she ever was of the ghost of Petronella De Meath.

"Please . . ." Nissa pleaded. "Take me. It's me you want, isn't it?"

The seconds ticked by. Mckenna looked around for something—anything—that could get them out of this.

Abby looked over her shoulder at Mckenna, like she'd finally awoken from her shocked state.

The elementals, Mckenna mouthed, gesturing to her surroundings. To her surprise, Abby nodded.

Simon screwed up his face, steadying his aim on Abby. "What are you looking at back there?" His eyes flickered to the precise spot where Mckenna stood.

Abby broke into a run. Simon fired, narrowly missing her as she dove behind the Scottish pine tree where Mckenna stood, landing at her feet. Breathless, she reached for her daughter's hand, pulling her to the ground. "Earth."

That was all her mother needed to say. Their four hands flat on the element beneath them, they beckoned it, and the creatures that embodied it. Mckenna thought of the sweet brownie who carved the Old Man of Storr, of the wood nymphs whose presence she could feel in their wake, too modest to reveal themselves, and of course, of the myriad faeries, who she could sense so strongly had been inhabiting the footbridge and stream that ran below it for centuries.

"Beings of the earth," Mckenna whispered. "We invoke thee."

The ground beneath them shook violently, and through the gap between the trees, she witnessed the terrible scene taking shape: Simon lost his footing. Andre lunged, knocking the gun out of his hand, but Simon was quick to retaliate, running head first into Andre's chest and tackling him against the bridge's stone wall. Nissa screamed—Andre's torso was hanging over the bridge, underneath which lay a blanket of jagged rocks below the shallow waters.

If Mckenna didn't act now, her dad's head was going to crack open. "Mom!" she called desperately. "What do we do?"

Abby muttered something, but Mckenna wasn't listening. Approaching behind her was a tall bombshell of a woman with the most commanding presence she'd ever come across: the High Priestess. And there, dangling from her neck, was the new stone carved from the legendary Misgaun Medb, glinting in the afternoon sun.

Maeve pressed a finger on her lips. *Shh*, she mouthed, and before Mckenna could decide whether to oblige or scream, Maeve blew gently into the wind.

Simon was thrown backwards hard, hurtling across the bridge

until he collided with a massive tree trunk some dozen feet away. He lay motionless on the ground, his body limp, blood trickling from a wound on the back of his head. Mckenna couldn't help but vividly recall sending her wren friend flying into Jared's skull in the schoolyard, yet again in Nissa's defence. Despite the sheer gravity of this moment, she nearly smiled at the poetic justice of it all—because she was not sorry for that bully then, and she was certainly not sorry for this bully now.

At first, Abby, Andre, and Nissa turned their gazes towards Mckenna with expressions of shock and awe, their wide-eyed reactions triggered by the apparent belief that Mckenna was responsible for propelling Simon to his tragic fate. But once the High Priestess emerged from the trees, all eyes were on her.

"Get up," she spat, delivering a swift kick to something hidden behind a sizable shrub. A groan echoed from the ground, and a young man tumbled sideways onto the earth.

"Cillian!" Mckenna shouted.

His mouth was duct-taped shut and his arms tied behind his back. Emotions swirled within Mckenna like a stormy tempest: love, hatred, guilt, fear.

"Maeve," Abby said, standing up. "He's just a lad."

"Abigail, you look well," Maeve said, her expression almost dreamy. "I've not had the chance to punish him for betraying me. I'm sorry, my dear friend—he's coming with me."

"Let him go, Maeve!" Andre yelled. "You're not a killer, are you?"

The High Priestess smiled at his words. "Pleasure to see you again. I do hope your partner is alright," she added with a nod at Seán's unconscious body. "How about I make you lot a deal? My former apprentice comes with me, *but* I will happily hand him back to you unharmed tomorrow. Meet me well before the sun rises."

"We will do no such—" Andre began.

"Or he dies."

Silence fell.

"Oh, and just the Wise One and her *twin flame*," she said, over-articulating and directing her gaze towards Abby.

Abby stared unblinkingly back. "Where?"

"The ancient passage tomb, of course. Surely, *she's* figured it out by now." She nodded towards Mckenna. The others looked from Maeve to Mckenna in bewilderment. "And I want my necklace back—the original. It was a gift, after all," she added before grabbing Cillian by the collar and dragging him away.

XVI

THE ANCIENT PASSAGE TOMB

DECEMBER 20, 1991

Seán's gunshot wound had gone untreated for too long. According to the ER doctor, he had experienced internal bleeding in his abdomen, leading to a perforation in his intestine and resulting in an infection.

The wait was unbearable. After what felt like an eternity, Mckenna, Nissa, and Abby sprang from their seats as they caught sight of Andre entering through the hospital doors and into the fluorescent-lit waiting room. "His surgery's tonight," Andre informed them. "I'm going to stay with him. You guys should go home."

"I'm not going anywhere," Mckenna and Nissa said in unison.

Andre sighed, looking too defeated to argue. "You need rest, Nissa. You were just treated for shock, and your father . . ."

"He was not my father."

Abby gave her shoulder an affectionate squeeze, and Mckenna took her hand. "He definitely wasn't."

Andre pulled Nissa into a hug. "You're right."

"The timing is dreadful, but . . ." Abby began, her forehead scrunched up in concern. "Maeve's transformation spell—it's ready."

Mckenna gasped. "Since when?"

"It's a bit difficult to put into words. It's like a puzzle. I've got all the pieces, save for one—been wracking my brain for weeks trying to sort it out."

"It's something Maeve said, isn't it?" Mckenna said, attuning to her mother's thoughts.

Abby nodded.

Nissa crossed her arms, looking from Abby to Mckenna. "I don't follow."

"I haven't been completely honest with you all," Abby said, inviting them to sit while she paced. "So much can go wrong, and, oh, I didn't want to burden any of you."

"You can tell us, Mom."

Abby took a deep breath. "Banishing part of Maeve's consciousness to another plane requires opening a portal first."

"A portal?" Nissa said incredulously. "Like an actual *portal*?"

Andre's jaw dropped. "That's really possible?"

Mckenna was getting *Star Trek* vibes again. "Wow, um okay. And what's the dangerous part?" She wondered if it was just as taboo as stumbling upon a farmstead in the 1950s.

"Aye," Abby said. "It needs to be swift—open, recite the incantation, close—meaning it calls for precision. We cannot predict what might come through from the other side."

"Yep, that's a terrifying thought," Mckenna said resolutely.

"There's more," Abby continued. "Opening a portal cannot be done just anywhere. Not only must the spell be cast at a spot that is *deeply* rooted in magic—I'm talking centuries' worth—but the spellcaster must have a strong connection with the place. A place that will not reject the magic being conjured."

Mckenna's voice dropped to a whisper. "The ancient passage tomb."

Nissa's gaze darted from mother to daughter. "Someone explain, please!"

"Newgrange," Mckenna stated simply. She remembered how it nearly left her breathless; how in awe she was of its alignment to the sun; how unique its spiral markings were; how her spirit quite literally wanted to soar, seemingly intertwined with the very stones that held it in place . . . The connection Mckenna held with it was undeniable.

Newgrange, she was certain, was moulded by magic itself.

"Mom, I have to tell you something. I know what the Scottish Scrolls say—"

"I ken," Abby interjected. In that moment, her amber eyes lost their glow.

Mckenna's heart plummeted. "How?"

"Ever since you dreamt it, swan. That day, you'd been thinking about it nonstop. I sensed your angst and . . . forgive me, but I snooped." She retrieved a neatly folded piece of paper in her coat pocket. "I found the paper you'd scribbled the Scrolls on in your room and copied them down."

Mckenna wasn't angry; rather, she felt foolish. "I should have told you right away. I was just seriously freaked out and . . . confused." Confused about which side she was on.

"I understand, swan." She rubbed Mckenna's arm. "Anyway, I've been deciphering the Scrolls ever since. There are many ancient passage tombs in Ireland, and several in Scotland. I had no way of narrowing them down. It wasn't until Maeve spoke that I realized you must've been to one."

"Yes, I can't believe I never mentioned it. The feeling I had at Newgrange . . . I have no words, really."

Abby placed a hand over her heart. "Well, then that kind of connection is just what our spell needs."

Mckenna wanted to bang her head against the wall. If she'd been honest, the spell would have been ready sooner. "I should've told you about going to Newgrange, too. I didn't realize it was so important!"

Nissa held her hand up. "Hang on, hang on. How does Maeve know which passage tomb it is?"

Mckenna had a theory. "Esme believes that Maeve found out what the Scottish Scrolls said when she forced Mom into a past life regression while she was pregnant with me—um, that's like a hypnosis session to remember a previous life," Mckenna added to Andre and Nissa. "Esme's theory is that during one of those sessions, she was able to tap into one of my past life memories."

Andre sat back down. "Before you were even born?"

Mckenna nodded. "And if she could do that, my guess is that she went even farther back to discover which tomb my soul has a history with. A connection with."

Abby nodded. "Exactly. The thing now is, going to Newgrange would also put us in grave danger. If we don't execute this perfectly, Maeve will have us exactly where she wants us. You and I—twin flames, the Wise One and her creator—united in the ancient passage tomb."

After a long silence, Nissa spoke first. "I'm coming."

Mckenna turned to face her friend, then placed her hands on her shoulders. "Nissa, I love you, but that's not happening."

"Kenna, Kenna, Kenna . . ." she said, shaking her head and making a clicking noise with her tongue. "When are you going to realize that we're a package deal, you and me?"

Truer words had never been spoken. From the very start of this journey, it was her and Nissa against the world, a cliché she embraced wholeheartedly. Her odds of triumph were destined to be greater with her best friend at her side. Just as it had always been.

Mckenna longed for nothing more than to end this battle for souls. She understood now—humans needed one another in order for their souls to evolve. Where would she be without Nissa? No, souls couldn't remain aimlessly adrift in the shadows of dark matter. They needed to reunite with purpose, perpetually returning to aid each other's progression, to resonate on a collective higher plane. To ascend, and ultimately merge into one—like her and Nissa's bond. Without a doubt, this was the reason their thoughts occasionally melded together.

Was this unity consciousness?

There was one thing Mckenna couldn't leave behind. "What about Dad?"

Andre, who'd been sitting in silence, his forehead pressed against his folded hands, finally spoke. "Your father is as strong as he is stubborn. He'll come out of that surgery tougher than ever. There's nothing more you can do here. When you do return, our Edinburgh plan is still on." He smiled in spite of the fear in his eyes, then glanced up at Abby. "I trust you'll bring my girls back safe."

Abby wrapped her arms around Mckenna and Nissa's shoulders. "You have my word. We leave tonight and arrive before the crack of dawn; I've no doubt Maeve will keep her word if we don't make it on time." Mckenna's being filled with dread at the realization that Cillian's survival hinged on them. "It'll be a long drive, and sunrise is 8:58 a.m. in the Boyne Valley."

DECEMBER 21, 1991

The High Priestess's houseboat swayed gently in the River Boyne, her favourite spot in all of Ireland. It called to her like no other place. Irish myth said that it was created by the goddess Boann, and while people only believed this to be a tale, she knew it to be true; Boann's life force was all over these waters. Maeve always admired Boann for following her heart, even when forbidden by her husband, the god Nechtan. Defying his orders, Boann approached the magical Well of Segais, challenging its powers by walking around it counter-clockwise, or *tuathal*, as the Irish would say. The well's response was a violent one—the waters rose up cruelly, rushing over Boann and whisking her off to sea. She drowned in the process, but the impact of her actions was most beautiful, for the River Boyne was forged. It was because of her sacrifice that nature thrived in this region. The magic in these waters was ever-present.

Behind Maeve, Cillian coughed. She'd nearly forgotten he was there, tied to the stern.

Maeve rolled her eyes, then walked over to him. "Here," she said, pouring water into his mouth. She held it in place as he gulped it down in one go.

"They'll come for me, you know," he said, his breath heaving.

"You'd better hope they do, or I'll truly have no use for you, will I?"

The day had finally come—the winter solstice. Everything she'd worked for, albeit with some help from the boy, would come to pass. As a gesture of gratitude, Gaia would bestow an abundance of power upon her, allowing her to harness all of the elemental magic she desired, without any debts to repay. Pravadi had seen it herself.

"I know what you're thinking," Cillian said, his words barely audible in the December wind. "But the Mother Goddess isn't so forgiving."

He knew her well, she had to admit. "You should be happy, Hayes. Proud. You believed in this initiative once before; you even devoted your thesis to the notion that humanity is actively destroying the planet! You wished for nothing more than to save the natural world because *your* world of government and policies was not moving nearly fast enough. What *happened* to you?"

His eyes, which were once hard and resolute, stared back at her with something more.

"Ah, you've fallen in *love*," Maeve said. "How sad for you to have given in to a human experience that amounts to nothing more than disillusionment. I thought you wiser than that, Hayes. I once believed we were kindred spirits—that united, we were what Gaia had been waiting for. I'm disappointed."

"I was wrong. This isn't the way it's supposed to go."

She didn't bother to argue. She merely turned her head and looked to the horizon, where soon the sun would rise and its magnificent golden rays would illuminate the ancient passage tomb.

On the drive to Ireland, Mckenna, Nissa, and Abby didn't have the luxury of taking scenic routes and making Cillian-style pit-stops. It was a ten-hour trip to the Boyne Valley—including a two-hour ferry ride from Cairnryan—where Newgrange had stood for five thousand years. With every passing hour, Mckenna felt increasingly drawn to the Neolithic tomb, beckoning her like a sail to the wind.

It was 8:00 a.m. sharp. Exactly fifty-eight minutes until sunrise.

Abby let out a deep breath. "To reiterate . . ."

"We got it, Mom," Mckenna said before Abby asked them to go over the plan for the umpteenth time.

"Again," Abby demanded. "We can leave no room for error. Nissa?"

"I wait outside the tomb with Kenna," Nissa said, "while you go in and try to get Maeve to see reason. Although, I really don't think—"

"Thank you, Nissa. Mckenna?"

"I wait for your signal."

"Which is?"

"You'll toss your hackmanite stone up the passage, where it'll glow pink. I'll enter, slowly."

"And you'll . . . ?"

"Stay back until your signal."

"Perfect," Abby said, releasing a long breath. "Once Maeve sees you, hold up her 'stone necklace,'" she said using air quotes, the reason being that the necklace would be a false one—Abby would be holding onto the original one. "And whatever you do, make sure the stone *does not* make contact with your skin."

"I know, I know, it'll make me drowsy."

"I'll have her release Cillian. He'll join you outside, Nissa."

Nissa nodded.

"The next bit is very important. Swan, when you described the inside of the tomb, you told me there's a large stone basin in each of the three end chambers, but the east chamber holds a wee basin within a bigger one." Mckenna nodded, remembering the Newgrange tour guide, PJ's, explanation perfectly. At the time, she'd wondered why that one was distinct. "Well, my theory is that the wee basin was meant for rituals. So, at my signal, you're going to distract Maeve by pretending to comply with whatever she wants you to do; in the meantime, I will place the *real* necklace in the stone basin." For her mom's sake, Mckenna made sure her nod was even more deliberate than Nissa's. "No matter what she says, swan, *do not* perform any magic. She needs both of our abilities to work simultaneously, timed with the sun illuminating the centre chamber."

"Simple enough," Mckenna said, though it was far from it.

"Before we continue, I have a question," said Nissa. "Why does she want both necklaces? The one she just forged and the original one that Seán and Andre took from her on Samhain."

"Because I gifted it to her."

Mckenna and Nissa exchanged curious looks.

"We were like sisters, she, Esme, and I, and for nearly our entire friendship, Maeve's deepest dread was that she'd never find love. I wanted to give her something that could reassure her, a keepsake reminding her that she could always find whatever she was seeking. I'd only ever heard whispers about Misgaun Medb's magical properties, and oh, it took me months to track it down. I did it out of love, friendship, sisterhood," she went on wistfully, "and because of this inimitable power, the stone's magic is ten times more potent. The new one she's forged will do the trick when she's dowsing, but not nearly with the same precision. The bond she shares with the original, nothing else could ever come close."

Mckenna was at a loss for words. She hadn't realized how close of a connection her mother had with the High Priestess. It both frightened and saddened her, deeply.

"So, she just wants her original necklace back—she doesn't need it to fulfill the prophecy," Nissa said, looking upwards as though doing mental math, "but we need her original necklace to complete our spell. Did I get that right?"

"Aye, that's right, we needed something precious of hers." Abby's dreamy expression hardened. "Once I place the original necklace on the stone basin, and Maeve puts on the false one, her energy will start to drain. She'll drift into a haze, and that's when I'll open up the portal. You'll then join me in the east chamber and recite the spell with me, where we beckon the Causal Plane to open. If all goes well, Maeve will slip into a trance, and a part of her consciousness will shift to the plane. We can only hope she'll awaken with the delusion of the Self cast aside."

"What do you mean by the delusion of the Self?" asked Nissa.

"It's a bit complex, but to put it as simply as I can, the Causal Plane is the realm of pure consciousness, where the soul first springs forth from the Soul Plane, and where it shapes its individuality and identity. You see, when souls arrive on Earth, they're pure, though they don't ken their purpose in this lifetime. Over time, our upbringing, milestones, relationships, tragedies, global events—anything we endure, really—changes us, influences us. We start to disconnect from our soul's purpose, and through rekindling our spirit, by following our excitement, it's up to us to find it again. That's why it's so crucial to follow our wee nudges." She winked, pointing to her heart.

"So," Nissa began, looking like she was solving a Rubik's cube, "are you saying that as a result of these outside influences, or ignoring our intuition, our Self here on Earth can just be a disillusionment? Like, not our *real* selves?"

"Aye. But I wouldn't worry, Nissa. You're as true as Ben Nevis."

The highest peak in Scotland. Nissa beamed.

Mckenna was both perplexed and fascinated. "Back to the Causal Plane thing—if I'm getting this right, the selfish, egotistical part of Maeve will get swallowed up by this plane, and she'll wake with her soul purified?"

"Not her whole ego—we're human, after all, so that'd be impossible. If all goes well . . . that's the gist."

If all goes well?

The clock hit 8:35 a.m. when Abby turned into the Newgrange visitor car park, which was completely empty. Mckenna remembered how packed this place was when she and Nissa visited just a few months ago.

"Look," Nissa said gently, nudging Mckenna on the elbow. She pointed to a handwritten sign hanging on the entrance door:

SITE CLOSED FOR MAINTENANCE.
SORRY FOR THE INCONVENIENCE.

"Maeve," Abby said under her breath. "Must've fooled the workers too somehow, on their busiest day of the year, no less."

Wouldn't put it past her, Mckenna thought as they stepped out of the car and made their way to the passage tomb.

Newgrange was as glorious as she remembered it, except winter had muted the mound's vivid, sun-kissed green. The size and structure were as remarkable as ever; upon setting eyes on the three vertical stones flanking the small opening, a wave of goosebumps prickled her skin. She couldn't help but feel overwhelmed by the sheer power, sacrifice, and determination it must have taken to move these massive boulders into place. Even after three months, the triple spiral—connected to shape a reversed triangle—etched on the Entrance Stone stole her breath away. *"There are theories about their meaning,"* their guide, PJ, had said. *"Spirals are often associated with infinity, and so some believe the triple spiral you see on the Entrance Stone represents the cycle of birth, life, and death. This ties into the theory that Newgrange was built as a sacred burial ground to transport the soul into the afterlife."*

Hypnotized by the spiral, she took a step closer. The stone glowed as the same unseen energy she'd sensed the last time surged outwards from the centre of the spiral, and back inwards. Whatever this force was, it felt ancient. She watched in awe as it encircled the stone like a current, forming a kind of energy field.

As if awakened by her return, the glow brightened.

The empty grounds around the tomb suddenly filled with hundreds of people; they appeared hazy at first, like a projector image that was not yet fully focused, but as their features sharpened, it was clear they were not of this age. Groups of men and women—who'd fashioned tunics, head dressings, and shoes made of animal hide and linen—were stationed at various parts of the tomb, which at this point appeared to be about eighty percent constructed. Not a few feet away from where Mckenna stood was a woman of tall stature, her hair particularly wilder than the others'. She was perched atop a handmade ladder, a sharp limestone in her hands, carving out the seventh X in a row over the legendary roof-box, a gap between two stone slabs positioned in perfect alignment with the setting sun.

Mckenna remembered those Xs well—there were eight of them in total, and she'd wondered what they could mean.

As though in answer, the woman spun around and met her eyes, which bore a striking resemblance to Mckenna's.

Eight Xs for eight gateways, a voice replied inside her head.

Do you see me? Mckenna thought.

The woman winked, then carved the eighth and final X.

What do you mean? Where are the eight gateways? How do I find them?

The woman flashed her one last knowing smile, her face suddenly flickering in and out of focus. Mckenna rubbed her eyes as the scene before her began blinking like an old television set struggling to hold onto a signal.

"No! Please, wait!" she shouted desperately, but her voice was swallowed up by the sudden silence that surrounded her. The woman, along with the entire prehistoric civilization that had been there moments before, was gone.

"Kenna? Why are you yelling?"

"Swan, are you alright?"

Mckenna couldn't tear her gaze away from the roof-box. "I . . . I think I just saw the past. It was so weird, it's like it was happening right now. The woman who built the roof-box, she could see me."

Nissa's jaw dropped.

Abby appeared enthralled. "You must have ventured into another dimension! Time's a funny thing. Everything's actually happening simultaneously, you ken? A concept that's challenging for humans to grasp."

Simultaneously. What if the triple spiral represented the past, present, and future occurring all at once? Separate, and yet interconnected, spinning in an endless cycle . . .

She had a million questions, but she would have to ponder them later—she had to mentally prepare for what they were about to do.

Abby approached the Entrance Stone, and stopped short of the small opening. "Stay here," she whispered to the girls. *Her* girls.

Mckenna and Nissa gave a nod. They knew the plan well—there was no reason for Abby to think that anything would go wrong.

She held onto this notion as she entered, flashlight in hand, illuminating the low, narrow passageway. The air seeped magic—a mixture of earthiness, mystery, and centuries of stories. Her fingers brushed the stones as she passed. They held secrets; she felt them whispering in a language beyond words. She was not merely navigating through a confined space, she was threading the needle of time itself.

With each advancing step, the anticipation within her swelled. As she reached the end of the passage, the atmosphere shifted from transcendent to foreboding.

"Abigail," Maeve said, greeting her like the old friend she was, her smile seemingly genuine. Did she really think Abby was giving in? She stood in the centre chamber, gripping Cillian's duct-taped wrists. "I'm so pleased you've come. Where is the Wise One?"

Abby looked from Maeve to Cillian. "Are you alright, lad?" Cillian nodded.

"You haven't just come for him, have you? I was hoping you'd come to your senses by now."

"I was hoping you'd come to yours. This isn't you, Maeve."

The High Priestess shook her head, her face marked with disappointment. "But it *is*. You of all people, so in tune with nature. An incarnated faery, to top it off—an earth elemental! You ken how vital it is for nature to flourish, to remain untampered. And yet, you're willing to let such devastation occur, when *your own child* has the power to stop it," she spat.

Abby's heart wept for her old friend. "It's not up to me to decide when a soul's journey has come to an end, Maeve. Nor is it yours."

"We're not killing anyone, Abigail."

"You're keeping souls from fulfilling their purpose, from ascending."

"Oh, not this again." Maeve rolled her eyes. "It's worth it if it means serving Mother Gaia."

This was worse than Abby had imagined. "This is what this is all about. You think she'll reward you."

Maeve shook her head. "I'm doing this for the planet." The words echoed through the chamber. "I'm doing this for what our ancestors long worshipped before *other* institutions took its place, going on a burning rampage to eradicate us. People have forgotten, Abigail." Her voice shook, and her eyes filled with tears. "They've forgotten the very thing that gifted us life to begin with, what's in our very *core*. They've forgotten that we come from the earth itself! Don't you care?"

"How could you ask that, Maeve? I'm telling you there *is* another way. Souls need to return to better this planet—"

"They will *not*. They will keep returning to DESTROY IT!"

She was too far gone. Nissa was right—there was nothing she could say that would make Maeve see reason.

"I've lost you, haven't I?" Abby said, defeated.

"You lost me long ago."

At these words, Abby tossed the hackmanite stone behind her, up the passage, then slowly paced around Maeve, towards the east chamber. "Just let the lad go."

"As usual, you're in Abby land, where everything works in Abby's favour. I ken Mckenna is here." Abby clenched her fists. "If she's not standing in the centre chamber when the sun hits, I'll kill this boy right in front of you."

Every second Mckenna waited outside the Entrance Stone felt like a minute, and every minute an hour.

"I should go in there, Nissa."

"No! We have to stick to the plan."

"What if something went wrong?"

"Your mom's got this, Kenna."

Clink. Her mom's hackmanite stone appeared a few yards away, glowing pink in the dark passage.

Nissa raised an eyebrow, giving Mckenna her best *Am I right or am I right?* face.

"Okay. I'm going in," Mckenna said. "Stay here," she added, grabbing Nissa by the shoulders. "Luv ya, sis."

"I believe that's the first time you've said the L word to me!" Nissa said dramatically, pulling her in and nearly squeezing the life out of her. "Be careful."

"Is it too late to call nincompoop?" Their "I'm uncomfortable" code word.

Nissa let out a snort. "I'm thinking a little late, yeah . . ."

Bending her head, Mckenna trod down the dark passage, letting herself feel each stone's magical essence as she passed, until she came face to face with her mother, the High Priestess, and Cillian, who looked terrified at the sight of Mckenna. His eyes widened as if to say *Get the hell out of here.*

"Swan?" Abby said, feigning surprise. "I told you to wait outside. Get out of here!" *All part of the plan*, Mckenna reminded herself.

"No, Mom. I'm here to do what the prophecy says."

"Mckenna," Maeve said, making Mckenna's neck hairs spike. "Right on time. You've done the right thing."

"First," Mckenna turned to the High Priestess, "you have to let Cillian go."

"Don't move any closer, Mckenna!" Abby shouted, but her eyes warned Mckenna not to waver.

She's near the east chamber. Good.

"I'll let him go," the High Priestess said icily, "when you've handed me back my necklace."

Mckenna lifted the false necklace over her head and dangled it in the air. "Untie him."

To her surprise, Maeve did so without hesitation. "Necklace?"

Just do it. Mckenna tossed it at Maeve's feet. "Run, Cillian!" He hesitated. "I said GO!"

Looking bemused, he staggered past Mckenna, back up the passage. As Maeve bent to pick up her precious trinket by its chain, Abby stealthily dropped the original stone necklace inside the basin of the east chamber.

Everything is going according to plan. Now, we just have to wait until Maeve puts it on . . .

The High Priestess widened the chain, and made to place it over her head.

XVII
ELEMENTAL CONSEQUENCES

Nissa was pacing around in circles, her mind swirling like the triple spirals etched on the Entrance Stone, when she heard heavy footsteps running towards her. It was Cillian, looking the worst she'd ever seen him—filthy and dishevelled, dark rings around his eyes. Thankfully, he wasn't hurt. The plan must be on track.

"Shhh!" Nissa hissed the moment Cillian spotted her.

"Nissa? What are you doing here?" he said, panting.

"Where Mckenna goes, I go, remember?"

He nodded, then sank to the ground. "I remember. And what exactly is going on in there?"

"Kenna and Abby have a plan. And under no circumstances can you go in there. Got it, Casanova?" she said, her eyes bulging in warning.

He gave a short laugh. "Got it." A silence hung between them. "Listen, I'm sorry about . . . about how things ended up. I shouldn't have lied. And once this is all over, I'm going to leave. For good."

Nissa nodded. "I think that's best." She couldn't deny that he and Kenna had a deep connection, but he'd been lying to them for months. She knew he wasn't all bad, but in her book, he was no longer trustworthy—and nowhere near good enough for her best friend. "Where will you go?"

"Back to Dublin, away from all of this. I'm going to run for the Green Party, make change the best way I know how."

"What you always wanted. I'm happy for you, Cillian. I think you'll be great." She meant it; there was no one more passionate about both politics and the environment than Cillian.

"For what it's worth, I'm glad Mckenna has you. I've never known two people to be so connected. When I found out you hadn't known each other long, I was gobsmacked. I was *sure* you were sisters."

Nissa smiled. "We totally are . . ." As his words sank in, a realization swept over her.

Mckenna watched intently as the High Priestess lowered the false necklace over her head. Just as it was about to settle around her neck, she abruptly stopped.

"This isn't right," the High Priestess said, lifting it off and dangling it in front of her. She examined it closely.

Damn, Mckenna thought, *she didn't touch the stone.*

Maeve looked to Abby, who was now in the east chamber, hunched over the small basin sitting within the larger one. "Did you not think I would know the difference? WHERE IS THE REAL STONE, THE ORIGINAL STONE?" The High Priestess bellowed, throwing the false necklace on the ground.

"Now, swan!"

Mckenna darted for the east chamber, joining her mother's side. Together, they chanted:

*"Caraid bliadhnaichean,
Na crionadh*

Ego air fhuadach
Ris an plèana adhbharach"

"What are you doing? STOP THAT!" the High Priestess bellowed.

Mckenna and Abby didn't waver. They repeated in English:

"Friend of old,
Do not wane
Ego be banished
To the Causal Plane."

The High Priestess acted quickly. Like the kiss she'd blown into the air at The Ford of the Three Burns, a short but strong gust of wind raged their way, sending the real stone necklace soaring out of the stone basin and into a crevasse in the chamber floor.

Maeve stuck both hands out below her torso, her palms parallel with the ground. "One wrong move, Abigail, and I make this foundation quake so brutally, this roof will come down on us all. Come, Wise One!"

Mckenna looked frantically from Maeve to her mom. What could she do? *Think.*

But she couldn't. Her mind was numb and her body frozen from fear, as the light of the morning sun was scarcely visible at the front of the passage. Trembling, she joined the High Priestess in the centre chamber, at the heart of the tomb.

"You next," Maeve said to her mom, and wrapped a cold, bony hand around Mckenna's wrist.

Abby hesitated but obliged. Maeve seized her wrist too, and the three now stood in the centre of Newgrange. Mckenna could feel her mother's dread and disappointment; she'd failed as a mother and protector, as a reincarnated elemental meant to guide people towards ascension . . . and as a friend.

Mckenna wished she was wiser, stronger, smarter. Any moment now, the sunlight would beam through the roof-box and illuminate the passage, as it did every year on the Winter Solstice. Maeve would have to act fast to fulfill the prophecy . . .

Which meant they had to act faster.

"Both of you, repeat after me: *Mother Gaia, I invoke thee.*"

Mckenna shook her head. "I won't do it." And then a light bulb lit up in her head; at the word *invoke*, she knew what to do. "Sylphs, I invoke thee!"

Maeve let out a shrill laugh. "When I'm near, the sylphs respond to *me*, Wise One. All the elementals do. We're well acquainted, see . . ."

Mckenna and Abigail gasped as, on the ground below, salamanders appeared like fiery sentinels, encircling them. A swarming dance of blazing spotted lizards, they spewed flames from their mouths, resembling miniature dragons.

Shit. "Wow. You must be really far gone to be best buds with the elementals," Mckenna said. "No wonder you're soulless. What d'you have to trade to even out the score, huh?"

Maeve scoffed, but Mckenna knew she'd hit a nerve. "Abigail, this one takes after your Irishman. Fowl-mouthed gype."

A flash of pink and green emanated from Abby, projecting onto Maeve like a shimmering veil of light. In an instant, the salamanders vanished, and the air filled with the enchanting aroma of wildflowers. Maeve's steely gaze wavered, her stern demeanor faltering as she stared longingly at Abby, her eyes glazed over.

"Remember, Maeve," Abby whispered. "Remember . . ."

"Mom, what's happening?"

"As an incarnated faery, I'm able to project feelings onto others by presenting them with their past memories, as a way of creating empathy."

Mckenna knew her mom had been holding back some rad magic skills. "That's badass. Why didn't you tell me, or ever use it—?"

"Because it's a way of manipulation."

The High Priestess's wistful gaze didn't last very long. Her expression hardened once more. "Nice try, Abigail, but an old memory won't change a thing. You leave me no choice. I'm going to count down from five, and when I say one, you will both do exactly as I say."

No. She's going to hypnotize us.

"Mckenna, block your ears!" Abby shouted.

Mckenna tried pulling her hand away, but Maeve's grip was too tight. She blocked one ear with her free hand.

"Five . . . four . . . three . . ."

Her voice was mesmerizing. Even with one ear blocked, Mckenna couldn't not take in the words; they were as silky as the hiss of a snake, and yet as soothing as a babbling brook.

"Two . . . one."

Mckenna was in the loveliest of trances. She felt weightless, as though she were adrift on a tranquil sea. Was she asleep? Whatever her state, she was content. So, so content.

"Say it with me," sang Maeve. "Mother Gaia, I invoke thee."

"Mother Gaia, I invoke thee," Abby and Mckenna repeated, unwillingly acquiescing.

The chamber was now bathed in luminance, and it was a sight to behold. Much like the enchanted evening she'd spent in the woods near the faery hill in Belfast, Mckenna felt a breath enter her body; her heart chakra burst open, and her breathing slowed, attuned to a part of herself that didn't belong on this physical plane. She felt more herself then and there than ever before, like she belonged to the universe alone—not bound by anyone or anything. She'd almost forgotten where she was when something even more extraordinary happened: From the sun's sharp rays arose a resplendent orb, radiating a golden aura. As the light revealed the figure of Gaia, the all-knowing, all-loving entity that governed the natural world, an ethereal voice boomed from the orb.

"What drives your quest for my power?"

"We wish to save the natural world by fulfilling the prophecy of the Scottish Scrolls," the High Priestess replied, looking entranced.

"This cannot be done, for you have not the Wise One's twin flame foretold by the prophecy."

The orb flashed once, its light merging with that of the Irish sun for a mere moment, and then it was gone.

"NO!" Maeve yelled, matching the Goddess in octave. "HOW IS THIS POSSIBLE?"

Out of her hypnotic state, Mckenna wasn't sure she understood what had just occurred. *As twin flames rekindle and the last living Wise One unites with her creator* . . . Evidently, her creator was her mother—was she not also her twin flame?

"Times have changed, Maeve," said Abby, though she, too, looked perplexed. "Destiny isn't written. The prophecy was an outdated prediction that has no part in the evolution of Earth."

"No, Pravadi's seen it! The passage stays illuminated for twelve minutes. We'll try it again!" she shouted stubbornly, nodding to herself. "Perhaps the sun didn't quite hit the centre . . ."

"The sun isn't the issue," a small voice said at the end of the passage. It was Nissa, Cillian at her heels. "I know why it didn't work."

"Nissa!" Mckenna shouted. "What are you doing here? Stay back, she'll kill you both."

Cillian stepped forward. "I tried to stop her—"

"Thanks, Kenna, but she won't want to hurt me." Why was Nissa being so calm? "Cillian, you should go," Nissa added. He hesitated. "Go, please." Mckenna had never heard Nissa speak so firmly.

When Cillian didn't budge, Mckenna, Abby, and Nissa shouted, "GO!"

As Cillian backed away, disappearing up the passage, the High Priestess's laugh filled the tomb. "And why wouldn't I want to hurt you, wee girl?"

"Because you need me. *I'm* her twin flame."

The moment the words escaped her, Mckenna knew they were true. "Nissa . . . how?"

Nissa met them at the centre chamber. "Cillian helped me realize it. He said he'd never known two people to connect so quickly—he thought we were sisters! And when I found out I was a faery, like Abby—"

"When did you—?"

"—I thought about those twelve beings of Elfame you described. And then I remembered." She placed her thumbs at the centre of Mckenna's forehead.

At her touch, Mckenna's mind flashed with a faraway memory.

Bessie sat near the cove in a daze, staring idly at the very spot where the twelve beautiful beings had appeared twice before. She wished she could speak with them, implore them to help her understand what had come over her at the village fair. What could those strange words she's spewed out mean?

Since that night, whispers flew about town that she was working with the devil. Though some were quick to defend her, others averted their eyes when they crossed her path. She mourned the life she once had, before being bestowed with the gift of Second Sight.

"Cheer up!" a jolly voice said nearby.

Bessie snapped out of her daze and came to realize she was not alone. The Elfame being with wispy rose-gold hair was standing in the cove, looking both delighted and cross all at once.

"Apologies, I—when did you arrive?" asked Bessie, standing up and dusting herself off.

What does it matter?

Bessie had nearly forgotten that these beings preferred communicating through thoughts.

Why so glum, Bessie?

Bessie swallowed the lump in her throat. *I feel like more of an outcast than ever. I'm now feared by many, including myself. I've foreseen a friend's end, and now, I've no command over my own words.*

Bessie, you cannot fear your own power. The world will need you in time, and you must *be brave!*

How could you come to ken such a thing?

Because the words you spoke bear the weight of a prophecy

destined for the twentieth century—a dire prophecy at that. And if you fail to understand your soul's powers, if you begin to stray from the light, it will come to pass.

Stray? Bessie thought, her chest tightening. *Do you reckon that in another existence, I might . . . turn to wickedness? Turn evil?*

It's not as simple as good and evil. Depending on the circumstances, humans can be swayed one way or the other.

How do I make sure I don't stray?

Bessie, I have known you in every one of your lifetimes—even the ones where your darkness has overshadowed your light. Your soul continues to evolve, and with it, so does the goodness inside of you. I've no doubt you will find your way.

We ken each other already? How, if you're a fae and I'm human?

I can't explain it other than that I hear your voice in Elfame. I feel called to you.

How strange, Bessie thought, though it somehow didn't feel strange at all. *When it's time, will you be there with me to ensure that I don't stray?*

The fae looked thoughtful. *I have never left Elfame before.*

But you know me best! Please . . ." she pleaded, *"promise to be by my side, in human form. I will need a confidante more than a fae keeping watch from a distance. I will need a sister.*

The Elfame being smiled brightly and held out her hand. *You have my word.*

Nissa was the twin flame all along. *As twin flames rekindle and the last living Wise One unites with her creator . . .* Mckenna had assumed her mother was both her creator as well as her twin flame, but she was wrong. Her reunion with Abby had led her to this moment, but it was Nissa whose magic the prophecy spoke of. It was Nissa who she was destined to meet in this lifetime. It was Nissa who was meant to be intrinsically by her side.

The boldest fae flees from our neighbour land
Her charge, the Wise One, and she the key
Whence the ancient passage tomb stands
United their magic, and so shall it be.

Nissa was the boldest fae, and Mckenna was her charge. It was their magic, *their* union, that was needed at Newgrange.

Despite the chaos amongst them, Mckenna beamed at Nissa. "I remember too."

Nissa turned to Abby. "Abby, open the portal, please."

"What?" Maeve said unsteadily. "What are you talking about? What portal?"

"Now!" Nissa shouted.

Mckenna and Abby began to chant:

"Caraid bliadhnaichean,
Na crionadh
Ego air fhuadach
Ris an plèana adhbharach"

"What is happening?" Maeve yelled, looking distraught.

"Oh, are you surprised?" Nissa said, revealing Abby's enchanted false necklace, touching it only by the chain. Mckenna hadn't even noticed her picking it up. "Kenna, catch!"

As though she'd been doing it for years, Mckenna extended her arm in front of her and stopped the necklace in mid-air. Then, with a swift wave of her hand, she launched it straight at the High Priestess.

Maeve instinctively caught it. "I'm not certain what you're up to, but I presume this false stone is enchanted, Abby's bonnie handiwork, no doubt," she said as she examined it, rubbing it between her fingers. "Did you think me stupid enough to put it on?"

"You're right," Abby said calmly, "about it being my bonnie handiwork. But there's no need to put it on, Maeve. It only takes a few seconds of contact with your skin before . . ."

As if pulled down by an anchor, the High Priestess collapsed to the ground. "I can't move. Wh-what are you doing?"

"We're banishing part of your consciousness, Maeve," Abby said, an underlying tenderness in her voice. "So you can be you again."

"*Friend of old*," Mckenna began, and Abby joined in:

"*. . . Do not wane*
Ego be banished
To the Causal Plane."

Several things happened at once: As the High Priestess fainted, Mckenna swept the real necklace—the original—off the chamber floor and dropped it into the smaller basin; at the *clink* of the stone on stone, a small hole in the atmosphere appeared above the basin, growing larger, widening, until a slender figure emerged from the opening. Her fair skin, delicate features, and thick wavy braid cascading over her shoulder were all too familiar.

"Niamh," Mckenna uttered in disbelief—the fae from the Inagh Valley who lured her into a shrub, transported her to the faery realm, and charmed her into removing her shoes.

"So pleased to see you again, Wise One," Niamh said in her honeyed voice.

Mckenna looked at Abby, perplexed. "Mom, did you mean to open up a portal to the faery realm?"

"No, there must be a mistake—"

"There's no mistake," Niamh said, turning to Mckenna. "The Causal Plane denied your request and sent me in its place as a consequence to invoking the elementals." Mckenna's whole body stiffened. "You've disrupted the balance in the universe, and I'm afraid one of you must come with me."

Abby put a hand to her mouth. "This cannot be . . ."

"Come where?" Mckenna asked, her heart thumping.

"To Elfame."

Nissa immediately stepped forward. "Kenna, I know how to

stop this." Nissa's eyes locked on her, and Mckenna knew the stupid, selfless thing she was about to do.

"No."

"It's the only way."

"No, Nissa. That's not happening. We've got the High Priestess. This is all over!"

Nissa's eyes swam with tears. "It's not, though. You have to repay your debt because of me."

"What the hell are you talking about?"

"You saved me from Simon!"

When she'd called the elementals. "Nissa, that's not the only time—"

"And besides, Kenna, we both know that if it's not the High Priestess, it'll be someone else with her ambition to banish billions of souls." She took Mckenna's hand, and said softly, "I need to go."

Mckenna shook her head frantically, like a child getting a time-out. "I said *no*. There's no way."

"The world needs you. And without me, no one could ever make the Scottish Scrolls come true. Those souls will be safe forever."

"Nissa, we will find another way," Abby said unconvincingly, her face wet with tears. "I will be the one to go."

Nissa took both their hands. "You belong here, Abby, with your daughter." Letting go of her hands, she turned to Mckenna. "Kenna, remember in Connemara, when I told you about that dream I had after I fell in that broken glass? Remember when I said that a voice was telling me to come back home—my *real* home?"

Mckenna couldn't suppress the tears any longer. "Nissa, I don't care. You can't leave me, do you get that?" She was shouting now. "I'm not me without you. I can't . . . you can't just . . . *please*. You can't leave me, please!"

Nissa chuckled through her tears. "Leave? Never. I'll always be with you in every other weird way, just not here. I don't belong here."

Niamh held her hand out to Nissa. "Are you ready, brave fae?"

Sobbing, Mckenna threw her arms around Nissa's neck. "No! Don't. Nissa, I'm begging you, don't leave . . ."

"It's okay," Nissa whispered in her ear. "Thank you for trusting a total stranger." She slowly pulled away, then embraced Abby. "And to you, Abby—for being my family."

Abby said nothing. She kissed Nissa's forehead, tenderly, like a mother would a child.

Nissa glanced at Mckenna once more and flashed the same illuminating smile she did when they'd first met in Mr. Heathley's classroom. "Please tell your dads I love them."

"Nissa . . ."

I love you too, sis, Nissa's dulcet voice said in her mind before she took Niamh's hand and crossed over to Elfame.

XVIII

Final Resting Place

The atmosphere in the inn wasn't what it once was. With Nissa gone, every room in the place was dimmer, every one of their meals was flavourless, and the days dragged on for what felt like eons. Life as Mckenna knew it and had come to love was over—she no longer had her best friend by her side to read her mind, literally, be silly with, whisper her dreams to. They were now separated by a veil she couldn't cross, no matter how hard she tried.

Her twin flame didn't exist on this plane anymore.

"She is still with you," Abby would remind her every day, and every day Mckenna would fight not to roll her eyes. What good was that if she didn't get to actually *be* with her?

Mckenna hadn't visited the faery tree yet. She was afraid she would completely break down and never recover. But that morning was the darkest of mornings, and this time it was both her dads and Abby who urged her to take a stroll up the path they'd walked countless times before.

"I'm not taking no for an answer," Seán said. He'd been on bed rest up until the day prior, having made a full recovery. "I promise, you'll feel better for it."

"Do you want us to come with you?" Andre asked, his hand warming up her shoulder.

Mckenna shook her head slowly. "That's okay." This was something she had to do on her own.

Bundled up in her mom's warmest coat, she ambled up the path, in no hurry to get there. She knew that the moment she spotted the bare branches of the faery tree, she would lose all control.

She was right. Her throat tightened and tears fell at the sight of the ribbon she and Nissa had tied together, and before she knew it, she was sobbing irrepressibly. She'd never felt so alone, even before she and Nissa met. Because at least then, she'd been used to it. She'd had nothing to lose.

She bent down to remove one of her shoelaces, then tied it to the tree branch that hung just above her head. "I know you can hear me, Nissa, and I'm sure you're feeling so at home where you are, among other beings that are special like you. Just come find me when you're ready. Where I go, you go, remember?"

A loud *chirp* made her jump. There, his small foot wrapped around her shoelace, was the wren that had guided her and Nissa's journey to Ireland.

A past conversation with Esme echoed in her mind: *Wrens are thought to be messengers. He helped lead you here because he was sent to do just that.*

By who?

The fae folk.

Mckenna's sobs turned to moans. Nissa really was here, somewhere.

The swishing of snow behind her made her whip around. She didn't even bother wiping away her tears as she turned to face a solemn-looking Cillian, his hands deep in his coat pockets.

"What are you doing here?" she said.

"I've come to say goodbye."

"Okay."

Silence.

"I'm going back to Dublin, to campaign for the Green Party. What I should've done instead of . . . you know."

She wanted to feel happy for him. She even wanted to feel pleased to see him, but in that moment, all she felt was pain. "That's good."

Another stretch of silence.

"I'm so sorry about Nissa."

Mckenna nodded. He may have meant it, but she didn't care that he was sorry.

"You know, while we were outside of the tomb together, I told her when I met you that I thought you were sisters. Do you know what she said? 'We totally are.'"

She stifled a small laugh, and it sounded foreign to her; she hadn't laughed in a whole week. "Not a bad imitation."

Cillian shrugged. "I tried to do her justice, but she's one of a kind." He took two steps towards Mckenna. "I hope we'll meet again, lass."

She wanted to hug him goodbye, kiss him like she never had before, have his arms wrapped around her until the sun set. But she stayed put, her mom's boots planted on the snowy ground. "Maybe in our next lifetime."

As Cillian made his way back to the guest house to gather his things, he contemplated turning back to beg for Mckenna's forgiveness a handful of times. But he knew it was too late; he'd screwed up in every way possible, lying so often he'd lost count. And each time, he'd convinced himself that it was out of fear of losing her.

The truth was that it had nothing to do with her. The High Priestess had made him feel so important, purposeful, like it was his mission to save the natural world—which had always been his mission, just executed by a vastly different means. Without hypnotizing him, she'd convinced him that her way, the prophecy's way, was the only way.

He'd never let himself forget who he was again.

Because that was the issue, wasn't it? He'd forgotten what he stood for. Along with a greener world, he also wanted peace—peace in Ireland and Northern Ireland, peace amongst humans and the environment. Without eradicating anyone's existence.

Now who was being idealistic.

He smiled to himself. He'd once loved the fact that he was idealistic, as did his professors at Trinity. It was what had driven him into politics.

He may not have Mckenna, at least not right now, but he'd found himself again—that passionate young lad whose quest for change meant the world to him.

His stomach fluttered with, dare he say, excitement. He was ready to fight the *good* fight the best way he knew how. And while he was doing this entirely for himself, for his soul, whose purpose he would never question again, deep down he longed for a day where Mckenna would be proud of the person he'd become, and possibly forgive him for all the terrible things he'd done.

Slipping his hand into his coat pocket, he crushed his very last cigarette, not the least bit tempted to light it up.

The aroma of Guinness mushroom pie hit Mckenna's nose—it was Nissa's favourite. Taking full advantage of his first day off bed rest ("I was legitimately losing my mind"), Seán announced he'd made it in her honour.

Seán hadn't talked much since the winter solstice. After Mckenna, he appeared to be the one who had taken Nissa's departure the hardest. But tonight, he seemed adamant not to just fill their bellies but also the dreadful silence that had been lingering all week long.

As they savoured Seán's delicious meal, Mckenna's gaze drifted around the room, settling on the vibrant glow of holiday lights that adorned every corner and the massive log burning in the hearth. Abby and Andre had taken it upon themselves to create an ambiance of cheerfulness, undeterred by Mckenna's own reservations about embracing the spirit of Yule; Yule, a celebration her mom observed every year, marked the winter solstice, symbolizing the return of light and warmth. The twinkling lights danced across the walls, casting a soft and comforting radiance that contrasted with the somberness of their recent days. Nissa would have loved it.

"Swan, we were talking," Seán said, topping off Andre's wine glass, "and your mum, dad and I agreed that some routine, and, well, normal kid stuff, might do you some good. We've enrolled you in school for the winter semester in Edinburgh—"

Mckenna's fork fell on her plate with a *clang*. "What?" School hadn't even crossed her mind these past few months. It felt far too ordinary for someone like her. After everything that had happened, how could she return to simply attending classes and doing homework?

"We know what you're thinking," Andre said, "but Mckenna, you need to at least finish high school. Or secondary school, as they call it in the UK."

"Agreed," Seán and Abby said simultaneously.

"I'll get homeschooled then. High school is *not* for me." If Nissa were around, it'd be a different story. But no way was she going to a brand-new school with a whole new band of human idiots.

"You might find lots in common with people at this school," Abby offered, squeezing half a lemon slice into her already lemony water.

Before Mckenna could retort, there was a knock at the door.

"Christ, it's dinnertime . . ." Seán said irritably, dropping his fork.

"I'll get it." *Saved by the bell*, she thought, making a mental note to grill her parents later about this ridiculous plan.

She opened the door to Mathis, looking tall and dapper in a knee-length overcoat, except for his pair of fluffy orange earmuffs. A small wooden box was tucked underneath his arm. "You're still here?"

Mathis chuckled politely. "A bit rude."

She shrugged, and pointed at his earmuffs. "Your human form's not used to the cold, I guess."

"Afraid not. Every time I return, I forget how unforgiving Mother Nature is—and how bloody cold the UK is in December."

Mckenna forced a smile, having never heard him swear before, then stepped aside to beckon him in. In no mood to exchange pleasantries, she went straight to the point. "The High Priestess is gone. Well, sort of. She's in a coma. We don't know if the transformation spell worked or if she'll wake up."

Mathis nodded, his knowing look turning intense. Weighted. He was holding something back. Again. Why did she get the feeling he was about to drop another truth bomb?

"All of this, it isn't over, is it?" Something had been gnawing at her the last few days, besides Nissa's absence; it was a terrible looming feeling, as though all of this—the Scrolls, Eachna's vision—was just the beginning.

"I'm afraid it's not." *And there it is.* "There's something I would like you to have. Several things, actually." He reached into his mysterious wooden box and retrieved a lustrous mossy-green gemstone, its surface glistening with a smooth, glassy texture. "It's moldavite—one of the oldest minerals on Earth. Some say it might've originated from space . . . Its properties are quite rare, and quite extraordinary. It's the most high-vibration crystal there is, and if used correctly, it can enhance psychic abilities." He dropped it into her hand, and a warmth immediately spread throughout her body. "It's more powerful than most crystals, so it must be stored properly and used sparingly. With caution." He extended the box, its lid ajar. As she gingerly returned the moldavite back to its place, she caught her breath. Nestled inside were three tightly folded parchments, their age seemingly spanning centuries.

"What's that?" Her heart pulsed in her ears. *Could it be . . . ?*

"These are the Scottish Scrolls. They belong to you."

Mckenna's stomach dropped. "There are three? And you're giving them to me *now*?"

"The Scrolls were hidden in Dalry—by me, as Thom, in 1572. I'd buried this box somewhere around the cove. It took me a bit to find it . . ."

She reached inside for one, careful not to damage the coarse parchment, which bore the stains and discolorations of age. Unfurling it, her heartbeat quickened; the script was written in an archaic hand, and the letters, though much more intricate than most calligraphy, looked rushed.

At last, there is not all but one course
For the Wise One's heart can be gently swayed
Through old magic harnessed and alignment with Source
The natural world can triumph both ways

This was the third Scroll. She stared blankly up at him, not knowing what to make of this.

"Lizbeth—I mean, Mckenna—this was not the main fight, this entanglement with the High Priestess. There is darkness in other dimensions that is already beginning to penetrate Earth, an evil far greater than any human can fathom. It is here to corrupt whomever it may, particularly those in power, and those who wield great power."

"Like Maeve. And me." Her head was going to explode at any moment. "So, um, what does that mean?" She placed her hands on either side of her temples.

"It means an increasing number of humans are straying from their soul's purpose. I've seen the path this world is headed down—greed has taken precedence over social and environmental sustainability, never mind the poverty and ecological destruction left behind. . . . and it will only worsen."

"What do you mean you've seen it?"

"There is something called the Akashic Records that only

beings in the fifth dimension—where I'm from—or higher, can access. Imagine one immense filing cabinet of past and future events, which changes according to the present-day reality. At the moment, with the route this world is currently on, the future does not look promising."

"I'm really tired of not being told the whole story, Mathis. Just tell me what you saw."

Mathis appeared shaken, his eyes burdened. "I witnessed the planet growing unbearably hot, reaching a point of no return. Wildfires wiping out entire regions, ice caps melting . . . and the damage is not confined to just the environment. I saw prejudice reach an all-time high, blatant dictatorship within a democracy, nations torn apart, a global pandemic, warfare—and all of this in a mere thirty years from now. The world is drifting farther from ascension, from unity consciousness, than ever before. During my visits to Earth, my mission always revolved around aiding in the betterment of the world, and I genuinely believed I was making a meaningful impact. But it's evident that I've fallen far short."

Mckenna could hardly handle getting out of bed, let alone the image of such a bleak future. "And where do I fit into this?" The throbbing in her head intensified.

"We need you. *You* are the bridge between all of existence."

There goes that vague, not-at-all-intimidating notion again. The goddam proverbial bridge.

He took a step towards her. "Your higher self has chosen this incarnation so you can help others to awaken to their full potential, to come into their mastery. It is *you* who is meant to unify the realms—to fight negative entities who are corrupting humanity, who are doing anything and everything to shield humans from the truth of what they are capable of. That is what will ultimately save both humanity and the natural word. Do you see? '*Through old magic harnessed and alignment with Source, the natural world can triumph both ways.*'"

Honestly, right now, her mind was drawing a blank. "How could I be the one? I'm not the greatest person, Mathis. Look at what I used to be," she said, thinking of Alice Kyteler. "And I almost went along with the High Priestess!"

"Mckenna, struggling to do what's right, falling victim to negative thoughts, that's simply being human."

She scoffed. "Don't talk to me about being human, Mathis. You can't relate to what it feels like to find yourself in a dark pit of mental despair."

"I can when visiting Earth. I'm here as a human, remember? I am no less affected than you are. What you must understand is, it is not solely the mind that's doing this; we are in duality—there is a positive and negative energy around everyone. Some are just better at protecting their energy fields. And a soul as steeped in ancient wisdom as yours, these lower frequencies, they will always impact you more profoundly. They want to stop you from bringing such sacred knowledge into this dimension, to keep the human race under their control."

"Who the hell are these assholes?"

"They are the Phainonians. These entities constantly manipulate humanity, feeding off humans' low energies through a kind of remote frequency band. And, I am afraid, they are prevailing."

And now she had to deal with invisible evil interdimensional energies.

Her eyes widened as she recalled those eerie green orbs that dove into her chest, the very ones that were messing with Maeve's mind, that nearly killed Mckenna in that dream-like state. They'd affected her thoughts, she knew they had—how else could she have even remotely considered siding with the High Priestess?

How was she going to keep up with all of this? Had she wasted these months playing house, pretending her life was normal, when she should've been finding ways to fight these things off?

"Clearly, you didn't just come here to see Cillian, or to warn me about him, did you? You came here to prepare me."

Mathis nodded.

"What do I have to do to beat these things?"

"First and foremost, you must understand your own mind more deeply than *they* understand your mind. When it comes to safeguarding the rest of humanity from their influence, your mission is to assist people in their awakening. Guide them on evolving towards unity consciousness."

"Doesn't sound hard at all," she said sardonically. "And how can I possibly do that?"

"There are gateways to other planes and dimensions, ones you can learn to navigate. Persuade the beings from these alternate realms to come together and devise a strategy to confront the Phainonians."

"Do you mean portals? Like the one my mom just opened?"

"Not exactly. Gateways are pre-existing—they do not require a complex ritual to access—whereas portals must be created. While Newgrange, in and of itself, is not a direct gateway, Abigail tapped into its ancient magic, combined with your inherent connection, to create a portal on the specific day when its magic is most potent: the winter solstice."

"Right. Not so easy to recreate."

"Precisely."

Did that mean she could pass through a gateway to the faery realm? Would she be able to see Nissa again?

"Accessing the gateways will take loads of practice," he added, likely sensing her longing.

She'll do anything to see Nissa again. "I'm in. As long as I don't have to face a dragon." She was kidding, but judging by Mathis's expression, she wasn't entirely convinced dragons were off the table.

"I'm relieved you're in agreement."

She was beginning to warm up to his refined manner. "Do I ever get to go, you know, up there?" She wondered if she'd ever get to see where the Galactic Council dwelled, or where this fascinating giant filing cabinet sat.

"I don't believe that's possible, unless you are summoned. However, I would like to show you the future I witnessed, to help you gain some perspective. First, we must practice shifting dimensions."

Like she'd done at Newgrange, when she found herself in

the Neolithic period . . . and likely what happened at the farm-stead. She recounted the strange encounter with the wandering *harry coo*.

"It appears you stumbled upon a nexus," Mathis explained, "a magical focal point shaped by the land's geological and his-torical significance. It is rare, but certain regions possess greater magical potency than others. If you found it more convenient to wield your magic within this nexus, imagine the possibilities, the potential access you might gain, in one that's fifty times more powerful—and without the need to summon elementals for aid."

Mckenna knew what was coming. "I'm not leaving my parents."

"You won't need to," Abby said behind her. Mckenna turned around to see her mom and her dads standing in the hallway, looking solemn. "We have a plan, swan. Mathis will come with you and your dads to Edinburgh, and you both will join me in Aberdeen for mid-term break in February. Between his and my instruction, we think you will be ready for Orkney by the spring equinox."

"Orkney? What's in Orkney?"

"It's part of the Northern Isles," Mathis said. "We think Orkney is where most of the gateways are."

Even for her, this was a lot. "When were you all going to tell me this?"

"Today," Andre said. "We wanted you to have some time to mourn."

"You've gone through more than what others go through in several lifetimes, swan," Seán said, then muttered under his breath, "Though, dropping in *after* dinner would've been nice, Mathis . . ."

Mckenna crossed her arms, wearing her best have-you-lost-your-mind expression. "And did you want me to save humanity before or after I handed in my lab homework?"

Andre squeezed her shoulders. "Glad to see your sense of humour is alive and well."

She rolled her eyes, turning to her mom. "Can't you come to

Edinburgh, too?" It seemed like it was only yesterday that they'd reunited. The last thing she wanted was to be apart again.

Abby tilted her head, stroking Mckenna's chin. "I'll come for the ride and help you get settled in, but then I'm off. It's time I return home to Aberdeen to settle a few things." She spoke with a glint in her eyes, making Mckenna think there might be more to the story than she was letting on. "I'm not far away."

"So," Andre said. "Do we have a plan?"

Seán clapped his hands together. "I think we do, luv. We'll need to rent a minivan, I think."

Mckenna decided that night that she was going to try something she never had before: dreamwalking into the past. She'd had a kind of divine nudge (a term she chose to use, as "Spidey Sense" felt somewhat understated) to do so. She had a strong inkling the woman carving out the Xs at Newgrange had been her past self, and if it was, then it was possible to speak with Bessie, too.

Not knowing whether this would work or made any magical sense, she plucked a few leaves of mugwort, which she remembered enhanced psychic powers and intuition, and tossed them in one of Abby's sachets—she chose purple for power—along with Mathis's moldavite. With the sachet resting in her palm, she meditated the way Abby had taught her, letting her thoughts drift in and out of her mind without judgement, and keeping her breathing steady and even. She held room in her heart for her past self—Elizabeth Dunlop—and when her eyelids grew too heavy for her to sit up straight, she tucked the sachet under her pillow and allowed herself to drift into sleep.

Almost instantly, Mckenna found herself standing in the cove she'd come to know well. There, standing idly by, was Bessie, who held an air of confidence she never quite had in Mckenna's vivid memories.

"I've been waiting for you," Bessie said, completely unperturbed by the fact that she was staring at a future version of herself.

"You knew I'd come."

"I had a knowingness. It is the *why* I am not certain about."

This is weird. "I'm not sure. I guess I wanted to speak with you."

Bessie nodded, a curious smile dancing across her lips. "I see we have not changed."

"How do you mean?"

"Our worry that we are not all good."

"A friend of mine told me we are neither inherently good, nor bad. It's the choices we make that define us."

"Your friend is wise. Why, pray tell, are you really here?" Elizabeth held her gaze, hard and true.

"I want to know how powerful we really are." This was it— what she'd been yearning to know all this time.

Elizabeth's smile broadened, and with a grace akin to a gentle breeze, her feet effortlessly rose from the undergrowth, hovering approximately a foot above the ground. She glided towards Mckenna, whose mouth was agape in stunned silence. "Extremely."

Within a few days, Mckenna and her parents were packed. Seán and Andre had arranged to have their belongings shipped from their former residence in Abredonia Woods to their new flat in Edinburgh, all expenses covered by the University of Edinburgh, which positively delighted Seán. ("They clearly want you badly, luv . . .")

"Mountains of boxes await us, so we'll need all hands on deck, please," Andre announced in some form or another every few miles. These things made him anxious, so Mckenna could see why he needed soothing. She was starting to think her "Yes, Dad" and "Don't worry, Dad" and "We got this, Dad" weren't helping one bit. Even Mathis promised he'd pull his weight, throwing sideways glances at Mckenna that made her feel both safe and perturbed all at once.

Some four hours into the scenic drive, passing the magnificent snow-glazed bens that she would never grow accustomed to, a road sign caught Mckenna's attention: *Torryburn, 2 miles.*

She turned to her mom, whose gaze seemed both focused and faraway at once. "Mom, do you mind making a pitstop?"

It took her a moment to register Mckenna's ask. "Sure, swan. Where to?"

"You can get off at the next exit."

She remembered Lilias's story—the poor, lost Necropolis ghost; how she was taken to Torryburn for her trial and disposed of, like she was nothing. It didn't sit well with Mckenna that she never got to have a final resting place.

One roundabout later, they exited and parked near a small beach. No one asked Mckenna why they'd stopped; they simply watched as she gathered a dozen or so pebbles, dug a small hole in the sand, and placed them inside. She swept the sand over it with her hand and formed the word *Lilias*.

"Lilias, we lay you to rest—finally. Let your soul carry on with its journey. So let it be."

"So let it be," Abby, Andre, Seán, and Mathis repeated in unison, their hands held together and heads bowed.

Mckenna's gaze rose towards the water, where she spotted the spectral figure of Lilias, her eyes fixed on the waves gently caressing the rocky shore. Upon seeing Mckenna and the resting place she could call her own, Lilias beamed. She then ascended gracefully, bathed in a radiant light that enveloped her form, and her silhouette gradually merged with the lowest cloud in the sky.

EPILOGUE

Nissa felt completely at home in Elfame, a realm of pure enchantment and wonder that surpassed any fantastical world she'd ever read about. Although she couldn't recall her previous life as a fae, she now knew this was where she belonged.

In Elfame, time held no sway, and the perplexing, paradoxical energies of the physical world were but distant memories. Here, she was in perfect harmony with every living entity. It was as if all beings in this realm were singing a harmonious tune, each contributing their unique instrument to a brilliant symphony. And the landscape of Elfame . . . it was dreamlike—sure to inspire one of Seán's illustrations if he were here. The sky overhead stretched into an endless gradient of colours, while crystal-clear streams meandered gracefully through the verdant, lush forests. Exotic flora and fauna, with hues and shapes unseen in the mortal world, painted a breathtaking canvas.

Nissa was keen on exploring the various regions of Elfame: the deep forests of Eberroots, where the nymphs danced among the ancient trees; Eelúmina, the sanctuary of the sprites below the water's surface, hidden from view; Eminus, a city cradled among the wispy clouds, the ethereal realm of the sylphs and devas; The Elkinglade, a cozy neighbourhood in the heart of Elfame shared by gnomes and brownies—Nissa could sometimes hear their laughter echoing through the valleys; the hidden boroughs of the leprechauns, beneath the Emerald Hills; and the Eldrith Alpes, home to the elves—the most powerful and revered of the fae, often graced with royal titles or bestowed with honour by the Elfame Court.

Since her arrival in Elfame, Nissa lived in Eventide Meadow, where the sun's glow softly bathed everything in a gentle, never-ending dusk—a place designated for faeries who had yet to choose their destined path. Here, the air was fragrant with the sweetest of wildflowers, and the meadow stretched on infinitely, inviting every novice fae to find their own unique purpose.

"What kind of faery was I before incarnating as a human?" Nissa asked Niamh one evening by her favourite hawthorn tree.

"We're not supposed to say, as it can influence your decision. You're a bit of a, hmm, unique case, Nissa. Because you've returned to Elfame as a human, you're still Nissa here, too. You've not been reborn, nor are you the fae you once were. All you can do is be true to yourself!" she said cheerfully.

"But I don't know anything about the other fae. How do I decide which path to take?"

Niamh, who Nissa learned was a nymph, smiled sympathetically. "You're never alone here. When you meet with the Elfame Court, you will be assigned a mentor."

Nissa nodded, wishing she could talk it over with Mckenna over a cup of coffee.

I know what you're thinking, remember? Niamh's voice said in Nissa's mind.

Right, I forgot we do that here . . .

You cannot pass the doorway to the physical plane—not yet. You've been brought back here to achieve balance; the Court will not allow you any visits this soon.

But when I was by the waterfall the other day, I thought I heard Mckenna speaking to me . . .

It's possible! That's the main gateway to the physical plane— that's different than a doorway, but you'll learn with time. When you stare into the water and listen, you'll hear certain humans calling to you.

I was trying to respond! Nissa thought excitedly, *to let her know I miss her.*

Mckenna received your message, Niamh said simply as a puffy-chested bird landed on her forearm.

Nissa stared incredulously at the wren's familiar tiger-like plumage. *How long do you think until I'll have permission to visit?*

Niamh squeezed her hands. *Patience, dear Nissa.*

Nissa nodded. *You know, even when Abby offered to take my place, I knew it had to be me. I knew this place was my home.*

Niamh looked down at the ground, suddenly taking interest in a caterpillar clinging to a dandelion. *We are delighted you have come back home.*

Later, Nissa sat by the waterfall, staring down at the pool, hoping to hear from Mckenna again. But a different voice beckoned Nissa—one she hadn't heard in some time, and that she missed dearly. As she gazed down at the ripples, the face of her grandmother, Arethusa, smiled back at her.

"Hello, my pet. Found your way back home, I see!"

At last, there is not all but one course
For the Wise One's heart can be gently swayed
Through old magic harnessed and alignment with Source
The natural world can triumph both ways

—Scottish Scroll III, 1576

Acknowledgements

A deep, heartfelt thank-you to . . .

Rachel, my trusted editor; I wouldn't dream of leaving my manuscript in anyone else's hands.

Carol, my eagle-eyed proofreader and dear long-distance friend.

Mickey, my publicist; your enthusiasm for this series keeps me going on the tough days.

Brenda (@sketchluv.mtl), who so beautifully illustrated my late Netherland Dwarf, Magic, to represent my imprint, The Magic Dwarf Press.

Bettie, for helping me out of my negative thought patterns.

My beta readers, Emily, Rachele, Samantha, and Anne—the story wouldn't be what it is without your insight and honesty.

The Nerd Herd, for letting me interrupt our twentieth anniversary trip to celebrate my book launch.

Riccardo, for your stunning maps (@fantacities), patience, and unwavering support.

Jennifer, Jessica L., Jessica C., Sophie, and Aly, for literally everything.

Chantal—your excitement for this book has made this journey all the more special.

My parents, for naively believing *The Scottish Scrolls* will be the next *Harry Potter*. (Hey, I'll take it!)

Nonna, for making me feel so much more brilliant than I am.

Andy, for filling in the blanks when I couldn't . . . and so, *so* much more.

About the Author

Katrina Tortorici Anglehart is an award-winning author from Montreal, with a multilingual prowess in English, French, Italian, and "Spanglish". A dedicated academic, she holds a Bachelor of Arts in Journalism, a graduate certificate in Scriptwriting, and a Master of Fine Arts in Creative Writing.

Inspired by the wizarding world, the land of Narnia, and parallel planes, she penned *The Wise One*, inviting readers to connect with nature and its ever-present magic. Her exploration of the landscapes and folklore of Ireland and Scotland greatly influenced her debut urban fantasy, marking the inception of *The Scottish Scrolls* series.

K.T. Anglehart is a passionate advocate for bunnies, thanks to her late Netherland Dwarf, Magic—the inspiration behind her imprint, The Magic Dwarf Press. When she's not writing or diving into magical reads, she revels in hiking, antiquing, and Netflix binges alongside her high school-sweetheart-turned-husband, Andy. They currently live in Toronto with their three pets: Nessie, a mysterious rescue dog from Puerto Rico, and their whimsical bunnies, Onyx and Stirling.

SUBSCRIBE TO K.T. ANGLEHART'S NEWSLETTER FOR EXCLUSIVE CONTENT, NEWS, AND GIVEAWAYS

SHOP BOOKISH GOODIES AND MYSTICAL MERCH